'An epic read that has a dystopian feel and makes you ask the question: What if?' *Sun*

'Fever bears comparison with landmarks in the genre such as *The Stand* . . . The novel explores humanity at its best and worst; the crushing loss of civilisation with everything that means for the structure of society . . . This great book asks us to reflect on our own hidden natures – how would we react if the world we knew came to an end tomorrow?' Vaseem Khan, author of *The Unexpected Inheritance of Inspector Chopra*

'*Fever* is one of the best books of the year. Deon Meyer is a masterful writer and has created a stunning epic that brims with emotion. The mystery, thrills, and action kept me riveted to every page. Highly recommended.' Adam Hamdy, author of *Pendulum*

'Moving and gripping.' *South China Morning Post*

'Deon Meyer should be applauded for this brutal, unflinching tale of the excesses of humanity coiled like a python around a coming-of-age tale; one that makes one think deeply about the human condition as it entertains as well as warns of the dangers ahead . . . Miss this insightful thriller at your peril.' *Shots*

'A thought-provoking, postapocalyptic examination of the human condition . . . With its stunning final revelation, this is a remarkable literary achievement.' *Booklist*

'[A] sweeping epic about a young Afrikaner boy's survival in a post-apocalyptic South Africa . . . The book is part ecological warning, part thriller . . . part adventure saga . . . and part coming-of-age story . . . Gripping moments and a haunting atmosphere.' *Kirkus Reviews*

'Tense, intriguing, and surprising, this thriller is a solid choice for readers who enjoy well-researched and detailed survival stories.' *Library Journal*

'I have been a Deon Meyer fan for some time. Fever is an interesting departure for him . . . and I loved it.' Thomas Perry

Deon Meyer is the bestselling crime writer in South Africa. This translation occasionally uses colloquial phrases from his original Afrikaans. A glossary of terms can be found at the end of this book.

Also by Deon Meyer

Dead Before Dying
Dead at Daybreak
Heart of the Hunter
Devil's Peak
Blood Safari
Thirteen Hours
Trackers
7 Days
Cobra
Icarus

FEVER

The memoirs of Nicolaas Storm, concerning
the investigation of his father's murder

DEON
MEYER

*Translated from Afrikaans
by K.L. Seegers*

HODDER

Originally published in Afrikaans in 2016 as *Koors* by Human & Rousseau
First published in Great Britain in 2017 by Hodder & Stoughton
An Hachette UK company

This paperback edition published in 2018

1

A CIP catalogue record for this title is available from the British Library

Paperback ISBN 978 1 473 61444 4
eBook ISBN 978 1 473 61443 7

Typeset in Plantin Light by Hewer Text UK Ltd, Edinburgh
Printed and bound by Clays Ltd, St Ives plc

Hodder & Stoughton policy is to use papers that are natural, renewable
and recyclable products and made from wood grown in sustainable
forests. The logging and manufacturing processes are expected to
conform to the environmental regulations of the country of origin.

Hodder & Stoughton Ltd
Carmelite House
50 Victoria Embankment
London EC4Y 0DZ

www.hodder.co.uk

The initial mystery that attends each journey is: how did the traveller reach his starting point in the first place?

— Louise Bogan

Memories of mortification persist for decades ...

— Oliver Burkeman, *Help*

Every autobiography is concerned with two characters, a Don Quixote, the Ego, and a Sancho Panza, the Self.

— W.H. Auden

Autobiography is usually honest but it is never truthful.

— Robert A. Heinlein, *Friday*

Down these mean streets a man must go who is not himself mean, who is neither tarnished nor afraid. The detective must be a complete man and a common man and yet an unusual man. He must be, to use a rather weathered phrase, a man of honour.

— Raymond Chandler

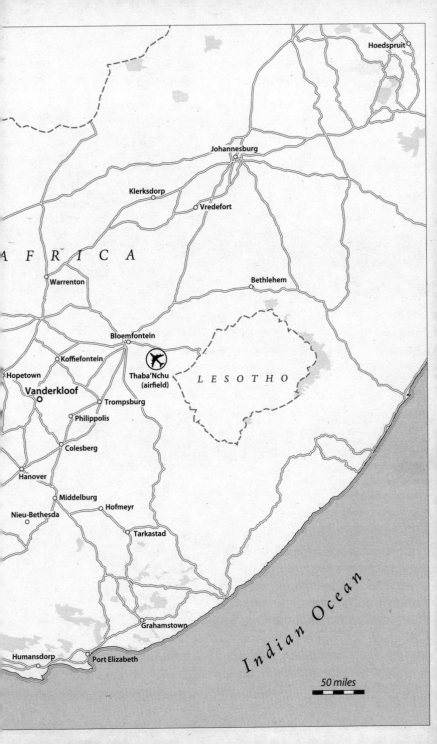

Hoedspruit

Johannesburg

Klerksdorp

Vredefort

A F R I C A

Warrenton

Bethlehem

Bloemfontein

Koffiefontein

Thaba'Nchu
(airfield)

L E S O T H O

Hopetown

Vanderkloof

Trompsburg

Philippolis

Colesberg

Hanover

Middelburg

Hofmeyr

Nieu-Bethesda

Tarkastad

Indian Ocean

Grahamstown

Humansdorp

Port Elizabeth

50 miles

I

I want to tell you about my father's murder.

I want to tell you who killed him, and why. This is the story of my life. And the story of your life and your world too, as you will see.

I have waited for a long time to write about this: I believe one needs wisdom and insight for such a task. I think one has first to get the anger – in fact, all the emotions – under control.

I am forty-seven years old today. The age my father was when he died, in the Year of the Lion. Perhaps that offers enough distance from the events of the time, though I don't know if I will ever develop the necessary wisdom and insight, but I worry that I will begin to forget many of the crucial events, experiences, people. I can't postpone this any longer.

So, here it is. My memoir, my murder story. And my exposé, so everyone will know the truth.

The Year of the Dog

2

20 March

The moments we remember most clearly are those of fear, loss and humiliation.

It was 20 March in the Year of the Dog. I was thirteen years old.

The day passed just as the previous day had done, and the one before that, to the dull drone of the big Volvo FH12 diesel engine, and the muffled rumbling of sixteen wheels on the long, enclosed trailer behind it. Outside, a predictable, forgettable landscape slid by. I recall the artificial coolness of the air conditioner in the cab of the 'horse'. The truck still had that fresh, new smell. A school textbook lay open on my lap, but my thoughts were wandering.

My father slowed the truck. I looked up, and out. I read the white lettering against the black background of the road sign: WELCOME TO KOFFIEFONTEIN!

'Koffiefontein,' I repeated out loud, charmed by the name and the image it evoked in my childlike imagination – a warm, aromatic fountain of simmering, dark coffee.

We drove slowly into town. In the near dusk of the late afternoon it seemed ghostly, bereft of life, like all the others. Weeds on the pavements, lawns thickly overgrown behind their fences. On the horizon, far behind the squat buildings of the wide main street, lightning crisscrossed in spectacular displays on a backdrop of fantastical cloud formations. The entire western rim was blooded a strange, disturbing crimson.

My father pointed. 'Cu-mu-lo-nim-bus,' he said, each syllable measured. 'That's what you call those clouds. It comes from the Latin. *Cumulus* means "pile". And *nimbus* is "rain". That's what gives us thunderstorms.'

'Cu-mu-lo-nim-bus.' I had a go at the word.

He nodded, deftly turned the big truck in at the filling station, and parked. He flipped the switch he had installed himself, to turn on the lights down the side of the long, enclosed trailer. Instantly the fuel pumps cast long shadows, like human figures. The engine off, we climbed down.

We were so used to our surroundings being safe.

The late summer heat beat up from the tarred forecourt, insect shrilling filled the air. And another sound, a deeper carpet of noise.

'What's that noise, Papa?'

'Frogs. The Riet River is just over there.'

We walked back along the side of the trailer. It was white, with three big green letters that looked as though they had been blown askew in a gale: *RFA*. They were spelled out on the back of the trailer – *Road Freight Africa*. We'd found it at a truck stop just outside Potchefstroom, with the Volvo horse attached, nearly brand new, full tank and all. Now we walked, father and son, side by side. His hair was long, blond and unkempt; mine was just as wild, but brown. I was thirteen, in that no-man's-land between boy and teenager, and for the moment comfortable there.

A bat swooped low over my head, through the pool of light.

'How does a bat catch its prey?' my father asked.

'With echoes.'

'What kind of animal is a bat?'

'A mammal, not a bird.'

He ruffled my hair affectionately. 'Good.'

I liked his approval.

We began to go through the familiar ritual we had performed at least once a day for weeks on end now: my father carried the small Honda generator and electric pump to the fuel station's refilling manhole covers in their colour-coded rows. Then he fetched the big adjustable spanner to lift up the black manhole cover. My job was to roll out the long garden hose. It was connected to the electric pump, and I had to push the other end into the mouth of the Volvo's diesel tank, and hold it there.

Refuelling in a world without electricity, or traffic.

I played my part, and stood there feeling bored, reading the letters on the white wall of the fuel station. *Myburgh Electric. Myburgh Tyres.*

I thought I must ask my father about that, because I knew that 'burg' meant 'a fort' – he'd explained that to me when we drove through places like Trompsburg and Reddersburg – but this was an unusual spelling, and not the name of this town.

Suddenly the hum of insects ceased.

Something drew my attention, behind my father, down the street. I called to him, in surprise at the unexpected sign of life, and a bit frightened by the furtive nature of the movement. My father hunkered down, pushing the pump pipe into the hole. He looked up at me, following the direction of my gaze, and saw the spectres in the deepening dusk.

'Get inside,' he shouted. He stood up, holding the heavy wrench, and ran towards the cab.

I was frozen. The shame of it would eat at me for months, that inexplicable stupidity. I stood motionless, my eyes fixed on the shifting shadows as they coalesced into solid shapes.

Dogs. Supple, quick.

'Nico,' my father shouted, with a terrible urgency. He stopped in his tracks, to try to fend the determined dogs away from his child.

The desperation in my father's voice sent a shockwave through my body, releasing my fear. And shooting the first dart of self-recrimination. I sobbed, and ran along the length of the trailer. Through the mist of tears I saw the first dog float into the pool of light, leap at my father's throat, jaws agape, long sharp fangs bared. The big spanner swung, a fleeting shadow of that motion. I heard the dull thud as it hit the creature's head, its curtailed yelp. At the step of the truck, I grabbed the silver railing, panic propelling me up into the cab. A dog lunged at me, as I dragged the door shut. The beast leapt up, high, almost to the open window, claws scrabbling on the metal door, yellow fangs gleaming in the light of the lorry. I screamed. The dog fell back. My father was down there. Five, six curs, creeping, crouching, circling him. And more darting into the pool of light, lean, relentless.

After that, everything happened so fast, yet it was also as if time stood still. I remember the finest detail. The despair on my father's face when the dogs cut him off from the truck, just three metres away. The whirring sound as he swung and swung the massive adjustable wrench. The electrically charged air, the smell of ozone, the stink of the dogs. They dodged backwards to evade the momentum of the deadly spanner, always too agile, just out of reach. But they stayed between him and the truck door, snarling, snapping.

'Get the pistol, Nico. Shoot.' Not an order. A terrified plea, as if in that moment my father saw his death and its consequences: his son, lone survivor, stranded, doomed.

His face contorted in agony as a dog attacked him from behind, sinking its fangs deep into his shoulder. That shook me from my trance. I reached for the Beretta in the compartment on the wide instrument panel, struggling to press the safety catch off with my thumb, as my father had taught me, over and over. Another dog bit into his defending arm, and hung there. Now I had both hands on the weapon. Two fingers to pull the trigger's first, stiff double action, the shot into the air, wildly, the blast deafening in the interior of the cab, so that my ears rang, all sound muted. Cordite stung my nostrils. The animals froze for a second. My father hit out with the wrench and the dog on his arm sank down. He took a step towards the door. The pack moved, and sprang. I aimed at the flank of one. Fired. The dog fell sideways. I fired again and again. The animals made high, barely audible yelps of pain, and the others began to drop back, for the first time.

Now my father was at the door, he pulled it open, jumped in, a dog hanging on his leg as he lashed out at it. It fell. With blood on his arms, blood down his back, he shoved me off the passenger seat, and slammed the door shut.

I saw my father's face, the loathing, determination, fear, revulsion, rage. I felt him grab the pistol from my hands. He ejected the magazine, pushed in a fresh one. He held the pistol out of the window and fired again and again and again. Each shot was merely a dull report in my ringing ears, the cartridges scattered silently against the windscreen, the instrument panel, the steering wheel, and dropped to the floor beside me, everywhere. I looked up at my father's tattered shirt, and the deep wounds in his back, the same crimson as the clouds.

The pistol emptied, still Pa kept pulling the trigger. Smoke filled the cab.

It was 20 March in the Year of the Dog.

Eleven months after the Fever.

*   *   *

My father slumped forward, with the pistol on his lap. He sat as still as death. I could not see if his eyes were closed.

Gradually the sounds outside returned, washing over us in gentle waves. The frogs, the early evening crickets. Far in the west, the blood-red horizon dimmed to black, and still he sat.

Someone sobbed quietly. It took a while for me to realise: it was me. I didn't want to let this happen now, it felt inappropriate. Ungrateful, in a way. But I had no control over it; the sobs came harder, more urgently. At last my father reacted, turned to me, put the pistol down on the dashboard, wrapped his arms around me. My whole body began to shake, my heart hammering in my ears. I smelled the blood and sweat on my father and I clung to him.

My ear to his chest, I heard his heart beating incredibly fast.

'There, there,' he said. I didn't hear the words, just felt the vibrations. *There. There, there, there.*

He held me tighter, till gradually I calmed down.

'You're my hero, Nico,' he said. 'You did well, you hear?'

At last I got the word out, the word that had stuck inside, for so long. 'Mamma.'

And when it reached my ears, the mortification burned through me.

'Oh, God,' said my father, and hugged me tighter. Then he turned off the lights down the side of the truck.

My father's name is Willem Storm.

In the light of a hissing gas lamp I cleaned the wounds on his back. My hands trembled. The antiseptic must have burned like fire in the long red gashes in his skin, but he didn't make a sound, didn't say a word. It scared me, strengthened my fear that I had failed him.

Later he opened two tins of Enterprise *Spaghetti and Meatballs*. We ate in silence. I stared at the blue and red tin, and wondered what was wrong with PORK. Because there was a yellow star on the tin, with fat red letters that said: *NO PORK*.

'I didn't think that would happen so fast,' said my father at last.

'What, Papa?'

'The dogs,' he said, and made a vague gesture with the spoon in his hand.

And then he went silent again.

3

21 March

In the morning Pa dragged the dog carcasses to the back of the filling station, and set them on fire.

We refuelled the lorry. Pa was quiet. Nothing felt right. The fear was like a shadow creeping along behind me.

We drove off, without breakfast. Pa said, 'We're going to eat at a special place.' He tried to make it sound like an occasion, but I was old enough to hear that his cheerfulness was forced. His wounds must have been very painful. 'Okay, Pa,' I said eagerly, as though I shared his excitement.

He drank water from a full one-litre plastic bottle. It wasn't long before he had emptied it.

An hour later we stopped at the special place. I forgot about the feeling of doom that had been with us the whole morning. I cried out like a child half my age, in total wonderment. It was so amazingly beautiful, so unusual and so loud – a bridge, a dam wall and a tremendous thundering. To the left lay the dam, perfectly calm, a huge outstretched expanse of water. To the right was the deep gorge of a river, veiled by the mist of water vapour, rising like smoke from the torrents roaring down the sluices.

Pa stopped the lorry in the middle of the massive concrete dam wall. He opened both windows. The sound of the mass of falling water filled the cab. It made the whole truck vibrate.

Pa had to raise his voice, as he pointed at the mirror of water: 'This is the Vanderkloof Dam.' Then he looked at the deep canyon: 'And that is the Orange River.'

'*Jissie.*' Yesterday forgotten, I was totally enchanted.

'I think they left the sluices open. After the Fever. Just as well.'

I stared in amazement. Until I realised that Pa had said the words 'the Fever' in a strange way. Not like he always did. Quietly, quickly and reluctantly, as though he didn't want to draw attention to it. I looked at him, but he avoided my eyes. 'Come, let's make coffee,' he said briskly.

We kept a gas stove and a big moka espresso pot under the bed, behind the seats. Along with a pack of biltong, sweets and rusks – the dry biscuits we dunked with our coffee. I clambered to the back, and got the process of brewing under way.

Usually we got out to eat, when we were on the road. But now Pa remained in his seat. He was being careful, after the dogs.

I passed him the rusks. He took only one. I ate three rusks, suddenly ravenous.

The moka pot sputtered. The aroma of coffee filled the cab.

I poured Pa's first, he drank it black and bitter. I liked mine with two spoons of sugar, and Cremora.

'Here, Pa.'

He turned to face me and I waited for him to say 'While we can.' He said that every morning, when we drank our coffee. He raised the mug high, as you do when you say 'cheers' and smiled crookedly. Because some time in the future the coffee supply would run out, and before it ran out it would grow stale, not taste as good, and that day was approaching. That's what Pa had explained to me, the first time he said 'While we can.'

This morning he didn't say it.

I noticed his hand was shaking. Then I saw the perspiration on his forehead, how red his face was. And his eyes, dull and out of focus.

Suddenly his silences, and everything, made sense. The shock of it, the fear, made the tears well up.

'It's not the Fever,' he said. 'You hear me?'

The fear was no longer just a shadow, it was all of me.

'Nico, listen,' said my father, his voice just as desperate as yesterday evening, with the dogs. It made me swallow back my sobs for a second.

He put the coffee mug down on the dashboard, and hugged me. I felt the heat burning him up. 'It's not the Fever. It's the dogs. It's just an infection from their bites, it's bacterial. I have to take antibiotics, and lots of water, and I must get rest. You hear?'

'You've got the Fever, Papa. I can tell.'

'I promise you, I've got a different kind of fever, on my word of honour. You've also had a temperature, from flu or a cold, from teething when you were little, there're many kinds, this isn't the one that everyone . . . The dogs weren't getting fed by people. They were eating carrion, or rotten meat, and then they bit me, and those bacteria are in my bloodstream now. That's where this fever comes from. I'm just going to be sick for a short while. I promise, Nico, I promise you. We've got the right medicine, I'm going to take it now.'

We drove up between the hills, into Vanderkloof town. It was an odd little place, a narrow higgledy-piggledy settlement next to the dam, sprawling high up into the *koppies*. Pa was looking for something. He found it deep in the deserted town, as silent as the grave. A modest house, paint peeling from the woodwork, a big steel security gate in front of the door, and burglar bars on the windows. Opposite it there was the only parking space on the street for our lorry.

Pa stopped. He got out, taking a pistol and a hunting rifle. I had to wait in the Volvo while he went to look in the house. I sat watching the front door. I was afraid he would never come back. What would I do then?

Everything was different now, after yesterday, after the dogs. And now, with Pa's fever.

But he came back. As he approached the truck, I could see he was unsteady on his feet.

'This place is good enough,' he said. 'Come, bring your books.' I put them in my rucksack, and climbed down. Pa walked slowly now, and he did everything gingerly and carefully, unlocking the back of the big trailer, pulling the ladder down. The contents of the trailer told the story of our life. It was an ever growing inventory, neatly packed and tied; we knew where every item was. Nearest the door were the boxes of tinned food and rice and flour and pasta, powdered milk, coffee, Cremora, hundreds of bottles of water. Then, in no specific order: books, hand-picked like the food wherever it was safe to browse. Do-it-yourself books about repairs and personal recovery and veld survival and *The Ultimate Beginner's Guide to Guns: A Green Light Shooting Book* from which we had both learned to shoot. Story books and school books and recipe books and how-to-slaughter-an-ox and how-to-treat-snakebite books. There were rifles, pistols, ammunition, hunting knives and slaughtering knives and kitchen knives, our equipment to pump fuel, and water purification filters. Medicine, bandages, ointments, sunscreen. A small tent, camp chairs, inflatable mattresses, camp beds, two folding tables, two large umbrellas, never used, still in their plastic Makro packaging. Three petrol power generators, ten fifty-litre jerry cans. Toiletries: more toothpaste than we could use in our lifetime, shampoo, soap, deodorant, toothbrushes. Washing powder, bleach. Laptop computers, printers. Cutlery, crockery, hand tools, power tools . . .

Pa assembled a few cartons of provisions, and he searched until he found the correct medicine. He climbed down, pushed the ladder in again, locked the trailer's back doors carefully. We carried the cartons into the house. The place was empty, and tidy, as though the people had cleaned up before they died. Every empty house we had been in had its own smell. Some were pleasant, some bad. This one smelled a little bit of rubber. I don't know why.

'The stove works with gas,' said Pa. I nodded.

'And there's water.' He meant the taps still worked.

Pa went back to our truck and locked the cab as well. He came inside again, locked the security gate of the house, then the front door. He gave me the pistol.

'Nico, I'm going to clean all the dog bites again, and I'm going to take the medicine. I have to sleep. There, in that room. Don't go out. If you see or hear anything, come tell me, straight away. Get yourself something to eat, there are tins, take your favourites. And biltong and biscuits. And soup. I'll have some soup with you tonight; come and wake me when the sun starts to set. I know you're scared now, Nico, but I'll just be sick a day or two, you hear?'

I touched him. He was fiery hot.

I didn't cry. I just nodded.

'How do we stay safe?' he asked.

'We trust only each other.'

'That's right. Come and look, so you can see where I'll be lying. If I'm still asleep when it gets dark: remember, no lights.'

He read something in my face. 'Everything is going to be fine,' he said.

*　　*　　*

Everything wasn't fine.

I unpacked some of my books. I sat in the sitting area of the open-plan living room. It was part of the kitchen and a dining room too. After what seemed like an eternity I couldn't stand it any more. I walked to the bedroom. Pa lay under the blankets. He was shivering uncontrollably, but it wasn't cold. He didn't even know I was there.

If he was going to die I didn't want to watch it. I walked slowly down the passage. I heard noises, in the roof of the house and outside. I tried to look out, through the other bedrooms' windows, but everything was quiet again.

In the sitting room I saw a movement through the lace curtain, an animal trotting down the street outside. Fear gripped me; was it a dog? I went and stood at the window. I saw that it was a bat-eared fox, tiny, with silver in its pelt. It halted suddenly, and stared at the house. It raised its muzzle, as though it had scented something. Then it trotted briskly away again, as if it were late for some appointment.

Dragging my feet in dread, I crept back to the bedroom. Pa was still breathing.

The house was laid out simply, a long rectangle, with the living area at the front door, three bedrooms and two bathrooms at the back. I explored all the other rooms of the house thoroughly, opened cupboards, looked under beds. There were no toys in the cupboards, there were no bookshelves on any of the walls. There were magazines in a wooden box beside a chair in the sitting room. *Sarie* and *Rooi Rose* and *You* magazine. I didn't like reading those because all the people in them were dead now; all the TV stuff and movies didn't exist any more. The whole world has changed.

I didn't dare look in the fridge, because as Pa and I knew, there was stuff that had gone rotten in all the fridges; it was better just to leave them closed.

High in a food cupboard were two large packs of Simba chips. Smoked Beef. I preferred the chutney flavour. A big slab of Cadbury chocolate. I tore open the chocolate wrapper. I knew it would have gone grey-white and unpleasant, but still I was hoping, because I was thirteen years old.

The chocolate tasted weird.

I ate a whole packet of chips. They had gone a bit stale, but they were crunchy and filling. I ate the other packet too.

I went to check on Pa. He had stopped shivering. He had thrown off the blanket and was sweating profusely now. The dog bites were fiery red and swollen.

I sat down against the wall of his room, and watched him. It was terribly quiet. Pa's breathing was the only sound. In and out. Too fast.

The fever had him in its grip.

4

The man under the mango tree

They knew the Fever came out of Africa. They knew it was two viruses that combined, one from people and one from bats. In those days they wrote a lot about it, before everyone died.

One doctor wrote in a magazine that nobody knew exactly how it all began, but this is how they thought it *might* have happened: a man somewhere in tropical Africa lay down under a mango tree. The man's resistance was low, because he was HIV-positive and not being treated for it. There was already one corona virus in the man's blood. There was nothing strange about that. Corona viruses were quite common. In the era before the Fever they knew of at least four that caused flu and cold symptoms in people.

Corona viruses also occurred in animals. Mammals *and* birds.

In the mango tree there was a bat, with a different kind of corona virus in its blood.

The bat was sick. Diarrhoea caused it to defecate on the face of the man under the tree, his eyes, or his nose, or his mouth. The second corona virus was now in the man's blood, the two viruses multiplying together in the same cells of the man's windpipe. And their genetic material combined. A new corona virus was born – one that could infect other people easily when inhaled, and with the ability to make them extremely ill.

The man under the mango tree lived in a poor community, where people were crammed together, and where the incidence of HIV was high. He quickly infected others. The new virus spread through the community, and kept on mutating. One mutation was just perfect. It spread easily through the air, taking long enough to kill for each person to have infected many others.

One of the family members of the man under the mango tree worked at an airport in the nearby city. The family member was incubating the perfect virus. He coughed on a passenger, just before the woman took the flight to England.

In England there was a big international sporting event.

All the first-world countries had a protocol for deadly, infectious diseases. Even most of the developing countries had extensive plans for such an incident. There were guidelines and systems for an epidemic. In theory, these should have worked.

But nature paid no heed to theories. And nor did human fallibility.

5

21 March

I sat on the floor beside the bed where my father lay fighting his fever and somewhere late in the afternoon I must have fallen asleep.

Something woke me. I heard a car. At first I thought it was my imagination. The sound grew louder. Quickly, but silently, I walked to the front room.

It really was a vehicle, the engine high-pitched as it raced up the hill to the town.

I ran back to the bedroom.

'Pa.'

He didn't hear me.

'Pa,' I said louder and more urgently. 'I can hear a car.'

Pa was breathing rapidly, his mouth open. He didn't move. I wanted to shout at him, I wanted to yell at the top of my voice, don't die, I'm scared, there's a car outside, we can only trust each other. Come back from the fever, I'm too small to be alone, Pa, please, just don't die.

But I was still shy about last night, about calling for my mother. I just stood there and stared and my father didn't wake up.

The car came closer.

I ran back into the sitting room. Outside the shadows were long, the sun dipped low. The car came closer and closer. It was moving slower now, I could hear. It was in the town.

I wanted to run outside, and say to them, 'Come help my father, he's sick.'

We trust only each other. Pa and I had decided that, after the people had tried to rob us, the other side of Bultfontein, five weeks ago. I couldn't go out.

The car came round the corner. It was out front now, in the street.

A black Jeep Wrangler, with an open top. It raced past. It looked like three people were in it. Then it was gone, down the street.

I ought to have stopped them, I thought. Pa was seriously ill.

I listened; the Jeep was coming back. I saw it stop opposite the Volvo, in the street in front of me. A man with very long black hair switched off the vehicle. He wasn't wearing a shirt, just trousers. He was lean, his chest hairs were dark and dense. He jumped out, and walked over to our truck. He had a gun in his hand.

I was going to call them. I was going to ask them for help. For me and my pa. I went towards the door.

I saw a woman in the back of the Jeep. Her head drooped forward. She had brown hair, very tangled. Her hands were tied to the roll bar. She cried out, as though she was very scared.

I stopped.

The other man, still seated in the front of the Jeep, was wearing a T-shirt with no sleeves. He had muscular arms. He hit the woman with the flat of his hand and she started to cry. He yelled to the man at our Volvo. 'When did we last come past here?'

'A week ago?' the one with long hair shouted back.

'This lorry wasn't here then.'

Long Hair climbed up to the Volvo's cab, tried to open the door, but it was locked. He climbed down again. He put a hand on the exhaust. 'It's cold,' he called to the Jeep. 'Are you sure? We were drunk, that time. It might have been here all along.'

Muscles laughed. 'That's true.'

I sat down on the chair, and looked over the couch, through the window, at them. People who would tie a woman to a car were not good people. I couldn't trust them.

Muscles got out of the Jeep. He said something I couldn't hear. He looked at our house, he looked straight at me. I sat dead still. I knew he couldn't see me through the lace curtain, but it felt as if he could.

Long Hair walked down the length of the trailer. He tested the door at the back, tried to open it.

'It'll do no harm to check,' Muscles called. He kept staring at the sitting-room window. Perhaps he could see me? Eventually he turned away, to the bound woman, and jerked on her arms. He called to Long

Hair, 'I'm going to take a look in this house, you look in those.' He pointed at the houses across the street.

'Okay,' said the other one.

Muscles approached our front door. He had a big shiny silver revolver on his hip.

The woman in the Jeep suddenly began to jerk at the roll bar with her hands. I could see her face now. There was blood on her cheek, and on her hair, just above her forehead.

Muscles laughed. 'You won't get loose.' He stood watching her, until she stopped struggling, and only made little whimpering noises, as if her heart was broken. He climbed up the steps of our veranda. He rattled the security gate loudly. I was frightened, but I kept completely quiet.

Our pistol lay on a low table in the middle of the sitting room, between the chairs facing the TV. I picked it up, held it in my hand, and sat down again.

Muscles came to the sitting-room window. He pressed his face against the glass, and cupped his hand to shade his eyes from the sun. I slid off the chair and lay flat, the arm of the couch between him and me. He couldn't see me, he couldn't see me, it was too dark here inside, I was sure. I stayed flat on the floor, until I heard him pulling at the security door again. I sat up. I saw him take a step back, take out his revolver, aim at the security gate lock.

The shot was very loud. This time I think I must have made a sound.

The bullet splintered the wood of the door and embedded itself in the sitting-room wall, just to my left.

Muscles wrenched at the steel gate. It wouldn't open.

'Don't worry,' he shouted to Long Hair. 'I'm just shooting off the locks.'

Then he fired again.

I held the pistol firmly in both hands. I shifted rearwards, so that my back was against the lounge chair. I raised the pistol. When he came through the door, I would have to shoot at him. If I could.

I heard him tug at the security gate, which screeched as it opened. Then the front door handle, turning as he grasped it. But the door was locked. He would try to shoot that open too.

I tried to aim my pistol at the door. My mind said no, I can't do it.

I didn't want to shoot a man.

I lowered the pistol again and squeezed my eyes shut. Let him come in. He would have to tie me up in the Jeep as well, with the woman. Maybe he wouldn't look further into the house. Maybe Pa would come to rescue me, if he didn't die from the Fever.

I waited for the shot, my eyes shut.

I felt a hand cover my lips. Startled, I tried to scream, but the hand was clamped tight over my mouth.

It was Pa. He took the pistol out of my hand, put his mouth close to my ear and whispered, 'Shhh.'

'What?' yelled Muscles outside the door, and looked across the street. He lowered the silver revolver.

Long Hair shouted something we couldn't hear.

'No, the whole place is locked,' shouted Muscles.

Pa lifted the pistol, as though it were very heavy. He aimed at the front door. I felt his whole body tremble, burning, behind me. I wondered if Pa would shoot a man like he had shot the dogs. After Bultfontein Pa had said, 'To shoot someone . . .' and then just shook his head, as if he wouldn't be able to do it.

The man with the muscles turned back towards the street. '*Ja, ja* . . . No, I haven't got the . . .' he said. He didn't finish the sentence, listening to what Long Hair said.

'Okay,' said Muscles, and lifted his revolver again.

He shot at our front door lock. A loud bang, wood splintering, plaster spraying.

Pa kept the pistol trained on the door, and his hand on my mouth.

Muscles just turned on his heel and walked away, down the steps, to the Jeep. Long Hair came from the other side of the street to meet him. Muscles smacked the woman on the head, then they got into the Jeep, started it, and drove away.

We just lay there, in the sitting room, for a while. Pa's breathing was rapid. 'I'm sorry, Nico, I heard you calling me, but I thought it was a dream.' He whispered. He had taught me, sound always carried further than you thought. Especially now, after the Fever, because there was no other noise about.

He said, 'You did very well. You can be proud of yourself.'

Later we got up. He drank lots of water from the tap, I heated the soup on the gas stove. Baxters Cream of Chicken.

While we ate, Pa said, 'We can't make any light tonight, we don't know how close they are.'

'And we won't be able to have coffee tomorrow morning,' I said. The smell of coffee betrayed the presence of people. Pa had taught me that too.

'That's right.' He tried to smile, but it seemed as if he just didn't have the strength.

I finished my soup.

'I feel better,' said Pa.

He was fibbing. He could see I didn't believe him.

'Okay,' I said. 'Those men had a lady tied to the Jeep.'

'I saw. We'll do something about that tomorrow.'

I lay beside him, throughout the night. He talked a lot in his sleep. Twice he cried out, my mother's name: Amelia.

6

The past is a river

It was Pa who said, the past is like a river. (That was in the Year of the Pig, if I remember rightly. I was seventeen.)

We were part of a greater group of people who talked till late one Sunday evening in the Forum and when he and I and Okkie walked home, I asked him, why does everyone still talk like that about the Fever, it's past after all, five years already.

Then he said, 'The past is like a river, Nico. We can't remember all the water that has flowed past. So, when we look back, we first look at all the driftwood, those bits of detritus that the storms and floods left behind washed up high on the riverbanks.'

'I don't understand what you're saying, Pa,' annoyed. My relationship with my father was already fractured, and I was a teenager. Adults in general irritated me.

'We remember the moments of great trauma the best. Fear, loss, humiliation . . . You will see, one day.'

Now I see. Now, as I try to write this memoir, now that I want to recall *everything*, not just the trauma. Also the events in between. It's not that easy. I quoted Auden and Heinlein on the question of autobiography, because the pitfalls they point out are genuine: when it comes to the memory river's more troubled waters, you are reliant on your own, sometimes unreliable and prejudiced memories, and the stories of others. You are exposed to the urges (and fears) of the ego, which wishes to include only select events. And exclude others.

Let me be frank: this is the story of what happened *after* the Fever, as *I* remember it. My truth. Subjective maybe, perhaps a little slanted. But I owe it to everyone who is part of this story to be as factual and honest as memory allows, especially those who are not here to share their testimony.

Truth was my single greatest incentive. I swear that.

7

I slept beside my father. He woke in the early morning, startled, bewildered, his hair unkempt and his eyes wild. It took him a moment to recognise me. He looked smaller, thinner, and in this sudden revealing moment he seemed vulnerable and fragile. Fallible. But it was as if I could not see that yet. Would not see it.

I made porridge oats for us, and Pa ate his in bed. Grateful. He said, 'One day we'll taste fresh milk again.'

He said that a lot.

And: 'I should be well tomorrow morning, Nico.'

'Will we leave again then, Pa?'

He shook his head, slowly. 'No. This is where we're going to come and live.'

'Here?'

'Not in this house, specifically. There are many to choose from. I mean, this place, this town.'

'But what about those men?' and I pointed towards the street, where the Jeep had been. We still spoke in low voices, as though they were close by.

'They are a . . . a complication.'

'A complication?'

'That's an interesting word. We get it from the Latin. *Complicare* . . .' Pa drew a few breaths, as if gathering his strength. 'It means "to fold together". You know, when you fold something, then you make it more complicated.' He tried to drum up his old enthusiasm: 'Neat, hey, the way language works. "Complicate" means "to make more involved" . . .'

'Why don't we just go to another place?'

'Because I think Vanderkloof is the best place in the whole country. For a new beginning.'

'Why?'

Pa ate the last of his porridge before continuing. 'Maslow . . . All the basic needs. Here we have structure and texture . . .' He sighed. He was tired. 'It's a long story. I'll tell it to you tomorrow. I promise. Deal?'

'Okay.'

He handed me his empty porridge bowl, and shook the pills out of the bottle. 'I'm going to lie down again. Remember to brush your teeth.'

In the afternoon I heard Pa talking. I went into the room to check on him. He had thrown all the blankets off, he was sweating, speaking wildly, his voice frightened.

Then he woke up. He sat up suddenly, turned his body so as not soil the bed and vomited on the floor.

I helped him to clean up. 'Sorry, Nico, sorry, my boy,' he said.

That night I made hot soup, but Pa slept through all of it.

The Jeep didn't return.

It was terribly hot and stuffy in the house.

8

23 March

In the morning my father slept long after I woke.

I ate rusks, drank water, looked out of the windows. I listened and couldn't sit still, something made me wander up and down, something more than boredom, more than the vague anxiety I had felt yesterday. I was thirteen, I didn't know how to process this.

I stood at the sitting-room window. My heart began to beat faster, my hands perspired, the earth was swallowing me up, the air, the walls; the day pressed heavily on me. I sat down and jumped up again, agitated. I didn't understand what was happening, but I didn't want to wake Pa, he had to get well.

I lay down in the other bedroom and the room shrank in on me. I squeezed my eyes shut. The dogs, the night of the dogs was in my mind, I saw it all again. The dogs, Pa's fever, the two men in front of the house, the shots though our door, the captive woman, I relived it all, the images, the smells, the fear, the distress. My father, two days ago, how he climbed out of the truck with his sore and injured body, how he looked scared, for the first time. Scared. The way he looked, the way he reluctantly touched the stiff, grisly carcasses as he dragged the dogs away. My heart wanted to burst out of my chest, my breath was not enough, it was all overwhelming me. There was a rage inside me, at the whole world. At the dogs that wanted to murder, who were so determined to kill us. Us, who after the Fever, out of compassion cut the fences of so many game farms and parks, who opened all the cages in the Bloemfontein zoo. We were animal lovers, why did the dogs want to kill us? Anger burned through me, an irrational fury. At everything, at the Fever that had destroyed my entire life. I balled my fists, I wanted to shout at someone or something for the injustice, while the room, the world, the universe became narrower and smaller and heavier, the pressure on me greater and greater and greater.

'Nico!'

Pa was suddenly beside me, and the heaviness was gone.

I looked at him as he sat down beside me. 'You were shouting. I think you're suffering from shock.'

My entire body was taut, cocked like a rifle.

'I'm here,' said Pa.

I had no words to say.

'My fever's broken,' said Pa.

9

24 March

In the early morning hours it rained, thunder and lightning, a drumming on the galvanised iron roof of the house.

There was a lot of moisture in the air, a certain pressure, as if something were brewing or fermenting. Inside me as well, yesterday's anger and fear had not disappeared completely, they were still lurking somewhere in the back of my mind.

Pa said, it's safe to make coffee when it rains, the aroma won't be detected that far. But we still had to keep the windows shut. We drank our coffee in the kitchen. He told me about Abraham Maslow's hierarchy of needs. Pa never talked down to me. He gave me almost all the information; I had to decide myself what I didn't understand. (Years later I realised he left sex out when he came to Maslow's list of physiological needs. I don't blame him.) He explained that Vanderkloof was ideal on the physiological level: all the water we needed, and good potential for the important forms of agriculture. The climate was reasonably good, irrigation was easy, and in addition there was hydroelectric power that we could redirect, if we could just find the right people with the right knowledge to change the system and maintain it.

He knew exactly what the question was on the tip of my tongue. He said of course there were other places, other dams and rivers, that offered more or less the same. But he knew this area so well; he had been here a few years ago. He knew: Vanderkloof was unique when it came to Maslow's hierarchy of security. Vanderkloof was a settlement, a burg, a natural fort, thanks to the hills with their cliffs, and the dam. There was only one easily negotiable road in, up the steep hill. There was only one flank to defend, unless the enemy arrived with a fleet of ships, which was most unlikely on the Orange River. Pa laughed. That was when I could see that he still wasn't fully recovered from his fever. His laugh sounded hollow. It was as if a part of him had not returned.

'But what about those two men in the Jeep? They live here.'

'Yes. The complication . . . I'm still thinking about that.'

The feeling of oppression in my head was an omen. 'I think we should leave, Pa.'

Pa didn't listen.

'They aren't going to drive around in that Jeep when it's raining,' said Pa. 'Let's go and fetch the arsenal.'

First we looked and listened carefully from the veranda before a dash to the Volvo to fetch our weapons and cleaning materials. We called our store in the truck 'the arsenal' ever since Pa explained to me where the word came from – 'warehouse' in the original Arabic, to Venetian Italian, to English and eventually to Afrikaans.

We laid out the couple of pistols and the hunting rifles on the kitchen counter. I wiped the raindrops from the dark grey steel. We sat side by side, and we cleaned and oiled the weapons thoroughly, one by one.

'We'll take a look tonight in the dark, if we can see their lights,' said Pa. 'Then we'll know how at ease they feel, and how near they are.'

I wondered why I hadn't thought of that.

'Then we'll do a little recce.' He thought a moment more. 'There might be more than those two men and the woman.'

'What will we do then?'

'Then we had better leave for now. The risk . . .'

'Why don't we just leave, Pa? Now. Tonight.'

Pa was quiet for such a long time I wondered if he had heard my question. Then he said, 'We want to make a new start here. We want to establish a community with morality, with the right principles, that cares for each other. So we had better get off on the right foot. We can't leave that poor woman like that. If there are just the two of them, we have at least to try. Even if it is just you and me.'

That was the first time that Pa talked about 'establishing a community'. My thoughts were on other things at that moment, so it didn't really register. Only much later did I realise he had thought everything through already. He had a vision, *before* the day of the dogs, *before* we arrived here.

By four o'clock the rain had cleared. 'That's a pity,' said Pa. 'It would have been a help.'

At dusk Pa dressed his dog bites with ointment, bandages and plasters. He swallowed some pain pills. He smeared black stripes on our faces with shoe polish from the kitchen cupboard, and we put on dark clothing. We each loaded a Beretta, and a rifle: the Tikka .222 with its long telescope for me, the .300 CZ for Pa.

'The sort of people who would treat a lady like that are . . . dangerous. We're just going to recce, Nico, that's all.'

'Okay,' I said and hoped Pa didn't hear the relief in my voice, because I just had this feeling things were not right, there was something bad in the air.

By ten o'clock it was pitch black, the moon not yet risen. We left the weapons in the house, and climbed up on the tin roof of the back veranda first. We saw them immediately. Their house was high up on the hill, about three kilometres away. They must have had a strong generator, because those were electric lights that were burning so bright. A big house, three storeys high.

'So sure of yourselves, hey?' Pa whispered, even though it was much too far for him to be heard.

Back in the kitchen he asked, 'You didn't hear any other vehicle while I was sick?'

'No, Pa.'

He was deep in thought as he handed the pistol and rifle to me. We walked to the door. 'Can they really be so careless?' I knew Pa was not expecting an answer from me.

He found his answer in the road.

Vanderkloof, in the Year of the Dog, was a jumble of a town, still in its pre-Fever form – a small unplanned, unfinished patchwork quilt that had been tossed over the hills. There was only one road leading to the upper suburb, and the Jeep men's castle of light. We crept quietly and cautiously through the darkness. I kept half a step to the left and behind Pa. Our trainers trod silently on the tar; I could hear my father breathing. At first we mistook the route, and had to turn back and try again. Find the right tarred street.

'Nico!' said Pa softly and urgently, startling me with the suddenness. He held out his arm to stop me. I couldn't see a thing.

'They've strung a wire across here,' he whispered.

He drew a finger through the air to show me the wire. I had to step closer, and look very carefully before I saw it shining with reflected light from the house up there, still over a kilometre away. Just above my head.

'No,' said Pa, 'it looks like fishing line.'

'How did you spot it, Pa?'

'I was thinking, what would I have done if I were in their shoes. If I had the lights on like that, like a candle attracting moths.'

'*Jinne,*' I said in amazement. 'But how will a fishing line stop anyone?'

'Come,' said Pa, and motioned for me to follow. He walked along the length of line, to where it stretched over the emergency rail beside the road.

'Look.'

I saw that the line was attached to something.

Pa held his mouth close to my ear. 'It's a flare. If you touch the fishing line, the flare shoots into the air. Then they know you are coming.'

He gave me time to have a good look. 'These guys . . . We must be very careful. Make sure you climb under the wire.'

We walked along, much slower now. I tried to be alert too now. I wondered, what did the Jeep guys do when they drove home to their house? Did they lift the line up?

Again Pa saw the next one first. Only a block from their house, scarcely two hundred metres. It was strung low, lower than my knees. He blocked me with his hand, pointed, didn't speak. I saw a few water droplets hanging from the line – dew or rain. That was how Pa had spotted it. I hadn't been looking so low down, I had assumed all the flare lines would be strung high.

We stepped over it. Walked on, three, four paces. Pa stopped, held up his hand to show I must stop too. He looked at the House of Light on the side of the ridge, shining so bright. It seemed cheerful, welcoming. But there was no movement or human sounds, no other sign of life.

Pa took the rifle off his shoulder, held it in his hands. He didn't move forward, just stared fixedly at the Jeep men's house up there.

Then to the left, at the row of smaller, dark houses that were strung along the side. And to the right, where there was only open veld.

Something was bothering Pa. Something was making him feel very tense.

A jackal called, just this side, against one of the slopes.

I wanted to turn back. I wanted to go to the Volvo, I wanted to drive away. The oppression, the humidity, that dark heavy feeling from yesterday stirred in me like a monster in dark waters.

I unslung the rifle from my shoulder.

Pa bent forward slightly, as if he wanted to make himself smaller. He began to walk again, more slowly this time. Every now and then he would stop. A hundred and fifty metres from the House of Light. An owl called from the veld, above the quiet hum of insects.

We just came to scout, why did he keep on walking?

At about a hundred metres from the house a hare flew out of the shrubs to our left. The shock made me gasp. Out loud. Pa just froze, looked slowly at me. I wanted to say, I'm sorry, but he squeezed my shoulder, to say he understood.

He turned to me, pressed his mouth against my ear. Very quietly he said, 'See that rock?' and he pointed to the right. A rock as big as a fridge had rolled down the hill, and lay on the pavement.

I nodded.

'Wait there beside it. I'm going a little way ahead.'

When I hesitated, he said, 'You'll be able to see me at all times.'

I nodded.

He waited. I went over to the rock, looking carefully where I stepped when I left the tar. The rock was as high as my chest. I put my rifle down on it, so that I could look through the telescope if necessary. I lay against the rock. It felt cold.

Pa took a step forward. Stood still. Another step, halt. Step, stand. The glow of the house stretched all the way here. I could see Pa in its light, his body a little bowed, his hair long and bedraggled.

He took a step forward, stood, listened and looked. Step, stand, listen, look. Further and further onwards, away from me. Why so slow and cautious? There was no movement, no sound, nothing, except the bright fort ahead. He would easily see a fishing line this close to the light. Maybe the Jeep people and the abused woman were long gone, maybe they forgot to turn everything off, maybe the flares were just a trick, a practical joke. It felt like an eternity, time standing still; he was ten paces away, then fifteen, twenty. I saw his back, ever smaller; we only came to recce, Pa, we've seen enough, that lady isn't here any more, let's go back, let's leave; twenty-five paces, Pa was a long way off, closer to the pool of light, he looked so small.

I didn't want to see Pa like that, I didn't want to be here now, it didn't feel right, something was eating me from the inside.

'Hey,' said a voice, and Pa jumped, and swung round to his left. I saw the man standing there. Muscles. He had the big revolver in his hand, and he was lifting it. He sounded surprised.

Pa had the rifle ready. He didn't shoot.

Muscles raised the revolver.

Still my father didn't shoot.

A shot boomed, reverberated. Pa fell.

IO

Pa fell. The universe stood still.

My whole body shivered, the echoes of the heavy revolver shot thundered over me and the rock, it shook free the heaviness in my head and at that moment I knew what I had experienced yesterday, that anxiety attack, the fury. I wasn't angry at the dogs and their treachery, I wasn't ashamed because I had called for my mother. I was angry with my father. I was angry with him because he had looked so small and afraid and lost at the fuel station, with the snarling dogs surrounding him. I was angry because, at that moment, he had needed me to help him, and I wasn't ready for that. I was angry because I saw him differently, the morning after the dogs, when Pa climbed out of the Volvo cab so carefully, with the .300 CZ hunting rifle over his shoulder and a Beretta in his hand. He walked through the dog carcasses with tentative steps, his body stiff and sore after the attack and the night of poor sleep. That was when I saw something, from the vantage of the truck, but I didn't want to see it.

Pa was smaller. Diminished.

Three nights ago, when he pressed my mouth shut at the last minute and the pistol shook in his hand, and the Jeep men were outside, I felt it, but I didn't want to feel it.

I was angry with Pa for being sick. For being weak. Now I was angry at him for falling in the darkness. His rifle was ready, he had seen that Muscles meant to shoot, but Pa couldn't shoot a human being. He just couldn't.

Three days ago, when he'd woken up so frantic, I knew, I understood then, but I didn't want to know.

All this fanned the flames of my anger. It made me want to stand up behind that rock and walk over to Pa where he lay on the tar in the pool of light cast by the house on the ridge. I wanted to scold him, though at that moment I did not have the full understanding and the capacity and the words to understand why. Years later it would make sense: that night, 24 March in the Year of the Dog, was the moment of the second great loss. The first was my mother and my life as I knew it. The dogs and their germs and the Jeep men and Pa's fever had robbed me again. They robbed me of the image of Willem Storm as the infallible protector, the all-knowing guide through life. They had robbed me of my father as a heroic figure.

Before the night in Koffiefontein he was big and strong and wise. Infallible. For the last time.

I lay against that rock, and looked at Pa where he had fallen. I saw his matted hair in the glow of the House of Light, and for the first time I saw my father as he truly was: a skinny man of average height. Fragile. Brittle. Fearful. Breakable. Mortal.

I shot Muscles. I could see him to the left of Pa in the untidy, over-grown garden of one of the other houses. He was etched against the light; time seemed to stop, his tall shadow seemed to move in slow motion, the big revolver still thrust out in front of him. I swung the scope on him, and I shot him, as I had practised, on tins and stones beside the road over the past five or six weeks. I shot him through the head, and I took my eye off the scope, looked at Pa, and saw another movement behind Muscles, deeper in the shadows. The man with long hair. He was coming towards the pavement. I swung the rifle, and I aimed and shot him with the Tikka .222. I shot him above his right eye, in the forehead, the blood making a dark spray against the light as he dropped.

It was the rage that made me shoot. The terrible rage.

I ran down the road to Pa. I nearly tripped over the low-strung fish-ing line. A flare hissed up into the air, and burst in a shower of light high in the heavens. Here below the shadows took on strange slow-motion life – trees, lampposts, houses, bushes, my father who lay there in the road. And then moved.

Pa staggered to his feet unsteadily. He held a hand to his neck. Blood was seeping through his fingers. It looked black.

'Pa,' I said. My voice sounded strange. To him too, I could see it in his gaze.

                            *   *   *

I was thirteen years old when I shot two people. Out of sheer rage. At the world and at my father.

That night I realised: *from now on, I will have to protect my father.* That would be my role.

II

Pa

(As I sit here writing, reliving that night, memories overwhelm me. They are jumbled, haphazard, the chronology confused. Chronology. I can't use that word without hearing my father's voice: '*Chronos* is Greek for "time", *logos* is derived from *legō*, which in ancient Greek means "I speak", which evolved to *logia*, the study of something. It's where we get the word and idea of "logic", for example . . .' And then he started to elaborate passionately on the Greeks and their civilisation, culminating with a sigh of deep regret: 'We were capable of so much, and so much, we lost.'

It's an odd thing, reopening the old doors, letting the winds of those past days blow in. Nostalgia and longing, pain and joy. Amazement: this is my life. This is how I was made and shaped. And the other great dilemma of this memoir: how to provide a readable framework for my narrative, despite the tricks of memory, and the complex navigation through the reefs of this emotional ocean.)

My father. Willem Storm. 'That damn polymath', as Nero Dlamini would often call him when Pa wasn't within earshot. My father was sensitive and gentle. He was a clever man. And wise. His qualifications as geographer and jurist – in that perverse order – were the official, academic indicators of his restless intellect, but they didn't tell the whole story. In practice, his interests and insight were much broader. He was half-historian, semi-philosopher, quasi-scientist. He had a huge appetite for knowledge, he was ever searching, constantly reading, and always questioning, completely buoyed up by, and totally in love with every aspect of *this* world. Not for him the narrow focus of a searchlight, but a brilliant lamp that illuminated everything around him. His perspective was always broad; it never excluded people, especially not me. Empathy was his core quality, that rare ability to see through others' eyes.

'What makes you like this, Willem?' Nero asked, shortly before my father's death, one evening in the Orphanage sitting room, each one nursing a glass of brandy.

'Like what?'

'You still look at the world wide-eyed, as if it's magical, everything and everyone. You live in wonderment, almost like a child, if you'll forgive me for saying so.'

Pa laughed, and he asked, 'Do you know the origin of the word "magical"?'

'You're not going to avoid the question.'

'Did you know the word "machine" has the same source as "magical"?'

'Why *are* you like this?'

'Because the world and life *are* magical, Nero. In a way. Because we can plan all we like, but the universe is indifferent to our schemes.'

'What made you this way?'

So Pa thought about it, and he replied that it came from growing up in a little town, the very last generation of children before the Internet. Oudtshoorn was big enough to have a good high school, yet still small enough and far enough from the city for country values to be preserved. At first Pa wanted to be a teacher, inspired by the good people who taught him. That was why he started off studying geography. But his roommate at university was a law student, and he began reading his textbooks, and Pa discovered another world that fascinated him. And in his third year he fell in love with Amelia Foord, and then he realised he would have to make something more of himself.

12

24 March

'My God, Nico,' said Pa. He moved his hand from the back of his neck, and looked in amazement at the blood on his fingers. His knees sagged. He sat down. 'I'll be all right in a minute,' he said apologetically.

I inspected his wound. In the light of the house on the hill I could see the tiny white tip of a neck vertebra, before the blood seeped over it. My father had been incredibly lucky. The bullet had grazed the back of his head, ripping through thin skin and soft flesh just below his skull. Millimetres from his brain stem.

'You're just badly wounded, Pa,' I said.

He nodded.

I could see Muscles lying on the pavement, his eyes wide, the back of his head a pulverised mess. The sight made me weak at the knees too. I stepped away from Pa. He looked at me with concern. I vomited, on to the tar road. Again and again.

Pa got up from his knees, and came to hold me. Looking back, I feel it was more a gesture of gratitude than comfort.

We smelled the liquor emanating from Muscles and Long Hair as we walked past them. That must have been the reason why Muscles missed.

The House of Light had merely been the bait. They were living in another house altogether, to the left of the street, the one they had come out from when Pa tripped a barely visible wire, and turned on a light inside.

The house smelled sour. There were empty bottles, tins and cartons and paper rubbish everywhere. Dirty clothes, dirty plates, dirty glasses.

Pa called out to the woman. No answer. We heard her whimper. Pa went ahead, he stopped at the threshold of the bedroom. 'Wait, Nico,' he said, 'the lady has no clothes.' I waited in the passage and could hear Pa talking quietly and gently to her in the room. She didn't reply. When they emerged, Pa had wrapped her in a sheet. Her body trembled just perceptibly. Her head hung low, but I could make out the purple and blue bruises on her face. Her hair was lank and greasy, and she smelled terrible.

Pa led her out, and down the street. We set off all the tripwire alarms on the way back, but we just didn't care any more.

13

The first woman

24 March

Pa offered the woman food, first in Afrikaans. She didn't hear, or she didn't understand. Pa tried English, then the smattering of French or German he could scrape together. That too produced no result. She just slumped on the couch cocooned in the dirty sheet, shivering and looking down at the carpet.

We warmed water for her in a big pot on the gas stove, and carried it to the bathroom, where we filled the bath. Pa led her to it and closed the door behind him when he came out.

An hour later he went back to check on her. When he came back out he said, 'She's still just sitting there, on the floor.' His voice was filled with pity.

We heated water again. Pa went in and bathed her, I waited in the kitchen. He helped her to dress in clothes that he found in a wardrobe in the master bedroom. Then he led her to the smaller bedroom. The clothes were a size too large. He tucked her into bed.

She still said not a word.

25 March

For many months it had been just the two of us travelling together. It felt strange now, knowing the woman was there.

Pa and I ate breakfast. The woman didn't move.

Pa was wrapped up like a mummy. The wound on the back of his neck was in an awkward place, and the bandage had to be wrapped around his forehead. And there were more bandages and plasters on the dog bites on his arms, back and shoulder.

I washed the dishes, Pa checked on the woman. 'She's asleep,' he whispered when he emerged.

We didn't talk about the previous night. Pa was changed. He discussed his plans with me. Before, he would have gone to bury Muscles and Long Hair on his own, to spare me the trauma. But this morning he took me along to help. It was a task that took hours, as the ground on the Vanderkloof hills was hard and very stony.

I threw up again when we dragged the bodies to the graves and covered them. Pa just said, 'Never mind, Nico. Never mind.'

We went back to the house, dripping with perspiration, dirty and nauseous. She was still asleep.

Pa took food to her in the bedroom. He woke her up. I stood at the door and watched. He had to feed her with a spoon while she stared at the wall with empty eyes, opening her mouth and swallowing, opening her mouth and swallowing.

Late in the afternoon we explored the town. We found a huge cobra in the OK Value supermarket. Pa said it must be after the rats and mice that were eating the meal and flour. The snake glided into the corner of the shop and then rose up with its hood spread. '*Sjoe*, what a beautiful animal,' said Pa. We walked warily back to the front door.

Pa couldn't kill snakes.

The shelves in the OK Value were pretty bare. Muscles and Long Hair must have carted most of the canned goods away.

The Alpha Pharm pharmacy was locked, the Renosterberg bottle store was almost empty, with the musty smell of stale, spilled beer left behind, and thousands of glass shards from broken bottles. 'There's a story here,' said Pa. 'I just can't decipher it.'

The post office was open, stacked with piles of undelivered letters and parcels. The police station windows were smashed and pigeons had made themselves at home inside.

On the corner the Midas spares and filling station was undamaged. We found a second desiccated corpse in the rear office. A man, his beanie still on his head. Pa said he posed no health risk to us, we would bury him another day.

Outside, on the pavement, he indicated I should sit beside him on the kerbstone. I watched him searching for words. Pa was almost never at a loss for words. I saw him quickly wipe his eyes. He said, 'I'm sorry. About last night. I . . .'

'It's okay, Pa.'

'I wanted to spare you that much longer.'

Pa took my hand. It was the last time in his life that he held my hand as if I were a child. He enclosed it between both of his, and pressed it against his cheek and just sat there like that. It made me uncomfortable, but I didn't move.

Pa dropped my hand again.

'The world now is . . . We'll fix it, Nico. We'll make it whole. You and me.'

'Yes, Pa.'

We stood up and went back to the house.

'I don't want us to stay in this house,' I told Pa and pointed at the place where we slept. Because it was here that he had been sick and weak.

The woman was still lying in the room. She didn't speak. Pa took her food. She only ate a little, but this time without his help.

In the night she started screaming. Eventually Pa managed to calm her down.

26 March

Pa was still in his room and I was brewing the morning coffee, around half past six. I think the aroma must have roused her. She came out of the bedroom and went to the bathroom and after a few minutes she came back. She sat down in the lounge area, sitting bolt upright, on the edge of the chair. She didn't look at me.

'Ma'am, would you like some coffee?'

She nodded.

I hid my surprise. 'With sugar?'

'And Cremora?'

She looked up at me. Her eyes were dark green, the bruises around them no better. She wasn't a pretty lady: she had a long face that made me think a little bit of a horse. I couldn't help it. She nodded a second time, and looked down.

'One day we'll taste fresh milk again.' I used my father's mantra, but she didn't respond.

I made her coffee and put it down in front of her. She looked at me again. I think it was her way of saying thank you.

Pa came in. He said, 'Morning, everyone,' breezily, as if everything were completely normal. He picked up his coffee, sat down with his back to her, and said, 'This morning we're cutting hair, Nico Storm, you look like a werewolf.'

She stood up and fetched the big pot and put it on the stove. I wanted to get up and help, but Pa put his hand on my arm. He said, 'We're going to make those recruitment pamphlets today. I want you to fetch the computer and printer. I have the wording just about right, and we'll write it in English only. Although I don't know what to call it yet. "Settlement" and "colony" are such loaded words in this country. Former country ... Maybe it doesn't even matter any more. Nonetheless, we want to attract good people of every sort ...'

Pa went on talking while the woman heated the water, and carried the big pot to the bathroom on her own. Once again, I wanted to help, but Pa just shook his head slightly to tell me to sit. I didn't really understand why.

I sat on a stool on the grass, bare-chested. Pa brandished a comb and scissors and began to cut.

The woman came out of the doorway and walked towards us. She took the scissors out of Pa's hand, and then the comb. Pa stood back and she began to cut my hair. You could tell straight away that she knew what she was doing.

Pa said, 'Maybe you can make him human again. Nico, call me when you're finished, I need a good trim too. I'm going to start writing that pamphlet.'

She touched my head. She was the first woman to touch me since my mother. I sat there, and missed my mother dreadfully. I longed for her to hold me. I wished that this woman would hold me tight, just for a little while.

She simply went on cutting my hair.

14

Ma

I can remember my mother's hugs.

Her name was Amelia, and her maiden name was Foord. We lived in a house in Die Boord in Stellenbosch, before the Fever.

She squeezed me tight when I cried. It made me feel completely safe. It was warm and smelled good, and for years I wished I knew what kind of perfume she wore, what made her smell like that.

Pa carried a photo of the three of us together. He kept it in a chocolate tin with two other pictures, and looked after this collection with great care. Back when we were still sharing a room, I would sometimes see him take out the photo and look at it. He grieved for Mother but he found it hard to talk about her. The photo showed a beautiful woman, with thick brown hair that she wore very short, and a wide, self-assured smile, as though she were exactly where she wanted to be, right there between us. Just as tall as Pa. In a summer frock that showed she was fit and strong. She was a provincial hockey player, and had nearly been selected for the national team, but she had to choose between her sport and her professional career. I remember the hockey stick that I found in a cupboard one day. It was battered, well used. I must have been eight or nine, and my mother took it out of my hands, and said, if you want to play hockey I'll buy you your own. But this stick belongs to me.

'Your wife?' people would ask Pa, the way everyone did.

'The Fever took her.'

I knew he mourned for her, and I tried to respect that, even when my own longing was fierce, when I wanted to ask him questions to refresh my memory or to ease my pain. Sometimes I just *had* to know, and then Pa would answer me. Sometimes he would also, in unguarded moments, mention or recall something about her. I collected every phrase, every scrap, like pieces of a jigsaw, so that I could preserve the image of her, and build on it.

She was a statistician at the university, and worked at a place called the Centre for Complexity Studies.

My wife was the clever one.

Pa said she'd been working on a project to relieve poverty; it was very important to her.

She had a good heart, a very good heart.

She had a strong personality.

And the one I wondered about most of all: *you are your mother's child*. That's what Pa said to me during that terrible winter of great hunger when I gave my food to the little ones. And he said it again when I shot the KTM off their motorbikes in the Year of the Jackal.

15

27 March

On the N1 beyond Trompsburg. Myself and Pa up front in the Volvo, the woman sitting upright on the bunk in the back, looking ahead through the windscreen. A straight section of road across the Free State plains. My hair was short and neatly trimmed, Pa's too. The woman had dressed Pa's neck wound and cleaned and disinfected the festering bite wounds on his back early this morning, but still she had not said a word.

I was bored after the excitement of the previous days. 'Let's play a CD,' I said.

'Let the lady choose,' said Pa.

I pulled the shoe box out from under my seat. We had found it inside a red Mercedes SL 500, near Makwassie. Someone had driven the expensive car until the very last drop of petrol was gone, and then just abandoned it. The box of music was the only thing in the car. There were nearly forty CDs in it, from pop to classics.

I handed the box to the woman. She held it on her lap for a moment, then looked up and saw me waiting. She opened it and looked at the contents, flipping through the spines of the CDs with her fingers, and reading the titles. She took one out, turning it over in her hands like something precious, then held it out to me.

It was one of Kurt Darren's CDs. *In Jou Oë*. In Your Eyes. Not one I knew. I wanted to take it from her, but she held her finger on the very first song.

'This one?' I asked. '"Heidi"?'

She nodded, the way she did when she wanted coffee. The slightest movement.

'Okay.'

The song began. An upbeat rhythm, and a cheerful tune. I turned up the sound. Pa shook his head, but he smiled and his fingers kept time on the steering wheel, and he pressed the accelerator more so the Volvo's big diesel engine joined in like a string of double basses. The music filled the cab with a jolly atmosphere. I grinned at the woman. Her eyes were closed.

When the song ended, she opened her eyes and she said her very first word to us: 'Again.' With a huge 'please' in her face and voice.

I played the song again, turning it up a little louder this time. I was catching on to the chorus now, and sang along.

Pa laughed. He glanced across at me, drove faster.

When it was finished the woman said, 'Again.'

I played it another time. Pa and I sang along. Loudly. The Volvo thundered. For the first time in a year I felt exuberant. Happy. The world wasn't such a terribly bad place after all.

The song ended. I looked at the woman. Her cheeks were drenched with tears, her eyes closed, and her body shuddered with weeping. She raised her palm to indicate I must stop the CD. I pressed the button.

Pa turned round to look at her.

I drew a breath to say something, because I couldn't understand why she was crying, she had wanted me to play the music after all. Pa squeezed my arm to stop me. The woman cried for a long time, maybe more than twenty minutes. Then she grew quieter and quieter, until she wiped the last of her tears away with the back of her hand.

Then she softly touched my shoulder.

'My name is Melinda Swanevelder,' she said.

At that moment, before we could react, an aeroplane flew over, from right to left across the road in front of us, very low and close to us. Pa braked sharply. '*Good grief*,' he said.

Everything always happens at once, just when you least expect it.

The plane was small, of the kind with the wing above the cabin, with a single propeller engine. It made a fancy turn in the air, and flew in the direction we were driving, parallel with the road.

'*Wooow!*' I yelled at the plane, and with sheer happiness that Melinda Swanevelder was at last talking to us. It was the first plane we had seen for ages. We used to hear planes in the sky until about seven months before, jets flying high and going somewhere far away. But it had happened less and less, and never so clearly right here in front of us like this one.

The plane was white, with a red tail. It flew ahead, parallel to the road, then turned and came at us from the front, straight down the road towards us. Flying low, and when he was a few hundred metres away, he waggled his wings as if to greet us. I opened the window and hung out, waving madly. 'Nico, don't lean out so far,' Pa said, as the plane shot just over our heads, and then he was gone beyond the trailer.

I closed the window. 'Ma'am, did you see?'

She nodded. A small smile played on her face, probably at my excitement.

'There's only one man in that plane,' said Pa. He looked in the rear-view mirror. 'Look, he's turning . . . Here he comes again.'

The plane came from behind. I could only see it once the belly swept right over us. He flew above the road now, ahead of us, slowing. He dropped lower. 'He wants to land, Pa,' I said. 'On the road.'

Pa took his foot off the accelerator. 'It's straight enough,' he said.

The plane dropped and the wheels touched down on the tar. Pa began to brake, keeping his distance behind the plane. He reached for his pistol in the door beside him, looking at the surrounding veld. I knew he was checking for a potential ambush.

The plane came to a halt, and so did we. The Volvo and the plane were about ten metres from each other. The door of the plane opened and a man jumped out. He was short, somewhere in his forties, an ugly man with a face like a pug dog, protruding eyes and deeply lined forehead. He was wearing flip-flops and shorts and a khaki shirt. He had a fat paunch and a wide grin. He waved and then walked towards us, lighting up a cigarette. You could just see he wasn't dangerous.

Pa switched off the truck's engine.

'Good day, people,' the man said.

Pa and I got out. Melinda Swanevelder remained sitting high in the truck cab.

I asked, 'What kind of plane is that, sir?' and went to peer in the windows. It was full of boxes, big ones and small ones. Cigarettes. 'Is that all cigarettes, sir? What do you do with all the cigarettes?'

Pa laughed, shook the man's hand, and said, 'Slow down, Nico. Excuse my son, you're about the first man we've spoken to in weeks. His name is Nico, I'm Willem. Willem Storm.'

The man told us his name was Hennie Laas, they called him Hennie Fly, and he was from Heidelberg in Gauteng. It was a Cessna 172; his pilot's licence had expired before the Fever, but who cares, there was nobody to enforce those things now. He flew back and forth these days, to all the small and medium places, the big places were dangerous, he felt. You couldn't see from the air whether the people were bad. But the smaller towns, if there were people, they came running out when they heard a plane, you could just see it was safe. He, Hennie Fly, was collecting 'ciggies' and pipe tobacco; he knew they would become currency, at least until someone began growing tobacco again in Zim and trade routes were re-established, almost like the Middle Ages. Did Pa smoke? Did we have something to barter? He would trade a few cartons of ciggies for a juicy steak; dammit, it had been a long time since he'd eaten a good piece of meat, not all this damned canned rubbish . . .

Pa said no, we don't have steaks, we're on a recruiting trip. 'We're starting a new settlement. Nico, fetch one of those pamphlets. We're setting up a place, a refuge, at the old Vanderkloof. We're going to need good people, pilots too.' Pa and Hennie Fly, both starved of adult conversation, stood between a big Volvo truck and a Cessna 172, in the middle of the wide N1 on the far side of Trompsburg, and they couldn't stop talking.

I fetched the pamphlet. He handed it to Hennie, as if he were proud of it. Hennie read aloud: 'A New Beginning for Good People,' with a heavy Afrikaans accent.

'Yes, it's in English,' said Pa. 'We want to reach everyone.'

'We are starting a sanctuary, a community that will have justice, wisdom, moderation and courage . . .'

'It's from Plato,' said Pa. 'From *The Republic*.'

'I see,' said Hennie, in a tone that revealed he had no idea what Pa was talking about, and he flicked his cigarette butt across the road. He read on: '. . . in a very safe place with more than enough water, shelter, and soon, food and electricity . . .' He looked dubiously at Pa. 'Electricity?'

Pa explained about the hydro-electricity. 'We just need someone to lay it on to the town. If you run into an engineer somewhere . . .'

Hennie Fly nodded, and read on: 'If you want to be part of this orderly, open, democratic and free new society, come to Vanderkloof (on the R48 between Colesberg and Kimberley). GPS coordinates are: 29.99952512 Latitude and 24.72381949 Longitude.'

He looked at Pa. 'You're taking a risk too. How do you know a bunch of *skarminkels* won't turn up?'

'What's a *skarminkel*, Pa?'

'*Lieplapper*. A layabout,' said Hennie. And when he saw I still didn't get it. 'A *maaifoedie*, a scoundrel. A rubbish.'

'We will *have* to run risks, if we want to rebuild something,' said Pa. 'If the majority are good people, it shouldn't be a problem.'

Hennie read the last lines of the pamphlet: 'Send these, the home-less, tempest-tost to me, I lift my lamp beside the golden door!'

'That's Emma Lazarus,' said Pa.

'Is that her up there?' asked Hennie and pointed at Melinda Swanevelder in the Volvo.

Pa said no, Emma Lazarus was an American poet. She wrote the poem that is engraved on the Statue of Liberty. The woman in the cab is Melinda Swanevelder. We found her in Vanderkloof.

Hennie barely heard him. He stood staring at Melinda. 'Pretty woman,' he said and lifted his hand to greet her. 'Shoo, very pretty woman.'

She waved back, a tiny motion of a hesitant hand.

'Where are you going?' asked Pa.

'Well, it sounds like I should go to Vanderkloof,' and Hennie reluc-tantly turned his gaze away from the woman to Pa.

'You don't feel like a bit of a detour along the way? We'll still be on the road for a week or two.'

'I can . . .'

'So, when you fly over the towns, the people come out of their hiding places?'

'If there are people. Most of the towns are totally godforsaken.'

'Yes, I guess the population density is less than one and a half per square kilometre now . . . Would you consider throwing our pamphlets out of your plane, where there are people?'

16

The Fever

I understand this, from what I experienced, from what Pa told me, from Nero Dlamini's sober judgement, and from each of the survivor's stories that Pa recorded or wrote down as part of the Amanzi History Project.

The Fever was a virus tsunami. Too rapid, too deadly.

Despite the protocols and systems and vaccines, despite the frantic scurrying of virologists and epidemiologists, centres for disease control, and governments and military intervention – and sometimes even *because* of some of these attempts – the Fever wiped out 95 per cent of the world population. All within a few months.

Five per cent of the world population, more or less, had the genetic good fortune of natural resistance to the virus. But not all those 5-per-centers survived the aftermath of the Fever. The catastrophe caused systems to collapse and released other disasters: industrial explosions, fires, chemical pollution, radioactive contamination, hepatitis and cholera. And the human element. In Domingo's words: 'Where the corona virus stopped, Darwin stepped in.' Greed and fear, crime and misunderstanding, ignorance and stupidity. Chaos. Some of the survivors were just too tiny to make a go of it alone, five years old and younger. Others were overwhelmed by the stress and trauma of unfathomable loss and post-Fever crimes. Thousands took their own lives. In the big cities especially.

Standing between the Cessna and the Volvo, Hennie Fly asked my father, 'Now how would you know there are less than one and a half people per square kilometre?'

Pa explained that approximately fifty-three million people lived in what was South Africa before the Fever.

Ninety-five per cent, or fifty million, were wiped out by the virus and its successors. And another million – more or less – died from other causes in the aftermath.

Hennie Fly nodded. That made sense.

'Two million left. It sounds like a lot of people, but if you divide that by the size of the land, it's less than one and a half per square kilometre.'

'Okay,' said Hennie Fly.

'Let me put it into perspective for you,' said Pa. 'South Africa was one point two million square kilometres. Before the Fever the population density was forty-five people per square kilometre. That's not so bad. Monaco, for example, used to have fifteen thousand people per square kilometre. Bangladesh more than a thousand, and Germany two hundred and thirty-two.'

17

Hennie Fly

As recorded by Willem Storm. The Amanzi History Project.

My name is Hennie Laas. Everyone calls me Hennie Fly.

Ja, *look, when the Fever came, I was a farm manager at the Nel farm on the other side of Heidelberg.*

I was divorced, my ex-wife was remarried to a Badenhorst from Centurion. We had two children, two girls, they lived with her and the Badenhorst guy. They all died in the Fever. I went to look, I went to the house in Centurion. There was nobody there. I mean, where do you go and look, if they are not at home? You know how it was, during that time . . . I'm getting too far ahead of myself, I suppose?

Anyway, I come from Heidelberg, I was born there. My father grew up in poverty, but he worked his way to riches. He used to supply the gold mines in those years; he made his money out of the props they used underground. Blue gum poles. He always drove Jaguars, he loved Jaguar cars. I think, if your father is rich, you are lazy, because you think everything will come to you. So I went to university to study for a commerce degree, but it didn't last. I partied too much. I dropped out before the end of my first year, and I begged my dad to let me fly, I was mad about flying. So I got my pilot's licence, and I went to work for Lowveld Air; they used to fly people to the Kruger Park. I was a co-pilot in the Beechcraft King Airs, hell, those were genuine royal planes those. And I wore a pilot's uniform and the girls loved that, and I gave myself the nickname of 'Hennie Fly', I told everyone, you know, that's what people call me. I lied. I thought I was this big shot, even though the captain wouldn't let me touch a joystick. Then I met Doreen, and she got pregnant on the third date, and we got married. But then Lowveld Air went bankrupt. I couldn't find work, and my father said I should come and work with him. After only a year he fired me. Total slacker. So I went to work for Justin's Cars, second-hand cars, and I worked for KFC as an apprentice manager, and my pilot's licence expired. Our second daughter arrived, and I was boozing too much, didn't come home at night, and Doreen left me. First it was just separate beds and tables, and she said, sort yourself out or I leave. Then she did leave. I don't blame her, I was bad, back then. So I worked a bit here and I worked a bit there.

It took me ten years to sort myself out, to quit my nonsense. To grow up, I suppose. Every year I had another job; for about eighteen months I was in Durban as well, trying to rep for Castrol. That didn't stick either. Jannie Nel was one of the big farmers in Heidelberg. He gave a lot of people a second chance. So I went and asked him for a job. Three years before the Fever. I used to drive a sheep lorry to the abattoir for him. And when he saw I had stopped my nonsense, he made me assistant foreman, and later foreman, on one of the chicken farms. They called it 'farm manager'.

Then I began to fix things with my children. Once a month, I drove to Pretoria, and I took them to the Spur restaurant. That was the beginning. I knew I had a long way to go with them. I began to fly again too, I tried to get enough hours to get my licence back.

Then the Fever came. How can you talk about the Fever? You can't describe it.

It must have been the same as it was for everyone. You watch the news on TV, and you think, no, they will stop this thing before it gets here, but you wonder, and you are a little bit scared. Just like with Ebola, a couple of years before the Fever. But you think, we live in a time of science, they'll do something, so you don't worry too much. Until England and America and all of them began to cancel flights and impose states of emergency. Then you worry, because it's never been this bad before. And then the virus was here, and you think, now they'd better do something fast, and for the first time you're really scared. And then the power goes off, and no one comes to work, and I phone and phone my children, but they don't answer their cellphones. And then the cellphone networks go down. I hid away on that chicken farm, I won't lie to you. I think I'm still alive because I lived there, slept there, and went nowhere. Then the radio went quiet, everything was quiet, and I sat and watched the road, but there was nothing. Then I took the pick-up and drove. And I smelled Heidelberg, from four kilometres away I smelled all those dead people. And I knew.

There's a time when you feel guilty for surviving, and you don't know why you were so lucky, because you were such a bad person. But then you get used to it. It's funny, hey?

I turned around and drove back to the farm, and I let all the chickens out of the batteries.

18

For a week we didn't see anyone.

We took the bypass around Bloemfontein, and went through Winburg and Senekal and Bethlehem; we pasted our pamphlets on stop signs and road signs and the doors of churches, we scattered them in the doorways of deathly quiet supermarkets and pharmacies. At every town library and school library we went in with empty boxes, and came out with boxes full of books. Half of the long sixteen-wheeler trailer was already full of books, the rest of the cargo was tinned food, coffee and medicine. 'For our sanctuary, for our future,' as Pa would say to spur me on to carry yet another heavy box out to the truck.

Near Bloemfontein we saw zebras grazing beside the freeway; they galloped off as we approached. I told Pa those were the animals we had freed.

Perhaps there were people in the towns, perhaps they hid away when we passed. We drove to Clocolan and Ladybrand and Wepener, Aliwal North and Adelaide. We didn't see another living soul, but we scattered our pamphlets in bottle stores, and pasted them on the windows of filling stations.

Pa slept less comfortably these nights, because Melinda Swanevelder and I shared the bed, and he had to make do with reclining his seat as flat as it would go.

Melinda communicated very little with her voice. Mostly she used her eyes and face. She took over some of my duties. She made the coffee, and she wanted to do the dishes too, but Pa said no, I have to do something. By the time five days had passed, it felt as though she had always been with us.

4 April

In the early afternoon, on the other side of Fort Beaufort, a big Aberdeen Angus bull ran across the road in front of us. His black hide glistened with sweat, he was bleeding on his rump and flanks. Behind him, snarling around him, was a pack of dogs, the same lean type that had attacked me and Pa.

Pa slowed down, the bull ran through the barbed wire to the right of the road. The wire cut him, held him back a moment. And the dogs sprang on him.

Melinda Swanevelder drew in a sharp breath. Then she looked away, she didn't want to witness it.

The bull shook off the dogs, he ran on, towards a dense thicket.

Then we were past, and we couldn't see any more.

'About twenty of them,' said Pa. 'Just like wild dogs. The same pack size.'

He was talking to himself, but he didn't try to hide his concern.

We were a few kilometres before Grahamstown, driving slowly past the golf course on the left, barely forty kilometres an hour. That was always Pa's way when we were near a town. He was looking out of his side window and Melinda lay sleeping in the back. I was the only one who saw the white vehicle approaching from the front – one of those little buses that have been converted into a caravan. Almost immediately it pulled off the road, and stopped.

'Pa,' I said excitedly, and pointed, sure that I was seeing the first signs of human life since Hennie Fly.

'What?'

'That bus thingy. It just stopped now.'

Pa braked. Behind us Melinda Swanevelder sat up.

'It's a camper,' said Pa. The vehicle was immobile and Pa asked, 'Are you sure?' I had sounded a false alarm once or twice before out of wishful thinking.

'I think so.'

Pa stopped the Volvo in the middle of the road. I passed him the binoculars without him having to ask. He had a look. The camper was parked on the gravel verge of the road, four hundred metres away, just before the long curve to the left.

'Can you see anything, Pa?' I was starting to doubt whether I had really seen the vehicle moving.

'No, son . . .'

Pa passed the binoculars to me. I looked. There was no sign of life. I felt embarrassed; I realised I had made a mistake.

Pa said, 'Let's go a little closer, maybe he's afraid of us, perhaps he's lying flat . . .' But I could hear that he was just trying to make me feel better. He pulled away, drove slowly closer.

We stopped beside the camper. On the door were the words *Ibhayi Camper Hire*. Down the side, near the back it said *Discoverer 6*. There was a Fiat emblem on the front grille. We looked down on the camper from the high Volvo horse. There was no one behind the steering wheel. The two windows of the living area were covered by curtains.

'The tracks are fresh,' said Pa quietly, and reached for his pistol in the door beside him, his left hand working the gear lever so that he was ready to pull away. 'See, behind the tyres.'

Melinda lay down and pulled the blanket over her. I stared. Behind the camper, between the wheels and the tarmac, were clear tracks from the tyres.

'What did you see, Nico?'

'He was driving, and when he saw us, he stopped quickly.'

The curtain of the camper's large middle window twitched a little, right in the middle, at the bottom.

'Did you see that, Pa?'

'Get your pistol,' said Pa. He released the clutch, and drove slowly forward, lifting his firearm to hold it against his window; he wanted to make sure they saw it. I took mine out of the cubby-hole. I knew I would have to shoot, if there was shooting to be done.

The curtain moved again. For a second there was a tiny face at the window. 'It's a child,' said Pa, and stopped again. He lowered his window. He called out, 'Hello!'

Just the big diesel engine idling.

'Hello, we come in peace, one man, one woman, one child here,' Pa called out.

Dead still.

'We have food and drink.'

The driver's door opened. A woman sat up, she must have been lying flat. She climbed out. She held a shotgun in her hands, double-barrelled. She pointed it at Pa. 'Let me see the child,' she said.

I wriggled in beside Pa, and hung out of his window. 'Hello, ma'am, we're good people.'

The woman was tall and brown, her hair was very short. She had a sturdy prominent chin, like someone with a very strong will. She wasn't convinced. 'And the woman?'

Pa looked back. Melinda still had her head under the blanket. 'That's not going to be so easy.'

The curtains in the camper drew wider apart. We could see more children inside, half a dozen or so of them. A few were a little older, six or seven.

'How many children do you have in the back?' Pa asked.

'Let me see the woman first.'

Pa said Melinda's name gently. She slowly emerged from under the blanket and I made space for her, so she could show her face.

'Are these good people?' the woman asked her.

I thought, please, Melinda, say something now.

'Very good people,' she said, barely more than a whisper.

The woman stood a while longer with the shotgun trained on Pa, and then lowered it. 'My name's Beryl Fortuin,' she said. 'Do you really have food?'

The children began to climb out behind her, a process that went on for a surprisingly long time: black, brown and white, until a large group of them stood in the road.

'How many are there?' Pa asked.

'There are sixteen children,' said Beryl.

We stood at the back of the Volvo's trailer, the doors open wide, tinned food and cans of fruit juice, rusks and biltong spread out on a camping table. We added our own spoons to all the ones from the camper, and still there were not enough. The sixteen children had to take turns. They were all much younger than me. Eleven girls, of whom the oldest was six, and five boys, between three and four. Some were loud and boister-ous, others clung timidly to Beryl's legs. A little boy of three walked shyly up to Melinda Swanevelder and looked up at her, full of hope.

'If you pick him up, another two will want the same,' said Beryl Fortuin. I could see how muscular her arms were, for a woman.

Melinda nodded, and picked up the boy. He put his arms around her, hugged her tight. She closed her eyes.

Beryl Fortuin said it was impossible to keep them quiet, to keep them obedient; she saw us coming in the big truck, so she stopped and lay down behind the camper's driving seat. She told them to be dead quiet, not to move. Then two of them peeped through the window. What could you do? And this after they had been robbed at the bridge over the Sundays River. Five men, or six, she couldn't, and she didn't really want to, remember. Men who used three children, those three – and she pointed them out, two black children and white-blond head – as bait, who made them stand beside the road and cry. So she stopped, and the men ran out and took the food and water she had. Food and water for the children. They wanted to do other things with her, if it hadn't been for the children and the elephants. The elephants, which emerged from the bush, and the children, who began to shriek and cry when the men grabbed Beryl by the hair . . .

That was when Melinda Swanevelder began to cry again. For the second time.

She was standing with the little boy on her breast, his arms around her neck, one moment with her eyes still shut, but when Beryl began to describe the men grabbing her by the hair, Melinda pressed her face against the child, sank to her knees and wept.

The little boy and some of the children came to comfort her, their faces worried. Some shed tears with her.

Beryl looked at Pa questioningly while she tried to console the children.

Pa said, 'Let her cry. There're a lot of bad things she needs to get out.' He went and stood beside Melinda and patted her awkwardly on the shoulder.

Only much later, when everyone had calmed down, Beryl said, *ja*, it was the elephants that saved her. The children's shrill screams, and the elephants that walked out of the bush across the river at that moment, and splashed loudly through the water towards them. It was as though the children's terrified screams had called the elephants. They must have escaped from the Addo Park. There had been a lot of rain in the area, the fences must have washed away. The men abandoned the three children with her too. Maybe that's what the gods intended, for her to protect the children. She, who was on record saying she didn't have time for children in the life she had planned.

'Where are you headed?' Pa asked.

She shrugged. 'To the next town. Somewhere safe, where I can feed the children. Where I can get help.' She stepped closer, speaking low so the children would not hear. 'Nobody wants them. Everyone is too busy trying to survive.' And then, more quietly, with a voice heavily burdened with guilt: 'But there are too many for me.'

'Come with us to Vanderkloof,' said Pa.

19

Pa and I drove in front. It was a couple of hours before sunset and we were on the lookout for a place where we could all safely spend the night. Melinda Swanevelder had switched to the front passenger seat of the camper and travelled with Beryl and the children.

On the road to Jansenville we saw the advertisement board for the Koedoeskop Game Ranch. We turned off, drove in. Blue wildebeest raised a cloud of dust as they dashed off. Further away a herd of springbok lifted their heads, and trotted lazily up a *koppie*, as if they at least remembered the harmless presence of tourists. Two warthogs occupied the veranda of the resort, reluctant to surrender the over-grown garden.

Pa said, 'Bring the Tikka.' He picked up his .300 CZ. We jumped out of the lorry. He jogged over to the women in the other vehicle. 'Just wait a bit, we're going to check the place out,' he said.

We walked side by side. We were the men, we had to do men's work: secure everything. I liked that. I mimicked Pa, and held my rifle in front of me. Cocked, finger on the trigger.

The buildings consisted of a pretty old farmstead that had been converted into a guest house. We opened the door. Pigeons flapped up suddenly in the reception area, startling us. They flew out through a broken skylight and we saw from the decor that it had been a luxury game farm. 'Probably for international tourists,' said Pa. There were hunting trophies on the walls: heads of kudu and buffalo and blue wildebeest, now soiled with pigeon droppings.

Everything was quiet, everything was safe.

Outside the back door, towards the *lapa*, we found a human skull and a few ribs scattered across the yard. The Fever had overtaken someone here. The animals had stripped the carcass and scattered the bones. We picked them up and threw them into the long grass.

*　　*　　*

We carried cartons of food to the kitchen. Pa stood and gazed out over the veld. He put a box down and said, 'Come on, Nico. We've got a lot of mouths to feed. Let's see if we can bring down a couple of springbok, then we can have a barbecue tonight.'

That was a first for the two of us.

We fetched the rifles and walked in silence in the direction that the buck had trotted off. The sun hunkered low on the horizon, the light soft, the colour of honey. The shrubs were overgrown and lush green in the late summer, the veld filled with the sound of birdsong and insects.

Pa stood still. He looked at the hills, the clouds, all the shades and textures. 'Hell, Nico, it's beautiful.'

I noticed something different about Pa. The people, Beryl and the children, seemed to have given him a purpose and a determination. I didn't understand why.

Pa cocked his head to one side to listen, and said, 'I think it must have been like this, before the Europeans came. You know, Africa.'

It took us twenty minutes to stalk the antelope. Pa gestured at me. I didn't know what he was trying to tell me. 'Take the shot,' he whispered.

It was years before I realised that this was also a pivotal moment. He had brought his rifle along, but I don't believe he ever intended to shoot. It was my job now. Later, around the fire, he took out a bottle of red wine and poured glasses only for himself and the two women. In spite of everything else, I wasn't old enough for wine.

Our first meal as a little family was not at Vanderkloof.

Melinda Swanevelder made *roosterkoek* dough with self-raising flour, sugar and sunflower oil from the game farm's untouched pantry. We cooked the dough over the coals and ate the hot buns with apricot jam. Pa and I barbecued the crudely butchered meat. The children played all around the building and outside in the light of the gas lamp and the campfire. Their high-pitched voices were exuberant, the little bodies active after sitting still in the camper all day. We all ate together around the fire in the *lapa*, under the stars. It was a delight, after months of isolation, to hear the babble of children and women's voices, the aroma of barbecued meat, and the taste of food that hadn't come from a tin or a carton.

When the children were asleep in the resort's spacious sitting room, sprawled higgledy-piggledy on sofas and easy chairs, and covered by blankets, I went back outside to sit with the adults, and Pa poured more wine and tossed some more logs on the fire. Then Beryl told her story.

She was a golf player, the resident female pro at the Pezula resort outside Knysna. She smiled wryly and confessed it was a profession that left her with absolutely no aptitude for a post-apocalyptic world, apart from fitness and some people skills.

Pa said those were probably not bad skills to have.

Her mother had been old and frail and one of the first victims of the Fever. Beryl went to Humansdorp to bury her. Then she went back to work, to keep busy, and process the loss, what else was there to do? The country was paralysed; chaotic. She had watched her colleagues and the hotel guests fall ill, while she remained well. She helped where she could, kept vigil, and watched them die, one after the other. Till she was the sole survivor. Then she felt the urge to go back to Humansdorp, where she had grown up. That was where she wanted to hide or die, or make a new start; everything was so horrible, painful and uncertain.

Beryl's voice was burdened that night at the campfire by the trauma of her journey, you could hear the hardship in every word.

She took an old, white Nissan 1400 pick-up truck; she had felt too guilty to take someone else's luxury car without their say-so. The first of the children was standing at the roadside at Harkerville. Six years old, hungry and thirsty, and completely alone. She stopped, and heard heart-rending weeping in a wooden house nearby. She found two more children there, family apparently, one sister, one cousin, or something like that, they looked so alike. They were too small to explain their relationship to each other. She thought the resistance to the virus must be genetic, because there was a woman who had survived the Fever as well. The mother, perhaps. Beryl found her two hundred metres into the Knysna forest. She had hanged herself from a tree.

Beryl Fortuin

As recorded by Willem Storm. The Amanzi History Project.

It was a very dangerous time, that time. The Fever wasn't completely burned out, you still found sick people on the roads, and sick people in the towns and so on. You couldn't yet tell who was going to survive and who wasn't. I think it was also because it was the Tsitsikamma, where people in the forest lived so isolated from each other that they only picked up the virus when they came out. Having the children with me, I had to upgrade to a bigger car. It was awful for me, it always bothered me to just take other people's stuff. How could you know that someone wasn't coming back to look for their car? But I took a minibus outside Plett.

So many odd things happened, so many things that you could never forget. Just before Storms River there was a man who was very sick, he drove his BMW right across our lane, as if he wanted to hit us. I think it was attempted suicide, and a case of 'I'm not going to die alone'. Luckily for us he missed, and veered into the forest, where he hit a tree and the car caught fire. I told the children not to look, but they did anyway.

I understand that people go out of their minds, really, I understand. But do you want to take a minibus full of children to the grave with you? That is seriously messed up, even under those conditions.

At the big filling station by the bridge at Storms River, there was a woman in a Fortuner; she came up to me, she could barely walk. You could see the Fever had her. And she said, come, see. I went to look. In her car Lizzie was lying asleep, four years old. And she said, I'm going to die, but there's nothing wrong with Lizzie; please, you already have three children with you, take Lizzie. And she turned around and wept terribly and walked into the forest, stumbling and falling. She left her child in the car. So then I had four. Me. I never wanted children, and then suddenly I had four. And I only knew the name of one.

Humansdorp in the immediate aftermath of the Fever was not a good place for children, not with all the decaying corpses and the madness of the few remaining survivors. For weeks she and the four little ones lived on a farm beside the Gamtoos River, until the worst was over. Then they went to Humansdorp, and all she found there was yet another child. And then on to Jeffreys Bay and Port Elizabeth, where the collection of children grew and grew. She said they became a sort of composite Pied Piper of Hamelin, because the voices of the children with her kept luring other orphans out of their hiding places. In Motherwell two men had five Xhosa children in their care. They pretended they were going to join forces with her, but the next morning the men were gone, and the children were still there.

Nobody wanted the children. Everyone was too busy trying to survive.

She just kept on the move.

5 April

Pa let the Discoverer 6 drive in front, because the camper was slow, it struggled to reach eighty in the head wind. We followed about a hundred metres behind. Pa gave Beryl a small Zartec two-way radio, so we could talk to each other. Just before Graaff-Reinet, he asked her to let us pass, to make sure the town was safe.

In the middle of the village Pa said, 'Good Lord,' and he stopped in the street and pointed.

I saw a painting, gigantic and colourful, spread across three old buildings. It was a herd of Nguni cattle on the veld, incredibly lifelike.

Pa raised the radio to his mouth. 'Do you see the painting?'

'It's amazing. Was it always here?'

'No,' said Pa. 'These are historical buildings. The Wijnkamer wine shop and the hotel. They always had white walls.'

I could see more scenes painted across the buildings ahead, to the left and right of the main street. And then I saw the church, half a kilometre further on, in the middle of the street, with its tall spire. The church building was now the shoulders of another Nguni cow, the tower was turning into a head and a single horn. There was a long ladder propped against the church spire, and a small figure at the top of the ladder. I pointed it out to Pa.

We stopped at the church. There was a man up the ladder busy with a big brush. He was a black man, tall and wiry. The only piece of clothing he wore was a pair of bright green gym shorts and he had brown sandals on his feet. He waved at us with the brush, his white teeth exposed in a grin, his left hand held tight to the ladder.

'You like?' he asked and gestured at his artwork.

'Yes!' Pa shouted back.

Beryl stopped behind us. The sixteen children burst out of the camper to have a look.

Later on, the painter turned down the invitation to go with us to Vanderkloof. He wanted to stay here, with his art. There were still a lot of paintings to do.

When we left, Pa said, be careful of the dogs.

20

Domingo

It's more than three decades since I saw Domingo for the first time. I think my memories today are strongly coloured by the huge impression he made on me as a thirteen-year-old. The reality was probably less dramatic and romantic, but allow me to tell it precisely as I remember it. At least I'm absolutely certain of the date: 7 April in the Year of the Dog.

I remember the dates, because I wrote them down in my diary. This journal dates from the first weeks of the Fever, when Pa and I lived in the caves of the Vredefort Dome. Or rather, hid there. I'm not sure how to describe it. Pa gave me the book, a yellow Moleskine journal, and a black pen. He told me that all the great explorers kept a travel journal. 'Just a few words every day, Nico, so that you will remember it later.'

On the evening of 7 April I wrote only one word: *Domingo*. It was all I needed to remember.

Late in the afternoon on 5 April we brought Beryl and the children and the camper to Vanderkloof. There was no one there. Absolutely no reaction to the hundreds of pamphlets we had distributed.

Pa hid his disappointment in frenetic activity. He decided we would move into the former Pride Rock guest house – it was simply easier to protect, care for and manage everyone that way. Early next morning he pumped the green, dirty water out of the half-empty swimming pool to make it safer for the little ones. I had to help him to connect a petrol generator, so the children could take a hot bath. It took a few hours to get all sixteen clean and dressed – it was weeks since some of them had had a proper bath.

We lugged cartons of food into the kitchen, carted books to the sitting room, packed them neatly, and cleaned the whole place.

Pa and I searched the houses in town for children's clothing, and for more food. We found a quadbike under a shed and push-started it by towing it behind the Volvo. Pa spent fifteen minutes teaching me how to ride the thing, and another hour to explain how easy it was to overturn the vehicle. He let me practise over and over, on the road and in the veld.

That night Melinda cooked pasta with a sauce of tinned tomatoes and meatballs. It was more delicious than anything that Pa had made us so far. We pushed all the four-seater tables in the guest house together. We ate together, as a community.

On the morning of 6 April Pa took me to sit with him in the garden, beside the empty swimming pool. He spoke earnestly. The Rolfontein Nature Reserve is here behind us, high in the hills, he said. It was two-thirds encircled by water, one-third by cliffs, superbly fenced, and almost unreachable by any road besides the one that ran through Vanderkloof. There were gemsbuck and kudu, springbok and impala in it. It would be our game farm, but soon our stock farm too. Because the dogs were busy exterminating sheep and cattle. The pair of us, father and son, would have to take a truck or something within the next week, and go and capture sheep and bring them here while there still were some left. Cattle too. But for those we would need help. Maybe Hennie Fly. Perhaps someone else . . .

But for now, for the foreseeable future, we would use the reserve as a source of fresh meat for the women and children. 'Take the quad-bike, and hunt for us. Take one of the radios . . .'

I was eager and excited. I was thirteen years old and I could go hunting with a quadbike. I leapt up before he had finished talking, but Pa called me back. 'I can see that you can't wait to ride the thing. Nico, be careful. It's a powerful vehicle, with that ratio of power versus weight. You are going to be tempted to do something with that power. But think twice. If you are lying bleeding under a bush up there in the mountain, and I don't find you . . . Stay on the tracks, so I can come and help you if something happens. And remember, there are white rhino too, some of the last survivors. Don't take chances.'

He talked me back down to earth. He said we had a whole lot of people that we were responsible for now. He was depending on me. 'But I know you will handle it with ease.'

Pa still knew how to manage me in those days.

On the morning of 7 April I was making a framework of sturdy sticks on which to stretch the skin of the springbok that I had hunted, just as Pa had explained to me. According to him it was the hunter's responsibility – the processing of the entire animal. In this new world we would have to use everything, the skins as well. I did not enjoy that part of the hunt. I worked alone in the yard beside the guest house, because the women didn't want the children to see the bloody hide.

I am sure sound travels further in the morning, before ten o'clock. The air is clear and still.

I heard the sound. It was high-pitched and very far away, but intense, penetrating. I halted my handiwork and straightened up, turning my head to hear better.

It was a man-made sound. The pitch was not constant. It rose and fell, from ecstatic crescendo to a lower, more animal growl, up and down the scales. It echoed over the plains, thirty, forty kilometres away. It disappeared entirely for a moment. And then it returned.

It was the sound of an engine. It was out of place, odd, curiously strange on this sunny, peaceful and perfectly still morning – almost a year after the Fever – in the deserted hills on the edge of the Great Karoo. And because it was the only mechanical music in the air, I could not identify or pinpoint it.

The sound came from the south, this side of the river. From the direction of Petrusville.

It took a few minutes before I realised that the sound was coming closer. I felt excitement stir. Someone had read our pamphlet. Someone was coming.

Instinctively I began walking down what used to be called Madeliefie Street, towards Protea. Because if he was coming to Vanderkloof he would have to drive up Protea Street. I heard footsteps behind me. I looked back. It was Pa. He had been trying to get a Tata Super Ace going, because the Volvo horse was too big to drive around town. We walked to the corner together and stood side by side listening to the noise get louder and louder.

'It's a motorbike,' said Pa.

I listened.

'Only one,' said Pa.

'Boy, it must be a fast one,' I said.

We waited on the street corner without further discussion, we just listened to the approaching rider. We could hear him shift down through the gears as he neared the traffic circle at the foot of the mountain outside town – about one and a half kilometres from us. The way the sound disappeared for an instant. Perhaps he was pausing to read a road sign? Then the revs rose again, higher and higher through the gears up the gradient. It sang a single note through the two wide curves as the road made a 'U', dropped uncertainly at the first fork, and then he was coming, and we saw him, a black apparition: black motorbike, black helmet, black rucksack, black leathers, boots and gloves.

He spotted us late. He braked, and stopped directly opposite us, on the other side of the road. There were thin, bright green contour stripes marked on the black of the bike. *Kawasaki* was spelled out in silver lettering on the tank. On the tail: *Ninja*. In a holster on the rider's right hip there was a big pistol.

The helmet's visor was dark, the man's face invisible. He moved slowly, with relaxed movements as he reached to switch off the key in the ignition. The engine hushed, just the tick-tick of the cooling metal between us now. He kicked out the motorbike's stand with his heel, swung his booted foot over the seat and stood next to the bike. There was, I saw, another pistol, on his right hip.

He pulled off his gloves, first the left, then the right. Put the gloves on the tank. Loosed the strap of the crash helmet under his chin. He put his hands either side of the helmet, and lifted it off his head in one flowing, practised movement. He shook out his long black hair as he put down the helmet on the tank and walked around the bike, to us. His walk was like a predator at the top of the food chain, nonchalant, supremely confident. He took off his dark glasses. His eyes were hypnotic, pale – a grey that reflected the environment like a chameleon, now faintly green, then a hint of blue, in strong contrast to his dark complexion. He walked up to Pa. Put out his hand.

'Domingo.' A deep voice. 'Tempest-tost,' and his eyes crinkled as though they could smile without his mouth.

Pa's face lit up. 'I'm Willem Storm,' said Pa. 'And this is Nico.'

Domingo looked me in the eyes and shook my hand. I noticed there was a tattoo on the back of his hand, two curved swords and a rising sun. I felt the heat and cold of his hand at the same time. A shiver went through me, because his smile and his eyes, in fact his entire presence, said he was deadly. I don't know why I experienced it at that moment. Childlike intuition? Perhaps because Domingo was in such sharp contrast to my father's peace-loving innocence. But I knew instinctively and without a shadow of a doubt that you wanted Domingo to be on *your* side.

Everything always happens at once, just when you least expect it. That was when we heard the plane. It came from behind us, over the mountain. Pa and Domingo looked up at the same time. It was Hennie Fly's Cessna 172. He swooped over us, and waggled his wings.

We drove down past the traffic circle outside town, to where the Cessna would land, on the nearest stretch of straight, level tarmac. We were in the Tata Super Ace pick-up truck that we had had to push-start. Pa drove, Domingo in the passenger seat, and I sat in the middle.

Domingo smelled of sweat and aftershave. Pa asked him where he had heard about us. He said he had seen our pamphlet in the Bethlehem Mall.

Was he from there?

No, he was on the way to Bloemfontein from Durban. That was all he said. But Pa wasn't deterred. Why? he asked.

Domingo gave Pa a long look, his own eyes invisible behind the dark glasses, but I felt that he was weighing things up. That he knew there was a price to pay if he wanted to stay with us. After a while he said the road surfaces in the wetter parts of the country were too unpredictable after the summer rain, so he came in search of the dry routes for his Ninja. He enjoyed high speed. While the roads and the petrol lasted. It might be the last summer that a man could enjoy a motorbike like that. No traffic, no speed traps. And he smiled that almost-smile, and looked at me.

'Where have you been?' asked Pa.

'Around Hazyview for two months. Those roads . . . Great. But it got rough. Heavy rain, flooding. People at Nelspruit shooting without asking questions. So I rode to Mozambique. Maputo. It's chaos there. I sat on my bike in the middle of Avenido Vinte e Quatro Julho, and a fellow ran naked across the street, with another man chasing him with a panga. And he . . .' Domingo looked at me and shook his head. 'Let's just say, chaos. And then I went to Durban . . . There must be fifty people living on the beach there. Flower power vibe.'

'Did you see . . . other communities?'

'Guy in Harrismith talked about people who started a place near Fouriesburg. In the mountains, whites only. I didn't go to look.'

'Were you in Bethlehem yesterday?'

'No. Four days ago. I went to the Cape first, to see if it was true about the radiation.'

Back then Pa and I had heard over the radio about the nuclear power station at Koeberg blowing up. There had been no one left with the know-how to turn it off.

'How are things there?' asked Pa, with great longing in his voice.

'Bad. Beyond Rawsonville, just before Du Toits Kloof Pass, the burned-out trucks and buses and cars are blocking the road. You can't get through. Charred bodies, it's pretty gruesome. And there are hand-painted signs saying danger, radiation, go through and die. The mountains are black, it looks toxic. I can only imagine what the Cape itself looks like . . .'

Pa was silent. Then he asked, 'Where are you from originally?'

Before Domingo could reply, we saw Hennie Fly and the Cessna. Hennie had already climbed out, and was standing next to the Cessna's engine; he turned and waved to us.

The first thing he said was, 'There are nearly two hundred and sixty people on their way, Willem. They should arrive tomorrow morning, if their petrol lasts. How is Melinda Swanevelder?'

21

Arrival Day

That's what we call it. Arrival Day: 8 April. A public holiday for the last thirty-four years.

Pa didn't approve. Nero Dlamini was against it. Both of them said it was nothing more than the day that the largest single group arrived. It was also too reminiscent of Van Riebeeck Day, when the first European settlers arrived in the Cape in 1652, in the era before the Fever. Which, coincidentally, was 6 April, very close to the date of Arrival Day. One doesn't want to sow a seed that might later sprout in division and discord.

But Arrival Day is what the people wanted, and Arrival Day it remained.

My Springbok hide was stretched on its frame and rubbed in with salt. My hands still stank of it, no matter how many times I scrubbed them with Sunlight liquid in the Pride Rock guest house.

I moaned and complained until Pa let me go and wait for the Arrival from a vantage point high up on the hill.

I rode the quadbike, and found a spot where I could look out over the dam wall, the road that my father and I travelled the first time we came here. This group too were approaching from the north.

Last night Hennie Fly said they were coming from Tshwane and Centurion, Johannesburg and Sandton, Lenasia and Soweto, Nigel and Standerton, Randfontein and Rustenburg. These were places where he had scattered our pamphlets from his plane.

At Westonaria, fourteen men with assault rifles had robbed the growing group. They were looking for jewellery. And money, can you believe it, they wanted money, said Hennie Fly. Now, in these days. At least nobody was hurt, though most of the food and water in the buses was taken.

On the road the convoy collected people in Potchefstroom and Warrenton. That was before Hennie knew about the group. He only spotted the procession of vehicles – a luxury tour bus, a suburban bus, a bunch of minibuses and pick-ups and cars – once they had passed Wolmaransstad, on his way to us. So he landed and they talked. From then on he provided air cover, flying ahead to check for trouble. There had been no more incidents.

Last night Hennie told us he had left them in Kimberley and come to alert us they ought to be here before midday.

Then Hennie went and sat with Melinda Swanevelder, and talked, and she just sat quietly listening to him. 'He'll need a lot of patience with her,' Pa commented to me and Domingo.

Pa asked Domingo, where are you from, originally? And Domingo replied, 'Here and there.' And he began to interrogate Pa about what he envisioned for the community, as if he weren't yet convinced whether he wanted to stay. I sat there hoping Pa would give all the right answers, because I wanted Domingo to stay.

That morning, when we had finished breakfast, Domingo said, 'I thought, being single . . . There's no point in taking a whole house. Is it okay if I move into the Orphanage for now? There are a lot of rooms open.'

And Pa said, 'Of course.'

That was how the old Pride Rock guest house got its new name. The Orphanage.

I balled my fist under the table and whispered, 'Yes!'

Pa asked me, 'How far are you with that skin of yours?'

On the hill where I sat waiting for the Arrival and looking out over the vast, deep Vanderkloof Dam, the water now not thundering over quite as powerfully as before, I thought it was a very good thing that Domingo was going to stay. We had to have him on our side.

By the time the convoy arrived around two o'clock, I was ravenous. I'd been reluctant to abandon my vantage point, in case I missed them, but was growing impatient. At last I spotted the bus coming around the hill on the other side of the river, taking the wide turns of the dam wall. Behind it, an older bus, and beyond that the cars and trucks. I grabbed the radio, and said, 'Pa, they're here. They're on the dam wall, I can see them.'

'Thank you, Nico.' I could hear him laugh. I was hugely excited.

I watched them stop midway along the dam wall, spend some time there, giving everyone a chance to see the water and the river gorge. Then they were on the way again. I hastily clambered down the hill over rocks and bushes, through thorn bushes and thorn trees to where the quadbike waited. It seemed to take for ever.

And then I raced back. To welcome them, and get something to eat.

I saw it all from some distance, and only years later would I think it over, and philosophise about the significance of the scene.

That day I was conscious that I was witnessing history, as much as an excited thirteen-year-old, starved for company of others and friends of his own age, could be. The true gravity of the moment and the people involved in it would only be impressed on me later.

The leading vehicle, the luxury bus, was already parked in the centre of the road when I stopped the quadbike. Two men got out and approached Pa, Hennie Fly and Domingo, Melinda Swanevelder and Beryl and all sixteen of the children who waited for them in the middle of Protea Street. The first man out of the bus was old, his hair snow white, wearing a white surplice with a golden stole and a peculiar hat. He carried a shepherd's crook, made of wood and silver. His left hand leaned on the arm of another – a younger, impressive man with a broad chest who was taller than everyone else.

That was what I saw, what I stored away to pass on one day, to tell others, I was *there*, I was part of it.

I ran over, and took my place between Pa and Domingo.

'The man in the dress, is that the bishop, Hennie?' I whispered.

'It's a surplice,' said Pa, with a chuckle in his voice.

'Yes, Nico, that's the bishop,' said Hennie Fly humbly. He had told us about the Anglican clergyman who was part of the group, who had become their leader.

The grey-haired bishop shuffled across the road to Pa. He opened his arms wide, smiled and said, in English with a faint Scots accent, 'You must be the author of the pamphlet.'

'I am,' said Pa. He stepped forward and shook the bishop's hand.

'Hallelujah!' the broad-chested man beside him called out, 'Hallelujah.'

'Amen,' said the bishop. 'I am Father James Rankin. This is my colleague, Pastor Nkosi Sebego.'

Pa shook the powerfully built Sebego's hand. 'You are all welcome,' he said.

'Praise the Lord,' said Sebego. He turned, and gestured to the other people in the bus to come out. He had a gracious smile on his face and an intense gaze. But then he turned back and focused on Domingo.

As people tumbled out of the buses and cars, calling out, talking, walking up to us, I think I was the only one who saw Pastor Nkosi Sebego's smile change to a frown of consideration, suspicion and finally an unfathomable dislike.

Domingo's face was stiff and unreadable behind his dark glasses.

22

The 256

Two hundred and fifty-six people arrived that day.

Number-crunchers in the community would later point out that 256 is a perfect square – sixteen to the power of two. The superstitious would extend this principle to call it a lucky number, a good omen. I suspect in a hundred years' time they will talk about the descendants of the 256, like the descendants of the *Mayflower* in what was once the USA. It might carry some sort of status.

But in that first week it was an unlucky number. We were totally unprepared for the influx.

A much better number in that time was thirteen. When you are thirteen years old, and you are the son of the author of the pamphlet, you are allowed everywhere that adults congregate, but at the same time you are invisible, as long as you sit still and keep quiet.

The first emergency meeting was late that afternoon on Arrival Day. It was about accommodation.

The problem was that the 256 didn't arrive in tidy family groups. In the entire group there were only three people who were related – old Mrs Nandi Mahlangu, her daughter Qedani, and her grandson Jacob. Three generations of genetic resistance to the virus, the only case recorded. (In the following months and years there were brother-and-sister combinations joining us, there was myself and Pa, eventually another four cases of parent and child.)

When the excitement of the Arrival trickled away and the 256 began to think of a place to sleep and live, it suddenly became a rush for the best, biggest or closest-to-those-that-I-know, without organisation or forethought. Some people wanted to share accommodation, there were many singles who moved into houses on their own, while there were arguments over who would claim the two luxury houses on the shore with a view over the dam. And six teenagers who had travelled together in the old municipal bus had formed new bonds of friendship which meant that they just had to stay together, without supervision, in the furthest, most remote house on the slope of the hill.

The Committee, as they later became known, formed in a natural way when everything had to be decided: the first three members were Pa, Father James and Pastor Nkosi. The fourth member was Ravi Pillay.

The bishop and pastor called all the 256 people together to discuss the accommodation arrangements. Pa and the bishop stood on the load bed of the Tata Super Ace in front of the Midas filling station to address them, and to see and hear everyone. Pa called for order. Pillay came out of the group to the front. He was a slight figure, greying at the temples, somewhere between fifty and sixty. He asked Pa if he could say something for a moment. Pa nodded, and helped Pillay to climb on to the back of the Tata.

He held up a hand for silence. He began to speak, his voice surprisingly deep and authoritative. It rang out over the group, it demanded attention. He spoke English with the characteristic accent of the South African Indian. He told the people that he had run a restaurant in Bedfordview for fifteen years. His initial marketing strategy was to offer a buffet on Sundays: eat as much as you can, at a fixed price. 'It worked. People came, they told their friends about the delicious food and good service. I made a solid profit. But two years later, I stopped providing the buffet. Many clients were angry with me. "Ravi, we support you. Ravi, the place is packed, why are you taking our beloved buffet away?" Then I told them, I couldn't stand the waste any more. Every Sunday I watched people piling up their plates, overflowing, excessive. But they didn't eat half of it. Rich people. Black and white and Indian, every last one of them. Every Sunday they wasted so much food, in a land where many of the poor are living below the breadline. But that's the way we are, our people. If we get something for free, we take more than we need. More than we can use. Come on, we have a new beginning here, let's not start out that way. Let's each just take what we need and what makes sense, what's best for our survival and our future and the good order here, including the houses and the accommodation. We're just the first of the arrivals, we won't be the only ones.'

From that moment on Ravi Pillay also became a member of the Committee. Only later would he tell us he had once been the mayor of Lenasia.

The second crisis was food.

The 256 had not brought food with them. Some of them had two, maybe three days' provisions, but most of them had assumed it would all be provided at Vanderkloof.

The evening of Arrival Day, Pa, Pillay, Father James and Pastor Nkosi held the second emergency meeting in the dining room of the Orphanage. I sat at the table and listened, Domingo sat to one side, busy cleaning a pistol and oiling it. Pastor Nkosi looked at Domingo every now and then with dislike, unease; it was hard to tell what he really thought.

Beryl Fortuin brought coffee to the table while they weighed various options of teams, groups and shifts – for food gathering and cooking. Beryl put the tray down hard enough to rattle the cups and then she sat down and said, 'A new beginning for good people, right?'

She had their attention.

She was angry: 'That's what Willem's pamphlet said. That's why all these people travelled all that way. As far as I can tell, it didn't say "A new beginning for good people ruled by middle-aged men".'

I saw Pa look around the table, and nod thoughtfully. Bishop James got a word in first. 'You're absolutely right. Join us; we need your wisdom just as much.'

And that was how Beryl became a member of the Committee.

All the while Domingo sat in total silence a few tables away, his hands occupied with some task, but he listened to every word.

The third crisis came two days later. The vehicles were lined up at the Midas filling station. They had to be filled up for the planned expeditions: the search for any still-edible packaged food in the towns in a two-hundred-kilometre radius, and the capture and transport of surviving sheep, cattle, pigs and chickens on what were once farms.

Then the fuel ran out.

The Committee had to rethink, reorganise manpower so that two groups of four people could go in search of a fuel tanker. One of those groups we never saw again, and we never found out what became of them. It was ten long days before the other group returned with a large, practically new tanker, full of petrol.

Most of our vehicles used diesel.

So on we stumbled, on the road to progress.

The Saturday of that first week a pack of starving, bloodthirsty dogs attacked one of our sheep capture expeditions, six kilometres east of Philippolis. The men – two adults, two teenagers – had cornered seven sheep in a camp. After such a long time without handling the sheep were fearful and jittery. The men planned to load the sheep on to the pick-up; their attention was focused on the sheep and they didn't see the dogs until it was too late. None of them were skilled with the firearms they had with them. They rapidly depleted their ammunition in their flight back to the pick-up and did little harm to the dogs. The dogs bit one of the men on the arm, and one of the teenagers on the leg before they could slam the truck door. Then they sat and watched the pack tear the sheep apart. They came home to Vanderkloof safely, but badly shaken.

The Committee conferred that night about the incident.

'We have to teach people to shoot,' said Father James.

'We'll have to collect enough ammunition first,' said Pa.

'Who's going to do it?' asked Beryl. 'We haven't got any extra useful hands or vehicles or fuel left over.'

'The people who are gathering food must also look for ammunition. Most farms have guns.'

The Committee members nodded in silent assent, as there was no other solution.

'Too many calibres.' Domingo's voice filled the silent void from his seat to one side of the room. It was the first time that he had uttered a word during a Committee meeting.

Five heads turned to look at him.

He explained: 'Guns on farms are mostly hunting rifles. There is a range of calibres. If we want to teach people to shoot . . . In three or four months we will have to travel a long way in search of ammunition.'

The Committee were silent.

'Don't look so worried, there *is* a solution,' said Domingo. 'We must standardise. The Defence Force depot at De Aar. It's an hour's drive from here. There should be a few thousand R4s. At least. And hundreds of thousands of rounds of ammunition.'

'R4s?' asked Pastor Nkosi.

'The army's assault rifle. Five point five six by forty-five millimetre, thirty-five rounds in the magazine. If we don't empty that arsenal, someone else will do it some time or other. And then we'll have bigger problems.'

'Will you lead an expedition?' asked Pa.

Domingo nodded.

In that first week I burned to go on an expedition too. Any expedition, but especially Domingo's. I had already shot dead two bad people, a few dogs and buck. I had some big adventures with Pa in the era before Vanderkloof. It was more than most people could say. But Pa just shook his head when I first hinted, and then asked outright.

I should have known there was something brewing.

On the Sunday afternoon the Committee held a meeting, but Pa said I should go and help Melinda in the kitchen.

That Sunday evening Pastor Nkosi made an announcement on behalf of the Committee that would change my life radically. They asked the whole community to gather in the parking lot behind the OK Value supermarket, the meeting place that later became known as the Forum. The pastor stood on the back of the little Tata truck. He spoke in his sonorous voice about the food crisis, and asked everyone to respect the rationing of available provisions. He said everyone was working hard on it, and as soon as there were enough reserves, they would begin slaughtering livestock.

He gave feedback on the various expeditions. There wasn't much good news.

And then he came to 'the children'.

According to their calculations, he said, there were forty-nine children between the ages of six and sixteen. The Committee suggested that all forty-nine gather at the old bowls club at eight thirty on Monday for school. Three people had been provisionally identified to work as teachers. 'Children, we want you to know, your education is extremely important to us as a community. Under normal circumstances we'd let you attend school exclusively. But we don't live in normal circumstances. Therefore, the children who are ten and older will receive one week of instruction, and the following week they will help with all the work that needs to be done.'

23

James Rankin

As recorded by Willem Storm. The Amanzi History Project.

I spent my whole adult life working for the Church. I was with the Anglican Diocese of Johannesburg for eleven years, but nothing prepares you ...

There was this moment, at the height of the Fever ... I was working, helping at the Milpark hospital, I was really just praying for people, for the dying, for their relatives who were being infected. It was ... There was this moment, I was standing next to a bed, holding a dying man's hands, in this six-bed ward, and I heard the shouts, there was a man with a gun, he was pointing it at me. He was saying, 'It's your God who did this, it's your God,' and just came closer and closer, with the gun pointed at my head. He was already sick, you could see that, he was in the first stage, the Fever had started, he knew he was going to die, and he wanted to blame someone. He stood right up against me, and he pressed the barrel of the gun against my forehead. And then he looked at me, and he realised I wasn't sick. So he started shouting, 'Why aren't you sick?' Over and over again. He was so furious, I was sure he was going to shoot me.

I was ashamed to say that I stopped praying. It was because of the fear, but mostly it was because I felt so incredibly guilty for not being sick.

The man with the gun, he just turned the gun around and shot himself.

I still feel this guilt, every day. But I keep praying, and I keep telling myself, the Lord spared me for a reason. Perhaps it was to help lead these people to Amanzi.

Amanzi

On 3 July in the Year of the Dog we all gathered in the Forum. We were more than three hundred strong. The first, democratic election of leaders was on hand. Pa stood on the back of the Tata. He said he thought we should have a new name for this place, Vanderkloof was in no way suitable.

In the silence that followed, the grey, bent Granny Nandi Mahlangu called out: 'Amanzi.'

There was a rippling of sounds through the crowd as everyone tried out the name on their tongues. Someone began to clap. Then a wave of applause and everyone was clapping. When it died down, Pa said, 'Welcome to Amanzi.'

No one explained what it meant, and I was too shy to ask openly. I asked Pa in a whisper only when we were walking home later – 'home' was, and would be for the next number of years, the Orphanage that we shared with Beryl and the children, Melinda Swanevelder and her hopeful suitor Hennie Fly Laas, Domingo and Nero Dlamini.

'It's the Zulu and Xhosa word for "water",' said Pa.

I chewed that over, but couldn't connect the watery name to the wave of applause. 'So why did everyone start clapping?'

'Because it's perfect.'

Nkosi Sebego

As recorded by Willem Storm. The Amanzi History Project.

I was the founding father and pastor of the Grace Tabernacle Church of Christ in Mamelodi. I kept the church open through it all. It was very difficult, because I knew it was God's way of telling us to change our ways. God sent the Fever, because the whole world had lost its way. But you cannot tell that to the people who are suffering so much, who are dying.

I thought I wasn't dying, because I was a God-fearing man, a righteous man. But then I saw that God was taking my wife, and she was a better Christian than I was. And he was taking babies, and little children, nobody was being spared the Fever. So then, I did not understand, and I was very angry at God. I shouted and I swore. But I think God knew that it was because of the pain of all the loss and the suffering.

The strange thing was, Mamelodi was a safer place, during and after the Fever, than a lot of the white neighbourhoods. I think most of the black townships were better, because the black people, the poor people, we were used to helping one another, we were much more used to loss and suffering and standing together, and sharing.

Three months after the Fever, we were twenty-nine people in Mamelodi who had survived, living together at the church, helping each other, taking care of each other. And then during that time, I went to Silver Lakes Golf Estate, and Faerie Glen, where all the rich people lived, mostly white people. I went there to look for food. There were no groups, nobody working together. Just a few people shooting at everything that moved.

Domingo

As recorded by Willem Storm. The Amanzi History Project.

I was born in Abbotsdale. It's the coloured township of Malmesbury. I went to school there. My mother worked at the Sasko mill in town. But I was there near Swellendam when the the Fever came. It had a sort of paramilitary occupation. No, I'm not going to elaborate. No need. Useless information.

Nkosi Sebego

As recorded by Willem Storm. The Amanzi History Project.

There is one sight I will never forget. It was when the Fever was at its worst. It reminded me of those black-and-white films about the atrocities during the Second World War.

I woke up in the morning, and I heard this engine. You have to remember, this was when the Fever was ... when it was really bad, so Mamelodi was much quieter than usual, and I heard this big engine. I walked in that direction; it was coming from the open ground between Khutsong and the Pateng Secondary School. This was about one kilometre from the Mamelodi hospital. The engine was a bulldozer. It was pushing people into this mass grave.

It is a terrible thing to see. People. People who laughed, who loved, who lived. And there they were, just rag dolls. Pushed into a hole in the ground. Like rubbish.

24

Nero 'Lucky' Dlamini

As recorded by Willem Storm. The Amanzi History Project.

Look, I was a dandy, a very snazzy dresser, make no mistake, I was the best-dressed psychologist in the greater Johannesburg metropolitan area. I know, I know, not a difficult achievement, but nonetheless ...

I don't deny, my lifestyle was a reaction to the poverty of my youth.

My father only had four years of schooling. He was a labourer, he worked at an auto electrician place in Braamfontein, and he did private auto electrician jobs in our backyard in Orlando East to keep the wolf from the door. My mother worked at Baragwanath, the hospital, the Chris Hani hospital. She at least had grade ten, she did administrative work at the Paediatric Burn Unit; so many nights she would come home, crying over what she had seen in that hospital, the township kids who got burned. Injury by poverty is what she called it.

My father believed 'Nero' was a great Roman emperor, classic case of a little knowledge being a dangerous thing. So he insisted on christening me that. But he meant well, and he was a wonderful man, he never left my mother, so I forgave him long ago.

Anyway, I was a clever boy, I matriculated in 1999, I earned bursaries, I wanted to do psychology, because I wanted to make sense of the world, really, everybody was so ... so angry. I went to Wits, in 2006, and then I opened a practice in Sandton. I treated all these nouveau riche black businessmen, and after two years, I thought this is as good as it gets, is this going to be the difference I'm going to make in the world? So I took a sabbatical for six months, I gave it a lot of thought, and I changed course ...

Long story short, I have always been fascinated by how we absolutely need to be in a relationship. I mean, it consumes us, that need, that terrible need to be loved, to be with someone. The disease of the last decades BF – Before the Fever – was loneliness, lack of being loved. To be with someone, *that's what it's all about, movies, books, TV, Facebook ... I had all these patients, rich people, Willem, very rich, highly successful. And so very unhappy. If you cut through all the crap, all they needed was love.*

So I specialised in couples therapy. Oh, the stories I could tell.

I liked Nero a lot.

My father liked Nero from day one. Because he was a raconteur. (The first time, when I asked Pa what it meant, Pa said it was a 'master storyteller'; the word originates from nineteenth-century French, *conte* meaning 'story'.) But also because he became Pa's intellectual sparring partner, because he was a good sounding board, often disagreeing with Pa, and later standing with Pa trying to resist the overwhelming spiritual onslaught of Pastor Nkosi.

In the raconteur version of his decision to travel to Amanzi, he said it was necessity, and the joy of the bicycle.

I wasn't a competitive cyclist. I was a weekend mountain bike warrior, it was my fitness regime, my way of staying slim to fit into all those snazzy clothes; did I tell you I was a real dandy? I never liked jogging, it's such an inelegant pastime, so much sweating and jiggling ... Anyway, my big hope was one day to do the holiday cycling routes in Europe. In the era BF. And then, first months AF, I didn't think about cycling, it was just survival. I lived in Sandton, and in the early morning I would go scavenging for groceries, because that was the safest, all the dangerous people stayed up late. And it was so damn inelegant to run from the dangerous people ... I knew I would have to relocate, the resources were dwindling and the dangerous people increasing, but where do you go? And how? I had no idea where and how I would find petrol. I'm not technically minded, despite what my dad did for a living.

Then one day I found your pamphlet in the street. Hennie Fly's airdrop pamphlet, and I thought, why don't I take a bicycle? Of course there was a certain risk, but I thought, who's going to rob a black man on a bicycle?

There's this cycle shop, the Cycle Lab Fourways Megastore, where I bought my Silverback Sola 4, my regular bicycle. Every Saturday BF I used to stand and drool over the Cannondale, such a love-hate relationship, you beautiful thing, but how could one pay a hundred and fifty thousand rand for a bicycle? In this country, it's plain vulgar.

Then I picked up your pamphlet and I liked what I read, and I said, okay, I'm going to that place. So I walked to Cycle Lab, and here's a fascinating statistic: after the apocalypse, nobody took a single thing from that shop. Nothing. I walked in there and I thought, the Cannondale must have been looted a long time ago, but there it was, together with every other thing that was in that shop, energy bars, water bottles, you name it. So I took the Cannondale bicycle and a Garmin Edge 810 and the very best, smartest and most expensive biking apparel, and I packed the rucksack and off I went. I knew nothing about the dogs; I didn't even see four dogs, the whole three weeks, the whole six hundred and twenty-nine kilometres; that is the exact distance from that bicycle shop to here, according to the Garmin GPS, before the thing's batteries went flat. After I got here, I heard about the dogs. And it gave me a fright, take my word for it, a big fright and I thought how lucky I was, how very, very lucky.

He arrived on 2 May in the Year of the Dog. The real reason for his coming we would only discover later. Because 3 May was the first of that bitter winter's cold fronts – a rare seven centimetres of snow in the autumn, on the edge of the Karoo. Within a day the temperature fell far below freezing, pipes burst, children shivered and romped about in the streets with snowballs. The entire community had to change gears, had to pay attention to emergency repairs, and the generation of heat.

And on 5 May the KTM came. For the first time.

25

The KTM

The Karoo, Pa said, got its name from the Khoi people. It means 'place of great thirst'. It is the great semi-desert in the western part of southern Africa, as big as California, bigger than the whole of Norway.

Before the Fever it might snow once in five or six years in the Karoo, Pa said. Mostly not actual snow, just half a centimetre of icy layer that they called 'kapok'. That word derived from the Malay, *kapoq*: there were certain trees in the tropics that formed a sort of woolly white fibre around their fruits, which local people used to stuff cushions and mattresses.

On 3 May of that year the snow in the morning formed a layer seven centimetres thick.

After the snow came the wind and sleet.

Our community didn't have enough warm clothing for the extreme weather. Nobody had thought to collect firewood for the winter either. For a few days the roads were almost impassable.

Jacob Mahlangu, grandson of old Granny Nandi, and I were appointed as shepherds, a task that we performed every second week when we were not attending school. But on 5 May there was no school for anyone, and we hitched a lift on the back of the old municipal tractor driven by Hennie Fly. It took over an hour to reach the reserve up in the mountains. In the veld we had to shovel and sweep snow off the grass so that our growing flocks and herds of sheep and cattle could have a few places where they could graze. Then we went to fetch wood, which we had to chop and saw and lug to the trailer. It was hard physical work; we were wet and cold and by late afternoon very hungry.

Normally we would help Domingo clean rifles in the evenings. But on the night of 5 May I was too tired. Pa and Nero Dlamini and

Ravi Pillay sat in a circle in the big sitting room of the Orphanage and debated the possibility that so much smoke in the atmosphere was responsible for this extreme and unusual weather – the smoke of fires all over the world, from hastily evacuated industries and over-heating nuclear reactors and uncontrolled forest fires and even the whole cities in densely populated countries that could go up in flames due to gas leaks, for example. Not one of them could remember this kind of intense cold, so much snow in southern Africa, so early in the year.

Domingo sat apart, as was his habit. He oiled and cleaned five R4 rifles, part of the arsenal that had been brought from the De Aar army base storage facility. Every evening he did five new ones, and in the morning he would take them back to our magazine. Domingo kept two hundred rifles and ammunition in the safe of the old police station – the guns that he cleaned. And another few thousand guns and a store of ammunition he kept quietly in a secret location that only the Committee – and I, the eavesdropper – knew about. The storage shed of the nature reserve, seven kilometres out of the town, up the mountain. Beyond the gate and the fence, remote.

Domingo's movements were rhythmic, ordered, practised. Soothing to an exhausted, dozing thirteen-year-old.

Then he stopped suddenly, and looked up at the front door. 'People,' he said.

Pa sighed. There had been people here all day, to come and report some new crisis, more damage or another emergency.

Domingo put down the gun, stood up, and went to the front door. Only then came the hard, urgent knock.

I was awake, I watched Pa and Ravi rise to their feet. Domingo opened the door, an icy wind blew in; a strange woman stood outside. She was tall and imposing and beautiful, with grey streaks in her hair, though she was not old. She spoke, but I could not hear. Domingo looked at her, and the people behind her. At last Pa said, 'Let them in.'

Domingo hesitated.

Then he stepped out of the way. The woman entered. Behind her, another four women, and three men, all under fifty years old, strangers. Pa invited them to sit. The woman introduced herself. She had a melodic voice, and said her name was Mecky Zulu. They were sorry to arrive so late, they had meant to arrive earlier today, but their minibus had broken down before Venterstad. A bearded man in his forties introduced himself as Hans Trunkenpolz. They'd found our pamphlets in Steynsburg; it had taken them two days to reach us, because of the snow and car trouble.

Pa welcomed them, invited them to sit near the fire, asked them if they had eaten and went to the kitchen himself to fetch rusks and coffee, while the bishop chatted to the new arrivals.

Domingo stood observing them. Then he went to the kitchen as well. I followed, curious, because I could see his unease.

'They're lying,' said Domingo behind the closed kitchen door.

'About what?' asked Pa.

'About the minibus breaking down.'

'How do you know?'

'Their hands are clean.'

'Domingo, we don't know what broke, it doesn't mean—'

'Where are the children, the old people?'

'What do you mean?'

'They are not a natural group. They are all ... fighting age. All alert ...'

'Five are women ...'

Domingo frowned. 'Willem, there is something about them ...'

Pa smiled. 'I appreciate your concern, but they seem to me to be ordinary, good people, and they are hungry and tired.' With that he carried the tray through into the sitting room.

Trunkenpolz and Mecky Zulu did most of the talking. They said they were all from the east coast: Margate, Durban, Umhlanga and Richards Bay. They'd found each other gradually after the chaos. And then they began to travel, in search of security. Mecky was a Zulu princess, said Trunkenpolz respectfully. And he was an engineer.

'That's very good news,' said Pa. 'We urgently need an engineer. What other professions does your group have?'

Before they could answer, Domingo asked, 'What was wrong with the minibus?'

'Excuse me?' said Trunkenpolz.

'The vehicle that broke down. What happened?'

'The carburettor ... We think the petrol in the filling stations is starting to degrade. We had to clean the carburettor. Totally. It took us a few hours to find the bloody cause ...'

Domingo nodded.

'Come,' said Pa. 'You can sleep right here in the Orphanage tonight.'

Domingo came knocking on our door when everyone went to their rooms. Pa opened up. Domingo entered, gun in his hand. 'I don't trust them.'

'Let's get some sleep,' said Pa, in his that's-enough-of-that voice.

'None of them smell of petrol. You can't clean a carburettor and not smell of petrol.'

'Please, Domingo, we talk about this tomorrow.'

The KTM robbed us just before noon on 6 May, but I wasn't there. Jacob Mahlangu and I had to take the quadbike up the mountain, to make sure the livestock had grazing, and to drive away any predators. We were late coming back in the afternoon, since the snow still lay deep up in the reserve, the ground roads were muddy, and very slippery.

When we eventually got back to Amanzi, we heard the whole story.

That morning Pa and Pastor Nkosi gave Mecky Zulu, Trunkenpolz and the new arrivals a substantial breakfast and a thorough tour of the town and all the key sights. They pretended to choose houses for themselves, came down to do the admin at the old post office and collected their rations where we stored most of our food in the old OK Value supermarket.

Domingo sat in front of the police station watching, R4 in his hands. He was the only inhabitant of Amanzi who was armed. Trunkenpolz and Mecky approached him. Trunkenpolz asked him a question about the gun to divert his attention. Zulu pulled a pistol out of her handbag and pressed it against Domingo's head and said, 'Give him the gun.'

Domingo just sat there.

Trunkenpolz put a hand in her bag and pulled out another pistol. He hit Domingo in the face with it. 'Give me the gun,' and he ripped the R4 from Domingo's grasp. Domingo's nose and eyebrow were bleeding. He just sat and watched Mecky Zulu give a signal to the two other men in their minibus. One of them produced a two-way radio, and barked orders into it.

Ten minutes later a lorry and eight motorbikes stopped in the street. The motorbikes were all bright orange and black. They had the letters KTM on their fuel tanks. All the men were armed. They carried our entire store of tinned and dried food out of the supermarket. They stole all two hundred R4 rifles and ammunition from the old police station, and packed them into the lorry. One of the men who had arrived that night climbed into the cab of our tanker and drove away with the diesel.

Trunkenpolz held the R4 to Domingo's head. He said to Mecky, 'We must shoot this one.'

People who witnessed all of it said later there was no trace of fear on Domingo's face. He just sat there with hatred and anger in his eyes, all focused on Trunkenpolz, his fists clenched, nails biting so hard into his palms that they bled.

The woman looked Domingo up and down, and sneered, 'Don't bother.'

And they left, their motorbikes roaring, in a triumphant convoy.

The Committee met that evening in the dining room of the Orphanage. Pa said, 'I was wrong. I should have listened to Domingo.'

'We're all too . . . trusting,' said Bishop Rankin.

'We'll have to correct that,' said Ravi Pillay. 'And quickly, too.'

'But how? We don't have the know-how,' said Pastor Nkosi.

'We do,' said Pa. He looked at me, where I sat in the corner listening. 'Go and call Domingo, Nico.'

I went to find him. He wasn't in the sitting room. I knocked on his bedroom door. He opened it. The wounds were thin bloody lines across his eye and nose. 'Pa would like you to come to the dining room.'

He nodded, as if he knew why.

In the dining room Beryl Fortuin asked him, 'What must we do, Domingo?'

He looked back at them. 'Are you asking me?'

'That's right. How do we make sure that it never happens again?'

'Come and sit down with us,' said Pa.

'I prefer to stand.'

'What must we do?'

'We must control access,' said Domingo. 'We must put armed guards night and day at an access gate.'

'We don't have a gate,' said Pastor Nkosi.

'We have the two buses that we can pull across the road, halfway up the first hill,' said Domingo. 'So that nobody can race through. And we park another car between them, one that has to be moved. It will cost us nothing.'

'Please sit down, Domingo,' my father said again.

'No, thanks.'

'Is that all? Is it enough?' asked Beryl.

'No. We have to train an army,' said Domingo.

'Sad,' said the bishop. 'But true.'

'It can be a tiny army to start with,' said Domingo. 'Small is better than nothing. A small one would have stopped the KTM scum.'

And so the robbers were first called 'the KTM scum', and later just 'the KTM'.

'Will you form a defence force? And train them?' Pa asked.

Domingo shook his head.

'Why not?'

'Defence is a symptom of a certain attitude. We want an attack force,' he said. 'That's what I will train them for.'

I remember: that night tempers were frayed in the Orphanage dining room. They argued over emergency measures, over priorities, over policy and the general philosophy of welcoming incoming strangers.

And Nero Dlamini, sitting to one side with a book in his hand and a sleeping child on his lap, broke the tension. 'My goodness, that woman was beautiful,' he sighed.

'What woman?' asked Pastor Nkosi irritably.

'That Zulu princess. If I have to be robbed by someone, I'd want it to be her.'

26

The sharpshooter

On 7 May work began in securing the entrance to Amanzi.

Before Jacob Mahlangu and I rode up the mountain to tend the animals, we had a quick look: Pa was standing with the bishop and Beryl on the slope. They were watching Domingo and the few men helping him set up the barriers. Pa looked vaguely nervous, and worried.

Domingo and the men parked the buses across the road, in the spot where it passed between two hills. It was a clever choice, because when he later stationed a sentry in the foremost bus, he could see at least three kilometres down the mountain. With more guards on the heights it would be extremely difficult to attack the new gate. Domingo removed the wheels of both buses so they couldn't easily be moved. He towed a heavy old Nissan pick-up between the buses to form the cross arm of an H. The Nissan would have to be moved before any vehicle could pass between the buses.

He had two people on sentry duty round the clock – one in each bus – equipped with radios to alert him and Pa if someone was on the road. Then Domingo and his team fetched rocks and stones to fill the gaps between the buses and the slopes on either side of the road. It took him three weeks to complete that task.

Under cover of night Domingo brought enough ammo and another two hundred R4 assault rifles down from the mountain. He restocked the arsenal at the police station. And in the course of the next week everyone in Amanzi had the opportunity to learn to shoot, and demonstrate their ability: men and women, boys and girls, anyone over the age of ten.

Those who were away on expeditions also had their turn when they came back.

Domingo set up a shooting range at the massive old gravel quarry near the dam wall. He gave each group of ten shooters an hour of basic instruction in weapon handling and safety. Then he let them shoot. Once everyone was reasonably proficient, he tested us: everyone had to stack five stones, more or less the size of a brick, at fifty metres and try to hit them with five bullets through open sights. And so he divided the wheat from the chaff.

I had my chance much later. I was driven by a fear of humiliation, because I had bragged to the other boys that I could shoot. And I was motivated by my desire to impress Domingo.

I shot all my stones to smithereens.

The next day I shot against all the other five-stone finalists – twelve of us. This time we had to shoot over a hundred metres. I went through to the next round, along with six others, to the hundred-and-fifty-metre knockout. Still six. At two hundred the brick-sized stones were almost too small to see. Only three of us went through. The other two were over twenty years old. I struggled to contain my pride. Every now and then I would glance at Pa, but he looked angry. He stood watching me with his arms folded. I couldn't understand why.

Domingo walked to his Jeep – the same one that the two original Vanderkloof inhabitants used to drive. He took out three other rifles, and gave us each one. They had telescopes attached. 'This is the DM variant of the R4. DM stands for dedicated marksman, these are sniper rifles. The telescopes have already been set in. Now you will shoot at three hundred metres,' he told us.

I was the only one to get five out of five. Domingo gave me a fist bump. I ran to my father.

'Pa, I'm going to be a soldier.'

He said, 'You're too young, Nico.'

'But Pa . . .'

'No. You're still too young.'

'Please, Pa.'

'We're not going to fight over this,' he said and turned and walked away.

Why did he do that, now? I won the shooting contest, it was my finest moment, the high point of my whole life. And he walks away? I experienced a moment of absolute and bitter disappointment before anger flooded me. It was so unfair. I wanted to scream at him, how can you say that, Pa? What about the two men I shot dead? When Pa couldn't, when Pa was too soft, too scared to shoot. I wasn't too young then. What about the dogs that I had to kill to save Pa? I wasn't too young then. What about the springbok, when we went hunting at the Koedoeskop Game Ranch? I wasn't too young then.

I drew a deep breath so I could let all my rage out, to scream all that at him, in front of everyone. I didn't care, he had betrayed me.

A hand on my arm, fingers squeezing hard. I looked up. It was Domingo. He just shook his head.

27

The perfect storm

Throughout that May and June the young settlement of Amanzi staggered on.

The first snow and cold, unusually bitter and totally unexpected, exposed serious shortcomings in our knowledge and skills, forethought and planning. I overheard one resident tell another that my father wasn't as clever as everyone thought; why choose a place for a new beginning if there weren't even enough trees for firewood in the winter?

In that foul weather we ate more, but had less opportunity to forage for supplies. Many people were called on to help to fix streets, roofs and burst pipes, cleaning chimneys, frequently without the right tools or knowledge. Others had to collect wood and saw it up, hard physical labour. Those who were out on food-gathering duty struggled to make progress on the slippery, rutted and sometimes impassable roads. School was suspended for three whole weeks, the children needed to help with the workload. Boys of fifteen and sixteen went with the adults on expeditions, searching for food, and sheep and cattle, pigs and chicken. But I wasn't chosen for one.

And still our numbers grew; every week there were new groups of weary, hungry arrivals.

If the unexpected icy temperatures and snow had been the only setback, I believe we would have survived and overcome them relatively easily. It was the raid by the KTM that changed everything, that made the dominos topple faster. The loss of weapons and security eroded the optimism and self-confidence of Amanzi. The loss of food and fuel pushed the community to the edge of collapse, hunger and deprivation fanned the flames of dissatisfaction and rebellion. Everyone knew we had to ration food. Everyone agreed that we could leave it in Pa and Ravi Pillay's hands for the division to be done fairly. In the first week or two after the KTM invasion everyone accepted this with resignation. Then hunger began to gnaw at their bellies, and the people complained: why couldn't we slaughter more cattle and sheep, or some of the hens that Hennie Fly was farming in the temporary buildings of the old holiday resort? Why couldn't we shoot more springbok in the old game reserve?

'Because it's not an infinite resource, and a long, cold winter lies ahead,' Pa explained patiently each time, and the committee members stood solidly behind him. 'We must manage sustainably, and that will require sacrifices sometimes.'

The pressure on Pa was immense. More than once I woke in the middle of the night and saw him sitting upright in bed staring into space. He had to make a new notch in his belt, because he was losing weight fast. It seemed as though he wanted to shoulder all the responsibility alone for the growing disaster. On 26 June, in front of the OK Value supermarket, a small crowd of residents complained about the size of the rations that were being doled out. Pa tried to explain about long-term planning.

'But who gave you the right to make that sort of decision?' a woman's voice cried out, caustic and anonymous somewhere in the queue. Other voices murmured in support, a growing wave of discord.

That was when Pa said the only solution was a democratic election. As soon as possible.

At a Forum meeting of the entire Amanzi community they decided to hold elections on 14 July for an executive committee of six people. Voting rights were given to everyone aged sixteen and older, you had to be at least eighteen to be nominated, and a nominee had to give their permission for that.

Many people asked Domingo to stand for election. Every time he just said, 'Sorry, no.'

In the evening Pa asked him, 'Won't you reconsider, Domingo? We need you.'

'I have done considering,' he said.

*   *   *

Twelve days before the election, 2 July.

Dusk was just falling when the expedition returned, three middle-aged men, two boys of barely sixteen, in an old ten-ton sheep lorry. They had been away for two weeks on a pretty fruitless search for food in the old Northern Free State: Welkom, Virginia, Kroonstad. Their harvest was small, their loss of heart great.

They came to the Orphanage to report first. Pa commandeered everyone to help off-load the lorry, because the workers at the OK Value supermarket had already gone home. I went with him, Beryl and Domingo, Pastor Nkosi and Hennie Fly and Melinda Swanevelder. Bishop Rankin was sick, he stayed behind.

We worked in the dark, in the icy cold. As we off-loaded and carried boxes, I listened to the expedition team describe their hardships, the giant potholes in the roads, the bandits, the supermarkets and cafés plundered and emptied by other people.

Domingo carried a big box into the store. He said, '*Ja*, well, it is because we are stupid.'

'What did you say, Domingo?' asked Pa sharply.

Domingo halted. 'We are stupid,' he said.

'What does that mean?' Pa approached him. I had never seen him look like that. Cold, an icy glare in his eyes. I knew it was the tension of the past few weeks, the pressure of responsibility. Everyone went quiet, everyone looked at Pa. And Domingo.

'It means we should have left the low-hanging fruit for last – the nearby towns – for the winter, for the bad times. We should have looked for food in the distant places when the weather was good.'

Pa stepped closer to him. 'And why didn't you ever say so?'

''Cause nobody asked.'

''Cause nobody asked?' said Pa. 'So we must ask before we can share your wisdom? That's your idea of a community? Of making a contribution?'

'Are you saying I don't make a contribution?' More surprise than aggression.

Pa took a deep breath, and reined in his temper. He said, 'That's not the point, Domingo. You sat in the Orphanage every night listening to us make plans, and you kept quiet. But now you stand there criticising. Now you tell us how stupid it was. You, who are not even standing for election.'

Domingo didn't answer. I could read his body language; he knew that right now he was in the wrong. I believe it was on the tip of his tongue to defuse the situation, in a way that would allow him to preserve his dignity.

He didn't get the chance. 'That's just cowardly,' said Pastor Nkosi Sebego. He stood, muscular and broad-shouldered, beside Pa. He looked so much bigger and stronger than the wiry Domingo.

Domingo's eyes narrowed. 'You calling me a coward?'

'I'm saying that a man, a real man, would put himself in the democratic firing line. Takes a lot more guts. So yes, I think you are a coward.'

Things happened in Domingo's face, possibilities moved across it like spectres: all of them frightened me. It was his eyes, those colourless light eyes of his, that darkened in fury. His hands dropped to the buckle of his belt. On the belt were two holstered pistols. He loosened the buckle, he was going to tackle the pastor bare-fisted.

Pa tried to defuse the situation. He walked in between them, speaking in a casual voice. 'We all know that Domingo is one of the bravest men in our community. I'm sure he has good reason for declining the nomination.'

Domingo's hands were on his buckle. He looked past Pa, at Pastor Nkosi. The moment, balanced on a knife-edge, seemed to stretch and stretch. The few bystanders stood transfixed.

Domingo drew a deep breath, relaxed, and said very quietly, 'Tell me, Padre, would you rather have a real man who lies about his beliefs?'

The pastor thought he had won the confrontation and his voice remained aggressive: 'What do you mean?'

'I declined the nomination because I don't believe in democracy. Not now.'

'What do you believe in?'

'Even in a perfect world, democracy is a messy business. This world is all screwed up. What it needs is a benevolent dictator.'

'You can't be serious?' said the pastor, triumphantly appalled.

'He has the Romans on his side, Nkosi,' said Pa, his voice light and pacifying. 'They chose a dictator in times of crisis. In those times the term "dictator" was a positive one.'

'Then call me a Roman,' said Domingo.

Nero Dlamini was the only one who laughed then, quietly.

The pastor breathed, calmed. But even he had to retire with dignity. 'You scare people,' he said to Domingo.

'I know,' said Domingo, as he turned and walked away.

On 4 July it snowed again.

Nero Dlamini called it the last straw that broke the Amanzi camel's back. Pa would later refer to the events, from the first snow and the KTM, to the last bad weather, as 'the perfect storm'.

Hennie Fly had been busy for the last two months with the only worthwhile farming enterprises in the community: a chicken and egg project, and a vegetable greenhouse, all in and around the asbestos buildings of the old sprawling holiday resort right at the top, near the gate to the nature reserve.

The seven centimetres of snow did general damage to buildings and roads, but the greatest damage was when the hothouse roof collapsed due to the snow's weight. All the plants were destroyed – tomatoes and sweetcorn, green beans and beetroot, two weeks before Hennie could begin harvesting. We had lost the Committee's food insurance policy.

The icy nights caused scores of hens to die. Our meagre egg production came to a halt. In the reserve a number of sheep froze to death.

The two oldest members of the community, sure candidates for the coming election, Granny Nandi Mahlangu and Bishop James Rankin, became seriously ill. Nero Dlamini was the closest thing to a medical practitioner that we had, and he kept repeating that he actually knew nothing. Out of desperation at the illness he prescribed antibiotics. That didn't help. He realised the two old people weren't eating, they were donating their food rations to the little ones. Nero put a stop to that. He put them each on a drip. It was too late for Bishop James. He died on 10 July. Everyone who wasn't out on expedition attended his funeral on 12 July.

Granny Nandi survived to be elected to the Committee. Along with Pa, Ravi, Beryl, Nero and Pastor Nkosi. Because we had no constitution, the community decided to give everyone a chance to be the seventh member of the Committee: every resident of Amanzi over eighteen would get a turn to sit on the Committee for two weeks, with full voting rights.

The chairman was to be elected by the Committee, and would serve for one year.

That same evening of 14 July, in the dining room of the Orphanage, they elected my father, Willem Storm, as the first chairman of Amanzi. Pa tried not to, but he shed some tears. He said in his speech that he knew it was a symbolic gesture, there were others who could do it better than him. But it was a great honour, and he pledged his loyalty and his best efforts to everyone in this difficult, difficult time.

Old Granny Nandi died on 29 July. Her funeral was disrupted when Amanzi's entire water supply collapsed on the 30th. In the following two weeks the whole community had to pull together to try to get it fixed.

The expeditions that returned brought only bad news, especially about the desperation and aggression of packs of dogs which were seen ever closer to Amanzi. Pa said it made sense, the big feast for these dogs was over, winter was also taking its toll. Domingo sent teams out to patrol the roads around Amanzi. In the second week of August a large pack of dogs was spotted in the distance a few times. When they went closer the animals melted away into the veld. Everywhere they saw evidence of the dogs' torn prey – small buck, springhares and an old, dying kudu bull.

By this time my father was barely sleeping at all. He was as thin as the last of our sheep, he worried about the more than twenty people who were sick from malnutrition and deprivation, and the fact that the end of the rationed food was in sight.

28

13 August

Jacob Mahlangu and I set a trap for the rock pigeons up in the reserve, a simple ambush of sticks and chicken wire and a long line. Birdseed as bait. We caught seven while we were guarding the sheep and gutted and cleaned them there. We were skilled at this, we had learned a lot in the past months. We could slaughter sheep and cattle, springbok and chicken and pigeons without mess or waste, without disgust.

The snowfalls were rare. On most of the winter days on the edge of the Karoo there were blue, open skies, sunny, though delicate, like something that you handled with care.

Jacob brought the salt, I recall. I remember the gnawing hunger and feeling of impatience while the pigeons were roasting on our spit over the coals. I remember saying, 'They're ready,' and Jacob saying, 'No, a bit longer, remember last time?' Last time they had still been raw, because we had been too hungry and greedy. Raw pigeon is not very tasty.

We sat and ate in the sun, like dassies on a rock. Afterwards we checked each other for any traces of our little feast, to be sure there were no signs to give us away.

At night it was cold in the Orphanage sitting room, as the fire only burned while the little children were still up, to save wood.

Domingo came to me, weapons in his hands. 'Come with me,' he said. 'We have to talk to your father.'

I was startled, he looked angry, and I thought at once, the pigeons, he knew we were eating alone, on the sly.

I forgot that Domingo always looked angry.

He sat down beside Pa, and put the two R4s on the coffee table. One was the DM sniper rifle with scope. He said to Pa, 'That's for Nico, and Jacob Mahlangu. The bus gate guards said they saw the dogs this morning on the side of the southern mountain, on the traffic circle side. They will find our stock up there, Willem. The night shift on the mountain are all armed and ready. The boys must also be able to shoot. We can't afford to lose more sheep. I want to request that Nico and Jacob be excused from school for now, until we have dealt with the dogs.'

Pa's mind was occupied by all the other troubles. He looked at Domingo. Their relationship was more formal nowadays. Pa looked at me. 'Very well.'

'Thank you.'

Domingo rose, picked up the rifles, walked across the room. He beckoned, inviting me to sit with him. He gave me the DM rifle, and a black canvas bag with eight magazines. 'You practise with this, you hear me?'

'I hear you,' I said trying to contain my excitement.

'Start at one hundred metres, and practise up to six hundred. Use all the ammunition, tomorrow I'll bring you another eight.'

'Okay, Domingo,' I said. 'Thank you.'

'Don't thank me. This is business. Those dogs can wipe us out if they reach the flock.' He passed me a smaller bag with magazines. 'This is for Jacob. Help him, so he can learn to shoot properly. You need him.'

'Okay.'

He just got up and walked away.

14 August

I helped Jacob first. He had very good eyesight, the ability to spot a springbok or even a little steenbuck in the grey winter grass from a long way off. But he was only a reasonable shot. I think he wasn't really interested in it.

After that I shot out all eight magazines.

That night Domingo brought another eight magazines to the Orphanage. 'How did you do?'

I told him, from four hundred metres I was having trouble. He asked where the bullets were going. I said a bit varied, but generally too far left and too short. He checked that my scope was correctly mounted. He said he would come and make a tour through the mountain tomorrow. The dogs had been spotted again.

15 August

He came at eleven in the morning and looked through binoculars where my shots landed. He said, 'You're just inconsistent. First thing to remember is if you shoot a lot of times close together, you are going to generate too much barrel heat, and you are going to get inconsistencies. Second thing is inconsistent trigger pull. Each one must be the same. Third thing is inconsistent shoulder pressure. Try to squeeze it a little bit tighter, and try to do it exactly the same way every time.'

I fired again.

'Much better,' said Domingo. 'One more thing. Your shot isn't over when you pull the trigger. It's like a golf swing. You must follow through. You must stay part of that rifle, you must visualise how the bullet strikes the target. And you look through the scope until it hits. Then the shot is complete.'

I shot again, a whole magazine.

'Perfect,' said Domingo.

I glowed with pride.

'Now both of you, remember, if those dogs come up here, you aim for the leaders first, the ones in front of the pack. You get them, the others will get confused. Keep shooting, we need to get them all. You hear me?'

We nodded, Jacob and me, and our hearts beat faster.

'Where did you learn all that?' I asked him.

His eyes were dark behind his sunglasses, as they always were in daytime. His face twitched a fraction into what might possibly be called a smile. 'You're talking to Davy, who's still in the navy.'

'You were in the navy?'

'No,' said Domingo. 'Billy Joel.'

'Who?'

He didn't say.

I didn't understand him at all. 'Were you with Billy Joel in the navy?' But he was on his way already, and I was none the wiser.

16 August

Some time after nine in the morning, Jacob Mahlangu and I were high in the mountain, near the sheep. It was his eagle eyes that spotted the dogs. 'Nico,' he whispered, and pointed. They came over the ridge, from the side, slyly, sniffing the breeze. I'd never seen dogs hunt in such broad daylight before, they must be starving in this dreadful winter.

I pointed the scope at them, Jacob looked through binoculars. 'You can see,' he said. 'They're killers.' There were nearly thirty of them, loping effortlessly, the pack close together, a small, highly efficient procession.

'You shoot,' he whispered. 'I'll pass you the magazines.'

'Okay.'

Two hundred metres from us the dogs picked up speed because the sheep were in sight. The flock saw and smelled the dogs, they jostled about in fear. Then I began to shoot.

The first shots weren't very accurate. I was too keen, too rushed, I didn't allow enough room for their movement.

The shots first brought the pack to a halt. Ears pricked, eyes searching for us where we lay downwind, while I kept shooting, and improved. I focused on the leaders. Domingo was right, it confused the pack more, so that they ran back and forth and eventually chose a direction away from the noise of the rifle.

I got the last one just before he was five hundred metres away. I was very proud of that shot, it was a moving target, very far. Jacob leapt up, yelling, punching the sky, then he slapped me on the back, shouting, 'Incredible shot, we got the bastards, Nico, we got the bastards, every one of them.'

We raced back with the quadbike to tell Pa and Domingo, to bring the first good news in a very long time. We found everyone in a crowd in front of the Midas filling station. There was rejoicing in the air, and most people were helping to unload bags from one of our returned trucks.

'Our hunger is over, it's maize meal,' someone said. 'Two thousand bags. They found it on a goods train other side of Warrenton.'

'We shot nearly thirty dogs dead,' said Jacob.

'Two thousand bags. And there might be more. They didn't break open all the train trucks. Isn't it fantastic?'

I went to look for Pa, to tell him about the dogs. I found him inside the OK Value supermarket. 'Pa!' I said, excited.

Pa held up his hand, the radio against his ear. Domingo's voice crackled over the ether: 'If you could come down to the bus gate, we have fresh arrivals.'

'I'm on my way,' said Pa. He always tried to get to the gate when new people arrived. He rode the Cannondale Scalpel Black Inc. Nero Dlamini had donated the expensive bicycle as Amanzi's 'official vehicle', for the exclusive use of the chairman – to save fuel and be visible everywhere. Pa liked the idea very much: he believed as leader he must remain humble, just one of the people.

Jacob and I followed on the quadbike.

It was Birdy who arrived at the gate then. Birdy and Lizette Schoeman.

29

Cairistine Canary

As recorded by Willem Storm. The Amanzi History Project.

It was that bloody Domingo who went and called me Birdy, I was christened Cairistine, and that's what people called me, in the old days. I don't know why everyone here is so taken with 'Canary', there were lots of Canarys before the Fever. I won't talk much about the Fever myself, I hope that's okay. It hurts too much even if it is a few years ago. My mother ... I just don't want to go there.

I come from Newtown, in Calvinia. I was doing my masters in high-energy physics at UCT when the Fever came. Early on, I already could see it was an ugly thing. I left the Cape before the big mess happened, I went home because I was very worried about my mother. At Clanwilliam, they opened that dam's sluices, seems they were afraid there would be nobody to do it; that was a sight to behold.

I saw everything happening from Calvinia. I lost all my family and friends. In the whole town there were only two survivors, myself and an obese white man by the name of Nelus Claassen who had Claassens Trading, a supermarket there in town; he was so fat from just sitting behind the till eating marshmallows. Now you must understand, his shop was the last one out on the R27, beside the Total garage, so it's the last place I'm going to look for food, because there are quite a few other supermarkets in Calvinia, and only two survivors, those first weeks, before the travelling scavengers turned up.

I got myself a scooter, a MotorMia that was parked at one of the garages, and rode around on it. I made myself a little hand pump that fitted in a backpack, for the petrol, very basic physics. I wanted to see how easy the petrol was at the Total, when that fat Nelus Claassen came out of his shop, and I nearly died of fright.

We were both so starved for conversation, for another living soul, and he said come, there's lots of food here inside. I said thanks very much, and got *myself a few tins of curried fish, and he said, that will be seventy-five rand. I kid thee not. So I said to him you really are silly, and he said, but it's my shop's stuff. And I said, do I have to go to the Total and take cash out of the till to pay you? You know, to point out how ludicrous he was. He says to me, no, he's already emptied the Total till, I will have to fetch other money. I just laughed and put the curried fish down. And when I wanted to leave he actually made a pass. He said, here we are Adam and Eve, we have no choice but to procreate, but a little more crudely than I said it. I was on the point of losing my temper, when I realised how hilarious it was. I laughed all the way back to Newtown.*

It was the last time I saw him. I still wonder if he survived the scavengers.

Cairistine 'Birdy' Canary and Lizette Schoeman arrived in a little silver Hyundai.

Birdy, the delicate, fine-boned, bespectacled Birdy with the braces on her teeth. I don't remember much of Birdy those first meeting moments, because I was transfixed by Lizette. It was what I later learned is called 'puppy love'. She was standing next to Birdy, looking tall and graceful; she was nineteen years old. She wore blue jeans that stretched tightly over her beautiful behind, and a thick cream-coloured wool jersey. Her hair hung very long down her back, the colour of walnuts, straight and shining in the sun. Her skin was smooth and flawless and her mouth wide, eyes big and beautiful, and I just stood staring at her, speechless, I could hear nothing, see nothing else.

She looked back at me, seeing the intensity of my attention and surely my admiration as well. She smiled, it was like the sun rising, her teeth were perfection. She said to me, in a voice filled with joy and music, '*Oh hi, sweetie pie.*'

I blushed, and looked away, but for weeks afterwards I wondered whether this rhyming greeting, the first poetic words from Lizette to me, were an insult, or had a deeper meaning. Until I heard that she greeted other people she liked in that way. Then I felt a little bit better.

But in those moments of falling in love other things happened of which I remember nothing. I heard them later, and they became part of the legend.

Domingo, the deadly Domingo, the emotional Domingo, had his own knee-buckling romantic epiphany. It wasn't the beautiful Lizette who stole his ice-cold heart, but the vulnerable Birdy.

The only words that Domingo could utter when he saw her – desperate to say something, make a connection – were: 'A Hyundai i10?' It sounded much more scornful than he'd intended.

'Yes,' said Birdy Canary. 'It's very energy-efficient.' Her voice was so completely unique, one contradiction piled on the other: half an octave too high, even for her plucky little body, but so full of self-confidence and wisdom. An accent that Pa said was 'pure Namaqualand', but she sometimes used long, learned academic words, and frowned irritably when you couldn't keep up or understand. And nearly every sentence ended on a higher note, as if it were a question.

Her answer had Domingo stumped for a reply and he could only respond with an 'Uh . . .'

'The brochure mentioned electricity,' said Birdy. 'Hydro, I assume?'

Domingo said, 'Uh . . .'

'It's more of a pamphlet,' said Pa. 'We hope to get the hydro-electricity working,' he added.

'Hope? You mean it's not working yet? That's false advertising.'

Domingo said, 'Uh . . .'

Pa said, 'No, the pamphlet speaks about "soon" . . .'

'Which is something of a relative term, apparently,' said Birdy.

Pa was also embarrassed now. 'We don't yet have the expertise to make the connections.'

'Well, I'm here now,' said Birdy.

'You know how to work with electricity?' asked Pa.

'Basic physics. I'll figure it out,' she said.

'Fantastic,' said Pa.

'Uh,' said Domingo.

'Shame, is he a bit soft in the head?' Birdy asked Pa, and pointed at Domingo.

The bus guards laughed. Pa laughed, some of the onlookers laughed. Birdy laughed and the braces on her teeth sparkled. And everyone looked at Domingo, who had never once laughed out loud since he'd arrived.

And then he laughed too.

30

Birdy Day

On 24 September in the Year of the Dog there were four hundred and one residents of Amanzi. Nero Dlamini orchestrated it so that they were all there that day – no one was out on expedition or patrol. He made sure everyone knew that they must be on the edge of the dam at 18.15, down by the boat slipway that looked out over the huge concrete wall.

He told Domingo the bus gate guards had to be there too, 'Because, really, Domingo, we're not going to be invaded on this day, and at this hour. And even if they do, so be it.'

Domingo growled and conceded, because, like everyone in the community, he too had an inkling of what Nero planned.

They began arriving before six in the late afternoon. All they could see was a big canvas tarpaulin draped over some objects – chunky shapes lined up in a tidy row a few metres from the water's edge. Beryl Fortuin and Dlamini directed people to sit down in a semicircle around the mysterious tarpaulin.

By ten to six they were all seated. There was a festive atmosphere, people laughed and chatted as they watched the sun dip lower towards the dam wall, until at twenty past six the rays just began to touch.

I sat as near to Lizette Schoeman as I could, and hoped and prayed that she would glance in my direction just once. Because I was big, I was fourteen; since 22 August I had been fourteen years old. To my mortification I saw Pa arrive, and he searched me out among all the people, and sat down beside me. What would Lizette think?

Nero walked to the centre, in front of the tarpaulin, and raised both hands in the air. Beryl walked to the back, out of our sight. More than three hundred and ninety people fell absolutely silent. Some of the little ones' voices could still be heard. Nero spoke: 'Today was Heritage

Day, in the time before the Fever. And Braai Day, when we celebrated with family and friends; it was a day of togetherness, not a day that honoured politicians or historical figures or events, it was a day that honoured ordinary people. And tonight we're going to do it again. Honour ordinary people. In a special way. Tonight sunset is at exactly twenty-eight minutes past six. Remember that, remember that you were here at that moment.'

Nero looked at his watch, and he waited.

Behind him the sun dipped behind the dam wall. The western horizon was a pageant of colour. Nero lifted his arm, his eyes still on the watch, and then he dropped it.

Beryl pulled the tarpaulin off.

Then came the music.

The notes moved over us, first the dystopic double bass, the ominous drum rolls, and the violins hinting at the beauty to come, like a battle between good and evil, until the good gradually overcame – all this emanating from the massive nightclub amplifiers that stood revealed there now. Those people who knew music gasped. We were dumbstruck, carried away, even the smaller of the children felt it was a sacred, charged moment, and they didn't make a peep. Beethoven's Ninth Symphony, the fourth movement, the chorale, the most beautiful music that I had ever heard in my whole life, like a thousand night birds flying over us, up to the stars which began, one after the other, to twinkle.

I sat beside my father and I heard him sniff. I looked and saw he was weeping. I wanted to give in to tears as well then, but I resisted, in case Lizette saw me . . .

We sat there, the music rising and falling, over and over, the orchestra, the choir, it was overwhelming and perfect.

And as the last note faded over the dam and the hills and the plains far away, there was another sound, a single deep mechanical sound, and then the lights of Amanzi went on, behind us, and in front of us, the length of the dam wall, and down there by the substation; for the first time in nearly two years after the Fever there was electricity again.

'Tonight we honour Cairistine Canary,' said Nero Dlamini. 'Our bringer of light.'

'Birdy Day,' shouted, of all people, Domingo, in a happy voice.

'Birdy Day,' the small crowd of Amanzi people cheered.

And so it was called from that day on.

(It may be the only thing that my father overlooked when he said what lasts: I remember those moments of great joy just as well as those of great fear and humiliation.)

31

Bits and pieces I: about Willem Storm

Nostalgia is the memoirist's great seductress.

I want to talk about the day the lights came on. It was a moment, and a day, that made a huge impression on me as a fourteen-year-old. It was a redemptive moment and a day of jubilation and huge significance for everyone in Amanzi: it literally and figuratively drove out the darkness. That winter's hardship was debilitating. The adults endured hunger for weeks on end, and there was the cold that crept into the marrow of your bones, the hours of back-breaking labour, the discouragement and eventual despair. And when the bishop and Granny Nandi Mahlangu passed away, there was fear of an outbreak of fever, of a new viral mutation, of another wave of death coming to engulf us.

Electricity changed all that. We moved with one flick of a switch from the Middle Ages to the era of technology. Among other things it brought more pure physical comfort. Lights, right through the night. Heaters. Electric stoves. Fridges. Oven-roasted leg of lamb! It made labour immeasurably easier: electric irrigation, electric saws and drills and food processors and vacuum cleaners. And a PlayStation in the Orphanage playroom.

But above all it brought new prospects. And that one ingredient that we needed more than any other: hope.

Cairistine Canary

As recorded by Sofia Bergman. The Amanzi History Project, continued – in memory of Willem Storm.

I want to say to you, that day the power came on should have been called Willem Storm Day. 'Cause, first of all, he had the vision. Not the short-term, small-time vision of flicking a switch and lighting up the ceiling. No, the long-term vision of progress, of reclaiming some of the lost time and technology. Sometimes I would think that Willem Storm viewed Amanzi as a struggle between man and virus, or at least between man and the devastation of the virus. And the hydro-electricity was a big score against the virus. He had so much drive. I won't forget that. Look, Willem wasn't a big man, but that drive gave him presence. He was everywhere, on that official bicycle of his – I'm the one who christened it Bike Force One – he was the chairperson, our Fearless Leader, but he didn't mind getting his hands dirty, he was just as happy to unblock a woman's drains, or dig potatoes on the farms, or to untangle electrical cables for me at the substation. And those cables were no joke, they cost us a whole lot of sweat. And then he'd go home at night and raise a child too. That night when we turned on the power, he was so on edge, I said to him, Willem, chill, what's the worst that could happen? If it doesn't work tonight, then it will work tomorrow or the next day.

But he said, it has *to work. We can't let the people down. That's the kind of man he was. He didn't want to disappoint his people.*

But what I loved most about him, he was so happy for someone else to get the glory.

In that first year I stayed with my father in a room at the Orphanage. A big room – only just big enough for a father with a son of thirteen or fourteen. It was purely an extension of our way of life before Amanzi, when we shared the Volvo cab, or rooms in empty houses in deserted towns.

Pa would fall asleep after me, and get up before me. Now and then I would still be awake when he came to bed. I would watch him making lists in his notebook, of all the things that had to be done in the next week or month or year. Some mornings I would wake before him, and see him lying there with his notebook, just as he had fallen asleep the night before. At the time I didn't think much of it, I didn't add up the clues to come to the conclusion that 'Pa was dead tired'.

It's too long ago to remember exactly what I felt for my father at that time. But I do remember the growing jealousy. It was irrational, as selfish as any teenager's, but in some way it was understandable. Before Melinda and Beryl and the children and Domingo, before the arrival of the 256, my father had been mine alone for nearly two years. Exclusively and totally mine. Not because I demanded it, but because circumstances dictated it. And suddenly I had to share him with everyone.

It wasn't a conscious jealousy, there wasn't a moment of realisation, of awareness of his general absence. It was a slowly developing abscess. It took a long time before it burst. Because, despite everything, I was secretly very proud of him.

When I think back, if I try to assemble the bits and pieces from memory, I can better understand Pa's sudden absence, his abrupt neglect of me. Birdy was right, he saw Amanzi as a battle between man and virus. And I believe on some level he believed he would personally determine the outcome of the battle. It was the reason he worked so hard, from early morning to late at night. It was his magnificent obsession.

Birdy was also correct when she said that Pa brought up his son in the evenings. Even though it didn't feel like enough to me, he did make time to sit with me, eat with me, talk with me. He asked questions about my day, my experiences, my feelings. At thirteen, and in the afterglow of our wandering Volvo days, I still had good conversations with him. Today I feel grieved and ashamed about the subsequent years when I did so much to damage our relationship.

If only I had known we would have so little time.

Hennie Fly

As recorded by Sofia Bergman. The Amanzi History Project, continued – in memory of Willem Storm.

At the time I was the manager of the hothouse with its tomatoes, salad greens and cabbage, and the chicken-keeping project, everything in the prefab buildings of the old Vanderkloof Holiday Resort. Later, we had to move it all – we were producing enough food, but living space had become a problem – but in the early days it was me and four other people who farmed the chickens and vegetables. Every second Tuesday we loaded chicken manure into the wheelbarrows with spades and pushed them over to the tomatoes. First thing in the morning. Now, Willem knew that, and he would arrive on his bicycle, and put on a pair of blue overalls, grab a spade and pitch in. He wasn't very handy with a spade, you could see that wasn't his strong point. But he came to help with the second-smelliest job in

Amanzi. He never made a song and dance about it. As far as I know, he never announced to anyone that he shovelled chicken shit every second Tuesday. So it wasn't a case of a politician wanting to show that he could get his hands dirty. I think he did it so that he ... When the tomatoes were ripe, then he would come, and pick one – always just one – from the vine and take a bite, with his eyes shut, and you could see the great pleasure it gave him. I think he came to cart chicken manure because it made him feel that he had a share in that tomato. He had helped to take us one more small step away from hunger and closer to civilisation.

Beryl Fortuin

As recorded by Sofia Bergman. The Amanzi History Project, continued – in memory of Willem Storm.

It was shortly after we got power, one of the expeditions returned with the box of digital voice recorders, must have been twenty in the box, all with rechargeable batteries. When they were off-loading they wanted to throw the box out, but Willem said no, and he took them, and brought them to the Committee meeting, and he said he was keen on having them, the voice recorders. He wanted to collect people's stories. He called it the Amanzi History Project. And he started carrying one with him at all times, in his pocket. And when he could, he would talk to people, and ask them, now tell us ...

32

Bits and pieces II: about Baruch Spinoza

The end of the Year of the Dog.

In less than five years my father would be murdered.

The guilty party has already appeared in these pages. And those that I view as accomplices, however small their role. And everyone that I would suspect, some to my later great shame.

I promised the reader that I would write this memoir with honesty – as much honesty as the pain and anger allowed, even now, after many decades. This honesty also includes the mitigating circumstances for those that I would accuse, and find guilty.

And the mitigating circumstances, both for me and my mistakes. My unforgivable mistakes.

So I would like to interrupt the sequence of events. In my haste and enthusiasm to get to the first great joyful event of Amanzi, to recall and relive the day the lights went on, on Birdy Day, in my concession to nostalgia, I skipped one of the smaller events. Things seeming unimportant on the surface, things that would become pointers to our future, our coming troubles, and the motive and motivation for murder.

Like the conversation on the night after we'd buried Granny Nandi Mahlangu.

It was in the darkest depths of that murderous winter, before the maize meal find at Warrenton, before Birdy's arrival. The Committee meeting was over, the members were still sitting around the ashes cooling in the hearth of the Orphanage sitting room. Nero Dlamini was trying to cheer everyone up. He brought the few flickering candles closer to us, and fetched a bottle of brandy on a tray, poured some for all the adults and passed out the glasses. As he did every evening, he raised the bottle and said, 'Domingo?'

And as he did every evening, Domingo just shook his head. He didn't drink. I lay on the sofa on one side and watched Domingo clean rifles, and thought, when I grow up, I won't drink either.

Pa stared straight ahead, tense and grim, cold and weary. And hungry too, I thought.

'Are you all right, Willem?' Beryl asked.

Pa sighed. 'It's my fault.'

'No, Willem, she was old and frail,' said Ravi. 'Nobody knew she wasn't eating her rations.'

'No,' Pa said. 'Not Nandi. This place. I chose this place. I lured everyone here with pamphlets. And I made a mistake, because I was so self-satisfied, too taken with my own reasoning . . .'

'What *are* you talking about?' Beryl asked.

Pa stared at the ash in the grate, his voice without expression. 'After the Fever, when Nico and I . . . When I realised we were going to survive, I spent a lot of time considering what would be the best place to take my son. To start a settlement. To . . . rebuild civilisation. It was an interesting exercise for sure, because my first impulse was to choose places that I knew. Places I had a positive connection to. Like Cape St Francis, where I spent holidays as a child. Or beautiful Knysna, a place of substance, texture, wood, shelter, water . . . The challenge, the scientific and intellectual challenge was to eliminate personal preference. I didn't much like Vanderkloof, back then . . .'

Pa looked at the people around him. 'You know that bunch of whites who wanted to live separately on their own just down the river from here, about thirty kilometres or so?'

'Yes,' said Pastor Nkosi. 'Orania. The last outpost of apartheid. I wonder if any of them survived?'

'Well,' said Pa, 'before the Fever, when I had the time, I would go by car on business trips to Jo'burg, and take a different route every time. About four years ago, I drove through Vanderkloof. Actually, I spent a whole day in town, because it was . . . different, I suppose. Unique. Like a seaside holiday town with no sea. Odd. A bit run down, a little sad. And sleepy. Very sleepy, two-thirds of the houses empty, just waiting for the holidays. With the vague sense of promise that it would come alive and transform in the summer vacation . . . It fascinated the geographer in me. I spoke to everybody I met. One local whispered to me that most of Vanderkloof's inhabitants shared the Orania ideology of whites only, or Afrikaner only, or whatever it was that they hoped to achieve. The only difference was, the Vanderkloof inhabitants didn't want the racist stigma. So, this town, Vanderkloof, was a sort of clandestine Orania, where the more cowardly separatists lived. That's why I didn't like the place very much.'

'But what has that to do with the fact that you say it's your fault, all the bad things that happened?' asked Beryl.

'The past months I have been so smug about my reasoning,' said Pa. 'I was so impressed with the fact that I could look beyond the stigma of Vanderkloof, at the bare facts, weigh it up as a place for a new beginning. Intellectual arrogance, because I was so sure that I had taken everything into account: enough substance for survival, security, water, the potential for agriculture, a good chance to generate electricity. I thought the distance from the cities would be an advantage. And it is, in a way. But then I stopped thinking because I was so pleased with myself. I failed to realise that you pay a price for the remote location, for the former low population density of the area. We should have foreseen those risks. As Domingo—'

Beryl gave Domingo a dirty look – which he didn't catch. 'Nobody can think of everything. Nobody knew that it would snow this much.'

'God brought the snow,' said Pastor Nkosi in his ringing preacher's voice. 'God brought the hunger, and the suffering. He's trying to show us that we're taking the wrong road again.'

'And how exactly is he doing that?' asked Nero Dlamini.

'Just look at all our troubles. Just look at all the sad things happening. Where is God when we have Forum meetings, Nero? Or Committee meetings? We don't pray together, we don't praise together. He is trying to tell us—'

'That's why Granny Nandi died?' asked Domingo, his hands still, his voice as keen as a blade. 'And the bishop? That's why the KTM robbed us? And it snowed? Because God wanted to make a point?'

'Tell us, Domingo,' said Pastor Nkosi, his eyes full of evangelical fire. 'Do you believe in God?'

'Yes, Pastor, I believe in a god. My god is Darwin. I believe in the survival of the most ruthless.'

'Then you have the devil in you.' Spat out with so much revulsion that the hairs rose up on the back of my neck.

'Are you going to exorcise him now?'

'Perhaps one day we will have to,' said the pastor, with much more courage than he usually showed in Domingo's presence.

'Nobody is going to exorcise anybody,' said Pa. His voice betrayed his fatigue.

Pastor Nkosi wasn't yet ready to drop the subject: 'Do you believe in God, Willem?'

At first Pa seemed to consider the necessity of an answer. Then: 'Do you know what Einstein said when a rabbi asked him the same question, Nkosi?'

'No.'

'Einstein said, "I believe in Spinoza's god, who reveals himself in the orderly harmony of what exists, not in a god who concerns himself with the fates and actions of human beings." '

'And that's what you believe?'

'That's what I used to believe. Now, I just believe in Spinoza, really.'

'I see . . .'

'Spinoza,' said Nero Dlamini, and sipped his brandy. 'He's the guy who first said religion and politics should be kept separate?'

'Yes, and with all due respect, that's why Nkosi will not like him,' said Pa, in an attempt to lighten the tone of the conversation. 'And the wonderful irony is Domingo won't like him either.'

'Why?' asked Domingo, who didn't like to imagine that he and the pastor might have anything in common.

'Because Spinoza believed that democracy is the form of government that would accommodate personal freedom best.'

'Personal freedom is overrated,' said Domingo, but his tone was gently mocking, like Pa's.

Pastor Nkosi was still deadly serious. 'I will keep fighting for God in this community. And in this Committee. One day, he will be our chairman. I'm willing to bet my life on that.'

33

Bits and pieces III: of love and desire

Nostalgia encourages triviality, self-indulgence. Nostalgia whispers, 'Tell them how Lizette Schoeman broke your heart when you were nearly sixteen.' It was, as these things go, utterly unremarkable: I was walking from the water tower on a late Sunday afternoon in August, in the Year of the Jackal and I saw Lizette in an embrace with Charl Oosthuizen, a man in his thirties who had barely been in Amanzi for two months. I wanted to burst into tears, I wanted to scream, to fall down at her feet, I wanted to attack him, I wanted to run away, escape for ever. But I just kept walking towards the Orphanage, my heart broken, shattered, in pieces. (Scarcely two months later it would make a complete recovery!)

They got married in the end, the two of them. Charl was a good man, he would go on to become a big sunflower farmer, and Lizette became our best honey producer. But I could only really start to like him once I'd also discovered the love of my life.

For two long years I'd been intensely and hopelessly besotted with Lizette. Hopeless, because I was still a child, and she was not. Hopeless, because it was unrequited. A futile endeavour.

Futile, as my infatuation meant that I missed out on the greatest love and lust bonanza of my era. Which was the result, first of all, of the phenomenon that Nero Dlamini called the 'baby boom effect', the evolutionary urge to drastically increase population growth after a bloody war – or a catastrophic viral epidemic.

Second, it stemmed from the intense desire people have to be touched and held, to connect, to cherish and be cherished, in a world where the usual sources of affection have been wiped out – parents, family members and loved ones. Nero called it the John Bowlby Effect, and said among young people who had in addition been severely trau-matised, it had an even greater influence.

And third, there was the fact that teenagers – in any case the world's randiest creatures – were statistically one of the largest groups in Amanzi. Because this cohort's youth, adaptability and physical strength had helped them survive the dangers of the post-apocalyse somewhat better than the rest.

That was the academic, Dlaminian explanation of the Sex Fest among young and old, but especially the young, and I missed out on it all, being so besotted with Lizette Schoeman. But not so Jacob Mahlangu. He took advantage of the excess on offer, yet never encouraged me to do the same. Years later he would confess: 'I didn't need the competition, Nico. I'm not stupid. If you knew how many girls had a crush on you . . . I had to console them.' And then he laughed in that deep Mahlangu way that made his whole body vibrate.

Jacob was my co-shepherd and my great comrade. Jacob was also my mole, my gossip link, my source of information about everything outside the Orphanage. As son of the chairman I had the advantage of inside knowledge during those early years: about Committee meetings and decisions, all the great questions facing our community, the undercurrents, the plans, the conflicts and the strategy. But the greatest disadvantage was that the people of Amanzi didn't trust me with all the gossip and complaints. Nor with their constant criticisms of the chairman and the Committee and all its members, regardless of whether they made good or bad decisions.

That was where Jacob played such a vital role. In many aspects we were opposites, and the perfect combination. Jacob was placid, patient, philosophical, easy in his own skin. I was none of those. Yet we both developed a love for reading, and an unquenchable thirst for juicy news.

It was Jacob who drew me aside one morning at school and breathlessly told me, 'Beryl and Nero are gay.'

At fourteen I had a somewhat loose grasp of the term. 'Gay? But they can't be gay together?'

'No, stupid, she likes women, and he likes men.'

'How do you know?'

'Miss Denise said so.' Denise was a forty-year-old woman who had been here since Arrival Day, one of Amanzi's biggest blabbermouths. 'She says Beryl was a golf pro, and everybody knows women golf pros are all gay. And you can still see it, from Beryl's muscles, and her butch ways.'

I thought of Beryl, and, looking at it like that, it made sense.

'And Nero?'

'Has he shown any interest in any of the women?'

'No . . .'

'And the way he dresses. And speaks . . .'

'Oh.'

'So, there . . .'

I believed him.

Sipho Jola was born on 26 December in the Year of the Dog, the first person to enter life as a member of the community of Amanzi.

His name means 'gift'.

The Sex Fest would produce twenty-four babies in the next twelve months – the Year of the Crow.

The Year of the Crow

34

Thielert's gearbox: I

Cairistine 'Birdy' Canary

As recorded by Willem Storm. The Amanzi History Project.

Yes, causality can be a pain. I mean, the story about Hennie and the plane and the petrol, and Nico and Okkie and all the drama started by all those companies who genetically engineered seeds. It's not as if they thought, hang on, what happens in case of a global catastrophe, what happens in a post-apocalyptic world? They modified their seeds so that you could only harvest once. Then you had to eat them, because you couldn't plant the seed from the first crop, they were programmed to fail. You had to buy new seed. Beautiful business model, but then all those companies were gone with the wind, but the seeds remained.

I told the Committee, that must be one of our primary objectives, if we were going to plan long term: develop a seed bank. Luckily we had Tony by then, Tony Mbalo, who had worked on a grain farm that belonged to the Premier of the Free State provincial government, back in the day, near Reitz. Tony was the farmer, as the Premier was almost never there. And Tony was a good farmer. When he came to us, he became the chief in charge of Amanzi's grain farming.

Tony and I talked a lot about the problem of the genetically modified seed. Tony told me he knew there were many Eastern Free State farmers who cultivated wheat for non-modified heritage seed. We should get hold of some of that seed.

But it wasn't a case of just going to collect some. At that stage the KTM controlled too many of the routes between the Lesotho mountains and Bloemfontein. If you wanted to pass through, you had to send an armed convoy, and we didn't have the people or the vehicles, and couldn't run the risk; there were too many other urgent necessities to see to before the next winter.

Then Hennie Fly said he could load four hundred kilos of seed in the Cessna. Would that help?

Hennie Fly

As recorded by Willem Storm. The Amanzi History Project.

I flew in from Bethlehem with the Cessna, on my own. I had over four hundred kilograms of seed wheat on board. It was seed that Amanzi sorely needed, and before winter, as they still needed to plough and plant. Now, four hundred kilograms is too much for the Cessna, if you take into consideration my weight and the odds and ends that I have to take along, and fuel as well. So I loaded the wheat, and then I pumped some of the fuel out of the tanks, to get the weight down. I left a good safety margin for the range that I could fly with the fuel, so I wasn't too concerned. But I was still about forty kilograms too heavy, not too bad, but it does make you watch the vitals, the instruments, it's like always in the back of your mind that you're overweight, you're flogging the old girl, so you have to keep an eye in case she starts to complain.

I was at ten thousand feet … that's about three thousand metres, it's a good altitude for the 172. I was cruising, a hundred and twenty knots, or two-twenty kilometres per hour. Around ten o'clock in the morning, in January. You know the weather can build up, that time of the year in that part of the country. And this morning there were already a few clouds and a bit of turbulence, but I ought to get back home before one, the big thunderstorms only arrive in late afternoon.

Anyway, I still had about seventy-five litres in the tank, enough for five hundred kilometres if I kept it nice and steady, and it was only four hundred back to Amanzi. Everything was hunky-dory, or so I thought.

Then it began to sputter. Out of the blue. At ten thousand feet.

At first I thought the engine would cut out altogether, the first sputter was so severe, and then it came back, and struggled. It was as though the fuel was gone, but both tanks showed just over half full. Sputter, sputter, and I was losing power, and losing altitude, and I was overladen.

I tried working the magnetos, that didn't help, then I knew it had to be the plugs that were dirty. Now, if the plugs are dirty you make your fuel mixture leaner and you give maximum power to see if you can burn the dirt off the plugs. It helped, but only for about five minutes, then the sputtering returned, and you had to burn them again.

I knew then, Hennie, you have to land, you have to clean those plugs.

Now the route from Bethlehem to Amanzi, as the Cessna flew, takes you between Bloemfontein and Botshabelo. When the plane trouble began I was about thirty, thirty-five kilometres north-east of Botshabelo, and probably seventy east of Bloem. It's all very well to say a 172 can land anywhere where the road is reasonably good and reasonably straight, but if you don't know the area . . . The trouble is wires. Power lines and telephone wires. You can't see them, and they are always beside the road and across the road, and you don't see them and you fly into them, and then you're in trouble. If you have time and lots of petrol, and not overloaded, you can take a good look for wires where you want to land. But if you don't have that, then you look for an airstrip. Quickly.

And the other thing is, at that moment I decided I definitely didn't want to be found fiddling with the engine somewhere to hell and gone on a stretch of road that was rotten with the KTM. If I could, I had to make a plan.

Before I take off, I look over the few maps I have collected to see where there are airfields. And the plan, the best plan I could come up with at that moment it began sputtering, was Thaba 'Nchu airport. Not the biggest in the world, it only had one runway, but it was good and long, and properly tarred. I remembered it was south of Botshabelo, but I didn't know exactly where. The old lady was sputtering, and I was losing speed and altitude, my glide ratio was bad, too bad for the distance, and I had to study the map on my lap to see where the hell Thaba 'Nchu airport was. Then I had to set course, and keep burning the plugs every five minutes, and I had to keep a sharp eye out for beacons, or the airport. I tell you, I was in a proper sweat. I thought, if I crash here, Melinda will think I've run off, and I can't do that to her. And Amanzi needs that seed badly. I prayed out loud, between burning off the plugs and checking my rate of descent.

And then I spotted it, but it only made the sweat pour even more, because it seemed just too far, and the runway was north-west to south-east, which meant I had make a wide turn as well. Now you should know, Thaba 'Nchu's airport was built under the old apartheid era, for the Bophuthatswana homeland, for the casino, really; back in those days it was quite a grand airport. But after apartheid the place went backwards. And now it was two years past the Fever, so there was no windsock, and I guessed the wind was blowing a bit north to south, so I turned to the south-eastern end of the runway, knowing full well that I might not make it, but if you don't try, hey ...

There's a little koppie, a hill that I had to get over, and I only just made it. I burned the plugs one last time and I opened up that engine, and made my last turn for final approach. Now I was ... I don't want to lie to you, but the ground was very close and the runway still too far; it was grassveld, long green summer grass, there could have been a buck hiding in that grass, and I realised, oh shoot, the wind was still from behind and I was coming in too fast. And then I saw the cows on the runway, far over on the northern end.

I put her down, must have been a good hundred and twenty metres before the runway started, in the long green grass. If I had hit an anthill at that speed, or an aardvark hole, then I and the wheat and the 172 would have been in our glory, but she rolled towards the tarmac, and then onto the tar, but we were going too fast and the wind was strong behind us, and we were too heavy to stop in time. I sat and watched those cows come closer. Two were standing on the tarmac, maybe ten more in the grass on either side of the runway. Now I ask you, what was a cow doing on the tarmac, there's nothing to eat, it's just fate. I braked as hard as I could – you can't overdo it, or you'll tip her on her nose – and the cattle kept coming closer, and I braked, and sweated, and the cows kept coming.

It's one of those things that you'll never forget. You think, I've just brought this aerie with four hundred kilos of wheat and a stuttering engine down safely, a huge achievement, if I have to say so myself. I'd sweated blood, but I was on the ground, and now I was going to crash into a cow. You could see her, up ahead, with that big fat stupid expression on her face and those long tart's eyelashes, and it's into this creature that you're going to smash yourself to smithereens.

Now that cow strolled out of the way, just at the very last split-second. I still believe it was because the noise of the engine was annoying her, and she wandered just far enough for me to swerve left, and I slid between the two cows, and stopped the Cessna and just sat there, my whole body shaking, my whole body, I'm telling you, but I just bent my head and said thank you, God, thank you. I had stopped at the end of the tarmac, the very end of the runway, and I could see there was an eroded gully just beyond the strip; I would have somersaulted her there if I hadn't got her to stop. It was destiny.

Little knowing the Lord and I still had a lot of work to do that day.

Cairistine 'Birdy' Canary

Petrol was made to burn easily. And that's precisely the reason why it doesn't keep for long. If you store it in a tank too long, some of the elements that burn most easily start to evaporate. And the other thing is, hydrocarbons in the petrol start reacting with the oxygen, and they change the chemical composition of the petrol. They contaminate the fuel; that is why Hennie Fly found that gummy stuff in his fuel system.

Hennie Fly

Standing on the end of the Thaba 'Nchu runway, I knew I had to do two things. I had to find out why the plugs were getting so dirty, and I had to clean them. The first part was the easiest – as soon as I began to look, when I ran some petrol out of the tanks, I immediately saw the petrol in the left wing was dirty, it had these little bits of gummy stuff in it. It had me seriously worried, and I ran fuel from the right wing tank, but that at least was clear.

Now, those 172s had three settings for the flow of petrol. You could select the left tank, you could select the right tank, or you could set it to use both tanks at the same time. You always used the last setting when flying. But with the left tank dirty, I had to set it to use the right wing.

The trouble with that was that it immediately halved my available fuel. I stood there thinking, how was I going to get home?

I emptied all the bad fuel out of the left wing, to make the aerie as light as possible, and I thought, if I work smart, I can make it. With a bit of luck. And a tail wind. And by the grace of God.

If the fuel does start to run out, I'll land as close to Amanzi as I can, and then I'll walk to get help from my people.

You know, what else could I do?

The clock was ticking, the clouds were building in the sky.

But first I had to get the plugs cleaned, and that's another story. A Cessna's plugs, as you can imagine, aren't just like a car's plugs with wiring that you can simply pull off, the wires are screwed to those plugs. I had a mini-toolbox in the aerie, and I knew I had a plug spanner, and I knew I had a three-eighths spanner, but I also knew that I didn't have a seven-sixteenths. And without a seven-sixteenths, I couldn't get those plugs out to clean them.

I looked around, and I spotted the airport Arrivals building; it was a ruin, everything broken. And there were several hangars, small ones, five or six in a row. I walked there, and saw the hangar doors were half open, and I knew then there was nothing in there. I was right, there were no planes in those hangars. But I hoped and prayed as I searched through them, and in the last one there was still a workbench against the wall. It was filthy, covered in a thick layer of dust and rubbish, and there were rags and empty cans, and part of an engine, and a bunch of spanners and pliers and screws and stuff, really rusty, and I began to scratch around and blow away the dust, and I realised that some of these engine parts were from a 172. I began to feel hopeful, and I continued to search and would you know, there was a seven-sixteenths. Let me tell you, I shed a tear when I held that spanner in my hand.

I began to remove the plugs and clean them – they were terribly dirty, but otherwise they were fine. Time passed, things always take longer than you think, and the thunderheads built up in the west. We're talking about serious weather, you could feel it in the air, there's that electricity, which means trouble.

I worked as fast as I could. I put the plugs back, and chased the cows away as far as I could, then I threw a handful of grass in the air to check the wind. It was still blowing north, so I could just turn round and go, and I took off, the plugs were clean and I got her in the air and turned and climbed. So it was one eye on the weather and one eye on the fuel gauge, because I had about two hundred and thirty kilometres to go to Petrusville. By that time I had already cleared and repaired the Petrusville airfield runway, which was where I kept the Cessna, about twenty kilometres by road from Amanzi.

Now I was flying, and it was going okay. With about a hundred kilometres to go, the wind turned. Now it was a head wind. I knew if it kept on blowing, the fuel I had would be just too little, and the clouds grew thicker and the turbulence worse and the wind blew harder from the front, but at least the engine was running smoothly. I did sums in my head, and I thought, higher or lower, faster or slower, what would be best? This was really going to be touch-and-go, hair-raising stuff. Very scary.

The Cessna's glide ratio was more or less fifteen kilometres for every two thousand metres altitude. Under normal circumstances. But this wasn't normal. By then, the load was much lighter due to the fuel dumped and the fuel used, but the head wind blew stronger and stronger.

And my glide ratio I estimated at, say, twelve or thirteen kilometres for every two thousand in altitude. So I was still positive, but hell, that petrol gauge was low, I never saw it so low.

You know how it is, how you remember some things perfectly? For me it's a lot to do with smells, I smell something, and the memory is so clear. But for that day I don't remember a smell, I remember a scene, because it was so incredibly beautiful, and because I thought I'd better store it in my mind, in case it was the last thing I was going to see.

Because twenty kilometres from the Petrusville landing strip, the fuel ran out. Completely.

35

Thielert's gearbox: II

Hennie Fly

When the engine died, maybe it was adrenalin, but I felt I could see more clearly: I was just over two thousand metres up. Down below was Amanzi's dam, stretching fifty kilometres from north to south, I was flying east to west, and that day the water was so very blue. The sun shone through the thunderclouds, like a beam of divine light, I'm telling you, such sunbeams, such rays, as if God were saying: I'm still here, Hennie, you just fly that machine. And the sun and the sunbeams shone on the surface of the dam. And the clouds were like, you couldn't describe it. And there I was, just beneath them, and they were ranked in rows, like an army approaching, like towers, dark grey at the bottom, so dark they were nearly black, but up at the top they were the whitest of white, and they rolled and whirled up there, and you knew that if the Cessna ended up in one of those, if that convection current grabbed hold of you . . . and you could also see the lightning strike past you on one side, from the cloud to the earth, you saw it hit the highest mountain just south of Amanzi, and you knew your Melinda and the little children and all the people must have seen or heard it, you are so close to home. And you looked out on the beautiful world, the hills down there and the plains of the Karoo stretching out to Petrusville and beyond, to where the world ended. It spread so wide. And you pictured yourself and that little Cessna against the clouds and the waters and the earth, you were just a speck, so small, so insignificant, and suddenly the sun shone on you and the light went golden. I'm telling you, man, it was so beautiful I wanted to cry.

But you couldn't cry then, because the engine was dead, the petrol was gone, and you had at least to try to land, even though you knew the chances were zero. Okay, not zero, but if you had to take a bet, the big money would have been on the side of a crash, because, as I said, the glide ratio said it's just too far.

If you're up there above the dam, on that specific spot, all your landing chances are equally far off. Because of the dam, and the hills, there isn't a piece of ground flat enough to put her down. And I was gliding and I thought, try for the runway, Hennie, you know the approach, you know it best. Just try.

I was floating. It was a weird sensation, to fly like that after the engine's long roar. It was suddenly so silent and calm and peaceful, and I could listen to the thunder. I flew into the rain, it clattered and spat, and then I was out of the storm again and it was quiet, and I looked at the beauty and looked at the instruments, and I thought, well, at least the wheat is here, if I crash this side of the runway, and the fuel tanks are empty, the Cessna won't burn, they will surely find the wreckage and the wheat.

The winds of the thunderstorms pulled me this way and that, nothing was constant, everything was crazy; the main thing was to stay calm, not to overreact or overcompensate. So I kept my head, I had to get the wheat on the ground, that was the thing, but I was down to a thousand metres and saw clearly I would be way too short, four, five kilometres too short, it was an eternity, it was coming-down-in-the-water too short. I looked out and saw: due east of the airstrip the dam makes this funny bay, like an arrow-head, and I knew there was a Jeep track running down to that bay, and I thought, if I can just get over the water, I can try for that; it was bad and full of stones and gullies, but at least I would keep the wheat out of the water. So I headed for that and I prayed, though I knew I couldn't make it, everything said that, the rate of descent and the distance and my own eyes and brain. No chance, I simply would not make it, I was going down in the dam, in the water. And then the convection current hit me, the turbulence lifted up the Cessna, like the Hand of God. Now, I know that does happen. I have flown on the Highveld in the old days, and a convection current would grab you and lift you up like an elevator one hundred, two hundred metres, it's not impossible. But there over the dam that day, with that load of seed, and the engine dead and no fuel, it wasn't coincidence; it was the Hand of God. It was no coincidence that it lifted me up, I'm telling you, five, six hundred metres. It was a miracle, nothing less than a miracle.

We crowded together in front of the old police station, around the bags of seed wheat. Pastor Nkosi spurred Hennie Fly to tell his story to the new arrivals as well. Hennie didn't need much encouragement. When he had finished everyone cheered, and clapped him on the shoulder. He didn't care about the admiration. Every time he just looked for approval in Melinda Swanevelder's eyes. And he found it.

Within a short space of time he had to tell the whole story all over again from the beginning, to a new group. And with each retelling the Hand of God lifted Hennie and the Cessna a little bit higher.

Birdy Canary said, 'That's the last flight, Hennie. The petrol is going to get more and more contaminated from now on.'

'What if I put it through a filter?'

'It won't help.'

Hennie looked crushed. Without a plane he just wouldn't *be* Hennie Fly.

'We need the plane badly,' said Pa, looking worried.

Ravi Pillay said, 'Indeed. It's one of our few strategic advantages.' He meant over the KTM and all the other evils.

'We'll just have to manage without it,' said Birdy.

'Look at the seed wheat. Look at the sheep,' said Pa. He meant the more than four hundred sheep that Hennie had spotted over the past months in remote areas of the Karoo using the plane, and led expeditions to them. 'Look at how much time and fuel we saved.'

'And lives,' said Beryl Fortuin.

Pa looked at Birdy. 'We have to do everything in our power to keep the plane in the air.' He would regret that a great deal later on.

Birdy shook her head. 'Planes don't fly on diesel.'

'That's not entirely true,' said Hennie Fly.

Birdy Canary was involved everywhere. She taught a science class to the oldest children, trained teachers, since December she had been a permanent member of the Committee, on the insistence of the whole community. Birdy was Amanzi's sharpest scientific brain, and her knowledge did not only include physics and chemistry but, thanks to her undergraduate studies, included a little botany, as with the genetically modified seed, and zoology.

Much to Domingo's frustration, she and Pa developed a close working relationship, because they shared a passionate determination to let this community survive and thrive. After the tragic loss of human lives, Pa once said, the greatest damage of the Fever was that it deprived us of so many scientific and technological opportunities – it could have been a much better world already. And Birdy said, 'Exactly! That's exactly how I feel.' And Nero Dlamini remarked drily a few days later that it seemed as though the two of them were trying to reclaim all the technological and scientific possibilities single-handed.

Among other things, Pa and Birdy were Amanzi's long-term planners. Pa supported her enthusiastically when she did a fuel presentation at the first Committee meeting in January. She explained why the petrol in filling stations and tanker trucks would become less and less usable over the next few months. She told them they would have to produce biodiesel. She described the difference between ethanol and diesel, and explained why the former was not suitable for Amanzi under our post-Fever circumstances (basically she said we couldn't easily or economically grow the necessary amount of sugar). Our future was in diesel. And that it was a hidden blessing, because all the agricultural equipment ran on diesel.

She said we must start collecting sunflower seed to plant, starting next summer. To produce diesel from the sunflower oil. It wasn't too difficult. And because diesel kept longer than petrol, we would be able to manage for at least another twelve months on old stored diesel. Perhaps even longer.

That was the reason Birdy told Hennie Fly there in front of the old police station that we would have to manage without our aeroplane.

She didn't know about diesel-powered planes.

'There are a few types of diesel planes,' Hennie Fly told the Committee a week later during an official sitting. 'But there were only two kinds imported into South Africa: the Cessna 172D – which is the same plane as ours, but with a diesel engine – and the Piper Archer DX. I don't know where the Piper is that they brought in. But just before the Fever, I was chatting to a guy at the Heidelberg airfield. He said he really felt like buying a TD-Cessna, and he knew there was one at the Western Transvaal Flying School at Klerksdorp, and at the Hoedspruit Flying Club in the Lowveld. Now, Klerksdorp's airfield is close by, just over three hundred and thirty kilometres from here . . .'

'That's a dangerous route, Hennie,' said Ravi Pillay.

'I don't want to drive, I want to fly,' said Hennie.

'After your petrol troubles of last week?' said Beryl Fortuin.

'I looked at our supply. We have enough clean petrol, the dirty fuel was in the tank at the Petrusville airfield. But we'll have to hurry, Birdy says the petrol is going to degrade faster and faster.'

'That's right,' said Birdy.

'So you want to fly to Klerksdorp first?' Beryl asked.

'Yes. And if that plane is okay, we'll bring it back. Otherwise we'll fly to Hoedspruit.'

'And if both planes are unusable?' Pa asked.

'Then that's the way it is. But if we want a plane, we'll have to go and take a look.'

'How far is Hoedspruit?' asked Pastor Nkosi.

'About eight hundred and eighty kilometres,' said Hennie.

'Can you fly that far?'

'Easily. The 172 has a range of about one thousand six hundred kilometres.'

'But you have to go there and back, Hennie, that is more than one thousand six hundred,' said Birdy.

'I know. But if I take a hundred and fifty litres of petrol, I'll make it easily.'

'What are the risks?' Pastor Nkosi asked.

'Oh, the usual . . .' Hennie tried to make light of it.

'And what would that be?' Ravi Pillay asked.

'Weather. Mechanical failure. Getting attacked when we land . . .'

'We?' asked Beryl. 'How many people do you need?'

'Only one other. You know how badly I shoot and fight. I'm looking for someone to cover me when we're on the ground. I'll have to take a battery along for the TD and install it. I have to check the tank drains, do a general pre-flight and I have to get the aerie going. It's going to take some time.'

'Can we afford to send two?' Nkosi asked.

'It's not really that dangerous,' said Hennie.

'Why do you say that?' asked Birdy.

'You've no problem with me flying with someone nearly every day, if the weather is good, two, three hundred kilometres to look for the

KTM or sheep or cattle. This may be just to Klerksdorp. About two hours' flying. Even if we have to go to Hoedspruit, it's just a few hours further. All the other risks remain the same.'

'That's true,' said Pa. 'We send four to six people out every day on the roads. We mustn't overreact because this is by air.'

'That's right,' said Hennie hopefully.

'And if they do bring back a diesel plane . . .' said Pa. 'It's a big prize. A very big prize.'

The entire Committee nodded.

'Shall we vote? Anyone opposed?' Pa asked.

Not a hand in sight.

'Fantastic!' said Hennie Fly. 'Thank you. Thank you very much.'

'It's we who must thank you, Hennie. It's a brave thing. Who did you have in mind to go along?' Pa asked.

I sat in the corner of the room. I saw how Hennie Fly took a deep breath and then looked at me and said, 'Nico.'

36

Thielert's gearbox: III

Sometimes I would fall asleep during the Committee meetings. Sometimes it would be so thoroughly boring to a fourteen-year-old that I would tiptoe out and help Domingo clean rifles in the sitting room. Tonight I had followed every word of the discussion because it gripped my imagination, especially after Hennie's wheat seed saga. When he said my name, I was mute with astonishment.

But then I imagined the adventure, and all the fame that would go with it, and I said, '*Yes*!'

'Be quiet,' Pa said to me. And then to Hennie: 'You can't be serious.'

'It's the only way we can do it,' said Hennie.

'The only way. Why?'

'I'll have to fill all the tanks to the top before I leave. I told you I would have to take about a hundred and fifty litres of petrol, in case I have to come back with the same plane from Hoedspruit, if nothing goes right, if both the diesel Cessnas are out of action.'

'Yes,' said Birdy. 'Makes sense.'

'A hundred and fifty litres of petrol is about a hundred and twenty kilograms. And then I have to take at least a hundred and fifty litres of diesel along, because we don't know if the TD has any diesel in its tanks, or how clean any diesel is that it may have. And we have to fly home.'

'Okay,' said Birdy.

'That's another hundred and twenty kilograms. And I have to take a spare charged battery along, because the TD's battery is bound to be flat. I weigh ninety-four kilograms as I stand here. Then there are the tools, and a firearm or two, and ammunition, and food and water and a few other things . . . The thing is, there won't be capacity for anyone heavier than forty-five, fifty kilos. Maximum. And the only guy in that weight category who can shoot straight is Nico Storm.'

Deathly silence. Then Pa shook his head. 'No,' he said emphatically.

I was fourteen that January in the Year of the Crow. Fourteen and a half, as I pointed out to Domingo.

A year or two later I would surely have thrown an adolescent tantrum – perhaps even in front of the whole Committee? – and told Pa precisely what I thought of such flagrant injustice. I would have screamed at him that at thirteen I'd been good enough to shoot two men dead to save his life, I was good enough to hunt buck and butcher them, get blood on my hands. At fourteen I was good enough for him to neglect me, so he could devote all his time to the people of Amanzi. At fourteen I was old enough to spend every second week up in the reserve with a gun and another fourteen-year-old; there was always the chance that the KTM or someone would get there and try to steal our livestock. But I couldn't go with Hennie Fly?

At sixteen I would have, in a seething temper tantrum, venomously told Pa that a few fourteen-year-olds, and many fifteen-year-olds in our community had already been out on expeditions last year, during and after that dreadful winter, when we were desperate. But those were other people's children, or orphans; did their lives matter less?

And then there was the fact that Pa, up to that day, had never told me he was proud of the way I had wiped out the pack of wild dogs so skilfully, and single-handedly, to save our flocks. It was a thing that I had been brooding over – why did Pa make little of it, why did he avoid the subject and not share the praise that was due to me?

I wanted praise and I wanted fame, like any fourteen-year-old. I wanted to be part of the legend of Amanzi, the legend of the First, the Pioneers, the History Makers, the Heroes. I wanted to impress Lizette Schoeman. At night I lay in bed before sleeping, and I dreamed about myself and Lizette, of how I would save her from the clutches of the KTM, and then she would say, 'Nico, you are the man for me,' and she would throw her arms around me and kiss me. If only I could fly with Hennie, Lizette would realise I was old and big and brave enough for her. I so badly wanted to be noticed, talked about, as they talked about Domingo's scornful stare when the KTM wanted to shoot him, like Birdy and the hydro-electric power, like Hennie Fly and the seed wheat. I knew I was destined for that kind of recognition. I *knew* it.

And now Pa was going to deprive me of that.

The crushing disappointment and frustration didn't evoke a teenage outburst, but a fourteen-year-old's tears. Which I had to choke back and hide. I got up and walked over to the door and out of it and kept on walking, through the sitting room of the Orphanage, past Domingo who watched me go, out of the front door and into the street, into the darkness.

Pa knew where I was. I watched him climbing up the hill in the darkness by torchlight, and eventually he reached me and sat down on the rock beside me. We stared out over the town on the right and the dam wall ahead, the streetlights looking like beads threaded in the night.

I could feel the tension in my father, I could feel the mass of words and emotions dammed up behind his silence. I waited for it to erupt.

He put a hand on my back, held my shirt as though he could hold me back. I heard him sigh. Pa, who always had the right words – and even knew where they came from – had nothing he could say to me now.

Later he shifted his hand, put it on my shoulder. We sat like that, for maybe a quarter of an hour, maybe half an hour, until Pa said, 'I understand why you're so disappointed.'

I said nothing.

'Come, we must go to bed. Tomorrow is a long day.'

They chose Little-Joe Moroka to fly with Hennie. Little-Joe because he was intrepid and brave, only weighed sixty-one kilograms and was a reasonable shot. Little-Joe was twenty-two years old. When Pa said fourteen was too young, the others asked him, how old is old enough? And that put Pa on the spot where he had to voice an opinion, and he said if it wasn't an emergency, older than eighteen, for sure.

Domingo took charge of Little-Joe. He gave him one of the few R6 assault rifles we had. The R6 was based on the R4, but it was smaller, lighter, shorter. And more suited to indoor work, for the circumstances that might be expected in aeroplane hangars in Klerksdorp or Hoedspruit.

I seethed with jealousy. I had never fired an R6 before.

Little-Joe's shooting didn't impress Domingo. The Committee said, 'Let him practise more.' Hennie Fly said, 'You're all so worried about the shooting. I'm going to fly over the places first to see if there is any trouble. We won't land if there is any danger. I'm not an idiot.'

Domingo made Little-Joe shoot more. He improved a little.

Little-Joe had never been in an aeroplane.

One morning in early February just after sunrise, Hennie Fly took him up in the Cessna, to get him accustomed to flying. Little-Joe perspired and started to feel airsick and then threw up on the floor of the plane. He begged Hennie to land. Back on firm ground he stood shaking like a leaf, and said he was terribly sorry, but he wouldn't be able to go. He would do anything else, really anything, but fly he would not.

'It's fear of flying, also known as aviophobia,' said Nero Dlamini. 'I can treat him, but it's going to take time.'

We didn't have the time, because the petrol was deteriorating a little more every week.

I wasn't speaking to my father.

Birdy had arrived at Amanzi with braces on her teeth, six months before. She would often say: 'I know these things have to come off, but where do we find an orthodontist?'

And Domingo would say: 'Let me take them off, Birdy.'

'You? I won't trust a former biker with my teeth.'

He grinned, a little patient smile. She was the only person who could talk to him like that, who made him seem just a little less dangerous. Everyone knew Domingo was in love with her, everyone knew he'd been trying for months to ask her out on a date. 'Will you go out with me, Birdy?'

Every time she would reply: 'What for? I see you every day. And where would you take me? There's nowhere to go out here.'

He would just nod and walk away.

She sat watching Domingo one evening in February as he was reassembling a pistol. She saw how delicately he worked, how strong his hands were, how precise his movements. She said, 'Okay then. Tomorrow you can take these braces off my teeth.'

He looked up. 'Why now?'

'It should have been done a long time ago, and I can see you can work with your hands. But let me warn you, if you hurt me, I'll cut off your water and lights.'

'Ouch.'

'My point exactly.'

'I'll get the pliers . . .'

'No, Domingo. Tomorrow when the sun is shining.'

'Tomorrow you'll get cold feet. Or a cold mouth . . .'

The next morning she came to call him, and she sat on a chair by the summer vegetable garden where the swimming pool used to be, with her face turned up to the sun. Pa and Nero Dlamini, Beryl and Melinda Swanevelder went along out of curiosity, and to give moral support.

I was at school. Afterwards Nero would describe how Birdy sat in the chair, small and vulnerable. Domingo loomed over her; if you hadn't known what he was doing it could have been mistaken for a torture scene. But he worked very gently, deftly and surely. Slowly, carefully, his voice soothing. He used a pair of wire cutters, long-nose pliers and his strong fingers. He told her: 'Don't worry, don't worry, I would never hurt you.' As he removed the wires and the metal anchors, he dropped each one into an empty teacup, each one tinkling delicately as it dropped, until the last bit of metal was removed.

He picked up the teacup and showed her the contents and said, 'There you are. Now you owe me dinner.'

'I owe you nothing, but I'll tell you what, if Hennie Fly and I come back alive, I'll have dinner and breakfast with you.'

'Where are you going with Hennie Fly?'

'We're going to get the diesel aeroplane.'

'Over my dead body,' said Domingo.

'Then you had better fall down dead already, Domingo, because I'm going. I had an epiphany last night: if I can prove to myself I have the guts to let you mess around with a pair of pliers in my mouth, then I have the guts for this trip. And here we are. I'm the smallest, lightest adult over eighteen in Amanzi. And you are going to teach me how to shoot.'

'No, Birdy,' said my father before he could stop himself. 'You're too valuable.'

She got up from the chair, feeling her jaw, and she said, 'So, Willem, some animals are more equal than others?'

On Friday, 12 February in the Year of the Crow, Domingo came to take me out of school at ten in the morning.

'You have to come and learn to operate the R6,' he said.

'Why?'

'You're riding shotgun for Hennie Fly on the Great Diesel Expedition.'

37

Thielert's gearbox: IV

We walked out of the school, Domingo and I. I was burning to know: 'But how did it happen? Did Pa say it's okay? When do we fly? Are we going now?'

'Not now.' Curt and cold, his eyes hidden behind the sunglasses.

I didn't really understand, but kept quiet. We climbed into his Jeep. He gripped the key, but didn't turn it. 'My pa was a vicious man,' he said.

I waited for him to explain. He stared into the distance, then he started the Jeep and drove towards the gravel road. I had a multitude of questions, I was bursting with excitement and now, suddenly, a little scared.

We didn't speak, until he'd parked in the gravel quarry. He didn't get out of the Jeep. He said, 'Your father is a good man. It must have been a very difficult decision for him. You're still a child.'

'But I already—'

'Be quiet. You're still a child. I scheme you want to play the big man really badly. We've all been there. But your pa knows, and I know, that being a child, that innocence ... once it's gone, you never get that genie back in the bottle. That's what your pa wants to do. Keep the genie there as long as he can ...'

I wanted to say that it was way too late; I wanted to tell him about the night that I shot two men. 'Domingo, I've already shot two—'

'Shaddup. It doesn't matter how many dogs you've shot, you're a child, and your pa is protecting you. But now the Committee and the community have played their trump card, and your father is sitting with a losing hand, and I feel for him, so you're not going to gloat, and you're going to be very, very humble. In fact, if I catch you gloating, I'll give you a hiding. Understand?'

'Yes, Domingo.' It was the longest talk he had ever had with me. I was intimidated and honoured. And excited, because it meant a whole lot of exciting things.

'And your father talked to Hennie Fly for two hours this morning, and Hennie convinced him that he wouldn't land if there was any danger. So your role is very clear: you're just the pass-me-the-spanner boy. Understood?'

'Yes, Domingo.'

He stared at me a long time. Then his voice softened. 'Now, take the DM along in the aerie. And behind the seat will be the R6. Why take the R6 too? Because if you are inside hangars and buildings, the R6 is the better choice of weapon.'

I didn't question why we had to practise with the weapon if I were merely the pass-me-the-spanner boy. I just listened closely, doing exactly as he said.

At three o'clock Hennie Fly came to fetch me: they wanted to be sure I wouldn't be afraid of flying or get airsick.

Hennie talked the whole time, telling me the purpose of each instrument and lever. I think he wanted to distract my attention, he was so eager for me to pass the test. I didn't hear anything, I just wanted us to take off, so that I could show him I was fine.

As the earth dropped away and my stomach turned a somersault, I was momentarily terrified that I would be sick. Then the beauty of it all overwhelmed me as the dam came into view, the landscape spread out below us. '*Wow*,' I said. Hennie Fly smiled.

He sought out some turbulence, found it. My stomach lurched. He kept an eye on me. 'No worries then,' he said. 'You're going to be okay.'

I found my father in the late afternoon, hard at work at his irrigation project. He saw me approach and stood up, clutching his back and wiping the sweat from his brow. I could see he was trying to hide his emotions.

'Pa, I'll make you proud of me,' is what I said; I had thought long and hard about what would be the right thing to say, what Domingo meant by 'humble'.

'I know, but I hope that won't be necessary,' and he took a step closer to hug me, but that was the last thing I wanted, because Lizette Schoeman was standing only two beetroot rows away.

Pa saw me dodge his embrace and for an instant there was a look in his eyes, a sadness, and then I thought he understood. He ruffled my hair with a soil-smeared hand. 'Listen to Domingo and Hennie.'

'I will.'

An uncomfortable silence. Pa nodded, bent down and pulled out another beet. 'I hear you had a good flight?' He had his radio on his hip.

'It was awesome, Pa.'

He smiled. Pulled up another beet.

'Have you told Lizette yet?'

'What should I say to her?'

He just smiled. 'Go on, tell her you're the one who's going on the flight.'

I was mortified that Pa knew, that he could read me so easily. 'I don't want to tell Lizette.'

But I did.

'Off you go,' said Pa. 'I have work to do.'

I dithered and blushed. First I walked back to the four-by-four, stopped, looked back at Pa. He was concentrating on the beetroot plants. I wandered a little in Lizette's direction. Then I lost my nerve.

In the morning, in the quarry.

'People are fragile creatures in a hostile environment,' said Domingo. 'Those are the words of my favourite philosopher.'

'Who is that?'

'Nathan Trantraal.'

'My father never told me about him.'

'Never mind, just remember his words, 'cause it's the foundation of survival. And we will be revisiting it, over and over again. Apart from a bullet-proof vest there is very little you can do about your fragility. So combat and survival are mainly about how you can make your environment less hostile. Understood?'

'Yes.'

'Okay.' Domingo handed me a knife. It was nearly thirty centimetres long and razor-sharp. Black handle, black steel blade. 'Flick-knives

are for posers and showmen. In a real knife fight there isn't time for
flick and show off. So I'm giving you this combat knife. You carry it on
your hip.'

'Okay.'

He drew in a breath to speak, thought better of it and shook his
head. 'You're too young for the things I have to teach you.'

'Okay.'

'Why do you keep saying "okay"?'

'I don't know.'

He took off his sunglasses. His eyes were steely-grey and very
serious.

'This is combat training. You only say okay when I say you can.
You're too young to learn these things, but it's another world, this, and
I'll just have to live with it. And it helps a bit that I can see you have
the restlessness. And the heart. Inside you is a predator, a warrior, but
maybe you don't know it yet. No, you're not going to say okay. You're
just going to listen. 'Cause here comes the big lesson now. The biggest,
for every first-time warrior: the other guy wants to kill me. You have to
understand that. With that first fight, with that first battle, there's a
moment when you're scared of what you have to do. It's a big step, to
kill another human being. Even if you have the heart. Even if it is self-
defence. A very big step. So, you will be scared, and you will hesitate.
And he who hesitates is lost. 'Cause you're not making your environment less hostile when you hesitate, you are making it *more* hostile. So
just remember: the other guy wants to kill me. If I hesitate, I die. To
indicate to me that you understand, you can say "okay" now.'

'Okay.'

'Okay. You've done a bit of shooting already. With a rifle it's easier,
there's this distance between you and your adversary. You can be
scared, and you can hesitate, but you can shoot, because it's not so
kwaai personal, and that distance buys you a bit of time. But a knife
fight is up close and personal. And dirty and messy and hectic and
chaotic. You've seen knife fights in the movies?'

'Yes.'

'Okay, now let me tell you, those guys who made the movies, those
guys were never in a knife fight. As a matter of fact, those guys who
made the movies were never in a fight of any kind. You know how the

guys in movie knife fights dance around each other, knife in hand? And then the hero says a cool thing, and then the baddy says a cool thing, and then you just see a blur and then you hear the knife go whoosh through the air, and the hero jumps neatly back, just his shirt ripped so you can see his six-pack, a little blood, that sort of thing? That's all bullshit. To indicate to me that you understand, you can now say "okay".'

'Okay.'

'The other guy wants to kill me. If I hesitate, I die. Say it.'

'Okay.'

'No, say: "The other guy wants to kill me. If I hesitate, I die."'

'The other guy wants to kill me. If I hesitate, I die.'

'If you take out the knife, you don't want to dance, you want to kill. Say it.'

I said it.

'Louder. Say it like you mean it.'

The night before we flew, Lizette Schoeman came to tell me: 'I think you're very brave, Nico Storm.'

And she gave me a hug.

I couldn't sleep a wink that night because of it.

Pa wrote me a letter:

My beloved son

The word 'responsibility' is an interesting one. We can talk about the root 'respons' from the Latin, it means 'accountable'. 'Responsibility' means in reality that we must eventually provide answers to questions that our loved ones, our neighbours, or our community ask us. (And now that I think of it, loved ones, neighbours and community should be synonyms of each other.)

Our community – and you – asked me a question this past week, and my response-ability was to agree to send you with Hennie. Now it's my turn to saddle you with a responsibility, by asking you: please come back safely.

I love you very much, and am very proud of you.

Pa

That letter is here beside me today as I write.

*   *   *

The story of Hennie Fly and the wheat made a big impression on the community. It was as if his survival and the safe arrival of the seed were a sign that we were destined for success. Add to that the search for the one to fly with him on the Great Diesel Expedition, and the interest in our mission took on epic proportions. Consequently, a crowd gathered at the Petrusville airfield, just before dawn on Saturday, 20 February in the Year of the Crow. They arrived in every vehicle from Amanzi that would still run.

Hennie Fly was unsettled. He looked across the crowd, frowning deeply. 'I really don't know what all the fuss is about,' he said to Pa. 'We're just flying a little way.'

When we took off, they waved, they cheered and clapped. I could see that Hennie enjoyed it just as much as I did. But his eyes sought out Melinda Swanevelder, and mine Lizette Schoeman.

38

Thielert's gearbox: V

Sunrise from the air, at our height of three thousand metres, was so beautiful that I cried out.

Hennie Fly took a pair of sunglasses out of his breast pocket and put them on. Then he reached into his other pocket and took out a pair for me as well. 'The light can be bright up here.'

I put them on. They were too big for my face and kept sliding down my nose, but I wished at that moment I had a mirror to see what I looked like. It felt even better than the sunrise.

Hennie talked a lot. He described other planes he had flown, and those that he still wished to fly.

He pointed out Hopetown below, the only town that we flew close enough to see, he showed me the Vaal River. The rest was just monotonous landscape far below. And then, barely two hours after take-off, we began the descent to Klerksdorp. He pointed at the gold-mine dumps that lay like white scars across the landscape. 'They dug all that up from underground,' Hennie said. 'It will probably lie there for a long time.'

We flew low over the airport. 'If there is anyone here, they will come out and look,' said Hennie. 'They always do.'

We saw no sign of life.

He flew back and forth over the airport. 'I promised your father we would be very careful . . .'

There were two aeroplanes parked outside on a tarmac square. One had two engines. 'Luckily neither of those is our TD,' said Hennie. 'If they stand outside for so long . . . Your big trouble is rain in the fuel tanks.'

There were a whole lot of big steel hangars, I counted more than sixteen, some long and wide, others small and square. 'Our TD could be in any of those hangars,' said Hennie Fly.

He turned and landed. Then he taxied the Cessna down the tarmac road that ran past the hangars. He was looking for something. 'There it is,' he said and pointed. On the side of the hangar I read *Western Transvaal Flying School*.

He turned the Cessna so that the nose pointed back at the runway, and then he stopped. He turned off the engine. He said, 'Can you see anybody?'

I had the R6 in my hands, and I wished there was someone to see how I looked with the weapon and sunglasses. In my imagination I looked just like Domingo. But there was nobody there to see. I heard Domingo's voice in my mind: 'People are fragile creatures in a hostile environment. Vigilance makes the environment less hostile. Use your eyes and your common sense.'

I looked. I asked myself, as Domingo had taught me, where would I hide away, where would I set an ambush?

I saw nothing. 'No,' I said to Hennie Fly.

'Okay, let's get out.'

I want to recall, while I'm writing this, precisely how it felt to be fourteen and a half.

I can't. I am blinded by the knowledge of who I am now, the man I have become.

I imagine I already had at the time the early signs of that dissatisfaction, the restlessness, the vague suspicion that I wasn't quite like Hennie Fly. Or Nero or the pastor, or Jacob. Or Pa. That I was different, that I was more like Domingo, or at least had the potential to become like him.

Perhaps it was true. Perhaps all that was dormant in me.

Or maybe not. Maybe those few days were the turning point, the fork in my road. Maybe I had equal ability to become my father; it might just have been the incidents involved in the Great Diesel Expedition that determined my fate and character.

At the deserted airport outside Klerksdorp Hennie climbed out of the 172 and immediately lit a cigarette. He inhaled the smoke deeply and with great satisfaction. I had the R6 and did what Domingo said, I examined all the places, all the signs just as he had coached me, but there was no danger, it was just the two of us.

I remember: I wanted something to happen, I knew I was relieved and happy when Hennie Fly pulled open the door of the hangar and said, '*Blikslater*. Damn.' Disappointed. I wanted this adventure to last longer, be more dramatic, offer some more opportunities for heroism.

'What is it?' I asked, still on the threshold.

'They . . . This thing won't be able to fly today . . .'

He disappeared into the gloom of the windowless hangar. I looked around one more time, at the other buildings, at the horizon. I followed him. There were three aeroplanes inside. The one in the middle looked a bit like our 172, but its engine had been removed: it was suspended from the ceiling by a strong chain.

'It's the TD,' said Hennie. 'We'll have to go to Hoedspruit.'

I was pleased. Childish and excitedly happy. Like any fourteen-year-old.

We flew over Johannesburg and Pretoria. At three thousand metres there wasn't much to see.

A moment of excitement. We saw four big trucks one behind the other on a double highway, as if they were driving in convoy. 'That's the N4,' said Hennie. 'I wonder where they're going. And what they're carrying.'

I was overcome with amazement for a while, because it struck home for the first time that there were other people, other communities that had also made a new beginning, who also struggled and fought and built and hoped.

At eleven in the morning Hennie pointed a finger northwards. Specks, a thousand specks in the air. We flew closer. The specks were birds. We flew over the swarm that swooped and turned and glided. Hennie passed me the binoculars.

'They're crows,' I said.

'Now I wonder why? They don't usually behave like that.'

Pa would have known. Or had a theory about it.

We began the descent for Hoedspruit.

Hennie found the Cessna 172TD in a single-plane hangar after he smashed the lock with a crowbar. He looked back at where I stood at the old petrol Cessna and he said, 'Come and look, Nico, this thing is brand new.' He had his pistol on his hip. Domingo had said: 'Hennie shoots okay.'

I was reluctant to go and look, to relax my vigilance, because this was a strange place. The sweat streamed down my back, it was steaming hot, oppressive. The runway was in the town, there were houses and what looked like a shopping centre right beside the airfield; we had flown over an ordinary filling station when we landed. People could hide anywhere. And I had a premonition, a sense of unease, something that said this was a very 'hostile environment'.

Hennie Fly jogged back, a cigarette between his fingers, to turn off our old Cessna's engine. 'Nico, come and see,' but in the sudden silence I heard the thick carpet of sound, insects, something else; it was like that day in Koffiefontein, that late afternoon when the dogs attacked us, very brooding and ominous. He pulled the hangar doors wide, I caught a glimpse of the Cessna. I pressed the safety catch of the R6 off and I wanted to say, 'Hennie, I think there is something here,' but I had no reason, apart from the feeling. We had flown over the town four times. He had pointed east and said, 'The air force base is there, only ten kilometres away.' He and I had looked carefully for signs of life and then we landed. The Cessna 172TD was in the seventh hangar that Hennie opened.

I took off the sunglasses, wiped the sweat from my brow, put the glasses back on, looked at the bush on the other side, looked at the bush on this side.

Someone was watching us, I could feel it. I stared, I searched, I turned round and round.

'What's the matter, Nico?'

'Nothing, sir,' and I walked into the hangar and there was the Cessna, snow white, with flashy black and grey stripes down the side.

'This aerie has barely been flown.' He had all the doors open, he got in, looked over everything, fiddled with something, and said, '*Ja*, I'll have to put that battery in.'

We trampled a path through the long, green grass between the runway and the hangar; it must have been a lawn once. I helped him carry the stuff – the tools, the battery, the cans of diesel. I put the R4 down against the inside wall. In between I circled the hangar with the R6, looked around. I couldn't shake the feeling that someone was watching us.

Hennie stopped in front of the propeller, he tugged and pulled at it with his hands, and said, 'Nope, the engine isn't seized, everything is hunky-dory.'

He had a hand pump, transferred the diesel into the TD's wing tanks. He said, 'I think we must go back to Klerksdorp, I think we should go fetch that engine . . .'

'All right.'

'. . . for the Thielert gearbox.'

'Sir?'

'Let me tell you something, Nico: when they started building propeller aeroplanes, they realised that if the propeller turned too fast, the tips turned faster than the speed of sound, and then the propeller didn't work so well.'

'Why was that?'

'I . . . If I remember rightly, the drag became too much. Something like that . . . In any case, the sweet spot is about two thousand seven hundred revs per minute, the prop worked the best there. But low revs need a lot of power, so the engines of the planes of those days were big. When they first started building these Cessnas, in the 1950s, petrol was cheap, so big engines weren't an issue. They built an engine of five point two four litres, that thing could make a hundred and sixty horsepower. But later, when petrol got very expensive, they had to rethink. The interesting thing is, if you run a diesel engine at five thousand revs, it makes the same horsepower as that big engine, but it uses much less fuel. Now your problem is, how do you make an engine that runs at five thousand RPM turn a propeller at only two thousand seven hundred revs, Nico?'

'I don't know.'

'You build a gearbox that brings the revs down. And that's what this German company did. Thielert. They built a gearbox for a diesel engine. There's a gearbox like that in this aerie I'm sitting in now.'

'Okay . . . But why do we have to go back to Klerksdorp?'

'Push that can of diesel closer.'

I did that. Hennie pushed the feeder pipe in and began to pump again. 'The problem with Thielert's gearbox was that you had to have it inspected every hundred and fifty hours. In Germany. Thielert didn't charge for the inspection, but it still cost you the postage and the time to get the gearbox from here to there and back again. And then Thielert went belly up, and suddenly it cost eight thousand dollars to have the gearbox inspected with other guys. Then only the rich guys flew their 172TDs, because it became just too expensive. That must be why this one was almost never used. We are going back to Klerksdorp to get that gearbox from that TD. So we have two. So that we can have one in the plane while I take the other one apart for inspection. Then the Cessna will always be ready for action.'

'Cool,' I said.

'It won't take us more than an extra half-hour. But look at that weather . . .' He pointed outside.

I looked through the open door, I looked up. But it was a movement lower down that caught my attention.

I gasped in fright: something, a shadow had moved in the long grass near us. I gripped the R6 tightly, finger on the trigger.

'What is it?' whispered Hennie.

I tried to motion him to keep absolutely quiet.

I saw someone jump up out of the grass. He ran straight at us.

39

Thielert's gearbox: VI

It was a child, a small boy, long light brown hair, his stark-naked little body walnut brown, his face and feet and hands filthy. He headed straight for me.

I thought of the ambush Beryl Fortuin had described to me, the men who used the children to get her to stop, I heard Domingo's training, 'make yourself a small target'. I dropped to my knees, the R6 pressed against my shoulder, and moved the barrel to cover the visible area behind the child.

'Look out . . .' I said to Hennie.

The little boy ran into the hangar, paying no attention to the rifle. His face was filled with fear and hope, he collided with me, threw his hands around my neck, squeezed me tightly.

There was nobody behind him.

'Hello,' I said.

'Hello,' he said. And he laughed with huge relief and joy. Showing two rows of surprisingly white teeth framed by the dirt around his mouth. Again he said, 'Hello, hello.'

He smelled of wood smoke and bananas and shit.

He was alone, there was no one else.

I asked him what his name was.

'Okkie.'

What was his surname?

He shrugged. 'Don't know.'

He said hello to Hennie, but he kept clinging to me.

I asked him how old he was.

He held up five fingers in the air. And then he closed one. Four. Perhaps. He didn't seem absolutely sure.

'Come. Granny,' he said, and tugged my hand in a direction.

'Wait, wait . . .'

'Come.'

'Are there other people?'

'Come. Granny.'

Hennie was standing outside the hangar now, and his eyes searched along with mine. He shook his head. 'I don't see anybody . . .'

I was uneasy, unsure.

Okkie held up his arms so I could pick him up. I looked at him. He was too small to carry out someone's ambush-instructions, much too small.

I had to shift the R6 to pick him up. 'Where's Granny?'

'There,' he said and pointed with his disgusting finger; we had to walk to the high wire fence, to the west. There were houses on the other side of the fence, across the street. I carried him on my left arm, while my right arm held the R6 ready. I stood and listened and looked.

'Come,' he ordered, impatient.

Only the buzz of insects. I walked.

'I'll carry on here,' Hennie called.

We squeezed through a hole in the wire, and crossed the street. To the left was the filling station, to the right were the houses. He pointed at the house on the corner.

I could smell death already, five paces from the front door. 'Granny,' he said. 'Granny sleeping.'

On the veranda were signs of activity – a barbecue drum with pots and pans and a kettle on. Cooking utensils. Empty cans, a water bottle, banana peels.

I opened the door. The smell was overwhelming. I could hear the flies and bluebottles. She lay in the sitting room. An old grey-haired woman. She had set out food for them, there were plates and a glass and a cup on the little table in front of the couch. She sprawled diagonally across the couch where she had collapsed.

'Granny sleeping,' he said again.

Beside the Total garage was a Spar supermarket. Okkie knew it, he pointed down an aisle. 'Sweets,' he said. 'All gone.' Resigned to his fate.

All the bottled water was gone, there was very little food left in the supermarket, but there was plenty of soap and shampoo, toothpaste and facecloths. I took some and walked back with him to Hennie in the hangar. I had seen rainwater in half of a plastic drum.

'Where's Granny?' Hennie Fly asked us when we arrived.

'Granny's sleeping for ever.' Okkie echoed the consoling words I had patiently explained to him on the veranda. He just kept on nodding in agreement, I couldn't tell if he understood and accepted it. Now he said the words naturally, though with a certain age-old wisdom.

'Come,' I said. 'Let's wash you.'

'Okay. Wash Okkie's bum-bum.'

I smiled, wondering if his late granny had taught him to say it like that. 'Yes, Okkie.'

I gave Okkie a good scrub, the water a deep brown when I was done.

Hennie Fly started the new Cessna, the TD, and the diesel engine ran well. Okkie was terrified of the racket.

'It's just the aeroplane.' I had to shout to be heard.

He jumped into my arms, his eyes wide in terror, and began to cry, his arms tight around my neck. His hair smelled of shampoo.

'It's just the aeroplane, don't be scared, we're going to fly in it, we're going high in the sky.'

He lifted his head from my neck, looked carefully at the Cessna. 'Aeroplane,' he said.

'That's right. We're going to Amanzi.'

Hennie turned the Cessna off. He pointed outside, at the clouds building up. He said, 'The weather . . . we mustn't go looking for trouble. I think we should sleep over, Nico. Then we can get away early tomorrow morning, and there'll be plenty of time to land in Klerksdorp and load that engine.'

'That's fine, Hennie.' Pa and everyone back at Amanzi knew chances were good that we would stay away overnight, we had discussed it.

'We have room for Okkie, hey?'

Hennie laughed. '*Ja*, he weighs less than that battery we brought along.'

*   *   *

I told Okkie I was going to look for mattresses to sleep on, and he should stay with Hennie.

He followed me.

'You've got a little shadow,' said Hennie Fly.

We ate before it was dark. We pushed the big doors of the hangar closed to keep the insects away from the candles. There were two small windows at the back, where moths gathered in their hundreds.

After dark, a deep, ominous sound.

'That's him,' said Okkie. 'Old Man Simba.'

'It's a lion,' said Hennie. 'The Kruger Park is just over there.'

'Lion,' said Okkie. 'Big one.'

I couldn't sleep. The night was hot, and Okkie insisted on cuddling right up to me. If I edged away, he wriggled closer.

I must have dozed off, because I woke with a start, hearing the sounds outside. Okkie was no longer beside me. I grabbed the R6, and saw through the rear windows something moving, something big and slow.

Okkie was standing at the window, looking out. I walked swiftly over to him, put my arm around him. He looked at me, put his finger to his lips conspiratorially. He whispered, 'Shhht. Elephants.'

The massive shapes were identified.

I heard an elephant's guts rumble, remarkably deep and loud, just the other side of the thin steel wall.

And then the elephant passed wind, an endless, rolling, rumbling, comical fart.

'Oops, 'scuse me,' said Okkie, putting a shy hand over his mouth and giggling.

I fought back the laughter, so hard that my eyes streamed.

Hennie was fast asleep beside us.

'He pooped,' Okkie whispered, eyes wide at the scandal of it.

We took off over the golf course. Okkie sat on my lap. 'Look, Nico,' he said. 'Look!' He pointed at the herd of elephants grazing, unperturbed.

'They must have flattened the game reserve fences long ago,' said Hennie. And then: 'Now I'm wondering how free and how close that lion was last night?'

Okkie mimicked the sound of the elephant's midnight wind, with astonishing accuracy.

We laughed uproariously, the boy and me.

The new aeroplane was in excellent condition, inside and out, quieter, nicer, better.

'Hell, the old girl flies like a dream,' said Hennie.

I no longer wished for something dramatic to happen. I wanted to get home, to show Okkie to Amanzi. And Amanzi to him.

'We better get a move on, I don't like the look of this weather,' said Hennie Fly as he flew low over the buildings of the Klerksdorp airport. 'Can you see anything?'

With Okkie on my lap it was difficult to see properly. 'No, sir, there's nobody here.'

Hennie landed, rolled to a halt at the hangar marked *Western Flying School*, turned the plane and switched off the engine. He climbed out, and first went over to check the engine that we planned to take along. He called back, 'Nope, nobody's been here.'

Okkie and I went in as well. The R6 on my shoulder. The knife on my hip. Hennie's pistol was shoved into his belt. He stared, hands on hips, up at the chain that suspended the engine. 'I'm going to lower it on to the tarpaulin. It will be too heavy for us, we must push it little by little, on the sail. The trouble will be getting it into the aerie.'

Okkie was frightened by the rattle of the chain as the engine was lowered to the ground, and he jumped into my arms. I laughed, put him down again, and said, 'Wait, I'll pick you up in a minute.'

Hennie unhitched the chain. He took two corners of the tarpaulin, I took the other two. 'On three,' he said. 'One, two, three.' We strained, and moved it three-quarters of a metre. My R6 fell from my shoulder. I let go of the sail, picked up the rifle and put it on top of the engine-less Cessna's wing, beyond Okkie's reach.

Hennie said, 'Yes, good idea,' and he took the pistol out of his belt and put it down next to the assault rifle.

We bent down again. 'One, two, three.' Shifted the engine. It was heavy. Hennie Fly was much stronger than me. 'One, two, three.' Dragged the engine a bit. My fingers and hands were cramping. 'One, two, three.' Shift.

Eventually we reached the door. We rested. We dragged it outside, nearer to the plane. Then right up to it. We rested for five minutes.

Okkie was inside, playing with something he had picked up there.

We lifted the engine to load it into the Cessna. Hennie's eyes and neck bulged, his face was red with exertion, he groaned, there was a moment when I felt I couldn't go on, then it was in and Hennie shoved it a bit deeper, and he said, 'Bless my soul, high five!' and he tried to, but his hand missed mine. We both laughed.

'Come, Okkie,' I said and we walked back to the hangar. We went inside. Okkie was sitting just inside the door, against the wall, playing with a little bottle of shiny bolts and screws.

Hennie walked into the middle and looked around. 'What else can we take?' he wondered.

I bent to pick up Okkie. I heard footsteps, and straightened up. Someone outside. I reacted too slowly, I was stunned, surprised and scared. I let go of Okkie, spun around to my weapon. A man in the doorway, pistol in his hand, another man behind him. The front one looked at Hennie, looked at me. He raised the pistol, shot at Hennie Fly. I saw the eyes of both men were at once wild yet determined, purposeful and angry. And they were grinning, as if they got pleasure from this moment, from our shock and fear.

40

Thielert's gearbox: VII

We remember the moments of fear, loss and humiliation most vividly. We recall the detail of movement, of expression, of emotion, or smell and sound and colour. The colour of blood, the taste of it, the texture.

The bullet smacked into the aeroplane behind, he missed Hennie. The man was too rushed, everything Domingo had taught me he did wrong. I saw that and knew, in that instant, with a fleeting sense of relief: we had a chance.

I reached the R6, and turned my back on them to pick up the short, automatic rifle. I swung round, my hands working the R6, I aimed, I shot.

Adrenalin hammered through me, I swung too far, hit the one with the pistol, but in the hip; the other two shots were wild, at the ceiling. I saw the man behind look down at Okkie there beside the door, his little face terrified and dumb. He stabbed the child with a long, thin sword or dagger, a home-made weapon, its handle dirty rags, thickly woven.

Why did he stab the boy? Four years old, why did he stab the child?

Something broke inside me, something that had still been whole. Rage erupted too, a dark destructive rage.

The one with the pistol jerked as the bullet struck his hip, he screamed shrilly, swung the pistol round to aim it at me. The fury and the shock of the dagger stabbing Okkie had paralysed me. The pistol man pulled the trigger. The weapon jammed with a metallic noise, a glitch. He realised, reacted, came charging down at me. His eyes were different now, wild, but fear-wild.

The other guy wants to kill me. If I hesitate, I die.

I came to my senses, I aimed the R6. He grabbed the end of the rifle, jerked it upwards, my finger pulled the trigger, the shot boomed, it hit his cheekbone, he screamed; he had the rifle in both hands, he was very strong, he had the barrel, and jerked it out of my hands.

The other guy wants to kill me. If I hesitate, I die.

I gripped my knife, pulled it smoothly out of its sheath, I pushed hard against him, hard against the man. I didn't want to give him a chance to turn the rifle around. I stabbed him.

There're six angles you can attack with a knife. This one is the forward horizontal strike, coming in parallel to the ground. You attack the soft, vital target areas. Just here . . .

He fell forward, on to me. I stepped back, grabbed the rifle. He clung to it. I stabbed again, stabbed him in the heart. He collapsed inwards, on top of me. I wriggled out from under him, leapt up, looked.

Okkie lay beside the door. There was blood on his tiny body.

The other man, dagger man, was on top of Hennie. Hennie gripped the hand that held the dagger, keeping it from being thrust into his chest. They grunted like animals. I looked down at the man at my feet. He lay across the rifle, still. I dropped my knife, grabbed my rifle, but couldn't pull it out from under the man. I forgot about Hennie's pistol on the aeroplane wing, so great was my rage. I picked up the knife, ran towards the dagger man, where he wrestled on top of Hennie.

In the neck, get the carotid arteries. Here, and here, both sides of the neck. They are good targets, body armour doesn't usually cover the carotids.

My combat knife was razor-sharp. I sliced the dagger man's neck, deep, first one side, and then the other. Blood sprayed over me, hot, wet and sticky. He fell. Hennie came out from under him, he gasped for breath, staggered to his feet, went to pick up his pistol.

I ran to Okkie. His eyes were closed. I could hear Domingo's voice in my head: *I'm going to teach you how to apply a few field dressings.* I ran out to the Cessna, my rucksack was there.

Shots inside.

I grabbed the rucksack, ran back in. Hennie Fly stood with his weapon in both hands, he had shot the pistol man in the head. Hennie was bent over, heaving, he wanted to vomit. I crouched down beside Okkie, pulled open the bag, found the small pack, the first-aid kit; my hands were shaking, slippery with blood, the man's blood and Okkie's blood. I found the bandages, wiped the blood away from Okkie's belly. There was the wound, deep and ugly and bloody. I grabbed the antiseptic powder, tore the packet open with my teeth, and sprinkled it over the wound. I looked up. Hennie was still standing there.

'Come and help me,' I said.

He didn't hear.

'Hennie!'

He looked at me suddenly. Then he came.

'Press the dressing on the wound,' I said.

'Christ,' he said, and did as I asked.

I pushed my hand into the pack, I was looking for the superglue, found it.

They invented superglue to dress combat wounds, you press the two sides of the wound together like this.

Two hours flying back to Amanzi. I sat with Okkie on my lap. His little mouth hung open, I could hear him battle to breathe, sometimes I thought he had stopped. I hugged him tight against me, trying to keep him warm.

I felt like crying, in those two hours.

Why stab the child?

I didn't cry. I wanted to kill someone, why had they attacked us? What did they want? Why had he stabbed the child?

I looked once at Hennie. He was very pale. He had dagger man's blood on his face, shirt and trousers. He saw me looking at him. He said, 'You know, I'm flying as fast as this thing will go.' He sounded dog-tired.

I spotted the dam. Amanzi's dam.

Okkie gasped in jerky breaths, shallow.

He must not die, he could not.

We started our descent.

Hennie flew low over the town. I saw people come out and wave. Joy.

He turned towards Petrusville's airfield. First he checked the windsock, then circled to come in to land from the south.

Hennie's pick-up was parked beside the hangar. He taxied the plane right up to it. 'Let's get him to Nero.'

* * *

Halfway to Amanzi, Domingo approached on the motorbike. He saw us, turned around, rode up beside us. He was invisible behind the helmet, but I saw him turn his head to look in. I knew he saw, the dried blood, the child in my arms. He accelerated, raced ahead.

Domingo stood at the door of the Orphanage. He was calling inside for Nero, Beryl and Melinda Swanevelder. I brought the child in my arms, I ran up the paved pathway. Domingo wanted to take Okkie out of my arms.

'No,' I said.

I wept. I have no idea why I began to cry at that exact moment. Later Nero, when he gave me trauma counselling at Pa's request, would explain that I cried because I could finally pass on to Beryl the responsibility of keeping Okkie alive. I could hand over the responsibility to Domingo of keeping him and Hennie safe.

Response-ability.

Nero would say it had been a mistake to send me. Nero would say we should have listened to my father.

Hennie followed us, he explained to Nero and Beryl that the child had been stabbed in the stomach, he said we had stopped the bleeding.

I laid Okkie down on the bed in the Orphanage sick bay. I said, 'Nero, you must not let him die.'

I remember the expression on Nero Dlamini's face. The despair.

41

Okkie Storm

As recorded by Sofia Bergman. The Amanzi History Project, continued – in memory of Willem Storm.

I can't remember anything from before Amanzi. Zero. Nothing. I can't remember anything about my granny and Hoedspruit and Klerksdorp and the aeroplane and the man who stabbed me. Look . . . Here's the scar. I don't know what my real name is. Ockert, maybe? I only know what my big brother told me. My big brother Nico. He isn't really my big brother, I know 'Storm' isn't my real surname, but it . . . I don't think it really matters. What matters is that Nico and Hennie saved my life twice. Once at Hoedspruit, when they took me along, and again at Klerksdorp, when Nico closed the wound with superglue. Nero said that's what saved me, because when I arrived, he just put me on a drip for hydration, and gave me antibiotics, there was nothing else he could do.

Ever since I was little Nico said he was my blood brother. That is what he is to me. My blood-brother big brother.

Okkie lived.

My head told me I should be happy. Nero said it was normal to feel so distant from everything. He said it was part of the condition, to feel afraid and sad, and anxious. And sometimes to feel nothing. But also angry, that was the biggest thing for me, the anger, at everyone.

Nero was a good man. He spoke to me with such kindness, reassuring me again and again that none of this was my fault.

Pa, my beloved father, came and sat beside me on the bed that first night. He held me and wept. He said, 'Tonight I'm the one wishing your mother was here.'

And later, when he had stopped crying, he said, 'Thank you, Nico, for living up to your responsibility.'

Pa was gentle with me. And patient, for weeks and months. He and Nero thought it was only the therapy that was healing me. It wasn't. It was Domingo as well. Domingo and his philosophy.

The crows lay dead beside the road. Several expeditions that came back out of the west reported the same thing.

Birdy said it had nothing to do with the road as such, it would be a scientific error to draw that conclusion, because the people drove only on the road, so that's the only place they saw the crows. She delivered a little lecture on scientific observation. She said the dead crows were an example of ecological correction.

My father agreed. He said they had been increasing for decades because they adapted so well to people, cities, towns and all the carrion from roadkill.

Yes, Birdy said, during and after the Fever there was even more carrion for them. And now it was all gone. People, cities, towns, carrion.

It was just an ecological correction.

A work week, close to the end of March. Jacob and I were up early and on the quadbike, lunch and rifles packed, ready to drive to the reserve. The child turned up too. 'Okkie wants to go too, Okkie wants to go.'

I picked him up. He hugged me tight. I said, 'Another day, Okkie. I'll be back tonight.' He squeezed me even tighter.

Domingo came strolling up. He said, 'Jacob, you're off today, I'll go with Nico.'

'Yay,' said Jacob, who was becoming more and more of a bookworm. Now he could spend the whole day reading.

We had talked once after Okkie came, Domingo and I. He wanted a detailed report on exactly what had happened. He listened, nodding his head a couple of times. When I had finished, he just stared into the distance, and then he got up and left.

The adults had come to me at the Orphanage in the evenings, a touch on my arm here, a pat on my shoulder there, Pa ruffling my hair, all to 'connect' with me, that was the phrase Nero used. Not Domingo. He just went his way as always.

So now Jacob took Okkie, and Domingo and I drove up the mountain. We drove along the boundaries to see whether all the fences were in order. He took me to a lookout point over a valley that lay due south of our town, at the back of the mountain. It was one of my favourite places, Jacob and I often went there.

We stood on the edge of the cliff. Domingo pointed, he said, 'That little Jeep track, that's the soft underbelly. That's the weak spot in our defences. That is the only other place you can reach us with a motorbike or a four-by-four. Not easy, but possible, if you put your mind to it. If they come, they'll come in there.'

'Who?'

'The KTM.'

'Do you think they will come?'

'Yes, they will come.'

'Why do you think that?'

A long silence before he said, 'Sit down, Nico.'

We sat side by side. We gazed out over the valley. It was late summer, the veld was green, lush and beautiful. We saw the valley stretching out below us, carved out by a stream that only ran when it rained, tumbling downward all the way to the dam three kilometres away.

'They will come, for the same reason that man stabbed Okkie. That's what I want to talk to you about.'

I stared at the dam far below, the water the drab green-brown of army camo today.

'I see you're suffering since you came back. And it's good and right that you're in therapy with Nero, 'cause there's a lot that's true in that therapy. Nothing that happened was your fault. That's part of my philosophy, and I'm going to give you that philosophy. You'll see, it's not your father's philosophy, it's not the pastor's philosophy. Nor Birdy or Nero's. It's just mine. You won't find many people in your life who share this philosophy, 'cause it's harsh, and it's trouble. I'm not trying to convert you; I'm just putting it on the table. Use it, don't use it. Maybe it can help with all that you feel.'

'Can I say "okay" now?'

He smiled behind his sunglasses. 'This isn't combat training, you can say whatever you want.'

'Okay.'

'We are like the dogs.'

'The dogs?'

'That's right. That's the essence of my philosophy.'

'Oh. No. It's not true.'

'I know it's harsh. But it's true.'

'Why do you say so?'

He paused. I think he was searching for words and ideas. He said, 'Back in the day, before the Fever, every month or so you would read about a dog attacking a child or somebody. Major outrage, lawsuits, always aimed at the owner of the dog. But what the people conveniently forget, dogs were once wolves. Before we tamed them. Wild wolves, predators, killers, hunting in packs. Which makes them social animals. And then we domesticated them, and gave them a veneer, a thin layer of civilisation. One degree away from wild. And what happened, when the Fever made that civilisation disappear? They went back to the wild. They killed each other, they killed everything they came across, they attacked their former masters, they became wolves again. Talk to the people here . . .' He pointed in the direction of Amanzi. 'Listen to the outrage, how could the dogs do that? How could the dogs just want to kill people and cattle and sheep, we were good to them, we domesticated and civilised them. Same outrage as back in the day. And nobody understands. Because they don't want to, they can't afford to understand. Just like no one can afford to understand when men do evil deeds. 'Cause we all believe man is the crown of creation, we're the animals who think and cry and laugh, noble creatures, how is it that we can murder? The one who murders, there's something wrong with his head. Screw loose, lights off, fuse blown, right?'

'Right.'

'Well, I'm not so sure. Here is my philosophy: we are animals, Nico. Social animals. Domesticated, social animals, thin veneer of civilisation. Gentle creatures if the world is fine, if the social conditions are undisturbed and normal. But if you disturb the conditions, then that veneer wears off. Then we go feral, we turn into predators, killers, we hunt in packs. Then we become just like the dogs. That is why my mantra is: *the other guy wants to kill me. If I hesitate, I die.* That's the law of the jungle, that's how it works with animals. That guy who stabbed

Okkie, those guys who kept Melinda Swanevelder tied up in the house, the KTM who robbed us, they are animals, just like you and me. There's nothing wrong with their heads, it's just the veneer that's worn off.'

I pictured the two men in the aeroplane hangar in Klerksdorp, their eyes, the look on their faces. And then I thought of good people.

'But why? Not everyone is bad? My pa—'

'That's a classic mistake. Very human reasoning. If we're good, we can't be bad, the one has to exclude the other. Just like with the dogs. That time before the Fever, if you told anyone their dog was bad news, they would look at you as if you were a serial killer type. How can you not love dogs? Then they would tell you dogs are noble. Dogs are loyal and loving and cute. They would ask: what about the brave police dogs, and man's best friend, all the feel-good things that dogs have done? I'm not saying dogs and people can't do good things. Remember we're social animals. That means we must be sociable from time to time, do nice things. But that also means that from time to time we must be animals.'

I sat there, processing it all.

'I don't need you to buy into my philosophy, I don't want you to,' Domingo said. 'I may be totally wrong. Go and find other views. The pastor, let the pastor tell you about God. Or your father and his thing for that Spinoza dude. Go and talk to him, talk to Nero. One of them may be right. Maybe none of us are right, then you just take the philosophy that works best for you. A lot of people do that. But do yourself one simple favour, just ask yourself one question: which philosophy explains everything about the human condition? No loose ends. No awkward, unanswered questions. Which one makes complete sense?'

'Okay.'

We sat there for a long time, side by side in silence. Until a butcher bird came and sat shrilling in a thorn tree right next to us.

'What must we do when the KTM come?' I asked him.

'We mustn't wait until they come, that's what we must do. But the Committee . . . They just don't understand the animal.'

42

Lizette Schoeman

As recorded by Willem Storm. The Amanzi History Project.

Romain Puértolas's books. And chocolate. And lipstick. And my iPhone. That's what I miss.

Cairistine Canary

I feel the way you do, Willem. I miss the potential . . .

Okay, I'll try to explain. The world before the Fever was a complex one. We had major problems, in our country, and in our world. The biggest one was global warming, because it would have a big impact on all the other problems – the poverty, the inequality, the extremism.

We were already at the eleventh hour when it came to global warming, but the thing is, we were getting closer and closer to a solution. There was the potential for fixing it all.

Now, you can say, yes, but that was just the potential for a solution, we were actually in very deep trouble. But look at our track record. Look what we've already done, mankind. Look at all the diseases we've eradicated. Look at the theory of relativity. Quantum theory. We mapped the human genome, we had it in us to solve all the problems, we had the potential.

So, that loss of potential, that's what I miss the most. The Fever robbed us of that potential. It doesn't matter how you look at it, it put human and scientific development back at least a hundred years. If not more.

Less lofty stuff? Okay . . . I miss the Internet the most. Not the stuff like Facebook or Instagram, but access to information. I miss that badly. Okay, and You magazine. And . . . this is probably not for public consumption, but it's the truth. I miss tampons. Lil-lets Nano Tampons.

Pastor Nkosi Sebego

Isidingo *on SABC1. I loved that show.*

And Saturday mornings at the Menlyn Mall. Me and my wife used to go and do our grocery shopping at the Checkers Hyper, and then we would wander around, that was one big mall. I loved Coricraft, and she loved @Home … I wanted one of those recliners at Coricraft, I wanted it real bad. We could never justify the cost, but I would go to look at it every Saturday morning. And we would have lunch at Panarotti's, and we would just sit and watch people.

Ravi Pillay

Newspapers. Especially the motor supplements. And new cars. New models, I mean, I loved to see what they improve on next. And fish tikka. I tell you now, that was the single biggest achievement of civilisation.

Melinda Swanevelder

RSG.

(RSG was a radio station before the Fever – W.S.)

Hennie (Fly) Laas

To be brutally honest, there's nothing that I really miss. I know the Fever was hugely tragic, but I'm very happy now. Rugby, maybe, Saturday afternoons in front of the TV. That's all I can think of now.

Beryl Fortuin

Oysters. With lemon and Tabasco, straight from the shell. My mouth is watering right now. Obviously a good round of golf on a clever, challenging, perfectly manicured course. And magazines. Fair Lady. Cosmo.

Nero Dlamini

Shopping for clothes? Okay, okay, seriously: the city. I loved the city. Friday nights in Sandton, man that place was alive … And I miss craft beer.

Imported cheese. Good cheese in general. No offence to Maureen and Andy, of course, they are doing great work. And those first few years, I really missed fresh croissants. Until our own bakery started doing them. That's when I knew we were going to be all right.

Domingo

You really want to know?

Friends *reruns. And a good bunny chow. And Bundesliga football. I was a Dortmund fan. 'Cause I like the underdog, and I liked their style. There is no justice in the universe: when the Fever came, Dortmund was in second place in the league, they could have won. That Thomas Tuchel, he was their coach. Man's a genius.*

43

The Committee meetings took place in the dining room of the Orphanage, just because it had been that way from the beginning, and nobody thought of changing it.

It was a spacious room, with square tables that could be arranged in different ways. Up to November in the Year of the Crow I attended all the meetings, unofficially, uninvited, invisible and silent. Because I was Pa's son, but also because it had been like that from the beginning, and nobody thought of changing it.

The meeting of 19 November was my last in this privileged position. It was my own fault when Pa sent me out and banned me.

The first item on the agenda was Domingo. They called him in, invited him to sit down. No, said Domingo, thank you, but he would stand.

It pleased me that he was like that. I don't know why. I sat to one side, far enough away so as not to be part of the proceedings, but near enough to hear every word. I slumped in my chair like any typical fifteen-year-old who wants to remain invisible, looking bored and disinterested.

'Domingo,' Pa said, 'thank you for coming.'

Domingo was silent.

'You wanted to address us about Amanzi's security.'

'That's right, I—'

'After driving us crazy for weeks,' snapped Birdy, 'with all your scare stories.'

'Birdy . . .' Pa soothed.

'They are not scare stories,' Domingo said. His voice was calm and reasonable.

'That's not the point,' said Pastor Nkosi, who was happy to gain an ally in his constant battle with Domingo. 'You've been trying to influence us one by one, despite the fact that we have asked you to make a formal presentation to the Committee.'

'It's called canvassing. Age-old democratic practice,' said Domingo.

'Ladies and gentlemen . . .' Pa admonished.

'You're starting to sound like the old apartheid government,' said the pastor. 'The Black Menace, the Red Menace, and now the KTM Menace . . .'

'And you don't believe in democracy,' said Nero Dlamini, tongue-in-cheek.

'Please, enough.' Pa called the meeting to order. 'We'll have to give Domingo the opportunity to state his case.'

The Committee members' body language said they probably had no choice. But they were quiet.

'The floor is yours, Domingo,' said Pa.

He nodded, and began to speak, with no notes. 'Like it or not, if I sound like the apartheid regime or not, the KTM are coming—'

'What makes you so sure?' asked Beryl.

'Give him a chance,' said Pa.

'No, fair question,' said Domingo. 'Let me give you the facts. Fact one: we know they're robbers and marauders. They've staged an armed robbery of Amanzi itself, they keep attacking and plundering our expeditions, surely I don't have to provide more evidence than that. Fact two: they don't plant, don't farm, don't build anything, they don't save anything. They are the modern-day equivalent of hunter-gatherers, but they hunt and gather other people's stuff. Fact three: we plant, we farm, we build and we store up for the winter. We've got a lot of stuff that they want. Birdy, what's that guy with the razor you talk about, that one who says the simplest explanation is the right one?'

'Occam's Razor, but that doesn't really apply . . .'

'Don't matter, this is very simple. We've got what the KTM want. And they're going to come and take it, unless we are prepared.'

'Well, I'm not so sure,' said the pastor. 'Their attacks on our expeditions have decreased. We haven't had one in more than a month. Everybody knows the roads are getting worse, especially for motorbikes. The petrol is growing increasingly useless, so they can't use the bikes anyway. And we now have a gate to keep them out.'

Domingo looked at the pastor, that cold stare of his. 'There are fewer attacks because it's summer now. Lots of low-hanging fruit.

Maybe they're focused on robbing other, more vulnerable communities. And the roads are worse, but they ride dual-purpose motorcycles, they can go anywhere. And who knows how long they'll stick to motorbikes? There are a lot of diesel trucks and cars and pick-ups out there.'

'What do you want, Domingo?'

'Another fifty people for our army. Fifty full-time people, selected and trained. And no old farts, I want young and able people. And radios for them all. And we must close the road over the dam wall, 'cause I'm worried about the security of the power station. That is our most strategic asset. There's just too much traffic past there. And I want another secret arsenal for the majority of our weapons, and a seed bank. And a back-up herd of cattle and sheep on Heart's Island. We don't have any insurance in that regard.'

Heart's Island is the biggest island in the dam. Beryl named it that, after the shape of it on the big aerial photo in the old municipal offices. It's about four hundred hectares in size.

'But you already have eighteen people,' said Birdy.

'Eighteen? Our total security force is me, and seventeen geriatrics. With all due respect, they're good people, but they're not fighting material, and they are not fighting fit: twelve men who are permanently on bus-gate duty, because they're not strong enough to work on the lands or in the town. Good people, but that sort we call cannon-fodder. Three old ladies on radio room duty. And two reasonably fit sixty-year-olds who do border patrol around the dam and the reserve fence line, but only in daylight. And last week, after the thunderstorm, I had to get four people to help dig border patrol's pick-up out of the mud. That's our army. That is our first line of defence, Amanzi's finest. Last time you said we have too few people, there is nobody to spare. Look where our population numbers are now. Surely we can spare fifty now. Fifty non-fossils.'

'We can't,' said Ravi Pillay. 'That's just too many.'

'Agreed,' said Pastor Nkosi. 'Way too many.'

'Why another fifty?' asked Pa.

'Twenty-five for defence. And twenty-five for an assault force. Twenty-five is the smallest unit that I can take if we are going to attack the KTM . . .'

There was a chorus of objections: attack? Who said we are going to attack the KTM? That would just be provocative, would cause greater trouble. We couldn't expect our people to risk their lives. The KTM robbed us, but they hadn't killed us yet. It was belligerent, irresponsible.

Domingo held his hands up in the air as if to fend off the assault. My father called for order, and when it quietened down, he said, 'Is there anything else you want to say? About your requests? Before we discuss it?'

'The KTM are coming,' was all he said.

'Why this obsession, Domingo?' Nero Dlamini asked, deeply sceptical. 'Why this obsession?'

A rhetorical question, I only realised later. Domingo did not respond, the silence lengthened. Until I couldn't contain myself any longer. 'Because they're animals,' I said.

Domingo's lip curled in a hint of a smile.

'Out,' Pa said to me.

That was my last Committee meeting as a child.

They informed Domingo afterwards that he could recruit only four additional men for his security team, but all four could be younger than fifty. They granted permission for him to close the road over the dam wall completely on the Luckhoff side – one less access route to defend. They let him know he could keep a small breeding herd of cattle and sheep on Heart's Island as an insurance policy. They also approved the seed bank.

But for the second secret arms cache they simply gave a blunt 'no'.

Pastor Nkosi summed up the sentiment of the Committee: 'We acknowledge certain risks to our community, but we're not completely paranoid.'

When I heard what the Committee had decided, I went straight to Domingo. 'I want to be one of your soldiers,' I said.

'What soldiers? The Committee gave me four security people.'

'I want to be one of the four.'

'Too soon,' he said. 'Go finish school first.'

'But—'

He put a finger to his lips, looked left and right, as if he were about to share a secret with me. 'I'll be needing a few guys I can trust. For a special mission.'

'You know you can trust me,' my voice just as low and conspiratorial as his.

He nodded. 'Can we trust Jacob Mahlangu?'

'Yes. But why?'

'All will be revealed. But it's going to be hard work.'

'Okay.'

'And if you or Jacob spill the beans, I'll have to kill you.'

'Okay.'

The 'special mission' was a huge disappointment after the excitement and glory of the Great Diesel Expedition. The 'special mission' was in direct defiance of the Committee's decision, because it involved moving a large part of our arsenal to a secret storage place. And the only role Jacob and I had to play was to look the other way when we were on duty as shepherds in the reserve. And to help load and unload the heavy crates from the trailer.

Over a period of a week Domingo and five of his security men moved hundreds of arms and ammunition crates from storage in the old warehouse in the nature reserve. Step one of the transfer was moving them through the back valley – the one he described as our 'soft underbelly' when we had our philosophy chat – to the edge of the dam. Via this route only the shepherds could spot you; and if you picked your shepherds right, they would never breathe a word.

At first we had no idea what happened to the arsenal after that. But I realised that Domingo left the Orphanage very late some nights, and stayed out till it was almost daylight. Sometimes, when he returned next morning, I could see that his trouser legs were wet. Then I knew they were using boats on the dam. And I knew it had something to do with the 'special mission'. I burned with curiosity, and made plans to slip out at night, but if you share a room with your father, that's impossible.

I heard him say to Birdy Canary one night in the sitting room: 'Trust is a two-way street, you know.'

The next morning at breakfast I went to him and said, 'Do you trust me, Domingo?'

'Of course I trust you.'

'And trust is a two-way street?'

His eyes narrowed; he knew I was trying to manipulate him, because he himself was a master of the art. 'So?'

'So, you trust me to keep the secret of the weapons being moved, but you don't trust me enough to say where to.'

He carried on eating. I waited.

Eventually he said, 'Sicily.'

'Okay,' I said.

'Not even Jacob,' and he drew the knife he was using to eat slowly across his throat. I knew what he meant.

Sicily was a smaller island on the dam, just west of Heart's Island, about two hundred hectares in extent. Pa had christened it that after he stood in front of the municipal aerial photo and the shape reminded him of Sicily.

44

In the Year of the Crow I turned fifteen. Crows died in an ecological correction. And Amanzi's population grew past one thousand two hundred. Twenty-four babies were born.

It was Jacob Mahlangu who said they should each have a label around their necks saying 'Made in Amanzi'.

In the Year of the Crow we gained a carpenter and a young geologist among the new arrivals. And a man who grew up on a dairy farm and remembered enough about it. And a plumber's assistant, a welder, two teachers, a sous chef and an amateur baker. And an electronic engineer, Abraham Frost, who would greatly improve our radio system. And the retired police sergeant Sizwe Xaba, known to all as Sarge X.

In the Year of the Crow we gained Okkie and the Cessna 172TD.

In the Year of the Crow Domingo demanded reinforcements, another fifty men. He longed for Birdy, I longed for Lizette. Neither of us made any progress on either of these fronts. The Sex Fest went on, without me and Domingo.

We irrigated the riverbanks with electric and diesel engines. We ploughed and laboured, planted and harvested: maize, beet, tomatoes, potatoes, onions, beans, squash and pumpkin. We planted Hennie Fly's flown-in seed wheat, and the yield was exceptional.

We started a little community bottling industry to preserve food for winter.

We started a small dairy.

Our sheep, goats and cattle grew in numbers, because our expeditions and breeding programme added more animals than we consumed.

And the plague of dogs became a thing of the past.

In the Year of the Crow we sent out expeditions for fertiliser. Hennie Fly rebuilt the chicken and egg farm in the old holiday resort. There were some who called him the Flying Hen. He just laughed it off.

Our economy was communist – everyone shared in the produce of expeditions and harvests. In October two people asked the Committee if they could start a capitalist, for-their-own-profit bakery in the old Friendly Craft Shoppe. They wanted to bake fresh bread daily to start, and later pies and confectionery too.

The Committee thought it was a good idea, but the big dilemma of capitalism was that Amanzi didn't have a monetary unit. Barter wasn't an option, because in the collective no one had anything to barter.

It was Pa who suggested we use salt. It was a scarce commodity, and it had a long and wonderful history as a currency. Pa said the word 'salary' came from 'salt', Roman soldiers were sometimes paid in salt. That was where the term 'worth his salt' came from. Salt was as valuable per weight as gold in those days. If you said someone was 'the salt of the earth', you meant they were priceless.

Birdy suggested we measure the salt in the little 125ml containers, the ones in which everyone bought Cerebos salt before the Fever. That's why the Amanzi monetary unit is still called the cerebos today.

The Year of the Crow was when we also realised our sugar would eventually run out, although we still had many bags stockpiled.

That winter it only snowed once, lightly. But we had electricity, so nobody was cold at night.

That November it rained non-stop for nine days. Heavy rain. The river and the dam rose higher and higher, the water thundered over the dam wall in a spine-chilling, rolling, churning mass; you could hear the noise ten kilometres away. We were all afraid. Nobody really knew how to work the sluice gates.

Birdy said not to worry, she would work it out.

Pastor Nkosi said he and his growing congregation would pray that the dam would hold.

When the waters subsided and the dam wall still held, both the pastor and Birdy claimed credit for the success.

The rain wreaked havoc on the gravel and district roads. Everyone said it was a good thing; it would keep the KTM away. Domingo shook his head. He said the KTM had dual-purpose motorbikes. Nothing would keep them away.

You're paranoid, said Birdy, Beryl and Pa, but in a sympathetic way.

Domingo said the KTM are animals. They would come. And he looked at me and smiled that smile of his.

The Year of the Jackal

45

In the Year of the Jackal the pedlars came. And death. And war. And horror.

And Sofia Bergman.

Sofia Bergman

As recorded by Sofia Bergman. The Amanzi History Project, continued – in memory of Willem Storm.

In the Year of the Jackal I realised the end was near, early in that year, January, probably. The end of me, Meklein and Vytjie. His coughing fits had become much worse. And Vytjie was as thin as a reed; I was convinced she wouldn't live long. She disappeared in the first week of the year, for ten long days. Meklein kept saying: 'No, don't worry, kinta, she does that, she'll come back,' but I had made peace with the idea that she . . . Remember, I was fifteen, and I had this imagination. I thought she loved Meklein so much, she couldn't bear to see him suffer. Or she wanted to die in the veld, become one with nature, in the way of dust-to-dust. Now that I think back, I feel silly, that I would think that . . .

Ten days later, she returned with plants she had been looking for. Plants that she infused into tea for Meklein's cough. All she said was that the plants were very scarce at this time of year, as if it were completely normal to be away for such a stretch.

The tea really helped for his cough. For a while.

46

Sofia Bergman

I was born in Middelburg, in the Cape. I was the youngest of four children, my parents farmed between Middelburg and Nieu-Bethesda. I had two brothers and a sister. My oldest brother was Dawid Bergman, who won silver in the fifteen hundred metres at the Commonwealth Games. He and I were both born with silver-blond hair. We were all good at athletics, and we were all at school in Bloemfontein. My brothers were at Grey College, my sister was in Oranje Girls High. I was in the Oranje Junior School when the Fever came. We were all boarders in the hostels.

My father wasn't your typical Karoo farmer. From the beginning he said his children would inherit equally, not in the traditional way where only the sons inherit the farms.

We were all raised equal. My brothers had to learn to cook, they had to help as much as we girls in the kitchen did. My sister and I learned to catch sheep and dip them, we drove tractors and pick-ups, rode horses and learned to shoot, from when we were little. Pa let us shoot, and I would sit with my back against the pick-up, and the rifle butt under my arm, the butt also pushed against the pick-up, because Pa said the kick of the rifle was too much for my shoulder. I learned to shoot like that, first with an open sight, later with a scope.

My sister was a sprinter, but I had Free State colours in cross-country, and in javelin when I was in Grade Six. And again in Grade Seven. That was the year the Fever came.

My sister was the first one in our family to get sick. In two days she was dead. Ma and Pa came to fetch us all from Bloemfontein, my sister in her coffin. They wanted to bury her on the farm and get us out of school and the city, so we wouldn't catch the virus. But they all got sick ...

Meklein and Vytjie were workers on the farm. They didn't get sick.

2 January

The room that Pa and I shared in the Orphanage was big. He slept on the double bed, I slept on the single, and we each had our own wardrobe.

On the morning of 2 January, at breakfast, Pa said, 'I think it's time you got your own room.'

I wasn't sure if he was serious. 'Really, Pa?'

'With Hennie Fly and Melinda getting married on Saturday, Hennie's room will be available. And you're turning sixteen this year . . .'

'Amazing! Thanks, Pa.'

15 January

Sometimes Nero Dlamini and I would chat in his 'office' at the Orphanage, when I was in therapy with him for my post-traumatic stress after the attack on Okkie. But often he would say, let's take a walk outside. Usually we would go down to the water and sit on a tree stump beside the dam.

On that day, 15 January, he said it was our final session for now.

'So, I'm cured?' I tried hard to hide the faint feeling of disappointment. The PTSD therapy was a bit of a status symbol and an extension of the hero worship of the Great Diesel Expedition.

'No, you're as nutty as a fruitcake, but sane is so boring, Nico.' He knew how to work with teenagers.

'Right.'

'In a perfect world, I would have asked you to continue to see me. But people with greater damage keep arriving, so it's a matter of priority. And it does seem that the fifteen-year-old psyche is quite robust, particularly when daily life is mostly a big adventure, and you have Okkie Storm as a little brother now.'

Okkie *had* played a big role in my recovery. Because Okkie Storm was my shadow. Okkie Storm worshipped the ground I walked on. Beryl said that from one o'clock every afternoon Okkie would ask her: 'When is Nico coming?' Okkie could not understand that every second week was a work week and I would only be back at the Orphanage late in the afternoon. On those afternoons he would sit by the gate of the Orphanage and wait for me, any time from four o'clock. And when he heard me coming in the spluttering, jerking dirty-petrol quadbike, he would jump up and run down the street.

I had to pick him up at the corner. His face would beam with excitement. 'Go, Nico, go fast!'

Okkie had an irrepressible *joie de vivre* and an infectious laugh. Okkie also always managed to be the dirtiest child in the preschool class, even when they played in the shallow water of the dam.

Okkie would run into the Orphanage sitting room every night with a story book held in both hands, his piping voice ringing across the room: 'Nico, Nico, read us a story.'

And then I would have to read, regardless of whether I was tired, or felt like it. Okkie and his band of followers would come and sit around me, on me, over me and I had to read. Domingo would watch us from where he sat on one side, and he would smile. No grimace. He really smiled.

Okkie wanted to know why he couldn't sleep with me in my new single room. 'There's lots of room here . . .'

'One day,' I said. 'When you're big.'

Okkie adopted me and Pa. 'Annexed' is perhaps more accurate. One day when new arrivals asked him who he was he just began calling himself 'Okkie Storm'.

A school-week summer's day in my life in the Year of the Jackal: Pa would knock on my door, six o'clock. I would get up, dress, wash my face and brush my teeth. I would go to the kitchen to cook the oatmeal porridge. That was my morning chore: to cook porridge for all the orphans. It wasn't hard, I knew exactly how much water, how much oatmeal and salt to put in the pot. I knew precisely how long it had to cook. I looked at my Rolex watch to time it right. We all had good, expensive watches. It was human nature for expeditions and travelling pedlars and foragers and fugitives to take the contents of jewellery shops – everything shiny – for themselves, or in the hope of trading. The concept of what was valuable stuck. I still have my Rolex today.

Part of my morning responsibility was to dish up the oatmeal for the orphans and, lastly, for myself. I also had to wash the pot and put it away.

I ate my porridge with Domingo, because I wanted to, and with Okkie, because he insisted. I could eat breakfast and lunch where and with whom I wanted. Dinner I had to eat with my father and Okkie, because we were 'a family'.

School started at eight o'clock. We studied geography, mathematics, biology, science and world history. And one 'skill'. My skill subjects were sheep farming and shooting. I wasn't all that interested in sheep farming, but you learned it outside, in the veld, you worked with the sheep. I don't like being indoors.

Normal school was from eight to half past one, skills school was from two to four. Fridays were my best day, because it was when the chosen ones went shooting with Domingo.

Only Domingo could shoot better than I could.

Community tasks involved relieving Beryl and Melinda with the orphans. Jacob helped me with that. In the summer we would usually take them to the dam, or to go swimming, or shoot catapults, or float stick boats in the shallow water. Or we would take them to collect eggs from Hennie's hens, or we would play with them on the lawns of the old bowling green – rotten egg or hide-and-seek. Okkie rode on my shoulders when we walked. He would not allow any other child to do that.

After six in the afternoon I would hang out with the other teenagers in front of the bakery, until just before seven. There were more than thirty of us between the ages of fifteen and eighteen. Jacob was actually my only close friend. To the others I was 'the chairman's son', the one who lived in the Orphanage although he was no orphan, and not a small kid any more. I really hung out with the other teenagers late in the afternoon in the hope of seeing Lizette Schoeman. Lizette worked at crop farming. They came back from the fields between five and six, and she and some of her girlfriends would come to sit at the bakery and chat. Sometimes.

At seven I had to be at the Orphanage with clean washed hands to eat with Pa and Okkie and the rest of the Orphanage.

I was expected to clear two tables before I could go to my room. Usually I would fetch my homework and sit in the dining room or the sitting room while I listened to all the happenings. I had always been very inquisitive. It would be then that Okkie would commandeer me for reading duty.

27 January

Hennie Fly flew patrol twice a week, just after sunrise on Tuesdays
and Fridays. On 27 January he saw a long procession, on the other
side of Luckhoff on the old R48, just thirty kilometres from Amanzi.
From the air, he said later, they looked like war refugees, a long, weary
worm of humanity. Most of them on foot, just the oldest and the very
young rode on the vehicles – battered pick-ups without engines and
small trucks pulled by donkeys and horses. Five hundred and eighty-
one people, most of them from Namibia, and a few who had joined
the group in the Upington district.

Forty-two horses, thirty-six donkeys.

Along with practically every teenager, I was at the bus gate when
they passed through. The refugees and their animals looked tired,
hungry, thirsty and fearful. The people meekly relinquished their
weapons to Domingo and his militia, as though they were relieved to
do so. Practically the whole of Amanzi gathered around the Forum, to
welcome them, to offer the arrivals food and water, to try to organise
accommodation, but most of all to hear their stories.

The Namibians said that most of them were from Windhoek. For
the past eighteen months they had tried to make a new life there. They
had a good supply of dry food, they planted a little and there was a
healthy flock of goats. And then the attacks began. Last September
was the first: a group of approximately fifty men from the north. They
were in pick-up trucks, they shot dead three of the Windhoek people
and stole a lot of food.

The big attack came in mid-October. Maybe two hundred people,
perhaps more, nobody really knew, it was at night, it was chaos,
everything happened so fast. The attackers were in vehicles and on
foot. A hundred and sixty residents were murdered. The entire goat
flock was taken, weapons and supplies of food and drink were
stolen.

They packed up and began their trek, south. Their city was inde-
fensible, it was too big, and there were too few of them. At the Orange
River they began to hear rumours of the Place of Light that you could
see a hundred kilometres away, the only place in Africa with electricity. At the old Vanderkloof. Amanzi.

Us.

A hundred and two of them had died during the Great Thirstland Trek, from privation and hunger and fatigue, lions and snakes and disease and age. And the human animals that attacked them.

47

The KTM come: I

Sofia Bergman

As recorded by Sofia Bergman. The Amanzi History Project, continued – in memory of Willem Storm.

Meklein, Vytjie and I took care of Pa and Ma, my two brothers and the other workers on the farm when they fell sick, and died. Today I'm glad I could do that. There were so many of the people at Amanzi who were far from their loved ones when the Fever took them. It was so painful to lose my family, but I could say goodbye to each of them. And I could bury them.

Of course I knew what was happening. The epidemic was on the Internet and the radio and television, it was all-consuming, it was everything. So I knew precisely what was going on.

Much later, Nero Dlamini and I talked a great deal about the influence of that sort of trauma on the psyche. I just believe a person has an instinctive primal ability to handle it one way or another, in the moment. To carry on. To survive.

My father was the last to die, he clung fiercely to life, fighting death because I suppose he felt responsible for us, wanted to protect us. Only then, after he was gone, did I realise that I wasn't sick yet, and maybe I wasn't going to die after all. And Meklein and Vytjie too. My own survival was the worst for me, the hardest to accept. It was as though I thought I would bury my family, and then Meklein would bury me, I would soon be with them . . . Nero Dlamini said it was typical survivor's guilt. It was the thing I suffered from most, to be honest. I felt so awfully guilty that I was the one who survived. I deserved it least. I was thirteen. I was still nothing.

Meklein and Vytjie . . . It was one of the great mysteries of the universe that they survived the Fever together. A statistical impossibility. They were *husband and wife. He was three-quarters Bushman, she was coloured. With Griqua blood, she always said. Meklein was my father's right-hand man. Vytjie was a free spirit. She was the veld doctor for coloured people of the whole district. And us children too. She knew the medicinal properties of each plant in the veld.*

Meklein rolled cigarettes from Boxer tobacco and newspaper. That's what killed him in the end, those cigarettes.

I believe the Bushmen have a genetic resistance to the virus, if I look at how many we've run into over the past years, how many of them survived.

The simultaneous arrival of the five hundred and eighty Namibians had consequences.

The Committee had to plan well for the use of food, as we now had to feed many more people through the coming winter. The second consequence was that all of Amanzi's available housing was suddenly full. To the brim. The Namibians took the last of the houses, even the smallest in the old township, the most decrepit in the main town, the few empty old shops and the last vacant rooms in houses.

Due to my banishment, and to my great chagrin, I could no longer listen to the great debate over the future expansion of Amanzi first hand. But the Committee gave public feedback in the Forum, and I drew my own conclusions. There were two schools of thought.

The first was to begin to develop and populate Petrusville. It was only fifteen kilometres from Amanzi, it was easy to connect the electricity grid, and only eight kilometres from the big irrigation scheme on the river. The great disadvantage was the town lay on the plain, with no natural defences.

The second school of thought was to immediately begin planning and working on the expansion of Amanzi itself – the development of a brick oven, the laying out of new roads, new plots of land for new houses, and all the necessary infrastructure. It would be more difficult, because we didn't have the knowledge or skills to do everything quickly, and it would take months of preparation before we could build houses.

In what Domingo called 'a typical committee decision', they decided to get both solutions under way in the meantime. Expeditions were asked to look for cement. Our young geologist who had arrived the previous year said no, if we really wanted, we could make our own. Or at least a basic, workable version of it. We would just have to fetch lime.

The third consequence of the Namibians' arrival was that Domingo got fifty people for his army. The Committee were shocked by the arrivals' tales of vicious attacks, and of course now there were just more people available to deploy.

They were all over forty, the oldest sixty-one. None had previous military experience. 'A real Dad's Army, for defence purposes only. I am sure the KTM are shaking in their boots,' grumbled Domingo to me during target practice, when he was sure no one else could hear us.

I envied every one of our new soldiers.

The fourth – and best – consequence was the addition of valuable new skills: a nurse, four experienced stock farmers, a nature conservationist, a mechanic and a nearly qualified diesel mechanic.

The final consequence of the coming of the Namibians was that Jacob and I no longer rode the quadbike to the reserve. We were each allocated a horse for our shepherding work, animals that we had to learn to ride, and to care for. We helped to build the stables, just across the T-junction at Heide Street.

17 February

Domingo and his soldiers managed three roadblocks: one just south of Petrusville, one about fifteen kilometres west of Amanzi on the old R369, and one on the opposite bank at the old Havenga Bridge over the Orange River, about a kilometre downstream of the dam wall.

On 17 February the four day-shift guards at the Havenga Bridge heard the deep rumble of a diesel lorry, its hooter sounding out cheerfully. Then the big ERF lorry with a long white trailer came into view over the hill, clearly not one of Amanzi's expedition vehicles. It stopped a hundred metres from the barricade – a safe distance.

A man and a woman got out of the cab, stood in front of the truck and waved at the guards. The man approached on foot, the woman stayed by the truck. The man introduced himself as Thabo. He pointed at the woman and said she was Magriet. They were pedlars. They heard we had a growing, successful settlement, with electricity. They sold medicine for people, and medicine for animals. They also had rice, some pasta and electrical appliances – kitchen blenders, washing machines and tumble dryers, fridges and stoves, everything spotless, brand new.

The guards called Domingo over the radio. Domingo said he was on his way. He drove to the bridge, met the man and woman. They were good-humoured, harmless. He looked at the white trailer. On the side was painted a big red cross, and in clumsy letters the words: *Medicine. For trade. We come in Peace.* Followed by a large peace symbol in bright green.

Domingo searched the lorry. Three times. He found only boxes and crates, all filled with medicine, rice, pasta and electrical equipment, neatly packed and marked.

'What do you sell these for?' asked Domingo.

'For whatever you have. We barter. We urgently need diesel. Vegetables and fruit are worth a lot to us, actually any fresh food. Meat as well, we have a fridge in the trailer.'

Domingo interrogated them for another fifteen minutes before he was satisfied. Then he gave the sign – the blockade gate swung open. Thabo and Magriet drove over the bridge, up the hill, and stopped in front of the old police station.

They were the first travelling traders since the Fever. Pa said it was the most encouraging sign yet of a normalising world.

That night in the Orphanage I hung on their lips as they recounted their story. They said they were both restless souls whose paths had crossed by accident.

Thabo Somyo was nearly fifty. He had always been in transit in some way, working in various places in South Africa. The few years before the Fever as a receiving clerk at the harbour in East London's container terminal. When the epidemic and the ensuing chaos came, he hid out there, because he knew of the thousands of tons of imported grain in the harbour silos, of the shipping containers filled with exotic foods, including rice and noodles from the East, and pasta and tinned tomatoes from Italy. Eventually there were close to sixty people making a living in and around the harbour, but Thabo was ready to move on again.

Twenty-something Magriet van der Sandt was a pharmacist from

Queenstown. She had been a backpacker when the world was still whole, and after the Fever she soon became frustrated by the constrictions of a life of mere survival. And she yearned for fresh vegetables and fruit. Eventually she packed a small truck full of medicine and set off. Everywhere she encountered people she traded medicine and medical advice for fuel, fresh food and security.

In East London she met Thabo Somyo. He asked why she was trading with such a small truck. She said that was all she could drive. He told her there were seven shipping containers full of medicines in the harbour. He said he would show her where they were, he would get them a big lorry, but he wanted to come along, and he wanted a full 50 per cent of the partnership.

The medicine in the containers was not just for people. Nearly half was dip and vaccines for sheep, cattle and pigs. They packed some of those in as well and left. That was four months ago. First they went to places like Port Alfred and Cradock, Mthatha and Port St Johns. Then further. To Durban. Pietermaritzburg, Manzini and Richards Bay. Then Nelspruit, Pretoria, Johannesburg, Polokwane, Gaborone, Vryburg, Kimberley and, eventually, Amanzi.

Yes, they had been shot at, some people had thrown stones at them in passing. They didn't stop if it looked very dangerous. They had been stopped many times, often by people with weapons, people filled with aggression or fear, mostly people who were aggressive out of fear. But nearly all of those people were in need of medicine, or advice about medicine. Or someone in that group was sick or injured. Or people were just eager for news about what was going on elsewhere in the world. And then they would barter, and each time Thabo and Magriet were permitted to continue their journey.

They said the world was changing slowly, it was stabilising. People were joining forces in other places, just like us. Around Pinetown in KwaZulu-Natal there was a large settlement that survived on cattle farming and bananas and pineapples. They were making ethanol from sugar cane. There had been an ethanol plant before the Fever, which they got up and running again. Initially their production was small, and the quality varied, but it grew and improved weekly. At first they only produced enough fuel to run petrol generators, but now many of their vehicles were running on it.

In Nelspruit there was a peaceful, growing community who traded mangos, avocados and macadamia nuts for medicine.

In the north of Pretoria a cattle-farming town was developing, and in Johannesburg two dominant groups had arisen, the Easties from the Kempton Park area, and the Westies from Soweto and Randburg. They had no agriculture, they lived by plundering the city, house by house, for anything edible or usable. The tension between the two gangs was growing as the loot diminished. 'There'll be war,' said Thabo Somyo. 'We got out of there pretty fast.'

Amanzi's reputation, they said, was widespread, as far as Johannesburg even. Communities spoke of 'the place at the dam that has electricity'. That was why Thabo and Magriet began to trade their medicines for brand-new electrical wares, everywhere they stopped.

'So you haven't been to Bloemfontein?' asked Domingo.

'No,' said Magriet. 'We hear there are bikers who control that area, and they're dangerous.'

29 March

Thabo and Magriet returned, this time from the south. They brought a whole load of rice. They came to trade it for bottled fruit, for bottled tomato and onion sauce; they said that was very popular, everywhere they went.

They said they came through the Langkloof and Oudtshoorn and Beaufort West, to avoid the bikers, the people we called the KTM.

They said their journey had been without incident.

48

The KTM come: II

Sofia Bergman

I want to say something that will sound strange, but it would be dishonest ... incomplete if I didn't say it: those three years that Meklein and Vytjie and I lived on the farm, there was something sublime, something biblical, holy about it.

The farm was very remote, it lay deep in a river valley, in mountainous country, north of Nieu-Bethesda. The geography there strengthens your feeling of ... loneliness is not the right word, because I was never lonely. Nor were the two of them, because they had each other, and they had me as a responsibility, a purpose, you understand what I mean? Nero said a reason to survive and keep living is a big influence on the lifespan of old people. I might have been that for them.

But I digress. The encircling mountains strengthen one's feeling of isolation, they make it easier to believe this is the whole world, this is all that exists, even though you know it is not. Does that make sense?

We saw nobody else in those three years. Nobody. In the beginning, in those early months after we had buried all our people, we still had satellite TV, at night we could watch the world collapse into ruins little by little. But the transmissions suddenly stopped. One evening when we switched on, there was nothing. We still had the radio, for a few weeks. And then it was just us, and the graves of our loved ones, and our simple lifestyle. Now I have to laugh, because one romanticises so easily: the people of olden times definitely did not have a wind charger or solar panels for power. But nevertheless we had an uncomplicated existence, we were ruled by the sun and moon, and the seasons.

We had milk cows, sheep. Pigs and chickens. And the bottled fruit and curried beans and sweet and sour beans and beetroot salad in Ma's pantry,

*and in the summer we planted again and harvested. Vytjie found edible food
in the veld in winter, plants that I never even knew were edible. We always
had more than enough to eat. And so there was time to listen to Meklein and
Vytjie's stories, and they could teach me things. Especially Meklein.*

*Vytjie couldn't understand why I wasn't as interested in her knowledge of
the plants and medicines. I preferred to learn to hunt from Meklein. Naturally
we had hunting rifles in the house, but between the five rifles there were only
about two hundred and fifty rounds left, and from the beginning we decided
to save them. For what I don't know. But there was a crossbow. My elder
brother bought it second-hand from someone, he had ... You know how someone is interested in something for three, four months, and then ... The crossbow was there, with exactly eleven bolts. I started shooting with the crossbow.
I can't remember why, I think it could have been boredom or curiosity, we
really definitely didn't need to think of self-defence or hunting.*

*When some of the bolts were damaged, Meklein said he could make
them. He did, and he taught me how to do it too. He said that was how his
forefathers hunted, with bow and arrow. And then he taught me what he
knew. He taught me to stalk and track, to survive in the veld. And at night
beside the fire he described how his people would run after a wounded buck
for hours and hours, how that was real hunting, the animals always stood
a chance.*

*So I began to hunt out of curiosity and boredom. Remember, I was a
cross-country runner, it was intense fun for me to run for hours and
kilometres.*

2 June

I was in school that day. Winter, a cold morning with frost, but a
perfect sunny day, not a cloud in the sky.

Amanzi was peaceful and hard-working, everyone busy with their
daily tasks.

Thabo and Magriet and the ERF truck with the words *Medicine.
For trade. We come in Peace* arrived in the morning between nine and
ten at the barricade south of Petrusville.

Domingo was in the old police station, still his headquarters at that
time. The roadblock guards asked him over the radio if they could
allow the pedlars through.

'Are they alone?'

'Yes.'

'Did you look in the back?'

'Yes.'

'Let them through.'

He knew Thabo and Magriet would have to stop at the bus gate as well, because the protocol was that all vehicles were searched there again. He notified the Committee members that the two traders were back, and would stop in Amanzi within the next half-hour. He walked from the police station across the street to our big new food store and bottling factory. It was where the old OK Value supermarket, the Ribbok restaurant and the Renosterberg bottle store used to be, but the Amanzi building team had converted it into one structure. It was reinforced and secured, with only one entrance. It was known among our people as the OK.

He went to tell the OK people that Thabo and Magriet were nearly here. Domingo walked back to the police station. Sixteen minutes later he heard the gunshots.

The bus gate is a kilometre and a half from the police station, behind a hill. But Amanzi was quiet, and automatic gunfire is a unique sound. Domingo knew his soldiers did not have target practice today. He knew it was something else, it was trouble, he knew it had something to do with Thabo and Magriet; he had his suspicions immediately, because that was how his mind worked.

Domingo grabbed his radio and his R4 and ran to his pick-up. He called over the radio for the bus gate to answer. All he heard was more gunshots in the distance.

He called his small garrison of twenty soldiers over the radio. They were the ones not manning the roadblocks today, they were busy with field exercises between the sewerage works and the dam. Domingo shouted into the mouthpiece that they must come to the police station. He jumped into the pick-up, turned on the engine,

Pa came running and asked what was going on.

'Keep everyone inside,' Domingo yelled. 'Keep everyone inside the houses. And keep your radio on.'

Domingo raced to the bus gate. He tried to raise the guards on the radio again. They did not answer.

Just after Heide Street the main road out of Amanzi makes a wide turn to the left – the first stretch of the road makes a U-bend – and runs down the hill. Domingo saw the ERF truck – horse and trailer – approaching. It was still five hundred metres away. The shots, the radio silence of the bus gate guards, the lorry coming fast, he was deadly certain it meant big trouble. Domingo braked hard, so that the pick-up's tyre skidded. He stopped across the middle of the road to prevent the lorry from passing. He jumped out and ran left of the road, up the slope. He fell flat behind a couple of rocks, looked through the scope of the R4. The truck was approaching fast, barely two hundred metres away. Neither Thabo nor Magriet was behind the wheel. There were two strange men in the cab. For a moment Domingo hesitated, and then he shot, four warning shots.

The truck did not stop.

Domingo shot again, single shots, aimed at the driver. The first one wounded the man, the truck swerved. It made Domingo's second shot miss. It seemed as if the truck would run off the road, but then it straightened out, accelerated, the driver crouching low behind the instrument panel. The man beside him returned fire.

Domingo kept on aiming and shooting as the truck accelerated towards his pick-up, and hit the back at high speed with a thunderous crash of metal on metal and breaking glass; the pick-up rolled off the road, the truck reached Domingo, then passed.

He fired, grabbed his radio, jumped up and ran. He screamed into the radio for Pa to raise the alarm, the system of car hooters that Domingo had devised for an emergency. He screamed over the radio for his garrison of twenty men to put the defence plan into action from the police station. He ran back to town, uphill, about a kilometre, as fast as he could.

I was in school. I heard the gunfire, but thought it was Domingo's soldiers practising in the quarry. I envied them.

I heard Domingo's shots, closer, just over there, barely four hundred metres from the school. I jumped up. The teacher told me to sit down.

I stayed on my feet, I knew something was wrong, because I knew Domingo. He would never allow anyone to shoot so near the town's houses and the Orphanage.

She told me again to sit down, in the sterner you-will-bear-the-consequences voice that all teachers use.

I sat down reluctantly.

The dull thud of metal on metal.

Some of the children drew in their breath. I stood up again and said, 'Miss . . .'

She was listening too now, her expression worried.

Deathly silence in class.

The alarm sounded, the hooters that Domingo and his men had attached to the high pole at the Midas filling station. Everyone knew what to do when the alarm went off.

I said to Jacob, 'Let's go,' and ran out of the classroom. I had to fetch my R4 DM and my R6, and Jacob and I had to get the horses and race up to the reserve, we had to defend the valley. That was our emergency task, as approved by the Committee, our part of Domingo's defence plan. We were sent to the reserve because most likely nothing would happen there.

I ran across the veld, over the hill. My weapons were in my room in the Orphanage, just a hundred metres from the school.

I heard the big diesel engine, but didn't know it was the ERF truck, because I couldn't see it. I ran across the Orphanage lawn. The little ones were there, with Beryl and Melinda. Okkie saw me. He shouted, 'Here I am, Nico!'

I ignored him, ran into my room, grabbed the rifles, the rucksack with the magazines and the radio. I raced out, hearing Okkie's little voice behind me, some of the smallest kids screaming shrilly. I was out, running to the stables across Heide Street T-junction. I heard Domingo calling me, he was down on the corner, rifle in his hand: 'Come here.'

I ran to him, he shouted and pointed: 'Go and cover the tarmac road, the road to the bus gate.'

'What about up top, what about the reserve?'

'Go and cover the tarmac road. Now. And if you see a biker, you shoot him. Give me the R6.' His voice was calm, as if he had everything under control.

I handed him the shorter assault rifle.

'How many magazines do you have?'

'Three for the R6, three for the DM.'

'Give me the R6 magazines.'

I took them out hurriedly, dropped one.

Domingo picked it up, put a hand on my shoulder. 'Stay calm, cover the tarmac road.'

He turned and ran towards the town centre, lifting his radio and talking into it.

I charged down Heide Street, and turned left, in the direction of the bus gate, I knew where I wanted to hide. I saw the pick-up, Domingo's pick-up, on the other side of the road; the tail was bashed in. I wanted to hide on the opposite side, on the ridge that looked out over the approach road's wide U.

Okkie's voice behind me: 'Wait for me, Nico, wait for me.'

I heard the sound of a motorcycle engine. I looked where the tarmac road came over the hill from the bus gate, about a kilometre away. I saw the first KTM rider. And the second and the third and the fourth.

49

The KTM come: III

Down on the plain was the big traffic circle where four roads joined:
the one from the dam wall, the one from the Havenga Bridge and the
one to Petrusville.

The fourth road ran up the hill to Amanzi. First to the bus gate in
the cleft of the two hills, four hundred metres from the circle.

Just after the bus gate the road turned right, and formed a big U
across the plain, before the second rise that led up into the town.

From where I was lying, the furthest visible point of the U was
about eight hundred metres away. I saw the motorbikes race into the
first leg of the U, heard the high-pitched scream of their engines. It
was too far, even if the target were dead still. I followed the first one
with my telescope, waited until he reached the first turn of the U, then
he would turn in my direction at an angle of about fifteen degrees. The
best place to shoot them was when they reduced speed for the second
turn of the U. It was just two hundred metres from me. The problem
was that I could now count twelve KTM riders. If I missed one down
there in the turn, and had to move the sights, and shoot faster, they
might get past me.

I would have to start shooting at five hundred metres, in the middle
of the second U leg. I would have to shoot rapidly. I would have to hit
the target.

Okkie lay beside me. When he arrived I had shouted at him: 'Come
lie down here, and shut your eyes tight and keep absolutely quiet, you
hear?' My voice sterner than I'd meant, due to my shock that he was
here, my fears for his safety. Okkie began to cry because of the sirens
and my response. I had never spoken to him like that before.

He lay pressed against my hip, his little arms over his eyes, whimpering softly.

The motorcycles were in the second U-bend. I tracked the first one, got a feel for the movement, calculated the shot. The sun was behind me, there was no wind. Perfect conditions.

I fired.

He dropped. The rider rolled, the motorcycle skidded and scraped across the tarmac, sparks showered.

The next one, I aimed for the chest, below the helmet. I shot.

He fell.

Another one and another one, and each time the shot boomed, Okkie jerked against me.

My world narrowed into the tunnel vision of the telescope.

The sixth one's motorbike burst into flames, and then exploded. Behind the smoke and flames I lost sight of the group; another one came racing through, nearer, almost at the second bend of the U.

I shot. He dropped. And again – the shot, the fall.

A bullet smacked against a rock beside me. Someone was shooting at me and Okkie.

I wanted to pull my eye away from the scope, I wanted to see where the shooter was, but I dared not, they were coming too fast, I had to keep my rhythm, I had to make sure not one of them got through.

The next one was in the turn below me, a hundred and fifty metres away. I shot. He fell.

Nine down. Three to go.

The next one I shot in the turn, another one when he was ninety metres from me coming out of the turn: he and his bike skidded across the road, narrowly missing Domingo's wrecked pick-up, and crashed into the rocks on the other side, and then there were no more bikes on the road and I thought I had counted wrong, I had seen twelve, shot eleven. And then another bullet smashed beside me and I realised one had stopped, one had holed up and was shooting at me.

It was the sudden silence that made Okkie jump up. 'Okkie!' I screamed.

'To Pappa,' he said and ran.

It would form part of the Domingo legend, what happened in the town on 2 June in the Year of the Jackal. It would fan the rumours about his past and his ability, become part of the myth of Amanzi.

The crossroad at the Midas garage up in town is misleading, because the streets come together like the beams of a three-point star.

Domingo had shot off the collar bone of the driver of the ERF lorry – before it hit his pick-up – so that he had to control the vehicle with only one hand, which was not good enough for the speed and the angles of the three-point star. At the last minute the driver tried to turn left, towards the dam. He lost control and the truck ploughed into the lamppost and olive tree in front of the police station. The pole and the tree could not halt the momentum of the heavy truck, and it rammed into the corner of the police station and broke through the wall.

The twenty Amanzi soldiers who had been on field exercises were back in the police station, arming themselves in obedience to Domingo's orders. The front of the ERF crashed through the wall and hit seven of our troops who were feverishly grabbing and loading firearms in the arms magazine. The other thirteen soldiers, who were in the room next door waiting for their guns, fell flat while the dust, noise and shockwave blasted through the building.

Domingo had already shouted his orders to me, grabbed my R6, and sprinted after the lorry. He heard the crash as it hit the wall of the police station, four hundred metres away.

By the time he reached the corner and could see the ERF truck, he was two hundred metres off. At that instant the back doors of the trailer opened, and revealed KTM men with guns inside the long trailer. Our rifles, the R4s that they had stolen from us more than two years ago.

Domingo had my R6 over his shoulder, and his R4 in his hands. His R4's magazine was nearly empty, just about six rounds left. He slowed from a run, walked down the street. In full view, he didn't look for cover. There were people who witnessed it, looking out of the windows of their houses. Later they would describe how Domingo seemed so focused, so determined, that he was oblivious to danger.

The KTM men began jumping out of the trailer.

Domingo raised the R4 to his shoulder, looked through the scope, and shot. Three measured shots.

Three KTM men dropped. But there were ten in the back of the lorry. And the remaining seven returned fire.

*   *   *

I knew the sharpshooter who lay down there somewhere would see Okkie running. I knew how it worked, how movement drew your eye through the telescope, how you instinctively aimed, measured and shot.

I shouted Okkie's name, leapt to my feet. He was running back towards the Orphanage. He was four paces ahead of me, I had the R4 in my left hand, reached out with my right hand for him, then something plucked my left leg out from under me. In that instant there was no pain, but I knew I was hit because I had been expecting the bullet, I was just thankful that it hit *me*.

I grabbed Okkie as I fell, a handful of his shirt in the scruff of his neck. I hit the ground, my shoulder hit Okkie, he was winded, I heard him gasp and wheeze for air. I turned over on the ground, felt the dampness of blood on my leg. For the first time I felt the burning pain, but only at the exit wound, and I wondered why, such an odd thing to think of in those circumstances. I knew I had to locate the sniper's hiding place, I had to shoot him.

Okkie panted, gasped for breath.

I saw the lightning flash of the shooter's gun. He sprawled flat behind his motorbike that lay on its side in the middle of the road. The man was barely visible through the smoke cloud of the burning bike.

The next bullet hit right in front of me, dust and sand and gravel in my face, my eyes.

Okkie still struggling to breathe beside me.

I wiped the eye of my scope, desperate. I had better shoot fast, he had my distance, the next shot would not miss.

I drew the sights on him, I shot. I had him.

Okkie drew a deep gasping breath. He wept, in loud, ragged bursts.

I looked down at my leg. I saw the pool of blood forming on the ground.

I was going to bleed to death here.

'Okkie,' I said, 'you have to call someone. Anyone at the Orphanage. Do you hear?'

The R4 was empty. Domingo threw it aside, swung the R6 off his shoulder. Bullets slammed into the tarmac in front of him, ricochets whined away.

Suddenly he dodged left, quickly off the street, behind the Midas garage building.

The KTM men all jumped out of the ERF trailer. Three of them crawled under the lorry, using the big wheels as shelter. Four of them ran through the gaping hole in the wall of the police station.

Those four spotted the movement of the thirteen Amanzi soldiers. One soldier tried to reach the arms magazine, through the dust and bits of plaster and brick, over the bodies of his comrades who had been trapped between the lorry and the wall in the collision. The KTM shot wildly. They mowed the Amanzi soldiers down – only four of the twenty would survive.

Domingo

As recorded by Willem Storm. The Amanzi History Project.

There's a lot of exaggeration and nonsense about that day. I did very poorly. Me and my whole team. Our losses were heavy. We had all the advantages, the high ground, the checkpoints, the gates. And we failed miserably . . .

They said he was like a shadow. He moved like a phantom through the garage, while the three KTM men hiding under the truck shot at him.

Domingo used the windows and doors, even the petrol pumps, and he got them one by one, with single shots from the R6. He didn't seem to hurry, he didn't seem afraid, he expressed only focus and determination.

He jogged to the truck, rolled under the trailer, picked up two of their rifles, took out the magazines, shoved them in his pockets. He disappeared into the open hole of the police station.

The people across the road in the OK heard the shots. They said the KTM shot wildly. And every now and then there would be a single shot from Domingo. The storytellers would say, remember there were four of them, and just Domingo, and the police station wasn't big. But it didn't take long, three minutes they guessed, and then Domingo emerged and walked to the horse of the ERF truck, and there wasn't even a mark on him.

Two KTM members were still in the cab, driver and passenger, injured after the crash into the lamppost and the police station. The two who had killed Thabo and Magriet. They were bleeding, broken, but still alive. Domingo opened the door on the driver's side. Bits of glass fell to the ground. The driver with the broken collarbone handed his pistol with the silencer to Domingo. He said, 'We give up, we give up.'

Domingo took the silenced pistol, and shot them between the eyes. One after the other.

50

The KTM come: IV

Domingo

Let me try to set the record straight.

The KTM were not trained. They were a bunch of amateur yahoos with assault rifles. And yet they managed to kill my guards at two gates, breach those gates, and get past me with the lorry. They managed to kill twenty-six of us.

And remember, their plan backfired. Their plan was the Trojan Horse, their plan was to hijack Thabo and Magriet. Then two men with silenced pistols hid in the lorry cab with Thabo and her, and ten were behind in the trailer, and the twelve on bikes followed. At the gate my guards saw Thabo and Magriet, and they didn't suspect a thing, but then the two with silenced pistols jumped out and told the guards to tell us everything was okay on the radio.

At the Petrusville checkpoint their plan worked well. They shot my guards and the motorbikes came through.

The motorbikes then waited where the bus gate guards couldn't see them, and Thabo and Co. drove the lorry to the bus gate.

At the gate, the plan went wrong, we know, 'cause one of my guards survived to tell the story. He said Thabo tried to grab one of the silenced pistols, and then everyone began shooting, and the guys in the back of the trailer popped out, and that's how they breached my bus gate. But now their plan was shot to hell, no more element of surprise. The big mistake they made then is they should have cut their losses, should have retreated to fight another day. But they didn't have good leadership. They shot everyone, my guards, Thabo and Magriet, and the lorry raced ahead to get into town. There was a big gap between the lorry and the bikes, and that's what messed it up for them.

But despite the fact that they were yahoos and their plan was messed up,

they still managed to kill twenty-six of my people. That's totally unaccep-
table. That's a defeat. That's shameful.

That's why people mustn't come and say I was a hero that day. I was a
total failure. The real hero is Nico Storm. You won't see shooting like that
again. Ever.

But nobody says a word.

That's messed up.

I took off my shirt, and tied it very tightly around my leg, trying to
staunch the bleeding.

I began to feel dizzy.

I couldn't hear any more shooting in the town. I wondered what
had happened.

I saw Nero running towards me. And behind him, a bawling snot-
nosed Okkie.

I lay in the sick bay. Domingo was standing beside my bed.

'Why did you shoot them? Those last two.'

'You know my mantra.'

'The other guy wants to kill me. If I hesitate, I die?'

'That's the one.'

'But they surrendered.'

'With concealed weapons tied to their calves?'

'Oh.'

'Nico, they're animals. If they don't get you today, they'll get you
tomorrow. Never forget that.'

I nodded.

'And what would we do with prisoners?'

51

Sofia Bergman

As recorded by Sofia Bergman. The Amanzi History Project, continued – in memory of Willem Storm.

I sometimes wonder if Meklein hadn't died that May in the Year of the Jackal, if they had lived another four or six or ten years, if we would have stayed on our farm, if I would have ever seen Amanzi ...

I don't know how old Vytjie was. Deep in her seventies, I think.

So many nights we sat outside by the fire. Meklein loved it, sitting under the stars.

I know it sounds romanticised, but I think he knew the end was near. That last night of his life we were around the fire. The nights were already getting cold, we huddled close to the flames. He coughed a lot, more than usual. Then Meklein said he thought the Fever came because people were hurting the earth so badly. He said, with a coughing fit for every sentence, 'Vytjie, when last did you see a gompou?' He was talking about the kori bustard, that's what we called it, a gompou. He said, 'It's been years, but we used to see a lot more of those big birds long ago. Remember the black eagles, when we were young? There were so many. Remember the bakoortjies, how often we saw them in the old days? Those little bat-eared foxes are termite eaters, scorpion eaters, but the people thought they caught lambs. They never did. You don't see them any more. So many things you don't see any more. The old people hurt the earth, a lot. I wonder, is it not maybe the earth that sent the sickness?

Late that night he stopped coughing, as if his body just had enough. That night Meklein died in his sleep, and we buried him, Vytjie and me, and we divided up the chores again, but not even four weeks later, Vytjie also died. That night she sat so quietly by the fire, it was bitterly cold, I remember. She went to sleep and she just never opened her eyes again.

I buried her, then, beside Meklein, on the side of the ridge where they loved to sit close together in the sun on winter mornings and drink their herbal tea.

For months after Vytjie's passing I didn't even think of leaving the farm. I wanted to stay. I did stay. Through the winter. It was a regular Karoo winter, that year, no snow, just what my father always called 'perfect desert cold'. I pruned the fruit trees in July, and made biltong from two springbok. I stayed through August and September. And when it warmed up, I had to start planting. I began work, and I began digging manure and compost into the vegetable garden. But one morning, I packed the seeds out on the table, and I looked at the vegetable garden, and I saw the seasons stretching ahead, and I pictured harvesting the vegetables and fruit, and realised there was no one to share. And that was the moment the loneliness hit me. Odd, isn't it, the knowledge that I would eat alone, all those fresh vegetables. I wouldn't hear Meklein smacking his lips in delight, or wonder how Vytjie could nibble the sweetcorn so skilfully with the few teeth she had left.

That was when I realised I would have to find some other people. It was like a dam wall breaking, suddenly there was a flood of insight: it was actually dangerous to be so completely alone on the farm. You could slip and fall in the veld, or in the bath, and there was nobody to help. It was just as dangerous to go somewhere now. Where to? And how? We never used the vehicles, the batteries were flat, the diesel was probably spoiled long ago, and I never even considered getting anything going. I would have to walk. But where to?

To Bloemfontein.

That was the place I knew as a child. It was my frame of reference for where you went when you needed something that you couldn't get on the farm. It was where people and goods and services were.

I know it will be hard for people to understand this, but I still imagined the outside world as it was before the Fever. You must remember, I had been on the farm for more than three years, without seeing a single other soul, apart from Meklein and Vytjie. I had been entirely alone for nearly five months. I was just sixteen years old. I was in a kind of daze.

I thought I should pack a rucksack, take a rifle, and walk. I knew the shortest route to the N1; by the farm roads to Hanover it was a hundred kilometres or so, not more than that. There would be cars on the N1, and at Hanover I would beg a lift to Bloemfontein. I could stay in the hostel at my old school.

Silly plan, I know. I was so naïve. So ignorant.

I thought if I took enough food and water for a week, I would be okay. I thought it wouldn't matter that my mother's hiking boots were a little too big.

The best decision I made was to take the crossbow at the last minute.

52

The coup: I

It took Domingo and his assistants four days to dig the graves in the hard ground of the Amanzi hills. I only heard about it. I was laid up in the sick bay to start with, and when the nurse and Nero were satisfied that I had 'stabilised', I moved back into my room.

My wound looked bad, but Nero said it was 'clean', there wasn't much tissue damage. It should heal well. That news I shared with no one.

On the fifth day after the KTM attack, the entire community assembled on the ridge for the funeral service conducted by Pastor Nkosi. I wasn't allowed to attend, the nurse said the wound wasn't sufficiently closed.

On the ninth day we held a community meeting in the Forum. Jacob Mahlangu trundled me down from the Orphanage to the Forum in an old wheelchair with a wonky right wheel, my leg tightly bandaged and sore. I didn't want to miss any big announcements. I didn't want to forgo the admiration of the people. After all, I had shot twelve KTM members off their motorbikes. I didn't want to miss out on Lizette Schoeman's sympathy for my injury.

We had to sneak out of the Orphanage so that Okkie would not see us.

I was the centre of attention in the Forum; residents who called out their congratulations or came over to shake my hand, ask how I was doing. Some patted me on the back. Some of the seven- and eight-year-olds accompanied the wheelchair through the crowd, touching me now and then, eyes wide in hero-worship. I liked that very much.

I didn't see Lizette.

The Committee was a united group beside the old Tata truck. Jacob and I and our entourage of admirers stopped just a short distance away. Pa climbed onto the back of the Tata, which still served as the podium in the Forum. He spoke into a microphone, the sound system carrying his voice easily over the crowd. Practically the whole population of Amanzi was there to listen.

Pa said we had bid goodbye to too many of our own last week. Today we must begin the process of making sure it would never happen again.

The people applauded. Sombrely, still feeling the burden of loss.

Pa said last night the Committee had decided to channel the full production of bricks from our brick ovens, stone from the stone quarry, and all the cement that our young geologist mixed and the expeditions brought home, towards a project to fortify Amanzi.

The applause grew louder.

Pa said the bus gate would become a firm fixture. The old, wheelless vehicles that formed the gate would be replaced by thick brick walls and large, double, steel gates. Watchtowers would be built. The number of gate guards would be doubled. And Amanzi's standing army would be reinforced as soon as possible to man the new defensive structures.

'What about the KTM?' someone shouted from the crowd.

Pa said as soon as the main gate was built, work would begin on the Petrusville blockade, and the one at the Havenga Bridge below the dam wall.

'What about hitting back?' shouted someone else. 'Attack the KTM.' More voices rose in support. 'Do what Domingo says.'

When I heard that, I knew the news had spread: Domingo had told the Committee that the only way to eliminate the KTM threat was to attack them, to wipe them out. I wondered who had leaked this information from the Committee.

Pa said, 'The safety of this community is our first priority. We're investigating all possible responses and strategies. I . . . The whole Committee share your rage, we share your urge for vengeance, to attack them—'

'It's war!' someone shouted. The chorus of support intensified. 'Attack!'

'Yes,' said Pa. 'It's war. And in war our first priority is to make sure our community is safe from an attack. We just ask for patience . . .'

Pa paused, as Pastor Nkosi climbed up on the back of the Tata too and whispered something in Pa's ear.

'Pastor Nkosi wants to have a word.' Pa took a step back from the microphone and the burly pastor slowly lifted a hand.

'The Bible says, an eye for an eye,' the pastor called out in his powerful preacher-voice that swept everyone along.

A chorus of support rose up from the crowd.

'The Bible says, a tooth for a tooth.' The words rolled down the hill, and across the expanse of the dam.

The chorus of approval grew more enthusiastic.

I looked at Pa. He was standing right beside Nkosi. He was a head shorter and much leaner. I recognised the look on Pa's face – he was bewildered, not grasping what the pastor was up to.

'There is a time for war and a time for peace. And the time for war has come,' the pastor's voice thundered louder and higher. The crowd's reaction followed. 'Joel three verse nine says: "Proclaim this among the nations: Prepare for war! Rouse the warriors! Let all the fighting men draw near and attack." '

I saw the concern on Pa's face, watched him raise a hand to stop the pastor, attract his attention.

The people of Amanzi cheered Nkosi on.

'Jeremiah twenty: "The Lord is with me like a mighty warrior; so my persecutors will stumble and not prevail. They will fail and be thoroughly disgraced; their dishonour will never be forgotten." '

The people cheered louder.

'But if we want the Lord to be with us like a mighty warrior, my brothers and sisters, we have to allow God to rule this community. We must elect him our chairman. Because I am telling you today, God sent the KTM as a warning. Just like he sent the Fever. He sent the KTM and he sent the Fever because we did not make him our King. How much more must he send before we listen, my brothers and sisters? When are we going to listen?'

Pa gripped Pastor Nkosi's arm and I could see he was angry. Pa shouted something, but his voice was completely drowned out by the full-throated roar of the hundreds of bystanders. Nkosi shook his head emphatically; clearly he did not agree with Pa.

Pa pushed in front of the pastor to reach the microphone. Nkosi, much sturdier, pushed him aside. 'Do you want to listen to our chairman now?' he asked the crowd. 'Do you want to listen to the man who does not believe in God?'

The noise was deafening, no one knew if it was 'yes' or 'no'.

'No, Willem, they don't want to listen to you. They want to listen to God. They want an eye for an eye. They want to elect God as the chairman of Amanzi. I say, let's have an election.'

A great clamour, shouting from the people.

'Yes. Let's have an election. I hereby resign from the Committee. I am herewith creating the Mighty Warrior Party. I hereby nominate God for chairman. Are you with me? Are you ready for a holy war?'

Deafening noise, everyone was shouting something.

'Right! Let's have an election. This week. This Friday. Let us get God on our side.'

Voices, hands, arms, a heaving mass of reaction.

And then the pastor stepped back and smiled at Pa. He walked to the side of the Tata, and jumped down.

I wondered where Domingo was. I hadn't seen him at all.

It was quiet in the sitting room of the Orphanage. They sat defeated: Pa, Birdy, Ravi, Nero, Beryl.

I sat close to Pa, my leg resting on another chair in front of me. The pain was bad in the evening. I saved my pills for the night.

Eventually Nero stood up and fetched the brandy bottle and glasses. He poured a drink for each one, then said, 'The pastor is an opportunist, like all good politicians and preachers. And this was the perfect opportunity. If we'd been paying attention, we would have seen this coming.'

Beryl said the preacher was a backstabber. Ravi called him a traitor. Birdy clicked her tongue. 'It's not opportunism, it's a disgrace. Exploiting people's fear and pain.' And then she shook her head. 'Einstein said: "Two things are infinite: the universe and human stupidity; and I'm not sure about the universe." Now I understand what he meant.'

'I'm a Muslim,' said Ravi. 'I'm the only Muslim in Amanzi. I'll have a bit of a problem if Nkosi gets what he wants.'

Pa sat motionless, waxen and distraught, as though he were suffering from shock. He let them vent. Then, in a quiet voice burdened with emotion, he said, 'Two hundred thousand years. That's how old our species is. That's how long it took to produce a Benedict Spinoza . . .' He saw it was just Nero who remembered what he meant. 'Spinoza was the first man who wished to separate Church and state, the first man who said the basis for all politics should be personal freedom, and that democracy is the form of government that is most compatible with personal freedom. And then it took another three hundred years for that principle to take root in this land. And now . . . Surely we can't regress, can we?' It was like a plea.

Nero tried to answer, but Pa was too lost in his concern and passion. 'Do you know why I wrote that pamphlet back then? Why I wanted to make a new beginning here? I am not this great altruist, I must confess. I came here for Nico, so he could see . . . No, so he could be part of this new journey of two hundred thousand years, so that the interruptions would not . . . I . . . Aren't you also amazed by what we're capable of? Look at our journey, Homo sapiens's journey, look at how incredibly far we've come, from savannah prey to a robot on Mars and the splitting of the atom and the decoding of DNA. And democracy, reason and rationalism. Science above superstition, facts above myth . . . The Fever, it's horrible, the billions who died in the Fever, I know, it's terrible, but I wonder if the greater harm wasn't the interruption of what we were on the road to accomplishing. We had such huge problems before the Fever. Political and social and ecological, but we were finding solutions, as we have always done. Technology, just in the last twenty years, the tremendous advancements and breakthroughs and discoveries, all to solve problems, to make the world a better place. *That* was the greater loss to me, that we never had the chance to continue all those developments, to use our ingenuity to solve all those problems. We would have, I know we would. I . . . I owe it to Nico. And Okkie. We owe it to all our children, all the people, to two hundred thousand years of struggle and strife, not to regress now. That's what Nkosi will do. We . . . We must talk to the people, we must explain to them, we must inform them. Before Friday . . .' And Pa was so swept up, so desperate, that he stood up from his chair, as though he meant we must start the campaign right away.

'Ai, Willem,' said Birdy. 'They don't want information. They're scared. They want someone to take the fear away. Nkosi's entire strategy is based on fear.'

'We're going to lose,' said Nero Dlamini.

'Unless you believe in miracles,' said Beryl. And she laughed quietly. It broke the worst of the tension.

53

Sofia Bergman

I walked away from the farm in October. Quite early in October. I didn't know what the exact date was, because I had long ago stopped following the calendar. I waited for the spring, for warmer nights.

Rucksack, hiking boots, rifle and crossbow.

My mother was a hiker. She had the big rucksack and the hiking boots, which she must have last used fifteen years before her death, but they were in the built-in wardrobe in their bedroom. I wore my mother's and sister's clothes, I had outgrown my own long before. I packed the rucksack with underwear, clothes and socks. A sleeping bag and food and water, matches, torch, Leatherman multi-tool. I took the rifle and ammunition, and the crossbow and bolts. And a cellphone, my father's. Can you believe it? I actually thought it would work in Bloemfontein.

I opened the pig sty and the chicken run, the stables and the gates of the camps.

And one last time I visited the graves, and then I walked away, at dawn one morning in October in the Year of the Jackal.

It was a curious journey. I walked along roads I hadn't seen in three years, roads that hadn't seen a vehicle or a person in three years. Everything looked just a bit different. The trees and bushes were bigger, the eroded dongas were deeper. In places the road had washed away. The farmhouses were deserted.

There was only the sound of insects and birds, only the scents of nature.

That first night, I dreamed I saw the helicopter.

I walked to Nieu-Bethesda first, to get onto the Doornberg road. My mother's boots were too big, and my feet hurt more and more as they bumped against the toes and rubbed around the ankles.

There was nobody in Nieu-Bethesda. Only birds and beetles and one little klipspringer buck I startled as I passed. The empty town was spooky;

two cars had just stopped in the middle of the street, and the olive groves and the quince hedges and irrigated lands that once had been so neat, they were all overgrown and neglected. It made me uneasy. I walked through quickly, even though I knew that was silly. I left the village, and about two hours later I turned right at the fork, on the Dassiesfontein road. That was the road my father loved the most. The Dassiesfontein road was a gravel road, which followed the river valley, twisting and turning, to the R398. There were at least ten farmyards beside the road, but I just walked past them, I didn't want to think that they were all dead. Increasingly, all I thought about was my sore feet.

Lunch beside the little river. The stream had stopped running. I stopped at a pool, saw the spoor of baboon, klipspringer and kudu. I pulled off the boots and stuffed some underwear inside to make them fit tighter. It helped.

I set off again. I felt strange. Sort of feverish. Not sick feverish, just strange feverish. Distanced, one dimension separate from this desolate reality. The rucksack grew heavier, the straps chafed my shoulders, the sides of my breasts.

In the late afternoon I was tired. I tried to calculate how far I had come. About sixty kilometres, quite a distance, but I knew I wasn't going to make it to the R398. I would have to sleep over somewhere. The sun was behind me. I saw the dam to the left of the road, a farm's storage dam; it looked pretty in the soft light. It was Welgelegen. Pa knew the farmer and his wife. The farmhouse was another kilometre away. I stopped walking, tired, very much alone; as the sun set it touched the mountains behind me. I found the farm buildings, five hundred metres from the gravel road, just before sunset. There were bats darting through the twilight. I couldn't face the farmhouse. I shone the torch on the shed. Bales of lucern, small animals or snakes rustling through the hay. I would sleep on the veranda.

Then I heard the sound, an unfamiliar one, and instinctively I looked up in the direction from where it came. I saw the stripe, the light, the fire, low over the dark eastern horizon, like a meteorite falling, but close, as if it were just nearby, above the ridge.

It disappeared behind the mountain, and then it was quiet.

I stood in amazement looking at the night sky. I listened, realised everything had gone quiet and now was waking up again, all the early evening noises that I knew. I stared at the eastern horizon, but there was nothing now, just the imagined smoke trail where the meteorite fell.

I had to prepare for night.

I went to inspect the big veranda of the house. I used the torch, found a rusty drum and firewood, and made a fire just to banish the loneliness, and the ghosts. The night sky was visible between the veranda wall and the roof. It was breathtaking, millions of stars twinkling. I ate and drank and wondered, what was it that I had seen and heard? And then I thought of all the satellites in space. And the space station! There were so many things that could fall to earth. I must have seen one of them.

My first night without a mattress, the floor of the veranda was hard and cold. I slept badly, restless and uncomfortable.

After four the noise woke me from a deep sleep with a start. It was a helicopter, I swear it was a helicopter. I jumped up, looked east, where the noise was coming from, the wap-wap-wap of a helicopter.

I saw nothing, just the stars.

The sound faded away behind the ridges.

I couldn't get back to sleep. I wondered if I had dreamed it. I wondered if I was here, if I still existed. I wondered, do we make our own reality? Do we see the same reality as other people? Does this world even exist?

Were there any other people left in the world? What if I were the very last one?

54

The coup: II

My father. My beloved father. My idealistic, pathetic, clever, frustrating father.

He came to me where I was lying in my room. He said, 'I am so glad the wound isn't serious.'

I so wished he would ask me to tell him exactly how it had all happened. He never did. Never the slightest prompting to tell him the whole story. He just put a hand on my shoulder and said, 'You're your mother's child.' There was a new tone in his voice, admiration, a touch of respect perhaps, but also an edge, I recall.

He never told me he was proud of my role in stopping the second invasion of the KTM. He looked on as people came to congratulate me. There was a benevolent smile on his face, that sort that said it was the right thing to do, to smile. But his heart wasn't in it. He never once said he was proud of me.

I was disappointed; I wanted very badly to hear him say it, but I wasn't really angry with him about it. The praise and appreciation and respect of the community stroked my ego sufficiently.

During Pastor Nkosi's coup d'état in the Forum, I had watched Pa from my wheelchair, ashamed that he could be so easily overshadowed and pushed aside by the preacher and the crowd. Yet at the same time I felt an overwhelming love for him, and a strong protective urge. I wanted to spare him the pain and humiliation. I wanted to jump up and take on the pastor. That was why I had wondered at the moment of Nkosi's victory where Domingo was. Because I was wounded, impotent, and perhaps Domingo could help.

That night in the Orphanage sitting room, as he talked about the human species' journey of two hundred thousand years, I forgot my disappointment in his lack of praise for my heroic deed.

I felt only pride and love for my father. And the need to protect him.

And I wondered again, where was Domingo? He was nowhere to be found that night. The rumour was that he hardly slept, that he drove ceaselessly from gate to gate, to protect us.

That same night they founded a political party in the Orphanage.

The process of deciding on a name for their party was so tedious that I kept nodding off. I recall some of their suggestions were the Freedom Party and the Democrats, or variations on those themes, like the Amanzi Democrats or the Amanzi Freedom Party.

Eventually they agreed on Free Amanzi. The founder members were Pa and Birdy, Nero, Beryl and Ravi. Pa nominated Birdy as chairman, she nominated Pa. They voted, and Pa was elected unanimously.

They had six days before Friday's election. There were just over one thousand eligible voters in Amanzi. Their strategy was for Pa to talk personally with every one of the voters. After all he was the founder of Amanzi, the man who had begun everything, the man who brought them through famine and snow, the man who commanded great respect from everyone. Pa's approach, they agreed, must not attack Pastor Nkosi or his religion. Pa's message must be simple, easy to grasp, pragmatic and unique. ('Don't give them a history lesson about Benedict Spinoza,' said Nero Dlamini playfully, but not entirely joking, because he knew Pa.)

Their chosen slogan was: *Yes! To retribution – after thorough prepara-tion*. It was weak and lacking in imagination, but it was the best they could do. Later Domingo would shake his head and call it 'creativity by committee'. In the election battle Pa and friends would remind the people that the storehouse was stocked for the winter, the power was on, and the first sunflowers for diesel production were drying.

They worked harder in those six days than I had ever seen them work. Pa talked to everyone, every resident, even those too young to vote. He explained, he pleaded, he begged. He was received every-where with courtesy and sympathy. Many people thanked him for all that he had done for the community.

And the majority of them said sorry, but they were going to vote for the preacher.

'Your dad's going to lose,' Jacob came to tell me on the Tuesday afternoon after school. He was the source of most of my information. 'The pastor just keeps telling people: "Twenty-six comrades are dead, go check the graves, that all happened on Willem Storm's watch." '

That Wednesday evening Pa told me he had no hope. He said it with resignation, acceptance. As if he knew he had done everything in his power, had remained faithful to all he believed in.

Early Thursday morning I lay on my bed while the nurse cleaned the wound and put on new bandages. I saw Domingo hurry past down the passage. It was the first time since the funeral that he had been back in the Orphanage. I called out a greeting, but he didn't answer.

As soon as the nurse had finished, I struggled up on my crutches and hobbled to the dining room. The door was closed. I heard voices inside. Pa's. And Birdy and Domingo.

'No, no, it's not democracy,' I heard Pa say passionately, the only words I could make out.

Shortly after that they came out, and I could see none of them were happy.

I shuffled back to my room.

Later Jacob came to ask whether I had heard: Domingo was going to address the people of Amanzi. Pastor Nkosi objected vigorously. But Domingo told him: 'Stop me if you can.'

Jacob pushed me down to the Forum in the wheelchair. 'An ill wind,' he said. It was gusty, cold and ominous.

The people gathered. It was obvious no one liked this election, this schism. There was a muted atmosphere, a sense of reluctance in the air. But everyone came to hear Domingo speak, because he was the one who kept them safe.

At five Domingo climbed on the Tata. He looked weary. He carried an R4 over his shoulder. He switched on the microphone, tapped it to hear if it worked.

I saw the pastor and his large band of disciples to one side, hands in pockets, unhappy faces. I saw Pa and a handful of supporters, to the right of the Tata. Pa stood with his head bowed, as if he had already lost.

'I'll keep this simple,' said Domingo, his words measured and crystal clear. 'If Nkosi wins the election, I'll be leaving Amanzi. You'll have to go to war against the KTM without me. Thank you.'

He switched off the microphone, jumped down lightly down from the Tata and walked away.

The next day Pa would quote Voltaire and say about Domingo: 'Clever tyrants are never punished.'

55

Sofia Bergman

I dreamed on that veranda in the small hours, that unsettling part of the night just before the dawn, I dreamed wild dreams, disturbing dreams, dreams that cling, only let go of you slowly, even after you wake.

My feet hurt. I didn't know how I was going to walk. But I would have to walk, I only had food for five days in the rucksack, I couldn't waste a day.

I hadn't brought plasters. There were plasters in the bathroom at home, I should have packed a few. The dreams and reality, knowing that something could so easily go wrong, that there might be more trouble and obstacles that I had not foreseen, gave me a hollow feeling in the pit of my stomach.

I ate a little and drank water. I picked up a stone in the overgrown garden of Welgelegen farm and broke a window. I went inside. There were always plasters in a farmhouse, I just had to find them. I felt very uncomfortable, being in someone else's house like this. There was a desiccated corpse on the bed in the master bedroom. A woman. Three years dead, it smelled of nothing. She lay with her hands folded on her chest. I walked out fast, and sat down on the veranda, my legs shaking. I drank some more water. I could picture the woman's story: she fell sick alone, her husband was in town, or in the veld when he collapsed. Maybe she didn't have a husband, maybe she was a widow and her children were in Canada or New Zealand. She fell sick, alone in the house and when she lay down she knew she was going to die, she had been following the news of the Fever on the radio. But she wanted to die tidy, she wanted to die pretty. She put on her make-up, brushed her hair and put on her best clothes, and she lay down on her bed like that, the bed she had made up with the best linen, and she died.

I wept on the veranda of Welgelegen farm. It was the first time I cried. I cried like someone whose heart was torn in pieces, for more than an hour. And then something happened to me. I knew I had to finish and be done with crying, and I must decide: was I going to tidy myself up and was I

*going to lie down beside that woman and wait for death to come? Or did I
want to* live?

I decided I wanted to live.

*It sounds like a small thing now that I'm telling it, but it was big, it was
a very big decision for me, and it was as though, there on that veranda on
Welgelegen, I woke up from a three-year sleep.*

*I got up then and went to look in the bathroom and the kitchen, and
eventually found the plasters in a cupboard in the passage, along with ointment and Disprin. I bandaged my feet carefully. Then I had the idea that
perhaps I wouldn't need to walk. I searched the outbuildings, and it was
odd, but now I was no longer afraid of the rustling and spider webs, the
silence and the desolation.*

*I found a bicycle in the garage, an old one, without gears. The tyres were
flat, but there was a hand pump. I inflated the wheels, and took the pump
and my rucksack and rode down the farm road, just after ten that
morning.*

*Every hour the bicycle wheels went flat. Then I would get off and pump
them up again. At the steep hills I would push the bike up as it had no gears,
and happily freewheel down the other side, hair blowing in the wind. I
turned left on the eroded dirt road, the R398, and a kudu stood in the
middle of it in broad daylight in and stared at me as I cycled up. Then it
lazily trotted away. I was probably the first person it had seen in thirty-six
months.*

*I turned right on the next farm road, to Hanover. This was another road
my father loved, because he could see how the farmers' veld looked, their
dams and sheep. I rode that farm road in memory of my pa. I rode nearly
fifty kilometres on the bicycle before the rear wheel wore through and the
pump wouldn't make the tyre hard again.*

*I picked a veld flower and stuck it in the bicycle bell and left it there lean-
ing on the fence, and I walked on until my feet began to hurt again.*

That night I slept in the veld, under the stars, without a fire.

Nothing fell from heaven, no dream-helicopters flew near me.

56

The coup: III

My father and his Free Amanzi party won the election with a two-thirds majority, but no one celebrated it.

Pa consulted with his party management before they offered a place on the Committee to Pastor Nkosi. He said he would think about it. He didn't think long. The Sunday evening after the election he came to the Orphanage. Beryl invited him in, said he must come in to the sitting room. I was reading Okkie stories. Domingo sat near us listening. The pastor was dressed in his formal church garb – black suit with the long frock coat. He saw Domingo. I looked up at the crucial moment, and I saw the loathing in the preacher's face, and thought he was going to spit on Domingo in passing. But he just walked on, to Birdy, Pa and Nero. The men rose, shook Nkosi's hand.

'You know I would have won the election if it wasn't for your devious and very undemocratic tactics, Willem,' the pastor said.

'You would have won, yes. But what Domingo did, he did on his own.'

'That's not true,' said Nkosi. 'I hear he came to talk to you before his little speech.'

'I implored him not to do it,' said Pa.

'I don't believe you.'

Domingo didn't stand up. He spoke from his armchair: 'He did. Now come and tell *me* I'm a liar, Padre. Come and tell me to my face.' His tone was laconic, as if he found it all faintly amusing.

Nkosi ignored him.

I knew Domingo understood that the pastor's dignity was everything to him. That was why he allowed mockery and laughter into his tone: 'You were the one to introduce scare tactics, Padre. I just gave them a variation on your theme,' said Domingo.

'I want two seats on the Committee,' said Nkosi to Pa.

'That's a reasonable request,' said Birdy.

'And I want to build a church.'

'We don't have enough resources, Nkosi. You know we have to build the gates first.'

'Security gates first, Pearly Gates second,' said Domingo, taunting the pastor openly now.

Nkosi continued to ignore him. 'The church is the very next priority?'

'We cannot commit to that now,' said Pa.

The pastor wavered. Pa realised the pastor had to gain a small victory. He said, 'Nkosi, you're a highly respected member of our community, and you have been a vital, wise and much valued part of this Committee from the start. I have the utmost respect for your beliefs, and the beliefs of the members of your congregation. I'm sure we can extend our invitation to two seats, and we can promise to put the building of a church on the agenda the very moment the gates are finished. I would also propose that you and I lead a subcommittee to write a constitution for Amanzi, now that we seem to have a party system. You and I both want to ensure religious freedom.'

Now Pa held out his hand for the pastor to shake.

Nkosi allowed the tension to build, surely to demonstrate that he could not be so easily talked round. Then he shook Pa's hand. 'In principle, I accept. But I want to pray over the matter. I will give you a final answer by tomorrow.'

Pastor Nkosi Sebego was on the way out when Domingo stood up. 'While we have the new Intergalactic Council all together—'

'Domingo,' said Birdy. 'Don't. Please.'

'There're things you have to know, Birdy. Like that the KTM are wired. Like that the KTM run on ethanol.'

That silenced them for a second.

'How do you know they run on ethanol?' asked Birdy.

'I took the bikes out on the road where Nico potted them. I wanted to know why they weren't battling with bad petrol. I rode four of them, up and down, not a single misfire. And I smelled it, the exhaust was sort of sweet. And the petrol too. So I took it to our mechanics. They said there were definitely a few modifications made, they think it's a mixture, fifty or sixty per cent ethanol to petrol.'

Pa said, 'Trunkenpolz said he was an engineer . . .'

'It's more than that,' said Birdy. 'It means they have technology. Know-how. Facilities. And for that they need a base. And a base means some kind of community . . .'

'No,' said Domingo. 'I grant you, this indicates a certain sophistication, and we will have to pay attention to the potential implications. But this trash doesn't have a community or a significant base. Their economy is based on hunting and gathering, marauding really, but mostly robbery. If that's your lifestyle, you can't afford to have a base, 'cause why, you're making a lot of enemies, and sooner or later those enemies are going to come looking for you. So you must do like Amanzi, invest heavily in defence, in human and other resources. Which is expensive for hunter-gatherer-robbers. They are not going to do that.'

Birdy nodded. 'Okay. But it also means they don't make the ethanol themselves, because you need a base for that too.'

'That's right,' said Domingo. 'And what will they use to distil ethanol anyway? They don't plant. So here's my theory: Thabo and Magriet said there are guys near Pinetown who make ethanol from sugar cane. I think those guys are exporting to the KTM. And the KTM hunt and gather and rob, and they exchange some of the proceeds for the Pinetown ethanol.'

Pa nodded, agreeing: 'So what you're saying is they will keep coming back, because they have to feed their economy.'

'That's right,' said Domingo. 'Unless we stop them. But it won't be easy, because when your enemy uses guerrilla tactics, you have to fight an unconventional war. They are wired too, they all have CB radios built into the motorbikes, so they can chat to each other, they can talk to a controller a hundred kilometres away, if there is a base-station antenna somewhere. They're becoming a bigger and bigger threat.'

Everyone seemed deep in thought.

'So,' said Domingo, 'that's why I thought, while we are all together discussing the grand future of Amanzi, I also want to table my demands.'

'Your demands?' asked Pastor Nkosi.

'Padre, we've just listened to your demands. Why not mine too?'

Pa sighed. 'Just tell us, Domingo.'

Angrily, Nkosi crossed his arms across his broad chest.

'Thank you. I'll keep it very simple. I'll be the one who has to carry out everyone's election promises once the gates are built. I'm the one who will have to take the war to the KTM. Unless, of course, you have someone else in mind for the job . . .' And he waited, to see what they would say.

'Carry on,' said Pa.

'Okay. Cool. Here's what we're going to need: three shifts of eight people for each gate. That's twenty-four per gate, times three gates, is seventy-two people. Plus three shifts of eight people to permanently guard the Jeep track running up the back of the mountain, into the reserve.'

'We never had gate guards in the reserve,' said Pa.

'True. But the KTM are not stupid. They know they tried a Trojan Horse strategy at our gates, and it failed. So what's the next option? Find the soft underbelly. There are two soft underbellies: the dam, and the Jeep track up the valley. The dam is highly unlikely, unless they teach fifty guys to swim three kilometres with weapons and ammo, and I don't think that's going to happen. That leaves them with only one option . . .'

'I see,' said Pa.

'Now, where was I? Oh, yes, that makes a total of ninety-six people. And that's just the defence force. I also want two teams of twelve for our Special Ops Team, our attack force. Another twenty-four, for a grand total of a hundred and twenty souls. It's not open to discussion or negotiation, those are the numbers. And my final demand: you don't allocate people to me. I get to pick people, from the ranks of anybody and everybody who volunteers. Also not open to negotiation, take it or leave it.'

'And if we leave it?' asked Nero Dlamini.

'Then I pack my bags, and I take two horses, and I head off. I wouldn't mind seeing the ocean again . . .'

I want to forget the next morning, that Monday morning.

Till this day the memory is a hard thing inside here, a beast that gnaws at my heart with its jagged teeth. I wish I could turn back time, walk into the dining room and sit down beside my father, and then I would do it all differently, I would tell him I love him, admire him, that I can only dream of one day being the man he is.

But I can't. The damage was done for good, and the pain can't be erased.

Here is my rationalisation, my explanation, my mitigating circumstances: I was nearly sixteen. The age of idiocy.

I was angry at Pa, an anger that originated in the days when he had fever, when we had to hide in the house, the one on the corner of Aalwyn and Gansie Street, Vanderkloof, the house I still feel uneasy to walk past. An anger that came from the day when he stood, bewildered, outside the truck in Koffiefontein, so small and vulnerable. An anger that was inflamed by the fact that I was forced to shoot the Jeep men, that he never gave me recognition for the dogs that I stopped in the reserve, for the KTM that I stopped in the main road. That I saved Okkie, that I helped to fetch the diesel aeroplane. Anger that he neglected me, that he gave his time and his dedication to Amanzi, the time and attention that once had been all mine.

And I was ashamed of my father. I was ashamed that he was so easily overshadowed and pushed aside by Pastor Nkosi, that last night he had caved in to Nkosi and Domingo when they made their demands and set their ultimatums. I suppose I constantly compared Pa and Domingo with each other, and saw Pa as the weaker one. Pa wanted to compromise, to accommodate, Pa saw people as people, wonderful beings that were capable of being noble. In my sixteen-year-old mind Pa was a weakling.

That's what I have to offer as an excuse. Here is what happened, that Monday morning.

I had to return to school, the wound had healed sufficiently for me to sit in class. But I was still excused from my Orphanage duties. So I dressed early, hobbled to the dining room on crutches, saw Pa and Okkie eating at a table.

I decided to inform Pa of my intentions now.

I sat down with them. Pa greeted me. I was so determined to have my say that I didn't notice how heavily responsibility rested on him, how bloodshot his eyes were from lack of sleep. Okkie was buoyant and bubbly as usual, he wanted to talk, he also wanted crutches, asked

if I really had to go to school, he had really liked it that I was trapped
in the Orphanage with the injury.

I hushed him. I said, 'Pa, I want to leave school in August. For the
Special Ops Team.'

It was as though Pa had to come back from somewhere in order to
understand what I was saying. He looked at me, then said, 'No, Nico.'

'Pa, you don't have a choice. I'm sixteen in August.' That was the
age restriction that the Committee had set last night when they
responded to Domingo's demands.

'No, Nico.'

Much later, when I think back to that conversation, I would realise
that Pa wasn't forbidding me with the 'no, Nico' he was shielding and
pleading with me. I would realise he hadn't set the age restriction the
previous night because he knew that I would be the first to volunteer.
He negotiated it as a broad principle, for the benefit of all. But all night
I had lain in bed trying to anticipate each of Pa's counter-arguments,
preparing what I would say, and now the words burst out, with teenage selfishness and insensitivity, along with all the anger and shame I
felt towards him: 'That's what I want to do, Pa, and you won't stop
me.'

I should have left it there. I should have stood up and walked away.
But no. Like an imbecile, I added, 'I'm not like you, Pa. I never want
to be like that.'

He looked at me in bewilderment. I expected him to lose his temper,
to shout at me, forbid me to join the Special Ops Team. I was ready for
all that.

He didn't do it. His face registered pain, as if I had physically
wounded him. Pa sat at the breakfast table and tears ran down his
cheeks. Okkie looked at Pa, and he looked at me, and he began to cry
too. He got up, walked around the table to my father, grabbed him
round the neck and comforted him, saying, 'Don't cry, Pappa. Don't
cry. I want to be like you.'

I hobbled away on my crutches.

On the way to school I felt guilty. Perhaps, thought the nearly-
sixteen-year-old me, it was necessary to say that. Then, to my greater
shame, I consoled myself. I thought, we are animals. None of this
really matters.

57

Sofia Bergman

Let me just go on a little bit more about the last day's walk, as far as Hanover, because an interesting thing happened, which had quite a surprising result.

I was walking down the farm road. A farm road. In the days before the Fever we talked about a farm road as a road that wasn't a provincial or a regional road. The farmers usually maintained them themselves, because they led to remote sheds or camps. Most of the time they were not wide enough for two vehicles to pass comfortably, and every few kilometres there would be farm gates.

The veld between the road and the fence was usually denser and greener than the other side of the fence, and often duikers or steenbuck would graze there, and when you approached in a car they would run away along the fences. Springhares too. At night many of them were run over.

I walked to Hanover on the farm road because it was shorter. And prettier, the road roughly following a small river. My feet were sore, but the plasters and the underwear in the boots and the Disprins helped. I can't say I looked around much. I can't remember if I looked behind me at all in those three days of walking and cycling. Why would you look behind you when you knew you were the only one in your world?

It was about eleven in the morning, such a beautiful day in the Karoo, not very hot yet. And something made me look back.

There was a jackal behind me. A black-backed jackal, a rooijakkals. My father hated the black-backed jackal with a passion, they were sheep killers, but more than that, they would kill a whole string of sheep and only eat a bite here and a bite there from the sheep. They were wasteful, Pa said, and in the Karoo you just can't afford to waste. But my father had a peculiar respect for those jackals. He always said it was our fault the jackals became so clever. Because the people, the farmers, shot out all the dumb jackal, and only the clever ones survived, and they bred with each other, and so the farmers unintentionally applied their own genetic manipulation and bred a super-jackal. That's why it became impossible to eradicate jackal in the Karoo.

When I looked back, the jackal was behind me in the road. Less than a hundred metres. A beautiful big rooijakkals, his neck and back pitch-black, the rest a shade of russet like the hair I always believed Esau in the Bible must have had. And that bushy tail. If you've seen a jackal then you know what a jakkalsdraffie is, the way they trot so effortlessly, sometimes at an angle, half skew. He was following me like that. All down the road.

I didn't have the feeling that he was anything more than curious. Really. And so we went on – I limped along, and he did his jakkalsdraffie – for more than an hour, all along the farm road. As if we were fellow travellers.

And when I looked back again, he was just gone, and I felt a little bit alone. But also blessed that we had spent that time together. What had been going through the jackal's mind for that hour? I still wonder today.

And here's the surprising result of that hour or so: when Nico and I began naming the years, I remembered the jackal. The Year of the Jackal was named after him; even though Nico and the Amanzi people had jackal losses in the flocks in the reserve that same year, it was the jackal on the road we named the year after.

It was Nico and I who began naming the years like that, mostly animal names. We told each other our stories of what happened to us after the Fever. And then we couldn't remember which year it was, and we would say: 'Man, that year of the crows.' And I think it also had to do with the fact that we and our generation were part of something new. We weren't simply an extension of the old era, we were the post-Fever children.

Oh, we had a set of Encyclopedia Britannica that they found in a store-room of the school library in Philippolis. The encyclopedia said the Chinese also named years after animals, according to their zodiac. Every twelve years they repeated it. They had the Year of the Rat, and then came the Ox, the Tiger, the Rabbit, the Dragon, Snake, Horse, Sheep, Monkey, Cock, Dog and Pig.

It inspired us to keep on with our own zodiac.

Our zodiac, mine and Nico's, doesn't repeat. It helps us to remember our life. And today everyone in Amanzi uses it. It's unique to us.

58

Sofia Bergman

The N1 was a main artery, before the Fever. A 'mad house'.

When we drove to Bloemfontein and Pa was in a hurry, he would drive to the N9 and from there via Middelburg to Colesberg. He always said you stay off the N1 as long as possible because 'it's a mad house'. That's how I remember the N1 as child-before-the-Fever: a very wide, busy highway with people racing between Cape Town and Johannesburg in cars, lorries, buses and vans. You could never be on the N1 and not see another vehicle, it was that busy, day and night.

By sunset on the Day of the Jackal I arrived in Hanover on the N1 and it was as quiet as the grave. It took me by surprise; somehow I believed there would be people there. I knew I hadn't thought it through properly, but still it took time to realise that nothing you remember is as it once was.

Nothing.

First I went to the Caltex garage beside the N1, on the southern end of town. There used to be a woman who made hamburgers, delicious hamburgers. Now there was nobody, but I could see people had been there, someone had made a fire not that long ago, right where the cars stopped to fill up, and I thought, boy, that's risky. I had no idea that the petrol had all been used up a long time ago.

There was nothing to eat, the little roadside café was entirely empty, just a lot of broken cold drink bottles in the corner.

Then I went into town, to the Exel diesel depot where the big trucks stopped, and there it was the same story, there was nothing, nothing but trash.

The sun set, and I saw the signboard, Hanover Lodge Hotel, and I went there. The hotel was on the corner, opposite the Pop-In supermarket. I went into the hotel. There wasn't any rubbish, everything was tidy, though dusty. I picked a room. It was deep dusk outside, I wanted to take off my shoes, rest my feet. The double bed was beautifully made up, all in white. I sat down on the bed, took off the rucksack, took out my torch and clicked it on. I pulled off the boots, that was a huge relief, and the bed was so soft.

I did a foolish thing. I switched on Pa's cellphone.

It said: No signal.

You don't think, you just keep going. I went into the bathroom. There was a little bar of purple soap, and shampoo and shower gel. I opened a tap at the basin and water gushed out. I turned it off straight away, and thought, I could have a really good shower, for as long as the water lasted.

I closed the door, undressed, and jumped under the shower. I washed quickly, the water was ice-cold, but it had been a hot day. I shampooed my hair, washed my body. I smelled fresh, and I realised that my clothes and socks did not.

I sat down on the bed, and then it hit me: there was nobody on the N1, and there was nobody in Hanover. I didn't have enough food to walk to Bloemfontein. If there was nothing to eat in the Pop-In supermarket or in the hotel or any of the houses in the town, I would have to make another plan.

There must be more people who survived, I knew there must. At Colesberg, perhaps? At the massive Gariep Dam on the other side of Colesberg – water was always something that attracted people, that helped people survive, make a life.

I didn't know ...

What I didn't know, was that was the last night of my life that I would be so completely alone.

59

The first KTM war: I

We were a divided community after the second KTM attack. Divided into two camps, Free Amanzi and the Mighty Warrior Party, and nobody was happy because our precious unity had been fragmented.

'Paradise lost,' Nero Dlamini called it.

And Pa and I had lost each other too.

Pa kept on reaching out to me, but I was an idiot. A sixteen-year-old idiot.

At least we were united in our urge to build the new gates of the town. Every able person helped: mixing cement, making bricks, collecting sand and stone, digging foundations, and building. The main gate rose up, an imposing structure where the old bus gate had been. People said it would take a tank to break through it.

Early in July – and in consultation with Domingo – the Committee appointed the former police sergeant Sizwe Xaba as head of the Amanzi defence force, so that Domingo could concentrate on the training of SpOT, as the Specials Operations Team soon became known. And the members of the attack force soon became known as the 'Spotters'. Although Birdy called them the Spotties, just to rile Domingo.

Their relationship was stormy; they had loud arguments that the whole Orphanage could hear, mostly over Domingo's attitude. And then they'd be seen later sitting on a rock on the ridge chatting calmly as though nothing had happened. Their relationship was still unusual, with its own unique logic: he asked her out, she said 'no' in a way that led him to believe she might say 'yes' tomorrow.

Nearly seventy people reported for selection for the Spotters. Domingo made them run, all the way up to the reserve, down the other side, along the shore of the dam back to town, over thirty kilometres, steep ups and downs, difficult terrain.

Half of them threw in the towel before they reached the halfway mark. Only twenty-six completed the course.

Domingo made them shoot. One of the strongest candidates, a big, strong Namibian, missed every target.

'What's wrong with you?' Domingo asked angrily.

'I lost my glasses, a year ago.'

'So you can't even see the target?'

'No.'

Domingo sent him away.

Twenty-one qualified. Three fewer than Domingo required. It made me excited. I wanted to fill one of those three vacancies. I couldn't wait until I was sixteen. I exercised my injured leg, I had less than two months to go. I knew I could shoot better than anyone except Domingo.

Outside the main gate, between the large traffic circle and the river, is a hill where the Department of Water Affairs' offices and stores used to be. It was now the headquarters and barracks of SpOT. On 22 August at six in the morning I reported at the front door of the large ugly old building, with my R4 DM and my R6.

The guard at the door looked irritated. 'What do you want, Nico?'

'I turned sixteen today.'

He nodded. He understood. 'Wait here.'

I waited a whole hour, until both the SpOT teams came running out in step, in uniform, with backpacks, rifles. Domingo ran in front. He saw me. He called halt.

'I hear you're sixteen today?'

He already knew that. I had told him the night before that I would see him in the morning. He had nodded. Why was he asking me now?

'Yes,' I said.

'Yes, what?'

'Yes, Domingo.'

The Spotters laughed. But Domingo didn't. 'You address me as "Captain".'

'Yes, Captain.' I couldn't understand why he was being so fierce with me. We knew each other, we saw each other every night in the Orphanage. At home we were friends.

Domingo called a team member. 'Take him to the Q-store. He can leave those rifles there.'

'Yes, Captain,' the soldier said. And then to me: 'Come.'

He ran, and I ran behind him. The Quartermaster's store was on the first floor. The soldier opened the door and pointed inside. 'Get yourself trousers and shirt, socks and boots. Don't mess up the store. Leave your firearms on the table.'

Everything was stacked on shelves in tidy rows. There were clothes and boots that Domingo had brought from the big army depot in De Aar. I began to look for my size.

'Hurry up,' said the soldier.

I wanted to tell him he was just a private. I was the chairman's son and Domingo's friend. I held my tongue, found things that fitted.

'No, put them on here and leave your clothes on the table. If you don't make it, you must fetch them here tonight.'

'I'll make it.'

He laughed quietly. He was three years older than me, but not much taller. And I knew I could run further than he could, and shoot much better. If he could do it . . .

At that moment I actually knew nothing about the Special Operations Team and their training. They were separated from the rest of Amanzi, and when they came to town at weekends, they didn't talk about Domingo or what they did each day. We civilians only saw them in their uniforms sometimes running off in step somewhere, or we would hear them shooting, both day and night.

It didn't matter. I was full of confidence. I was the hero of the Great Diesel Expedition, the eliminator of twelve KTM bikers.

I folded my clothes, put on the new kit. The starched green and brown camos were tight against my skin and smelled of mothballs. We walked out and he closed the door behind me. The private and I ran down the stairs again and outside. The two SpOT teams were practising drills in front of the building. We ran to Domingo.

'That one is yours.' Domingo pointed at a rucksack and R4 that were leaning against the wall.

'Yes, Captain.'

I picked up the rucksack and rifle. It was a common R4, scratched and dented and neglected. The rucksack was heavy.

Domingo took a stopwatch out of his pocket. He turned to the two teams. He shouted, 'It's now seven o'clock.'

Both SpOT teams shouted back, loudly, in perfect time, 'Yes, Captain.'

'How far is Luckhoff?'

'Thirty kilometres, Captain.'

'How much time does he have?'

'Seven hours, Captain.'

Domingo looked at me. 'You heard that?'

'Yes, Captain.'

'You have to run to Luckhoff, and back again. To here. Sixty kilometres. In seven hours.'

'Yes, Captain.'

'Seven hours.'

'Yes, Captain.'

'You may not use the road. If anyone sees you on or near the road, you'll be disqualified. Understand? If you disqualify yourself, you can come back when you're seventeen.'

Why was Domingo talking to me formally now? He'd always talked to me like best buddies, now he seemed to want to exclude me from something.

'Yes, Captain.'

'On the corner of Fowler and Barnard in Luckhoff there's a stone. Under the stone is a letter. Read the letter, put it back as you found it. Come and tell us what the letter says.'

'Yes, Captain,' I shouted, like the Spotters shouted, but I was hurt. 'Come and tell *us*,' Domingo had said. He was with them, against me.

'What are you waiting for?'

I stood, unsure that he meant me to start running. The Spotters laughed.

I swung the rucksack on to my back. I picked up the rifle. I began to run.

'You can use the bridge,' said Domingo, and pointed at the single-lane bridge below the dam wall.

'Yes, Captain.'

'The stones in your rucksack are marked.'

'Yes, Captain.'

'Seven hours.' He clicked the stopwatch.

The Year of the Jackal, 22 August. It was late winter, that was the only thing in my favour. Summer heat would have made it impossible. Because the sixty kilometres between Amanzi and Luckhoff wasn't really sixty kilometres. It was sixty kilometres if you looked on the one-dimensional map. It's more like seventy if you take the terrain into consideration. A difficult seventy, if you can't use the roads. It was a rough landscape, hills and stream beds, up and down, stones and rocks, thorn bushes, gullies and sometimes soft sand. It wasn't a straight line and I didn't have a compass. And I was carrying a loaded rucksack and a rifle and heavy military boots.

For the first fifteen kilometres my anger at Domingo spurred me on.

Why was he treating me this way? I was the one he took to look out over the dam from the reserve, I was the one he had talked to there about social animals. I was the one to whom he had first taught military tactics, when I had to go with Hennie Fly. I was the one he had told, 'You have the restlessness. And the heart. There inside you are predator, a warrior . . .' He had shared his mantra with me: 'The other guy wants to kill me. If I hesitate, I die.' And now he treated me like this?

The greatest injustice of all: I had to run sixty kilometres. All those troops had only done thirty. And I had to do sixty?

I would show him.

For fifteen kilometres I ran as I had practised, one foot in front of the other, my focus ten paces ahead of me, not looking further, just running the next ten steps. The rifle rested on the back of my neck, I watched my step, trying for the most direct line. I was doing nearly nine kilometres per hour. I would make it.

The rucksack grew heavier. The rifle too.

I had run thirty kilometres before, two weeks ago, as part of my preparation, but then I had water with me. And I ran on Jeep tracks. After twenty-five kilometres I realised how clever Domingo was. The R48, the tarmac road to Luckhoff, ran past a large hill. If there were people on that road, they would see me, whether I ran over the hill, or around it. Over was tough, it was high. Around was far, it would add another five or six kilometres.

Two difficult alternatives.

I chose to go over.

It sapped my strength. What if I left the stones in the rucksack here, and picked them up again on the way back? No. What if someone was waiting in Luckhoff to see if I was carrying the stones?

Down the other side, I could see the town down below; my knees wanted to give way down the slope. Then my leg began to hurt, that one that had been wounded. A faint ache, a dull throb. I thought it had healed completely.

I was worried. How much more was it going to hurt? I ran more slowly. I had enough time.

I ran into town. I saw that it had taken me three hours and thirty-one minutes. I would have to run back faster. I didn't know if I could.

Beside the stone on the corner of Fowler and Barnard Street was a military water bottle. It was full of water. I unscrewed it and drank. The water was lukewarm and tasted of copper. I lifted the stone. The message in the letter was: *Shake a leg. Time's a-wasting.*

60

The first KTM war: II

Sofia Bergman

A deserted town at dawn is a much lonelier place than a one-man farm.

I was up early, I washed and dressed and went looking for food in the Pop-In supermarket. There was nothing. Literally nothing on the shelves. The shop had been thoroughly and systematically emptied.

I walked down Market Street. A family of meerkats scampered across the street. I went into houses and guest houses, looked in kitchens and pantries. Nothing to eat, everything taken. I walked back to my hotel room.

I collected all my things and walked down to the hotel dining room. The tables were set with white tablecloths and small white salt and pepper pots, cutlery that didn't shine any more. Everything under a layer of Karoo dust. Animals and insects had nibbled on the tablecloths and place mats.

I ate my biltong and drank my water and imagined it was a banquet in a castle. I checked my supplies. I had rations for another two days. I couldn't remember how far Bloemfontein was from Hanover. Three hours by car? Four hours? Let me be conservative and say it was four hundred kilometres. That wasn't so far. And there were towns along the way. Colesberg was a bigger town, there might be someone there, or something to eat, and it might be two days' walk away. Three, if I had to hunt food as well. I could hunt, I could survive.

I stood up, determined to face the challenge that lay ahead.

I heard the sound of engines in the distance. A whole lot of engines.

I ran towards the N1.

I didn't make it. Not even close. I ran the sixty kilometres that were more like seventy in just under eight hours.

'Ran' is not the truth. The last fifteen kilometres I jogged and stumbled and staggered and walked and fell.

It was the boots and the rucksack and my leg that sank me. The boots chafed more and more, until the pain in both my heels became unbearable. After nearly fifty kilometres I stopped and pulled off the boots. The blisters on my heels burst, bits of skin stuck to the socks, they bled, burned like fire. I put the socks and boots back on. I should never have stopped, they hurt more than ever. The rucksack jolted and chafed and the weight felt like lead. And my leg throbbed, excruciating, as I stumbled on.

When my watch told me seven hours had passed, the pain of humiliation burned through me as well. I had told my pa I didn't want to be like him and now I was. All my heroic deeds would be forgotten now. I would just be the little brat who thought because he was the chairman's son, and sat near Domingo at night, he could just become a Spotter, like that.

And the pain of betrayal. Domingo had betrayed me.

It was to preserve the last shred of honour that I kept on. At least I could show that bunch of troops who had looked down on me this morning that I could finish the sixty, even though it was twice as much as they had had to do. But I would never speak to Domingo again, he was dead to me, he had stabbed me in the back in every possible way.

The hardest was the last two kilometres, through the gap of the one-lane bridge, across the Havenga Bridge, and up the hill to the SpOT headquarters. Exhaustion was greater than the pain.

I hobbled the last two hundred metres, there was nothing else I could do.

I saw them waiting for me. Two teams, in line, standing at attention. Domingo in front of them, stopwatch in hand. I walked up to him. He pressed the stopwatch.

He shouted so that everyone could hear: 'Seven hours, fifty-seven minutes.'

I stood, my head bowed.

They began to clap. First slowly, and, I thought, sarcastically. But then louder and faster. I looked up at Domingo. He face gave nothing away behind the dark glasses.

The applause subsided. Domingo said, 'It's the sixth fastest time.'

I didn't understand.

Domingo looked at the two teams. 'Was it good enough?'

'Yes, Captain,' they shouted back.

Domingo nodded and thrust out his hand to me. 'Welcome to the Spotters.'

On 23 August I moved to the barracks of the Special Ops Team. I was assigned to Team Bravo. My life changed irrevocably. SpOT was my new home. My room in the Orphanage was given to a child who had grown too big for the children's communal dormitory.

The Spotters were my new kin. Team Bravo was my new family. Some weekends when we were off I would go and visit Pa and Okkie, but it wasn't the same any more, even though Okkie was over the moon when he saw me, even though I tried to spend as much time as possible on Saturdays and Sundays with him. Because the bond between Pa and Okkie had strengthened. As though Okkie were taking my place with Pa. And Pa with Okkie. Pa seemed to have made peace with the fact that he had lost me. He was courteous to me, warm even, but not in the old way.

I was still only sixteen, but I was old and intelligent enough to know it was Pa's way of handling and processing the pain that I had caused. It made me feel guilty, but I didn't dwell on it, I rationalised it and worked it away. And boy, did Domingo make us work. Long, intense days, and often nights too. The longer our training continued, the more I was certain he had a military background. Not just what he taught us – the drills, the discipline, tactics, weapons and hand-to-hand combat, map reading, veld survival, action and reaction – but also the way he taught us, the methods, the jargon, his skill and the quiet self-confidence, everything together said he knew exactly what he was doing.

On 24 March in the Year of the Dog I shot two men in Boom Street, Vanderkloof. I was thirteen years old. That was the first day of the end of my childhood.

And 22 August in the Year of the Jackal was the last day of my childhood. From the next day on I was a soldier. We were in a war and many battles lay ahead. And it was good and right, because in my heart I was a predator, a warrior, and I would remain that for the rest of my life.

19 November

I was the youngest member of SpOT Team Bravo. We rode in the trailer of the Volvo truck – the same horse that Pa and I came to Vanderkloof in that first time. But with a different trailer. Shorter. Modified. There were hidden peepholes and camouflaged firing holes. There were steel plates welded over to protect us. There were racks for guns and ammunition, and air vents so we wouldn't suffocate or get too hot. There were bins for food and water and personal possessions, as we might have to spend hours or days in there, who knew. There was an electric hot plate and a kettle and a small fridge.

The lorry was a copy of Thabo and Magriet's, it was the bait; down the side were the words: *Peace to you. We Trade Food.*

Up front in the cab were our two oldest Bravo members, Cele and Brits. Cele drove. They had let their hair and beards grow, they looked like gypsies, like pedlars.

Team Bravo.

Domingo broke down my impetuousness, my pride and my individuality. He reduced me, like all his troops, to just a member of the team. That was all that existed for us, all that was important to us. The team. It was our world. Cele and Brits. Jele, Taljaard, Esau, Ximba, Aram, Masinga, Jakes, Wessels and me. I was now only known as Storm, as Spotters had no Christian names.

We hunted the KTM on the N1. We knew they were there. We knew they had lookout posts and radios. We knew their strategy was first to observe. Two or three motorcycles: Domingo called them the Scouts. So we all called them that. When the KTM Scouts were satisfied that their prey could be caught, they let the others know by radio. Then they sent the Shepherds – six motorcycles that followed a vehicle and drove them on, like a shepherd, into the ambush.

We knew, because that was what they did with our expeditions. Those who survived told us.

Today we are taking the war to the KTM, today was our first revenge attack.

Sofia Bergman

I reached the N1 just in time to see them arrive.

If you stand in the middle of the road and look to the south-west, the road makes a turn to the left. So you can hear them coming, but you can't see anything until they are relatively close.

I stood there out of breath from running, the noise of the engines growing, closer and closer, and my heart sang; there were other people, there was life on the N1, everything was going to be okay. I had my rifle over my shoulder and my crossbow on my rucksack, in the middle of the N1. I smelled the tarmac heating in the early summer morning sun, and the unique Karoo dust smell of roads, and then I saw the first one come around the bend and I jumped out of the way. It was a motorcycle, the rider lying low as he took the bend, approaching at high speed, then another and one more and another. I stood on the edge of the road beside the N1 and waved as they shot past – one, two, three, four, five, six, seven, eight, nine, ten, eleven, twelve; the wind from each one moved my hair so that I had to brush it back. I stood and waved my hand like a child at a parade, and I thought, if they don't stop, that meant there were lots of people in this new world, it was nothing strange to see a girl standing beside the N1 here near the deserted town that once was Hanover.

Then they turned around.

Team Bravo had eleven members. Plus Domingo.

We should have been twelve, but not enough people could complete the selection trials. They tried – new arrivals, people who turned sixteen, others who had tried before and failed and wanted to try again.

We were the crème de la crème.

Two were in the cab in front. Nine at the back. Plus Domingo. Each of us had our full fighting kit on. Helmets. Earphones so we could hear each other – and the two up front.

Team Alpha were at the base in Amanzi. Domingo had flipped an old five-rand coin to decide which team would take part in the first operation. Bravo won. Now we believed we were the better team.

'Contact,' said Brits from the passenger seat up front. 'From the rear.'

Our hearts all beat a little faster.

We took up our positions at our peepholes. Mine was at the port side of the trailer. Domingo taught us to talk about port and starboard when we worked with vehicles. When Pa heard me say 'port' he said, 'Oh, that's left. Do you know how I know?'

He said that to Okkie, not me.

'No, how do you know, Pa?' I asked.

Pa kept looking at Okkie. He said, 'It comes from the days when ships were steered with a rudder that was fixed on the right side of the boat, so the ship tied up with the left side against the dock when it was in port. So port side is the left. Cool, hey?'

'Cool!' Okkie chortled.

I was no longer part of Pa's Team Alpha.

My spyhole in the port side of our assault vehicle, our Trojan Horse, was the one that no one wanted. It was the one that you could see nothing through, except the veld beside the road. The best spyholes were those that looked to the front and the right and the rear. But I was the youngest member of the team. My teammates sometimes called me the 'Beardless Wonder' when I beat them on the shooting range. I got the peephole that nobody wanted.

'Two bikes,' said Domingo. He looked towards the rear. He could look through any spyhole, as he pleased, because he was the captain. 'It's the Scouts.'

The question was, would the KTM Scouts see there was something special about our lorry? Or something suspicious?

Domingo quickly moved to a peephole on the right side. 'Here they come . . .'

And then to the one looking forward.

'They're studying our merchants up front,' he said. And then to Cele and Brits in the cab. 'Just wave at them, nice and friendly.'

I could hear two motorbike engines above the drone of our diesel. Our Volvo was running on the very first diesel that had been produced in Amanzi from sunflower oil. So far it ran as smooth as silk. I stood and listened while the seconds turned to minutes, Domingo still looking out, the KTM still beside us. Why so long? What did they suspect?

'There they go.'

The tension ebbed in the trailer. We heard Brits let out a breath in the cab. 'Wait and see,' he said.

'So far, so good,' said Captain Domingo.

61

The first KTM war: III

Sofia Bergman

*They slowed and turned, all twelve of them, then stopped next to me, revving
their bikes, making an incredible racket. I laughed, I was so happy to see
them, to hear the noise, the sound of human activity. They turned their bikes
off, removed their helmets. They all had black helmets. All had firearms
fastened to their backs. Long hair and beards, all men.*

*'Doll,' said the one in the middle, with a touch of grey in his long hair,
and what Pa used to call a whisky nose. His small brown eyes sparkled
mischievously, like a naughty boy. He seemed to be the oldest, and at that
moment I liked him. 'Where the hell did you come from?'*

'From the farm,' I said.

*'You've got to be kidding me,' said Whisky Nose. And his companions
laughed, all of them having a good laugh at me.*

Nine a.m. We were driving on the N1 between Three Sisters and
Richmond. We ate our rations (rusks from our own bakery, biltong
from the butchery) and drank tea with no sugar (but with milk from
our own dairy). We waited to see if the KTM Scouts had taken the
bait. The Volvo growled on at eighty kilometres per hour.

Our entire plan of attack was aimed at driving into an ambush.
Over and over we had practised shooting from inside the trailer, how
to jump out. How to go into nearby buildings, sweep and secure them,
room by room.

We learned to cover each other in the veld while moving forward,
on flat terrain, in hills, from above or below.

My rifles were beside me, an ordinary R4 and my R4 DM. I
was the sharpshooter, the sniper. I was the team member who had

to cover everyone. They trusted me, believed in me. We trusted each other, we were brothers and sisters. Esau and Masinga were the women in Team Bravo. Esau held the record for the most sit-ups in one minute. Sixty-one. At nineteen years old she was a machine.

We collected every single report of every expedition, vehicle and arrival that had been stopped or attacked by the KTM. And everyone who had been led into an ambush by the KTM. We knew the KTM were clever. They didn't use the same spot each time. Sometimes the ambush was in a town like Hanover or Colesberg on the N1, or Middelburg on the N9, or Smithfield on the N6. Sometimes – especially on the district roads – the ambush was where people were forced to slow down, like a mountain pass with its sharp bends, or a place where the road surface had eroded badly. Sometimes it was just a random place.

We believed the KTM consisted of eight or ten separate cells, because they were active over such a wide area. We suspected that the main concentration was in and around Bloemfontein, but the different cells covered different routes.

We wanted to take some of them captive so we could get more information. To do that we had to drive into an ambush first.

Our battle cry for today was 'Don't let a single one get away.' That was what Domingo made us shout out loud, for hours on end, on the parade ground. If a single one of them got away, he would tell the rest there was a war on the way. We wanted to maintain the element of surprise as long as we possibly could.

Just past Richmond Cele called from the cab, 'Here they come. Up ahead.'

Everyone with a forward view went to a peephole. The rest of us heard the roar as they raced at us, then past us. 'I count ten of them,' said Brits.

'So do I,' said Domingo. I heard the satisfaction in his voice, as if he were looking forward to what lay ahead.

I couldn't say that I looked forward to it. I was afraid, but I hid it well.

Sofia Bergman

Whisky Nose pushed his motorbike stand out with a booted foot, climbed off the bike and walked up to me. I put out my hand to greet him. 'I'm Sofia Bergman, sir,' I said.

The men chuckled. A few said 'Sir!', and then they guffawed louder. He didn't shake my hand, just looked me up and down. He was a big man, much taller than me, his belly hanging over a thick black leather belt.

'Sofia,' he said, 'you're a pretty little doll, aren't you?' and he raised his hand and squeezed my breast. I was shocked, enraged. How rude. I smacked his hand away and he hit me full in the face, his fist connecting with my cheekbone. I stumbled backwards.

To be honest I still wasn't afraid at that point. I just hadn't expected it, because he had such mischievous eyes, and now I was furious, because he was a disgusting swine. And my cheek hurt.

More laughter from his cronies, mocking, jeering now. Whisky Nose grabbed my rifle. 'Don't want you to shoot me, doll,' he said, tugging me off balance, the rifle still strapped over my shoulder.

'I think Number One will want this one for himself,' one of the other men said.

'Number One isn't here,' said Whisky Nose, and he grabbed me by the hair and yanked me upright. It hurt like crazy. I saw red, and shot up and hit him in the face with my fist, right on his ugly nose, because he was a disgusting swine.

More jeering, as Whisky Nose hit me back, so hard on the head that I fell to the ground, dazed.

'The radio,' said one of them loudly. 'They're calling us on the radio.'

The laughter and mockery stopped. I lay on the ground, dizzy, a rushing in my ears. I heard a faint voice over the radio. 'There's a truck coming, ETA Hanover thirty minutes.'

I looked up, saw the man with the whisky nose walk away from me, pick up the handset, speak into it: 'That's too close to us, we'll ambush in Colesberg.'

'Roger,' said the radio voice.

He walked back towards me and I tried crawling away from him on my hands and knees, but he grabbed me by the rucksack and dragged me to the other motorbikes. 'Cable-tie her hands, let's go.'

When the KTM shepherds positioned themselves behind us, Domingo gave the order: 'Battle stations.' That meant we each had to buckle ourselves in to our places, so that no one would be hurt if the driver braked suddenly.

Domingo described what he saw through the peephole: they rode in formation, one up ahead, three side by side. They kept a distance of nearly two hundred metres from the Volvo, also travelling around eighty kilometres per hour. Each KTM rider had a rifle slung across his back.

'Stand by, Hanover coming up,' said Cele from the front.

'Stand by,' said Domingo.

My heart hammered in my chest.

The Volvo slowed.

Nobody said a word.

Eventually: 'Nothing,' said Brits. 'Not Hanover then.'

Sofia Bergman

They tied my hands behind my back. Whisky Nose climbed on to his bike, and one of the others manhandled me on to the back of his motorcycle. They tied us together with a length of rope. I still had the rucksack on my back. The crossbow was strapped to it, but I didn't know where my rifle was.

Whisky Nose said to me, 'You can try whatever you like, doll. But at a hundred and sixty the tarmac road will make mincemeat of you.'

I was bound so close against him I could smell his foul breath, and his body odour – old sweat and booze. He put his helmet on and pulled away, so fast that I was jerked back and would have fallen off if I hadn't been tied to him.

He rode fast, my hair blew in the wind, I thought, now it's going to get full of knots. At least I couldn't smell him now.

Cele said, 'That sign says ten kilometres to Colesberg.'

Dead silence in the back of the trailer. We had been waiting more than forty minutes. We were uncomfortable, wound up, set to go, yet nothing had happened, except for the Shepherds behind us.

'Stay sharp,' said Domingo.

In my mind I ran through everything I must do when we made contact.

One. Open the firing hole beside me, the one facing portside.

Two. Look. If I saw an 'Ali Baba' – the term that Domingo used for the enemy – and I could hit him, then I had to shoot. Single shots. Disciplined. Accurate.

Three. When my port sector was completely clear, I had to shout 'port side front clear'.

Four. When Domingo shouted 'deploy', I would know Phase One of the attack was successful. Then I had to free the ladder. It was suspended from the roof, I had to pull a rope that withdrew the locking pin. I had to pull that ladder down, take my R4 DM and climb up the ladder. I had to open the hatch in the roof and first make sure it was safe to stick my head out.

Five. I had to give sniper cover to Team Bravo.

We had practised it over and over. I was as ready as I ever would be.

Minutes dragged by.

Domingo said, 'The Shepherds are falling back. This is it. Cele, maintain your speed, and then drive a little bit faster as if you're glad they've lost interest.'

A moment of silence, then a sharp warning from Cele, 'There they are!' He hit the brakes. My back slammed into the seat behind me, my helmet hit the steel panel.

62

The first KTM war: IV

Sofia Bergman

There, on the N1, on the back of that motorcycle, I realised I was in trouble.

It's hard to explain quite how naïve I was. I grew up so sheltered, my parents, my brothers . . . And then the three years on the farm with Meklein and Vytjie, two loving people, it made you believe all people were like that: caring. Gentle and harmless. The things that happened at Hanover happened so fast, so unexpectedly, that I couldn't process it. And then the blow to my head as well. But when I had been on the back of that motorcycle for half an hour, I had time to think, and I realised I was in deep trouble, these were not good people. And then I knew I had to get away. They had to stop somewhere, somewhere I would find my chance. And I thought, okay, I've got the Leatherman in my rucksack, in the side pocket. That Leatherman had blades and screwdrivers and a file and everything in the handles, but the pliers themselves would easily cut the cable ties. I could threaten this disgusting swine with a blade. Or something. I must just get to those pliers.

I wriggled and squirmed, to see if I could. But old Whisky Nose hit me with his elbow. So I sat still again.

I didn't have a crash helmet on and they were riding very fast; the rushing wind made it hard for me to see, but I knew we were on the N1, I knew the next town was Colesberg, and I thought, if they go on to Bloemfontein there will be people who can help.

As we reached Colesberg they suddenly slowed, at the big junction that was built before the Fever, where the N1 and N9 crossed. Pa always filled up with fuel there, I thought the bikers were also going to fill up, perhaps there would be someone at the garage – can you believe anyone could be so silly as to think that?

They rode under the N9 flyover, and they stopped at the second flyover that bridged the N1. Whisky Nose untied the rope that bound us and he dismounted, and dragged me, and he ran, they all ran. I could see that the road under the bridge was blocked, there were two sections of old lorries blocking the road, right beneath the bridge. Some of the bikers ran up the embankment to sit on top of the bridge, and others hid away behind the lorry parts. All of them had their rifles ready and they called to each other, and Whisky Nose had his radio in his hand. We ran up the embankment to the top of the bridge.

He spoke into the radio. Someone told him, 'No, you've got a good half an hour, the truck isn't in a hurry.'

Whisky Nose yelled to the others, 'We've got half an hour!'

On the bridge there was an old Toyota Prado, its tyres flat. Whisky Nose pushed me into the back door and he said, 'You sit here, and sit still, or I'll belt you again.' He walked to one of the other doors, picked up my rifle, and inspected it. Then he took his weapon and there were these big fuel drums on the side of the bridge that had been placed upright two by two, and on some of the drums there were car doors or corrugated-iron sheets, with stones to keep them in place. I saw Whisky Nose sit down between two drums, under the corrugated iron, and he rested his rifle on the railing of the flyover. That's when it dawned on me they were setting up an ambush. And if you saw everything that had been arranged here, it wasn't the first time they'd done it. They were organised.

But I was alone in the Prado, and began to carefully shift and move and pull and stretch to get the rucksack off my back, or at least my hands on the Leatherman.

My hands were tied behind my back, so it wasn't easy.

But we had half an hour.

The reports on our expeditions that had been led into KTM ambushes varied.

Sometimes the KTM didn't shoot at all. They just threatened, and stole everything that was edible or usable. Sometimes they took women too, or the people under twenty. We never knew what happened to these people.

Sometimes they fired warning shots. Sometimes they would shoot one of the men because he looked dangerous.

We didn't know what to expect. We all wore bullet-proof vests.

Domingo told us you could prepare for contact, you could train as long and as hard as you liked, but when it happened, it was absolute chaos and everything went wrong.

Our Volvo braked, the tyres screeched. It came to a stop. We all regained our balance. Domingo stood in the back of the trailer, looking at the Shepherds. He said, 'Hold your fire.'

I looked out of my peephole. I couldn't see any target. And then Domingo said, 'Fire,' and all hell broke loose.

Afterwards everyone would tell their battle stories, everyone would embellish and embroider, because no one could remember the details exactly. A skirmish is an overdose of adrenalin, it is naked fear, high stress. And it happens faster than you could ever expect, much faster than you can be ready for, in the eye-blink of chaos. But basically what happened was that Domingo waited for the Shepherds to close the cordon around us. And then we started shooting, deafening explosions of sound in the enclosed trailer, the smell of cordite choking us, and smoke, so that I could see nothing outside. Suddenly something ran into my field of vision and I aimed and shot and missed completely. The crack shot of the SpOT team, and I missed. I fired again and again, too quickly. Domingo had told us to fire disciplined, single shots, but we all forgot, everyone except him; we all emptied a magazine in seconds and had to reload. Domingo shouted, 'Single shots, single shots!' Nobody heard him. But I got my man, he was fifteen metres away and I saw the blood spray, I saw the fear and surprise, the way his legs still pumped, trying to run, but he was down. I felt nothing. I felt like an animal. The other guy wants to kill me. If I hesitate, I die. I felt disconnected from that man's death. I forgot to shout that my sector was clear. My ears buzzed, my blood boiled, everyone shouted into our radios.

Cele said, 'I'm wounded, I'm wounded.'

Domingo shook my arm and yelled, 'Is your sector cleared?'

'Yes, Captain.'

'Deploy, deploy, deploy!' shouted Domingo.

I stood rooted to the spot.

Domingo shook me: 'Get your ass up there.'

Shame engulfed me. And doubly so, as I forgot to take my DM, and Domingo had to pull me back and hand the rifle to me.

The rear door was open, daylight streamed in, Team Bravo jumped out. I was up the ladder, and lifted the hatch. I spotted one of the KTM on the flyover in front of the Volvo, sixty metres away, I saw him firing at my comrades, I heard the lead smacking down in front. I got him in the sights, easy shot, and shot him through the forehead.

The rest of Team Bravo advanced, as they had been trained, covering each other, running, covering fire, running, to cover all the sectors.

I looked for targets, I scanned three hundred and sixty degrees, and saw nothing except fallen KTM members.

And then I saw the girl with long blond hair.

At first I just sensed movement, far to the right; out of the corner of my eye, I saw someone running, three hundred metres away. Then I pointed the telescope, and I saw her.

I had never seen anyone run like that, with so much rhythm and grace. She was wearing shorts and boots, and her legs were indescribably long and tanned, and her long blond hair streamed out behind her as she ran. In her hand, she was carrying a wheel spanner.

I realised she was chasing someone with that wheel spanner, her body language showed she was chasing someone, and she was going to hit him with it if she caught him. I moved the scope. There was a KTM man with a fat belly running away from her. He had a crossbow, and was about ten paces ahead of her. She was closing the gap.

Our battle cry was: 'Don't let a single one get away.'

The girl and the KTM man were in the town, in a Colesberg street, between the houses now.

He mustn't get away.

I made the shot.

Sofia Bergman

Yes, I was furious that Nico shot Whisky Nose, because I wanted to hit him with that wheel spanner, the disgusting swine.

I was sitting in the Toyota Prado, in the half-hour we waited, and I wriggled and struggled, but eventually I did get the Leatherman and I cut my hands free, very quietly. Whisky Nose got up and came to check on me, but I lay still, and he touched my leg, pushed his hand up there. You must know, my hands were already free, and I had to clench my teeth not to try to stop him, I knew I had to wait until the right time. But then he left me alone again, walked away and went and sat under the corrugated iron between the drums, and the radios were talking to each other, and I heard the big truck coming, and I heard the big truck braking. And Whisky Nose saying over the radio, 'Okay, Kelly, get those people out of the lorry.'

Suddenly everyone was shooting at each other. Bullets were slamming into the Prado and I dived between the seats and lay wondering what was happening.

But then I felt something tugging at me, and I looked around, and saw Whisky Nose. He was trying to pull the crossbow off my rucksack, which was still on my back. He had used up all his ammunition, now he wanted my crossbow. I realised suddenly that the man was afraid, I saw it on his face, as he wrestled the crossbow free and ran. The others were still shooting, but this guy runs off with my crossbow, the disgusting swine.

So I thought, I want my crossbow back, it was my brother's crossbow. I lay in the Prado with shots going off and bullets hitting all around, and I kept alternating between being scared and angry, so that gave him a head start. Also I was looking for ... I can't say a weapon, 'cause that's not completely true, I was looking for something to sort of give my anger some-thing to hold on to, if that makes any sense. And I saw here under the Prado's seat something sticking out, and I grabbed it, it was the spanner, and it gave me courage to jump out, God knows why. And I jumped out and saw the whisky-nose man was already quite a long way away.

He wasn't that fast, but the rucksack was holding me back. So I threw it off and I ran, spanner in hand. He heard me coming, he heard my boots on the gravel and the tarmac, he looked back, and then he screamed, I don't know what he screamed, but it was the scream of a man who knew he was in trouble, and it was the most beautiful sound that I ever heard in my whole life.

I was catching up with him, and I knew I wanted to whack him with the spanner, just a few times before I took my crossbow back, and then the bullet hit him. It's an awful sound to be so close to someone and hear a bullet hit them, a sick dull sound, and he fell just like a sack of potatoes, just dropped down in the dust.

And then I was furious, because I had wanted to hit him first. He had hit me, he had squeezed my breast and groped my leg, he was a disgusting swine, and I never got the chance to hit him.

★   ★   ★

I had the long-legged girl with white-blond hair in my telescopic sights. I saw her look towards me, with a furious expression. She bent down and picked up the crossbow he had been carrying. I assumed that she was with the KTM. It was a semi-logical assumption. I couldn't let her get away. She was more than three hundred metres away, between houses, chances were good that she was going to disappear from view soon.

I aimed, drew the sights on her, I squeezed the trigger.

63

The first KTM war: V

But I couldn't shoot. Not a girl.

I don't know why.

I released the trigger, and watched through the scope, saw her disappear behind the concrete wall of a house.

Don't let a single one get away.

Everything was suddenly quiet, nobody was shooting any more. Domingo stood beneath the flyover, between the truck wrecks strategically positioned there. He held a fist up in the air. I heard his voice in my earphones: 'Hold your fire.'

I said over the radio, 'Captain, there's a girl who got away.'

'Where?'

'In the town. East.'

'One girl?'

'Yes, Captain.'

'Then go fetch her, Storm.'

I slid back into the trailer and ran to the rear door and jumped down. She had a head start on me and I had seen how she could run. I wouldn't be able to catch up with her.

I ran around the Volvo. I saw Aram and Wessels lift Cele out of the cab, Cele was bleeding from the arm, lots of blood.

I ran. I used the embankment to get up the bridge, where I saw the motorcycles that had been left there.

I swung the rifle strap over my shoulder, jumped on to the nearest motorcycle, started it and raced after the girl.

Sofia Bergman

Now you have to understand, I heard a motorbike coming, and this time I wasn't just a silly farm girl beside the N1, I knew what these men did. So I stopped, and pulled a bolt out of the quiver – the quiver is fastened to the crossbow when you carry it – and I cocked the crossbow, and waited, just around the corner of the wall, and I waited. I heard the engine coming closer and closer, and I held the crossbow ready and I stepped out around the corner and shot the bike rider full in the chest.

She appeared in front of me all of a sudden and shot me with her crossbow. The bullet-proof vest stopped her killing me, but the impact of the bolt was so strong that I fell backwards off the motorcycle, my battle helmet smacked on the tarmac. I was winded, and it felt like my heart had stopped, it was one helluva blow. The motorcycle sailed past her on its own, and I saw her coming. My rifle was behind my back, I gasped for air, saw she was fitting another bolt into the crossbow. This girl was going to kill me. I rolled, heaving, I had to get my rifle free, but there was no time. I stood up, I was slow and winded and sore, but I knew my life depended on how fast I could move.

I was up and charged at her and tackled her to the ground. I sat on her and held her hands down.

Then I had a good look at her. I could see she wasn't afraid, just angry. It was a splendid fury, like a force of nature, a source of magnificent pure energy.

I realised she was the most beautiful girl that I had ever seen in my life. Breathtakingly beautiful.

In that instant I fell in love with Sofia. That was the moment I knew I was going to marry her.

Sofia Bergman

I screamed at him, 'Get off, you disgusting swine, get off.' He just sat there making croaking noises as he tried to breathe, and he smiled, such a stupid smile.

I did not fall in love with him at that moment. Absolutely not. If I had been able to get free I would have shot him dead.

64

The first KTM war: VI

The blond girl and I walked back to Team Bravo and the battlefield. She carried the crossbow and her shoulders in a way that showed me she didn't trust me, and she didn't like me. Even though I kept trying to explain to her we were on the same side.

The bolt was still lodged in my bullet-proof vest, the arrow point enmeshed in the material. I tried to pull it out, but it was stuck fast.

My comrades looked at the bolt, and then at the girl with the crossbow. Then they burst out laughing. Uproariously, the post-adrenalin laughter of survival and relief.

Domingo told us to 'shut the fuck up'. He was furious. He called us pathetic. He said the only goal we had achieved was not letting any of the KTM escape. And that was only by accident. Where, he asked, was the KTM member we could interrogate? Where was the discipline, the control, the presence of mind that our repeated drills had tried so hard to establish?

We stood with heads bowed. The girl stood gaping open-mouthed at it all.

Domingo said we had failed miserably. To defeat a bunch of amateurs in a skirmish in *such* a chaotic fashion, when you had the advantage of total surprise, was nothing less than a disgrace.

He said he was taking us back to base so he could train us from scratch again, because we were hopeless. So that he could fetch Team Alpha, hopefully they would be slightly better than our bunch of morons. So that Cele could see a doctor. So that we could get this 'girlie' – and he pointed at the blond girl, my future wife – out of harm's way. 'Or,' said Domingo and glared angrily at the arrow lodged against my heart like an affront, 'to get Storm out of harm's way from a girlie with a crossbow.'

'I'm not your girlie. I'm Sofia Bergman.'

Domingo glared at her. We all thought for a moment that he would spontaneously combust. Or explode. But he shook his head, looked hard at us and ordered Esau and Masinga to take care of Cele and make him comfortable. The rest of us had to dig graves for the dead KTM members, in the rock-hard ground of Colesberg, out in the veld behind the Merino Inn Hotel. And we were to ride each of the motorcycles over the mountain east of town and hide them away at the water reservoir.

While he sat in the shade and talked to Sofia Bergman.

I wished I could have sat with her. I could think of nothing else besides that girl.

Lizette Schoeman was already completely forgotten.

65

What do you miss the least?

Domingo

As recorded by Willem Storm. The Amanzi History Project.

There was nothing to like before the Fever. Nothing. It was a mad, bad world. Everyone hating everyone else. White and black, haves and have-nots, liberals and conservatives, Christian and Muslim, north and south, I scheme people were just looking for reasons to hate each other: you're taller than me, so I hate you for it.

So I don't mind that that world is gone.

Yeah, of course I hated too. Facebook most of all, if you have to know. Facebook. Hated it. For me that was the epitome of what was wrong with society. 'Cause why, you've got all these friends, but they're not real friends, just people you can post photos for, of your breakfast and your lunch and your cute kitty. I ask you. Like they really cared. They only cared because they needed you as an audience. Facebook friends were an audience, that's all. And it made me sick how they all needed an audience. Society got so impersonal, so don't-care, till we had to validate ourselves on something like Facebook, to an audience of people who don't give a flying ... Let me just say, that's sad. Tragic.

But I'm not saying I'm glad about the Fever. I'm just saying I've got no nostalgia for the time before the Fever. Nothing. Nada.

Cairistine Canary

No, I can't ... Let's just say ... The beggars at the traffic lights in the morning. They were the worst part of the old world for me. And then you can extrapolate to inequality in general. I don't miss that deep inequality, and the guilt. But this is a very philosophical question, and I don't think you *must compare the world before and after the Fever, I don't think you should ask yourself what you miss the most or the least. Because somehow you end up thinking that the one is better or worse than the other. Comparisons can be misleading, and they can lead you to bad places. Every world was what it was. And it's what we make of it, isn't it?*

I guess that's not much of a contribution to your history project, is it?

Lizette Schoeman

I think society was much more ... like, in silos, if you understand what I mean. Like the way we are now in Amanzi, there's a strong sense of community. Of 'we depend on each other'. You understand? It's probably also because here we all know each other, because our world has become so small, but I like it. Before the Fever you saw hundreds or thousands of people every day who you didn't know, who you didn't greet. You walked or drove past, you didn't even look at them, there was no connection between you. Nothing. You might as well have been on different planets.

That's what was wrong with the old world. That's what I don't miss.

Pastor Nkosi Sebego

I don't miss that world. Because it was a godless world. And that's why I am working so hard to make sure that we don't live in a godless world again.

Before the Fever, our president, our government, our media and our businesses were all godless. But not only in our country. In every country, all over the world. Everybody just wanted one thing: money. To get rich. Even if you had to take it or steal it, even if you had to pull other people down to get it. We were in this vicious cycle, we were prisoners of the system. That's why God sent the Fever. To break the shackles.

Abraham Frost

Just a few months before the Fever, I read an article about bananas. They said bananas as we know them are in danger of dying out. And it's the second time.

Apparently there was a species of banana called Gros Michel, a delicious, creamy, sweet banana. About 99 per cent of all the bananas that were grown in the world used to be Gros Michel. And then in the 1960s a fungal disease appeared, and decimated Gros Michel completely. The banana farmers of the world had to get another species; they found Cavendish, which wasn't as delicious, but it was resistant to the fungus.

And so Cavendish became the one that produced 99 per cent of the world's bananas. And then a fungus appeared, a year or two before the Fever and began to wipe out Cavendish as well.

What I'm trying to say, is that we as people created a world that was very unnatural. We created a big imbalance. And then exactly what happened to bananas, happened to us.

That's what I don't miss about the old world. It just feels that now things are back in balance.

Ravi Pillay

I don't miss the traffic jams. You had to see it to believe it. All that time lost, sitting in traffic. Time we could have spent with our loved ones. Or just being productive. We lived in this high-tech world where they put little robot cars on Mars, but they couldn't sort out the traffic jams. They couldn't fix bad driving either. There's another thing I really, really don't miss: those idiots who clog up the fast lane, and when you dare to flash your lights – which is absolutely within your rights to do – they give you the finger. That used to really . . . I was sure I was going to die in a road rage incident some day.

Hennie (Fly) Laas

No, like I said with your previous question: that world before the Fever was a bad one for me. If you ask me, Hennie, what I don't miss, then I want to say: everything, Willem. I don't miss any of it. I know it was all my own fault that I was unlucky in that world, I made my own bad luck. So I don't blame anyone for it. I'm just saying, I'm happy now. And you know why? Because I feel I mean something now. I have worth. It's funny, hey?

Beryl Fortuin

Life before the Fever was like living in the city, and now it's like living in a small town. Literally too, for sure. What I really mean is, there are pros and cons on both sides. I don't miss the hectic lifestyle of that time. The rat race. The competition. I don't miss the scattering of all the people that you love. I mean, you grow up with your people, your family, your community. And then, when you finish school, you have to leave. You have to go and study, or you have to work. Humansdorp was too small to support all of us, so everyone you love, everyone you know so well, scatters. And then you have to start from the beginning again to gather up people to love, but it's never the same.

I don't miss that. I like this about Amanzi: we're not going anywhere soon.

Oh, and then there is the detox myth. I can't tell you how glad I am that I won't read anything about detox this and detox that in a women's magazine or on the Internet again. Lies, damn lies, and detox. Legal fraud, that's what that was.

Nero Dlamini

Interesting question. Okay, I'm going to . . . Just bear with me. There was this recurring theme in therapy that I found interesting . . . No, wait, let me just take one more step backwards, because I really want this to make sense:

The world before the Fever was truly complicated. In the words of the great M. Scott Peck: 'life was difficult.' You could not believe the stress levels ordinary people had to cope with. Just for getting through the day, for navigating all the social and professional and relationship reefs. And then they worried about all the stuff that was happening in the country: politics, and poverty and the economy. And then they worried about all the things happening in the world: terrorism, and recession, and running out of fish to catch, and more plastic than fish in the sea and global warming . . .

So, getting back to that recurring theme: a disturbing number of my patients had this wish, this fantasy, this urge for a new beginning. Just to walk away from their old lives, their old worlds and their old planets, and start over. Free from the worries.

Now, here's the interesting thing: Amanzi's world is not stress-free. Just forget about the trauma of the Fever itself for a minute, and look at this environment right here where we are now. It's not stress-free, we've got a lot to deal with. But I see a huge difference in the stress levels, in the type of stress. *It's as if people can cope better with the simple challenges of feeding themselves, keeping warm, dodging dogs . . .*

So, here's my answer: it seems to me that all of us don't miss those old complexities. And those fears about the world and the planet, those threats that we felt were too big for us to fix.

66

In the Year of the Jackal I turned sixteen. Lizette Schoeman broke my heart, and Sofia Bergman made it whole again, for a while.

In the Year of the Jackal my youth ended, and we fought back for the first time against the KTM.

Okkie turned five. Or six. We will never know exactly.

In December of the Year of the Jackal I began to have Sunday breakfast with Pa and Okkie. It gave me the opportunity to walk past the place where Sofia Bergman lived. That whole month long I didn't see her at all. I cautiously asked other people if they knew where she was.

They said she was mostly in her room on Sundays, reading a book. Apparently she was not a very social person.

Breakfast with Pa and Okkie was uncomfortable. Pa and I had nothing to talk about. When I wanted to tell him about Team Bravo's skirmish with the KTM, he shook his head. 'Not in front of Okkie.' But actually he was the one who didn't want to hear it.

In the Year of the Jackal we made diesel from sunflower oil, cheese from milk, and a bit of sugar from sugar beet for the first time. Our economy shifted more in the direction of capitalism when a bunch of the Namibians established their own irrigation farms further down the Orange River and started selling vegetables on the free market – beans, peas, broccoli, lettuce. Some of them even competed with Hennie Fly's chicken farm by producing ducks and turkeys, and offering them at high prices on the farmers' market that sprang up in the Forum.

We had seventeen marriages, thirty-nine births, and our number grew by more than a thousand people who came to us from all across the subcontinent. The town was bursting out of its seams, and we built gates and fences and houses.

Our first victory against the KTM was small in scale, but immense in what it did for the morale of Amanzi. We became a much more united community so that everyone, to a man (and woman), pagan and believer, big and small, all gathered in the Forum on Christmas Day to listen to the beautiful words of Pastor Nkosi's sermon. Even though he claimed, much to Domingo's exasperation, that it was just their prayers and the Divine Hand of the Lord that helped us win that first battle against the KTM without a single Amanzi loss.

But then, in a much smaller church gathering of his congregation, beside the dam on New Year's Eve, Nkosi preached about his dream of a land of Canaan for the first time, a settlement where no person ruled, only the Divine Hand. A purified community where only Christians would be allowed, that would stand in permanent penance for the sins that unleashed the Fever and the KTM. 'So, let us pray, my brothers and sisters, that the war against the devil will end soon. So that I can lead you to a new beginning, a Promised Land.'

That is how the Year of the Jackal ended.

The Year of the Pig

67

The first KTM war: VII

1 February

Team Alpha's first battle was smaller, shorter and much less intense
and dangerous, despite their best attempts to exaggerate and drama-
tise it with the retelling. But they – Domingo actually – got one thing
right that we couldn't.

On 1 February they drove the Volvo into an ambush, at the place
where the N10 winds through the mountains near Ludlow Station,
just before the N9 junction between Noupoort and Middelburg.

There were no KTM Scouts, there were no KTM Shepherds, just
the sudden roadblock in front of them on the pass. Domingo kept
them calm. When the driver in the Volvo cab said, 'There're KTM
here,' Domingo said in his commander's voice, 'Stay calm, stay calm,
battle stations, they don't know we're in the back here, we still have the
element of surprise.'

Team Alpha made the same mistakes we did. They got just as
carried away, they descended into the same chaos. They were up
against only twelve KTM members, and they very nearly let one get
away. A terrified young KTM rider saw near the end of the skirmish
that the writing was on the wall. He managed to escape on his motorcycle, east, in the direction of the N9.

Our Alpha mates told us Domingo saw it. He jumped on one the
dead KTM men's bike, and set off in pursuit. All that the Alpha
members could do was to listen in the following silence to the high-
pitched whine of the two engines echoing off the mountains, and then
disappearing.

They waited. They checked all the enemies' bodies to make sure
there were none still alive, they began to dig the graves and hid the

other motorcycles in a dry streambed. Twenty minutes. Half an hour. They were worried, they considered sending out some of the team who could handle a motorbike. But then Domingo reappeared around the corner of the twisting road on the KTM bike, and he stopped and told the Volvo driver there was a prisoner of war about thirty-five kilometres away on the N10 on the far side of Middelburg. Fetch him, he's alive, and he'll talk.

They found the prisoner there, tied to a road sign. The motorcycle stood on one side with a bullet through the radiator. The surviving member of the KTM was called Leon Calitz. He was twenty-two years old. He was tall and skinny, with a prominent Adam's apple, sticking-out ears and a gap between his front teeth. He talked fast, incessantly, in wide-eyed amazement, describing how Domingo had put the bullet through his radiator, the two motorcycles side by side, at two hundred kilometres per hour. 'I never saw a guy ride like that.'

Domingo shook his head. He said it wasn't *that* fast.

It all became part of the legend.

2 February

Team Alpha paraded their KTM prisoner and their victory through Amanzi. For that day they were our community's heroes.

Domingo and the Committee interrogated Leon Calitz on 2 February.

Calitz was eager to tell his whole story, to switch his life as a highwayman for the safe haven of our community. He seemed relieved and grateful to escape the clutches of the bikers. With words tumbling out of him like a sigh of relief, he sketched the facts about the KTM. It wasn't like any of us had imagined.

We in the Special Ops Teams would hear it all afterwards: the KTM did not exist.

What did exist was a loose network of plunderers. 'Clans', Calitz called them, with a respect in his voice, but Domingo said, 'Crap. They're a bunch of common gangs.'

Most of these gangs were on motorbikes. There were others that used pick-up trucks, in the eastern parts of the country. Even horses. Or a combination of vehicles.

These gangs robbed, stole and collected, using most of their edible loot themselves, and delivered the rest to a central buyer that – ironically it seems – was known as the 'Sales Club'.

Leon Calitz said he had been a member of a biker clan, the Marauders, for the past nineteen months – the gang that Team Alpha had practically wiped out near Ludlow Station on the N10 the previous day. Calitz came from Vereeniging, he had heard of the biker clans there, and had gone to look for them on his Honda CRF450; he wanted to be part of something exciting, something strong. The first bikers he encountered were the Marauders, on their way from Kroonstad to Cradock 'after a Sales Conference was over'. The Marauders interrogated him, roughed him up for an hour and threatened him, then watched him suspiciously for two weeks before he was initiated in a ceremony involving enormous amounts of liquor. They promised him a bigger motorcycle, an automatic assault rifle, fraternity, food security and lots of 'good times' and adventures.

There were other gangs, for example the Tribe, the Vikings, the Freedom Riders, the Death Squad. Some were big, up to thirty members, others considerably smaller, but none fewer than ten members. The Marauders usually had between ten and sixteen members. Some members deserted, some had accidents and were injured, died during robberies, or were lured to other, bigger gangs. Occasionally gangs amalgamated.

Each gang's hierarchy and ranks varied. The Marauders were led by a 'captain'. There was also a second-in-command, who was known as the 'roady', an abbreviation for 'road captain'. And a 'sparky', who could work the big radio, and one or two 'drivers', the men who came to load the gang's loot with a lorry.

Their life consisted of plundering their region of everything of possible value, especially weapons, ammunition, food, gold and diamonds, power generators, solar panels and specific car and motorcycle spares. The Marauders' region stretched from Aberdeen in the west to King William's Town in the east. That was why they were a small clan: their area was poor in the most precious resources and their numbers were too few to challenge another gang for a larger area.

They collected their loot at a temporary base, a safe, secluded place until they heard where the next Sales Conference would be. The Sales

Conference was held by the Sales Club, 'But that's really just the name we use on the radio, the Sales Club is just this man and woman and their . . . their bodyguards who are sort of wholesalers, they buy our stuff, and they sell it on to other guys,' said Calitz. And then he added with effusive respect, 'The woman is a Zulu princess.'

Our Committee members looked at each other; that rang a bell.

'Wait,' said Domingo. 'Have you ever seen her?'

'Yes. At Maselspoort. At the last Sales Conference,' said Calitz.

'What does she look like?'

Calitz described her.

'That's Mecky Zulu,' said Pa.

'No, they call her the Chair, but her name is Dudu Meyiwa,' said Calitz.

'And the man with her?'

'Clarkson. That's what they say, his real name is Clarkson. He's this terribly clever engineer . . .' And according to the description Domingo and the Committee knew they were the pair who had introduced themselves as Trunkenpolz and Mecky Zulu. Leon Calitz said he had never heard those names before. The man and woman's radio call signs were 'Number One' and the 'Chair'. They used many hiding places and Sales Conference venues. They were very clever, because everyone wanted to eliminate them. They were the middlemen, they had all the contacts, they controlled everything.

Number One and the Chair told the gangs what 'products' they wanted most. The nature and value of these goods had changed in the past nineteen months. Tinned and dried food had been very popular and profitable at first, but nowadays the emphasis was on ammunition, alcohol, spares, motorcycle and truck tyres. There was also a great demand for solar panels and batteries. A good set could easily be worth six hundred litres.

'Litres of what?' Pa asked.

'Ethanol,' said Leon Calitz. There were four ways the Sales Club paid the gangs: in information and skill to convert vehicles to ethanol, in ethanol fuel itself, in vehicle parts, and in ammunition.

'How exactly does it work?' asked Pa.

'The Sales Club lets us know when there will be a Sales Conference, then we take our products in the lorry to barter . . .'

'How does the Sales Club let you know?'

'Over the radio.'

'What radio?' asked Domingo.

'The radios that Number One gave us.'

'Those CB radios that are built into the bikes?'

'No, we only use those to talk to each other, or to our sparky. Number One calls us on the big radio. It's this big . . .' Leon Calitz gestured with his hands, about sixty by sixty centimetres.

'Wait a minute.' Domingo stopped him. 'How far away is Number One when he calls you on that big radio?'

'I don't know. We never know where they are. But the big radios can talk over hundreds of kilometres.'

'Yes,' said Domingo. 'A ham radio can do that, but then you need a long aerial.'

'We have one.'

'Where?'

'At our base camp. That's where the sparky lives. At the big radio and the CB base station, and the products that we collected.'

'Where is your base camp?'

'On the other side of Tarkastad.'

Pa started to say something, but Domingo stood up, a worried look on his face. He held his hand up in the air.

'That sparky is still sitting there?'

'Sure.'

'And every biker gang has a sparky and a base station?'

'Yes.'

'Does every gang have its own frequency?'

'I don't know. Our sparky always talks about forty metres, there's nothing on the forty metres.'

'Have you heard, recently, of gangs that just . . . went quiet?'

'Yes, the Road Rage Kings.'

'The Road Rage Kings?'

'Yes. Their territory was the N1 between Beaufort West and Colesberg. They were a big clan, more than twenty. And then they just disappeared. Our captain said he thought they were just fed up because everything was gutted, stripped, you can't make a living in this business any more.'

'How did you hear that they just disappeared?'

'Number One asked us over the radio if we knew anything, because the Kings' sparky said he couldn't make contact with his captain at all. With none of the Kings. Number One said they would give two thousand free litres for information about the Road Rage Kings. But our captain said we didn't know anything.'

'And then?'

'Then Number One said the offer stands, we must keep our eyes and ears open. He thought another clan might have taken them out. For the territory. But our captain said territory be damned, they were just as fed up as we are.'

68

The first KTM war: VIII

Domingo brought Leon Calitz to SpOT headquarters so we could listen to the interrogation. We sat outside on the parade ground in a semicircle, Domingo and Calitz sat on chairs.

'Tell us about the radio base,' Domingo said.

That was the first time I saw Calitz close up. He looked like an ordinary guy, a good man. Like one of us. I heard he had been training to be a fitter and turner before the Fever came. *This* is my enemy, I thought. He could have been me.

'Ach, there's really nothing,' said Leon Calitz. His big Adam's apple produced a deep baritone, but he looked like someone who suddenly had stage fright.

'Tell us.'

'It's a poor little farm, that's all.'

He saw this wasn't going to satisfy Domingo. 'It's near Tarkastad,' he added.

'Where near Tarkastad?'

'About twenty, thirty kilometres.'

'Give me detail.'

'There's a farm, we lived on the farm . . . The radio tower is on the mountain just beside the farmhouse. If you climb up to the tower, you can see a long way. You can even see the town, and all the roads leading to the town.'

'What roads?'

'The four tarmac roads that run to Cradock and Queenstown and Adelaide and up the mountain.'

'How far can you see on those roads?'

'The one that leads to Cradock . . . Actually to Hofmeyr, you can see for at least fifty kilometres. Maybe even further, I never measured it. But that's why our captain chose the mountain. To see far, and for the altitude, to get the radio aerial high.'

'What's going to happen if the sparky up there on the mountain doesn't hear from you gangstas for a day or two?'

'Oh no,' said Calitz, 'it happens often. He won't do anything.'

'And if we are only four or five bikes that he sees coming? Your bikes, your leathers?'

'He'll wonder where the others are.'

'But he won't do anything?'

'No. What can he do?'

'And if a few bikes arrive at the farm with two guys on, and the sparky sees them coming?'

'It's okay, the bikes break down, and we have to pillion the guys.'

'He won't be spooked?'

'I . . .' Calitz seemed to be getting more and more tense. He just shrugged, a gesture that indicated he really didn't know.

'Leon, what will he do?'

'He might try to call us on the CB radio, but often when we're riding fast we don't hear when someone uses the CB.'

'Will he tell the other gangs or Number One over the ham radio that there is a problem before we get to him?'

'No. It doesn't work like that.'

'Are you sure?'

'Yes.'

'Why?'

'We never . . . We don't talk to other clans, and you don't call Number One if you have trouble, he's not our boss. He only talks to the clans about product and Sales Conferences and stuff.'

'Okay. You're coming with us, we ride tomorrow.'

'No.' Leon Calitz shook his head.

'You don't have a choice,' said Domingo.

'I don't want to.' And he crossed his arms in finality. It wasn't just determination, there was something else too.

'Why not?'

'I don't want to see them ever again. I'm finished with them.'

'But it's just the sparky?'

'I don't want to see him again.'

Domingo stood up and walked over to Calitz. 'Are you lying to us?'

'No, I told you the truth.'

'Are there more gangstas beside the sparky at the radio base?'

'No, I swear, it's just him. But . . .'

'But what, Leon?'

'If you . . . If he . . . What if something goes wrong, and he lets Number One know?'

'Why are you suddenly afraid of Number One?'

'You don't know them. They've got bodyguards, they're psychos. Murderers. They . . . Some of the clans . . . There were clans who wanted to take them out, Number One and the Chair, clans that wanted to become wholesalers. The bodyguards hanged those guys in the trees, with their tongues pulled through their throats . . .'

'How is Number One going to know about you? About us?'

Leon Calitz just shook his head, refused to say more.

'What could go wrong, Leon?' Domingo was suspicious and aggressive now. He stood directly in front of Calitz. 'What is it you don't want to tell us?'

Calitz's voice rose in pitch. 'I . . . Nothing. I swear I told you everything.'

'What could go wrong?'

'I don't know. Anything. There're no guarantees in life.'

'Guarantees schmarantees,' said Domingo. 'Tomorrow you're coming along. If I get there and there're more than just the sparky, I'll shoot both your kneecaps off. Understand?'

Calitz studied Domingo as if weighing up one threat against another. He dropped his head, shook it gently as though he were being done a great injustice. But he said, 'I understand.'

3 February

At four in the morning Team Bravo stood at attention and in full combat gear beside the Volvo.

'I'm expecting you to do a lot better today,' Domingo said.

'Yes, Captain,' we shouted.

'We've worked hard.'

'Yes, Captain.'

'We've learned a lot.'

'Yes, Captain.'

'We're going to stay calm.'

'Yes, Captain.'

'We're going to be pro soldiers.'

'Yes, Captain.'

I glanced surreptitiously over to where Leon Calitz stood to one side, staring at us dumbfounded, his eyes wide in amazement. Or maybe just fear.

'Let's go,' said Captain Domingo.

We drove to where Team Alpha had had their skirmish. There Domingo, Calitz and four Spotters climbed on to the motorcycles that had been hidden in the dry stream bed – the only four of us who could ride well. The rest would remain in the back of the Volvo until Hofmeyr.

It was a tiny hamlet. Leon Calitz said it was totally deserted. Domingo didn't believe him and made Team Bravo scour the place, the beautiful old municipal buildings, the little park with the monument and the old slave bell, the peculiar church with its four ugly pillars. We saw that the village had been ransacked of anything the Marauders could sell.

We found no one. Calitz had a wounded I-told-you-so attitude.

The Volvo and the rest of Team Bravo were to wait in Hofmeyr.

The six motorcycles rode on – three now with passengers. I was one of them, thanks to my marksmanship skills. Domingo was in front, then Calitz. Jakes – who was driving – and I rode alongside Calitz. Domingo said if it looked like Leon Calitz was veering off, I was welcome to shoot him. The other three bikes brought up the rearguard.

69

The first KTM war: IX

We rode into Tarkastad. In the middle of the town was the only traffic circle. Leon Calitz stopped there. 'I'm not going any further,' he said when Domingo approached him angrily to ask what was going on.

'You're riding.'

'No. I'll explain to you how to get there.'

Domingo was suspicious. 'Can he see us, Leon? Is this a sign for your sparky? I'll shoot you, Leon, you hear me? I'll shoot you easily . . .'

'No, no, I swear, but I'm a traitor, I can't look Loots in the eyes. I'm staying here.'

Domingo swore.

'Curse me if you want,' said Calitz. 'I'm staying here.'

Domingo climbed off his motorbike, drew his pistol, grabbed Leon Calitz and shot off his little finger. Calitz screamed like a girl.

'You're coming,' said Domingo.

'No,' said Calitz.

Domingo shot off his ring finger. Calitz screamed, wild with fear, but he shouted, 'Okay, okay, okay!' His hand dripped blood on the handlebars of the motorcycle.

'Ride in front,' Domingo said and pointed with the pistol. That was all he needed to do.

Calitz led us up the mountain. It was an old tarmac road, riddled with potholes and gullies, that turned into a bad gravel road. On top of the mountain the road forked. Calitz kept left. He rode slower and slower, looking at me more often where I sat behind Jakes with my rifle ready to shoot Calitz.

Into the yard of the farm Bergfontein.

The man must have heard us coming, he came running out of the farmhouse, calling, 'Captain, Captain, there were guys here, Captain, there was a chopper,' his face twisted in excitement. He was a tall man, wearing only old jeans, a bushy black beard over a skinny chest, his head clean shaven.

We all stopped, the man ran up to Domingo's motorcycle, still babbling on about the 'chopper'. Domingo removed his crash helmet and aimed his rifle at the skinny man.

When the man saw it wasn't his captain he stopped talking, bewildered. He reeked of stale booze.

Leon Calitz climbed off his bike, trembling like a reed. 'This is the sparky,' he said to Domingo. Then he took off his helmet and told the sparky: 'Loots, everyone is dead, I'm the only one left.'

It was as if the sparky didn't register what Leon was saying. His eyes darted from Calitz to Domingo, the rest of us, then back to Calitz. 'Leon, there were guys here . . .'

'What guys?' asked Calitz, his voice full of tension.

'Chopper guys.'

'What chopper guys?' Domingo asked.

'I don't know. Who're you?' the sparky asked Domingo.

'Were you drunk?' asked Domingo.

'It's war, Loots. They shot us,' said Calitz. 'They shot us all, I'm the only one left,' an emphasis in his voice, as though he were trying to give Loots a message. But Loots was too upset and confused to pick up on it.

'Are you the chopper guys?' he asked.

Domingo grabbed Loots-the-sparky by the scruff of the neck and he asked, 'Who are the chopper guys?'

Loots was scared of Domingo, dazed, in shock. 'They came last night. Middle of the night. One a.m. I heard the chopper, so I got up, and I saw it land. Just over there. And four guys jumped out with night sights and laser lights and they saw me and shot at the door, look, here are the holes. And I held up my hands, and they came and pushed me on the ground, and I was lying there, I thought they were going to shoot me. And they were shouting stuff, they were asking me stuff about people I don't know, and I said I don't know, I swear. I thought they were going to kill me, Leon. Then they looked for the radio, and they just left everything again, and they got in the chopper and flew away. Chopper guys, Leon, I think it's Number One's chopper guys . . .' A light went on in his eyes, he focused on Domingo: 'Number One sent you.'

'No,' said Domingo.

'Did they take anything, Loots?' Leon Calitz asked. With a sly, meaningful tone.

'No,' said Loots. And then, without thinking: 'Everyone is still here.'

Domingo tackled him to the ground, he pushed his pistol against Loots's temple, and shouted, 'Who's everyone?'

Loots was confused. 'The girls,' he said.

Leon Calitz gave a despairing groan.

'What girls?'

'There in the store.'

Domingo told me and the other troops, 'Bring Calitz. Be careful.'

Domingo grabbed the sparky by the beard and dragged him in the direction the man indicated, to the outbuildings beside the farmhouse.

Calitz resisted. Jakes and I each held an arm. We had to drag him, until Jakes lost his temper and grabbed Calitz by his bleeding fingers and said, 'Now you come with us.'

One of the outbuildings was a storeroom with a padlock. 'That one,' Loots said.

Again that despairing sound from Leon Calitz.

'Open up,' Domingo said.

Loots's hand shook as he took the key out of his jeans pocket. He unlocked the padlock. Domingo walked in. The others waited outside.

Domingo came out, pistol in hand. He was beside himself with fury, I had never seen him like that before, his breath fast and ragged, his eyes wild with rage. He walked up to Loots, pressed his pistol against the sparky's forehead and pulled the trigger. Loots collapsed.

Calitz screamed shrilly and in terror, 'For Number One, they're for Number One!'

Then Domingo shot him too, between the eyes.

The rest of us stood, turned to stone.

Domingo spun on his heel, walked away, came back, walked away again.

Domingo turned towards us, said to Brits, 'Go and fetch the Volvo.'

Then to the others, 'Get them out of there. Fetch food and water. See if there are clothes for them. And soap and water.'

There were seven women in the storeroom.

Actually three girls and four women.

The three young ones were the only ones with clothing on. The rest were naked. There was no water or toilet, they had been kept for weeks in the storeroom, they had been kicked and beaten, given only scraps of food, and were allowed to wash once a week, from a bucket.

We helped them out of the storeroom. They stood in the bright sunlight, blinking, huddling together, shrunken and forlorn. Beyond fear, they stood waiting for something, orders perhaps, or a blow to the head. They looked at the bodies of Loots and Calitz, which our troops were dragging away.

Domingo could not look at them, he walked away, towards the mountain. Jakes came out of the farmhouse with a pile of blankets and towels and some items of clothing and began draping them over the women.

They just stood there.

There were three girls between the ages of eleven and fifteen, and four women between nineteen and forty.

We led them to the farmhouse, gave them the food and water that we could find, and showed them the bathroom.

The older women began to weep first, then the others broke down too.

The oldest one told us later that they were kept like that because the Marauders couldn't leave more men at the base to keep them captive in better conditions. The storeroom only needed one guard.

The captain of the Marauders told them it was only one more week till the Sales Conference. They must just stop whining, shut up till then.

We found two Nissan UD40 trucks in the shed. One was stacked with solar panels and batteries, the other contained drums of diesel and ethanol and leg shackles. We discovered a heap of empty booze bottles and over two hundred still full brandy bottles.

I found Domingo on the mountaintop behind the farmhouse, at the foot of the antenna we were going to dismantle to take back. He stood staring at the horizon.

'Captain . . .'

He didn't react, just kept staring into the distance.

I went up to him. Then he said, 'So now you know, Nico. I have a bit of an anger management problem.'

70

Team Bravo started digging graves for Calitz and the sparky. Domingo stopped us. 'No. Leave them,' he said, his lip curling with contempt.

I wondered how he could hate so purely.

We broke down the radio mast on the mountain. We took it, the radio equipment in the farmhouse, and the women and drove back to Amanzi.

In the back of the Volvo I kept an eye on Domingo. He sat dead straight, taut as a wire. He didn't look at the seven women, he didn't look at us.

On the other side of Petrusville I looked through my portside peephole. I saw our irrigation projects, the fields spreading out beside the river, the crops of sunflowers and maize, vegetables, I saw the people of Amanzi working in the fields, the gentle, good people. I saw the electric pumps, the tractors, a few pick-up trucks, a lorry, the technology that we had up and running again.

How could such different worlds exist? How could there be such barbarity, the viciousness of the men who had stabbed Okkie, and now the Marauders? While there was this oasis? That my father had created.

Were we even of the same species?

We erected the radio mast on the highest hill at Amanzi. Our engineer and his team connected it to the electronics of the shortwave, amateur radio. Domingo called it a ham radio. They turned it on, heard only hissing noise, though they searched through all the frequencies.

Domingo said, 'You have to get it right. I'm looking for Number One. He's mine.'

Birdy said, 'Patience. We'll figure it out.'

Between her, Hennie Fly, Domingo and the engineer they decided to concentrate on the forty-metre wavelength, which according to Leon Calitz was the frequency that the Marauders had to listen to.

★   ★   ★

The community took the seven women to its heart.

They were treated like family, nursed, nurtured, pampered and counselled with a dedication and focus that tried to show that we were different, that not all people were like the Marauders.

And their arrival and their experience and history changed something fundamental in the dynamics of Amanzi.

It was my father who noticed it, who put it in words, placed it in context. He shared it with me over a few Sundays, when I had lunch with him and Okkie. I think he was reaching out to me, very gently. I listened closely, encouraging him, because I wanted to restore our bond, and to lighten my burden of guilt.

Pa's way was to talk through an inkling of a new intellectual insight or point of view, worrying at it like someone who knew there was a golden thread in a crow's nest of wool, and then carefully plucking and tugging at it until he found and unravelled it. Sensing there was something precious there, though he wasn't yet sure what.

He slowly came to the realisation that the presence of the Seven Women changed us. He realised that, despite our internal division, it began to bond us as an entity, as an idea: 'the people of Amanzi'. Pa told me he suspected Leon Calitz's description of the motorcycle gangs as a loose collection of wild, disorganised plunderers had deprived us – at least for a few days – of a single enemy, a simple embodiment of evil. And people united more readily when threatened by another unified force.

We could add the things that the Seven told us to Sofia Bergman's brief experience of being captured, and catch a glimpse of a new, purer evil: an opposing entity that had descended to the barbaric level of human trafficking. Pastor Nkosi gave sermons about 'The devil who locks children in cages'. Domingo as well. His naked hatred for Trunkenpolz and Mecky/Clarkson and Meyiwa/Number One and the Chair was contagious, and he had a big influence on public opinion. Pa said this was how we became more united. We were the polar opposite of the evil. We were the counterweight and the counterbalance that had to keep the scales of the universe in balance. We discovered our identity in our difference: we were the Place of Light, we could only be that when 'they' represented the Darkness.

Us and them. Now more purely formulated and defined.

Pa told me about the historian Yuval Noah Harari who wrote that all animals could only experience major behavioural shifts when their genetics changed.

All animals except humans.

Pa said that for hundreds of thousands of years humans were just one of the many species on the globe, our numbers varying according to drought and flood, famine and surfeit, but the numbers were always under control and in balance with nature.

But then, about twelve thousand years ago, it all altered dramatically. Humankind began to multiply exponentially. And it wasn't a genetic change, it wasn't a climatic shift. It came with our ability to tell stories.

Pa said we are the only organism whose behaviour can change dramatically because we create fiction. Fiction that is so great and powerful that it bound people in larger and larger groups, to accomplish greater and greater things. Yuval Noah Harari described these as imagined realities, social constructs and myths. These stories of ours, these social constructs, were ideas like nationalism among people of different tongues and cultures, or religions, or political ideologies. Communism. Capitalism. Democracy. Imagined realities, because they only arose in people's minds, they had no scientific basis.

The French Revolution was a perfect example of a myth that changed human behaviour overnight: in 1789 a large number of the French rejected the myth of the divine right of kings to rule, and adopted the myth of the sovereignty of the people.

That fact, said Pa, this human ability to create a social construct, an imagined reality of myth, and believe in it, led directly to our ability to cooperate in our thousands and later in millions. As peoples, nations, as allies. Pa laughed and said that the one that was the funniest was the sports team. He said there were some of his colleagues at Stellenbosch who lived in Cape Town, but supported the Blue Bulls rugby team only because they had been at school in Pretoria. Or were Arsenal fans, even though they had no connection to Britain. Sports loyalty, Pa said, was the most inexplicable fiction and social construct of all.

But these constructs gave us cooperation, and cooperation made us the mightiest species on the planet.

'Clever, hey?' Pa said, as always ready to be awed by the inspiring world we lived in.

'Yes,' I said. At sixteen and a half I had perfected the art of hiding my enthusiasm.

Pa said he was still pondering how exactly it had happened, but the seven women had somehow changed Amanzi into a social construct. A myth. Before them there were two factions – the Free Amanzi Party and the Mighty Warrior Party – with a common, shared urge to survive. That was the reason we worked together.

Now there was a growing awareness of the myth of us as Amanzians. About who we were and what we stood for.

'I think . . . it feels as though there's momentum in this, Nico. It's as though the momentum of Pastor Nkosi's rhetoric is waning. His influence as well.'

Afterwards I wondered if it was just that Pa wished it so strongly, or whether it was really so. Then I saw the signs. And the momentum carried us into the winter.

It carried the Special Ops Team through intensive training, spurred more people to attempt selection for the unit, so that by July we were complete, two teams of twelve men each.

It sent us out on more missions, further, longer. We drove as far as Harrismith in the east, Willowmore and Beaufort West in the south, Williston, Brandvlei and Kimberley and Upington, on crumbling tarmac roads and increasingly impassable gravel roads. Alternating between Alpha and Bravo, every fortnight, slow days of frustration and boredom and lukewarm drinking water and bland food in the back of the truck, and the same old weak jokes and irritating personalities and comments and jibes until you felt like slapping your comrades, until you wanted to scream, until you learned to sleep sitting up and disappear into your thoughts to try to break the mindless routine.

Only twice was there an explosion of adrenalin when new gangs led us into an ambush, but they were the ones surprised by the ferocity of our response, as we destroyed them. We were more skilled and confident now, and blunted to the scenes and smells and sounds of battle and death.

The gangs were small and stupid. Neither of them had radios, neither had heard of Number One and the Chair.

It was as though the Sales Club had smelled a rat after the disappearance of the Road Rage Kings and the Marauders. We didn't hear a peep from them on our ham radio, we saw not even a shadow on the highways.

The arrival of the Seven Women, the shock of their appearance and the inhumane treatment they had received from the Marauders, was probably the main reason we completely ignored the sparky's babblings about 'the chopper'.

Perhaps we just forgot to talk about it.

I didn't know what Domingo thought in the weeks that followed. Perhaps he – like the majority of Team Bravo who had been present that day – imagined that the sparky had hoped to distract attention from the girls with his chopper talk. Perhaps Domingo thought it had something to do with the dope that we found in that farmhouse.

His reasoning might have been that we had no reasonable explanation for a helicopter and laser-vision-equipped soldiers there, with those 'small-time yahoos', and therefore it had probably never happened.

Nobody asked the Seven Women about it, no one asked them if they had heard the helicopter in the night. Maybe at first it was to spare them the trauma of remembering. And later . . . I don't know. Perhaps we forgot.

That's all I can say.

Sofia Bergman

I never heard the story of the women and the gang and the helicopter. I mean, not at the time.

Would I have said anything about my helicopter dream if someone had told me about the helicopter at Tarkastad?

I don't know. I really believed mine was just a dream. And the events were separated by months and a few hundred kilometres.

And that year, my first year in Amanzi, wasn't a good one for me. I didn't like anybody. A couple of times I very seriously considered running away.

71

3 July

We left at ten at night, Alpha and Bravo, in two separate lorries. Domingo drove with Team Alpha in the ERF, Brits was our commander in the Volvo. We drove through the night, keeping radio contact, five kilometres apart, via Koffiefontein and Petrusberg to avoid the N1. We were on our way to Bloemfontein, to stick our heads into the hornets' nest.

Over and over in the deserted streets and through the crumbling houses of Luckhoff we had practised night manoeuvres and urban warfare. We were going on the offensive for the first time, without our Trojan Horse strategy. We were going on foot through the suburbs. It was an expedition of intelligence gathering, literally and figuratively a shot in the dark.

We knew there was life in Bloemfontein. We had heard from the migrants who had to pass through the city or close by it on their way to us. We didn't know what form and structure that life was taking, because the stories of the travellers differed so much. They talked about a few frightened inhabitants living like hobos, but also of an organised group who lived in a settlement near the city centre, and shot at anything in the vicinity that moved.

We had avoided Bloemfontein so far. Domingo believed the risks were too great. He didn't have enough information about the city, nor was he satisfied with our training, and nobody knew whether we would really benefit from a mission like this.

Until now.

Domingo now believed the radio silence of the Sales Club and the complete absence of bandits on the roads were part of a deliberate strategy, a portent of an invasion. He displayed no emotion, but we suspected that behind those dark glasses burned a white-hot hatred for Number One and the Chair. Hatred for Clarkson/Trunkenpolz, who had intended to shoot him in cold blood, and Mecky/Meyiwa, who said, 'Don't bother,' as if she despised him as equally unimportant, dead or alive.

We thought we knew Domingo. We thought we knew what he felt. We thought that was one of the reasons we were driving to Bloemfontein in the freezing night of 3 July.

In the hour after midnight we stopped one street away from the N8, near the old Makro hypermarket outside the city. From there we walked in two patrols. Both teams walked from west to east, in separate streets, about half a kilometre apart.

It was nearly four years since I had last been in Bloemfontein. That had been only months after the Fever, when the infrastructure still looked normal.

The change was shocking, especially now in winter. Gardens and pavements were overgrown, the streets were cracked open by tree roots, dry grass and weeds, and storm water drains were blocked, which had caused flooding and erosion.

Some lampposts leaned askew, trees had lost branches in storm winds and they littered the streets collecting wind-blown leaves, dust and sand. Team Bravo's route took us past the rugby field of the Jim Fouché High School, which now served as a pasture for a few sheep and cattle. Further down the street was a hockey field – the frames of the goals still standing – dug over into a summer vegetable garden, now stripped and deserted.

There were people here. They were somewhere in houses nearby, but they gave nothing away, everything was dark and silent.

We crept on through streets as silent as the grave.

Team Alpha smelled the smoke from a wood fire. We followed it slowly to the old Mangaung cricket oval, and we saw two men warming their hands at the fire beside a sky-high floodlight tower. Both were armed, both carried R4 rifles. On the field where once international cricket matches were played, a motley little herd of dairy cows grazed.

The men chatted loudly in the darkness. We overpowered them with ease and confiscated a two-way radio from one of them.

They were shocked by our skill, weapons, military equipment; terrified by the pistol that Domingo pressed to the temple of one.

They answered our questions willingly, telling us almost everything.

They were sentries. The floodlight pole was their lookout tower, they could see for kilometres from up there. But it was freezing cold on top, and the night was always uneventful, so they came down to light a fire, just for the darkest hours. They'd been standing guard. There were two other places with permanent guards, both on Naval Hill, all for the protection of the community at the Mall. The old Mimosa Mall was a settlement now, there were armoured vehicles and tanks at the entrances, and sandbags, with machine guns and guards; it was where 'all the people sleep'. The community consisted of over one thousand people. During the day they came out and tended their sheep, cattle, goats and pigs. In the summer they planted crops in what used to be parks and sports fields. They had restored the water supply from the Welbedacht and Rustfontein dams, using a series of man-powered pumps – that was how they irrigated the crops. The only electricity was in the Mall, where they had hundreds of solar panels on the roof.

Where did they get the solar panels?

The first ones they collected here in the city. Later they purchased more, from the Sales Club.

Where was the Sales Club?

Nobody knew. The Sales Club called them over the radio. The radio was in the Mall. Only the Mayor listened to the radio. The Mayor was their great leader, who had started the Mall, and ruled with an iron fist.

How did they pay the Sales Club?

With food.

And what else?

Sometimes they caught people who came to Bloemfontein. The Mall didn't have room for more people, the Mall was full. And the Sales Club paid a lot for people.

Women?

No, men as well.

How were people and food exchanged for solar panels and batteries?

Lorries came, sometimes only one, sometimes even five.

Who rode in the lorries?

Guys with guns.

Did they know about Number One, and the Chair?

Yes. They were the people who had the Sales Club.

Where were they?

Nobody knew.

Domingo asked them about the Mall's defences and their weaponry. They grew more and more uneasy; they said everyone who worked outside the Mall carried firearms during the day. All the weapons were from the School of Armour and 1 SA Tank Regiment and 44 Parachute Regiment and 1 Infantry Battalion.

Were the tanks and armoured cars in working order?

One nodded, the other shook his head.

Don't lie to me.

No, the military vehicles in front of the Mall didn't work. The diesel had run out a long time ago, the vehicles were just parked there as a deterrent. Some of the cannon still worked. All the guns could shoot.

Domingo stood thinking about what he still needed to know. One of the Bravo team asked, did they have schools, doctors and ministers?

The two looked dumbfounded. No. Everyone worked. Everyone had to work to build up the food supplies. The Mayor was strict, if you wanted to live there you had to work. Who were we? one of them asked. Where did we come from?

'I think we should shoot them,' said Domingo, but we knew him, we knew it wasn't an order, it was a strategy.

They pleaded, both men. Please, they said, they daren't tell anyone we were here, they daren't admit that they had been captured and interrogated. If we went away, no one would even know that we had been there, they wouldn't tell a soul.

Domingo thought about it. He ordered four Bravo members to stay with the men, with instructions not to say a word about who we were. He led the rest of us on to the Mall. We studied it through night sights and binoculars from a safe distance. We could see the tanks and armoured cars, there were people moving at the sandbag barriers, people who were awake and ready.

We walked back to the cricket oval to fetch our comrades. Then Alpha and Bravo took another route back to the lorries.

*   *   *

The notorious attack, that famous battle where four members of Alpha and three of Bravo were wounded, took place in Bloemfontein, just across the N1, in the veld between Langenhoven Park and the Makro hypermarket.

Years later we would hear that it was such dangerous territory that the inhabitants of the Mall never dared go there at night, and in daytime went armed with guns.

We were on our way back to the trucks. It was an hour before sunrise, after a long, hard night. The tension wore one out, the worst was behind us and we had left the built-up area, starting to relax, sleepy, not as alert as we had been earlier. Bravo walked ahead, in V-formation, Alpha was a hundred metres behind us.

Pitch-dark.

We only heard them at first, frightening sounds, beastly, aggressive, malevolent. Bloodthirsty sounds. Then we saw, between the two teams, the dark shadows start to move, low on the ground, but incredibly swift. An attacking horde. Before anyone could react or Domingo could say a word, they were among us, and they knocked us from our feet, massive monsters of three hundred kilograms or more, snapping at us, fangs ripping through flesh and crushing bone. We couldn't shoot, for fear of hitting one another.

Domingo screamed orders and clicked on his torch. He was at the vanguard of Bravo team and had to turn around to confront the danger. He aimed the torch and in its beam we saw the pigs – not wild boar, not warthogs or bush pigs, but farm pigs. American Landrace, and Cinta Senese and hybrids of unfathomable genes, massive and ferocious. Later the farmers among us would identify them from the carcasses we took along, those that we managed to shoot before we drove the rest away with the clamour of our R4 rifles. They said there must have been piglets nearby that had to be protected.

Farm pigs. Domestic animals gone wild, perhaps the descendants of pigs that had been farmed somewhere in the area.

They wounded seven of us, and one soldier's femoral artery bled so much that we thought he would die before someone managed to staunch the bleeding.

The Year of the Pig.

72

Sofia Bergman

No, I didn't like Nico. Not at all.

And I felt lonelier in Amanzi during that first year than when I had been completely alone on the farm. I know people will say, come on, how is that possible, but you must understand the way it was. You arrive there and you're the flavour of the month, your story is the big one of the moment. And mine was. I was the one who was captured by the motorcycle gang, and I was the one who chased that disgusting swine with the spanner, the one who shot Nico Storm in the chest with a crossbow. Everyone thought that was the coolest thing ever, everyone wanted to talk to me and be my friend. Until the next group arrived, with another epic tale. Everyone's story was epic, in those days. And then everyone would want to be their friend.

That's the problem, if you're new, you can't be friends with everyone, and I saw that happen a lot in Amanzi, then in the end you're friends with nobody. I think it's the most peculiar situation, a community like Amanzi, where actually everyone is new, but . . .

The other thing was that, as far as I know, I was one of only a handful of people who arrived at Amanzi alone. Nero Dlamini, too, of course, but 98 per cent arrived in groups. Sometimes quite small groups, but at least they were groups. So when their fifteen minutes of fame was over, they at least had each other, until they were absorbed by the group as normal. But for me it was different.

I was overwhelmed. Try to imagine being secluded on the farm for so long, and completely alone for months, and then all those things happen at once, and you're thrown in with people and getting lots of attention and it's overwhelming.

I was sixteen, remember that, sixteen and socially inept.

At first they said I should live in the Orphanage. Then, just after New Year, I had to move to Groendakkies. Just below the Orphanage in

Madeliefie Street there's a whole row of town houses or terrace houses, I don't know what they called them in the old days. That's where they let most of the teenagers – the orphan teenagers – live. The houses all had green roofs, and Groendakkies was apparently a nickname for a mental asylum before the Fever. In any case, it was . . . Today I know it was the best possible system. Nero Dlamini managed it, he trained the adults and advised the adults who acted as foster parents or sort of mentors to us. But in any case, I moved in with others, who were anything from twelve to seventeen, girls one side, boys the other. And they told me I had to go to school one week, I had to study mathematics, biology, science, geography and world history, and two 'skills'. They suggested I take needlework and food technology as a skills.

Maybe it would have been okay if I'd had a bit of school before. But I had gone four years without attending school, and they tested me and told me I was to be in a class with the fourteen-year-olds, and I also had to take needlework or food processing. I refused to attend school. Nero came to talk to me, and I told him I walked from the farm in boots that were too big, and I was okay. Now that I had shoes that fitted, I would rather walk back to the farm than sit in class with little children, and I wasn't going to study such stupid skills.

He negotiated with me. He must have been laughing up his sleeve at me, I was so silly, but needlework and food processing? Please!

So he asked what skills I would prefer to study. And I said what is there? And he listed them all. I said agriculture and shooting. And he said okay. And would I just do six months of class with the fourteen-year-olds? Just for review. Then he would personally see to it that I was advanced, and then we would make a plan.

I agreed to that. But I wasn't at all happy.

The only thing that kept me from derailing entirely was running. Most afternoons after school I went running. For kilometres and kilometres.

I never could understand why Sofia Bergman was so angry. At everything and everyone, but especially at me.

At weekends if we wanted to go to Amanzi, we Spotters had to walk there, since Domingo forbade the use of the horses or the vehicles. It wasn't far, only about three kilometres from the SpOT barracks to the Orphanage, but it was uphill, and it was often very cold or very hot.

Sometimes it rained. But every Sunday I walked there to have breakfast with Pa and Okkie, and to try to have a word with Sofia Bergman.

But she would ignore me. Clearly she hadn't yet realised she was supposed to be my future wife.

Sofia Bergman

Of course I ignored him. He used to be a real little show-off.

He would stop there in front of Groendakkies and the other girls would say, 'Ooh, ooh, here's Nico Storm,' and they would bat their eyelashes and grab the nearest hairbrush or lipstick, and he would stand there in his uniform like he was God's gift to women. He had a real attitude, he can say what he likes, he did have this way of walking; the other girls thought he was the sexiest thing they had ever seen, but I thought he was just arrogant and vain.

He would come and hang about on the pavement in front of Groendakkies and ask if I was there, and the girls would come and call me, and when I went out he would say, 'Hi, Sofia,' in that funny way. He must have thought it would make my knees buckle, but all it did was annoy me.

I asked them if Sofia was there. I'd been thinking about her all week. I would fantasise about her, how I would heroically rescue her from the clutches of a biker gang. Or something. All week I ached to see her.

She came out on to the veranda at Groendakkies, with that long, blond hair of hers, and her slim body and skin that was sheer perfection. I drank her in, that beauty. My heart hammered in my chest, it squeezed my throat closed, paralysed my tongue and my brain, and all I could get out was 'Hi, Sofia.'

Sofia Bergman

Then I said, 'Hi, yourself,' and I turned around and walked to my room, and my roommates and my Groendakkies friends came to say, it's Nico Storm, he can shoot better than anyone, and he rescued Okkie and helped get the aeroplane and he shot so many KTM guys, it's Nico Storm.

Then I said he's a braggart. And one of these days I will shoot better than him. Because I was a good shot. Very good.

I didn't even know what a braggart really meant, but it sounded just right.

'Hi, yourself.' With huge irritation in my voice. At sixteen. Today I'm mortified.

I was angry at everyone when I was sixteen.

73

The first murder

They found the body of Matthew Mbalo just beside the crumbling parking lot near the gate to the reserve. On 2 August. He was sixty-one years old, a quiet, simple man; before the Fever he had been a janitor at the municipal offices of a small Free State town. He was one of our night shepherds, a duty that he had asked for and carried out diligently. They found his horse, still saddled and bridled, in the veld nearby.

Everyone liked Matthew. Everyone who was aware of his existence.

The cause of death was a blunt instrument that had smashed his skull with two violent blows.

Our first murder.

The Special Ops Teams were busy in Luckhoff. The town was our training ground. Some of the houses were shot to pieces, and our regular run up the mountain beside the town had worn footpaths beside the whitewashed stones that used to spell out the town's name.

We were running down the mountain with rucksacks, rifles and helmets. We saw Sarge X – Sergeant Sizwe Xaba – down below in his pick-up, the one with a hand-painted police star on the door. He drove into Luckhoff and parked beside the old, dried-up and broken-down sewerage works.

Sarge X had been our police chief for seven months. The Committee reported that he had said during his interview for the job that 'Eighty-five per cent of all crime is domestic in nature, drug- or alcohol-related, and happens mostly in disadvantaged communities. Amanzi is one big, domestic, disadvantaged community. Of course there will be crime.'

He managed law enforcement along with his responsibility as chief of defence, and he and his slowly growing team of people had caused the crime levels to drop dramatically since January.

Crime in Amanzi was nothing new. It began back in the Year of the Dog.

At first it was just petty theft, people nicking minor, trifling things, especially food. They were hungry, and accustomed to taking whatever they found, or hadn't grasped that private and personal ownership had been restored after the Fever. Nero Dlamini said post-traumatic stress had a negative effect on decision-making, which also contributed to crime.

In the beginning, small infringements were overlooked. People confronted and rebuked each other directly. Later they brought their differences to the Committee, which sometimes had to act as judge and jury. But in the Year of the Jackal there were simply too many people and incidents for that informal system. Consequently, Sarge X was appointed head of law enforcement. A twenty-four-year-old aspiring lawyer, who had not even completed her articles, became our first magistrate. The Committee became the court of appeal, for the time being.

The most serious incident that the APS – the Amanzi Police Service – and the court had to handle in the preceding six months was an assault, when two drunk dairy farmers came to blows over a bull that broke through a fence.

Domingo called Alpha and Bravo to a halt a hundred metres from Sarge X and his pick-up. He walked alone to the police chief while we stood watching. We knew something must be wrong, because it was exceptional for Sarge X to drive all the way out here. It had never happened before.

We saw the body language, Sarge X half apologetic, Domingo's at first neutral, then indecipherable, then aggressive, his hands and arms demonstrative, Sarge X defensive. And then tempers seeming to cool.

They spoke for another ten minutes, then Sarge X climbed into his pick-up and drove away. Domingo came walking back to us. Poker-faced, as usual. He stood in front of us, called us to attention. He waited, his eyes as always hidden behind dark glasses.

'There was a murder last night. Old Matthew Mbalo. They found him at the game reserve gate. Does anyone think they might know something about this?'

'Captain, permission to ask a question, Captain,' called Jele.

'Permission granted.'

'How did he die, Captain?'

'Why do you want to know, Jele? Are you a detective?'

'No, Captain.'

Domingo allowed the silence to lengthen. 'Blunt force trauma to the head.'

We stood there, wondering about many things. Later, back at the barracks, we would ask ourselves the same questions that everyone in Amanzi was asking: Who? Who would want to murder old Matthew Mbalo, surely the most harmless of all our inhabitants? And why? He had nothing, he had never offended anyone.

And why in such a way? With violence and rage and a weapon that one might believe just happened to be nearby, a piece of wood or something. As though it were spontaneous and unplanned.

And why there?

It was soon obvious that no one believed the murderer was an Amanzian. The general argument was that everyone knew everyone and we *knew* there were no murderers among us. Fighters, yes. People who were petty thieves, people who distilled moonshine on the sly and damaged property or disturbed the peace in their drunken state, yes, we had those. But murderers? No. It was simply unthinkable.

It must have been someone from outside sneaking in. Not impossible for one or two people, if they came on foot over the hills at night. Or rowed a boat across the dam. The main theory, entertained by most, was that Matthew surprised intruders, stock thieves or poachers. The old reserve was still securely fenced, it was the place where most of our livestock were kept, and the main gate was the exit where it would be easiest to take out a few sheep or a cow carcass.

And Amanzi's success was widely known, it must have been someone who had been planning it for a long time and watching, envious of our abundance. Someone from outside. But it wasn't one of us.

There was another theory held by just a few of the more disillusioned residents. That Mbalo may not have been as harmless we thought. That it might be a case of quiet waters run deep; Matthew could have been involved in something bad. With someone from the outside.

The investigation into his death drew a blank. Nothing.

The only additional clue was that at about one o'clock that night Matthew Mbalo told his fellow shepherds that he wasn't feeling well. They told him to go to bed, they would carry on. He rode away on horseback. That was the last time that anyone saw him alive.

Pastor Nkosi took advantage of the situation. The arrival of the Seven Women and the renewed sense of unity it gave us had lost him support, so he exploited the murder, warning his congregation that the devil was (still) running amok in Amanzi.

There was one thing that no one speculated about: Sarge X had fine-combed the scene of the crime the morning that the body was discovered. He found no sign of the murder weapon, even though he and his people had searched the area within a radius of two hundred metres. He ascertained that there had been no eye-witnesses. And then he got in his police pick-up and drove to Luckhoff to talk to Domingo.

Why?

And what was said at the police vehicle that made Domingo so angry?

We would imagine that we knew the answers to all those questions, six months later, in February of the Year of the Lion. We would all be wrong.

The full truth would only emerge after the murder of my father.

74

Twenty days after the murder of Matthew Mbalo I turned seventeen.

On the Thursday morning of my birthday Domingo woke me in the barracks, before six, when it was still dark outside: 'Happy birthday. The chairman wants to see you. Go on foot.'

Since I had become a Spotter, my relationship with Domingo was one of commander and soldier. It had taken me months to grow accustomed to it. Now I didn't want it any other way.

'Thank you, Captain.'

'You must be there by half past seven, Storm. Get a move on.'

'Yes, Captain.'

'You have the day off. Make sure you're back by six o'clock tonight.'

'Yes, Captain.'

'You're not eating my breakfast this morning.'

'Yes, Captain.'

Domingo left the room, and my SpOT comrades sang a dirge-like 'Happy Birthday' to me from their beds, in the exaggerated, morose fashion of funeral-goers, the way we young men celebrated the birthdays of all SpOT members.

I was still the youngest Spotter, but no one remembered that. I was the best shot in the unit. I ran the thirty kilometres between our base and Luckhoff in the second-fastest time now. Aram the Namibian still beat me, but every week I closed the gap by a minute or two. It was only a question of time.

I got up, washed and dressed. My fellow soldiers teased me. 'Shame, Storm is going home to Daddy. It's the only place he gets love. Say hi to Sofia. And then goodbye to Sofia.' That sort of supportive talk. They found it excruciatingly funny. I laughed with them. What else can you do with family?

I walked the three kilometres to town.

I reported at the main gate, where the old bus gate used to be. It was a sturdy structure of brick and concrete now. The guards were alert, disciplined and armed. They greeted me by name. They didn't know it was my birthday. They opened the first gate for me, then the second. They made quips about Sofia. Everyone knew I was in love with her. Except Sofia herself.

I walked briskly through the wide U of the tarmac road up the slope, my hands shoved into my pockets in an attempt to keep them warm in the icy cold of late winter. Two tractors with trailers were driving out of town. Both trailers were packed with people, wrapped up in warm clothes and blankets. They were on the way to the fields and fruit orchards. It was almost the end of pruning time for the peaches, pears and plum trees, and the table grapes that we had fetched with an expedition from Kanoneiland. The people greeted me loudly, smiled and waved. They all knew who I was. I smiled too, because it was good to hear their *joie de vivre*, and I waved back.

I passed the place where Okkie and I had lain when I shot the KTM, and they shot me. My leg had completely recovered now, only an ugly scar remained. Past the stables where the children worked as grooms during their out-of-school week. The system was still operating, some of them were leading horses out of the stables. The animals snorted and neighed, their breaths small volcanoes of steam in the cold morning air. The grooms greeted me. I greeted them in return.

I thought about Bloemfontein, I thought about a thousand people or more who were sleeping in an old shopping centre there. In my imagination I pictured everyone side by side on the floor, perhaps on battered mattresses. All the humidity of so many bodies, the shared toilets and washbasins, showers and baths, having to listen to the men snoring and the children crying at night. I thought of broken-down armoured cars guarding the the Mall entrance, of a despot in power, and I looked at the peace and space of Amanzi ahead of me, the security, the happiness and I was proud of what we had achieved. Proud of everything that this town and this community represented.

I knew why Domingo had woken me and sent me to Amanzi. Pa and Okkie wanted to celebrate my birthday with me. Pa had tentatively probed whether I would be okay with something like that. He wasn't a man who was comfortable with secrets or white lies, even when it was socially acceptable.

I turned into Madeliefie Street, the Orphanage was at the end of it. My heart beat faster. Sofia Bergman lived here, in the second-last Groendakkie on the right.

I carried a letter in my pocket. I had spent weeks writing it, one version after the other. In secret, in barracks. It wasn't an easy task, everyone wanted to know what you were doing, especially if you were doing something out of the ordinary.

It was a very, very difficult thing to write, a letter to your future wife. Think for a moment, what should the very first word be?

'Darling?'

No, no, it was too . . . loving.

'Dear?'

That was too I-like-you-as-a-friend. Or worse, we-could-have-been-brother-and-sister.

'Hi' was not even an option. 'Hello' wasn't much better.

Complicated. If you're seventeen.

Every Sunday I wanted to give it to her. Or push it under her front door. But my courage deserted me. What if she read the letter out loud in front of everyone, in the same voice she said things like 'Hi, yourself'.

I stopped in front of her house. The letter was in my pocket.

I had written it over thirty-four times.

Sofia
I don't know what I did to make you so angry. Whatever it was, I am sorry. I really want to talk to you. I really wish you would go horse-riding with me into the reserve just once. There is a spot that looks out over a valley and the dam. It's one of my favourite places. I would love to show you how beautiful it is.
   Will you let me know when you're not angry with me any more?
   Regards
   Nico Storm

In an earlier version I had the postscript: *P.S. I am going to marry you anyway.* I decided it was better to leave that out.

I took the letter out of my pocket. I stared at her front door.

No. I shoved it back into my inside pocket and walked on to the Orphanage.

Okkie was six. He was worse at keeping secrets than my father. Okkie sat with me and Pa at the breakfast table and he couldn't keep his eyes off the kitchen door. Every now and then he would cover his mouth with his hand, like someone stopping themselves from saying something. I knew what had happened. Okkie had seen the cake and candles in there. He had asked whose it was. And they said it's your brother Nico's. It's a surprise, you mustn't tell, or you won't get a slice. Now Okkie couldn't wait for them to bring it out, and the knowledge of the cake was wound up like a jack-in-the-box inside him.

The door behind me opened.

'Look, Nico, look!' The jack-in-the-box jumped out with a bounce and a scream; Okkie pointed his finger.

I turned round to look.

'Wow!' I pretended to be amazed and overjoyed.

Okkie was in seventh heaven. 'It's your cake, Nico!' His voice was shrill with excitement. 'I didn't tell, I didn't tell, it's your cake and your candles, you're seventeen, that's very old. I didn't say anything, Pappa, I didn't tell, I'm not a tattle-tale, can I have a piece?'

We remember the moments of fear, loss and humiliation best. But sometimes, also the moments of intense, pure joy. Like when you look at your father and see the lines on his face are a bit deeper, the grey temples a lighter shade of silver. You knew the burden of responsibility of the community, the recent murder, and his son's rejection have all contributed to this. But now you see the happiness reflected in his eyes, the way he looks at his adopted son and his flesh-and-blood son, from one to the other, happy. And proud. Of us, I hoped. Perhaps of everything that he had achieved here, everything that I had noted that morning. And Pa laughed because his planned surprise had worked, because he had both of us here with him, because he had set the whole day aside for just his two sons, and it stretched out lazy and sweet ahead of us.

I have to confess, there was also humiliation in that moment. I felt shame again for what I had said to him, more than a year ago. I felt ashamed because he – the one whom I had wounded – was using the occasion of my birthday to try to build a bridge, to stretch out a forgiving and reconciliatory hand.

But mostly I felt joy, because I was being offered a chance to make it right.

I hid my feelings by laughing at Okkie, by grabbing my blood brother and pummelling him. It camouflaged the tears in my eyes when the cake was put on the table, and the people gathered round, and of course Okkie, the loudest and shrillest of all, sang to me, and then told me to blow out all seventeen candles.

When they had finished, Pa put out his hand to me and said, 'Happy birthday, Nico. I hope it'll be a good year. I hope you continue to make a difference in people's lives.'

Pa had planned the day well. He took us fishing. He had earthworms and curried porridge for bait, birthday cake and ginger beer, a basket with fresh-baked bread and yellow salted butter, apricot jam and cheddar cheese, biltong and dried sausage. Everything had been made by Amanzi's people.

He had prepared a small boat for us, that we rowed out to the middle of the dam. We baited our hooks, tossed the lines in the water. We chatted, laughed at Okkie, and we didn't get a single bite. We ate and drank. It was like the old times, just him and me. And Okkie to break the ice. It was a good day.

Sofia Bergman

It was that morning that I first started to think of Nico Storm differently.

I was on the way to school. I came out of the door of the house and saw Nico and his father and little brother coming down the street from the Orphanage. I really didn't want him to see me, so I stepped backwards and stood inside the door, waiting for them to pass.

I studied them. Now you must understand, Nico didn't know I was watching him. So I was sure that what he did, he did from the heart. That's the important thing. I saw how he talked to his little brother. Okkie. I knew the story of Okkie, everyone knew it. But the story didn't say how Nico and Okkie felt about each other.

So I stood and watched, and I saw Nico look at Okkie with so much love. He said something to him, I couldn't hear it, but it was obviously something really nice. Nico laughed with Okkie, and with his father. And then he bent down, and picked Okkie up, and hugged him tight to his chest. And then he hoisted him up on his shoulders. And I looked at Okkie, and I saw how completely besotted he was with Nico.

And Willem . . .

There was something about that scene. Something that said they were . . . special people. And that Nico wasn't just a braggart. Even though he walked and talked and acted like a show-off when he was with his friends, in that moment Nico Storm was a very good person.

And I thought, okay, if he talks to me again, I'll try to remember that. I would give him a chance.

75

We were in the rowing boat, lines in the water, the fish not one bit interested.

A soft breeze came up. In August, in this part of the Karoo, the wind blows south-westerly. It pushed the little boat nearer to the far shore, away from Amanzi.

We were aware of it, but not concerned. We could easily row back. And even if the wind picked up later, as it often did in that month, we could always go ashore and hike the kilometre or two to the concrete dam wall, and from there back to Amanzi.

Pa described the trading network they were planning, now that the roads were safe. Our food surplus was large enough for that, and our biodiesel stocks too. In October they wanted to send out the first scouts to Johannesburg, to see whether we could begin bartering with other communities. He wanted my opinion, as if it really mattered to him.

Okkie kept a close eye on his fishing rod and the water; he was constantly imagining he had a bite, and would hook the 'fish' with a dramatic jerk of his rod and scream, 'I've got him, I've got him!' Only to see there was nothing on the hook. Then we had to pull the line in, attach bait and throw it back in.

It was the best day I'd had in years.

Somewhere in those few hours on the water I came to understand certain things. Not necessarily with crystal clarity and blazing insight, but I came considerably closer to certain truths. The first was that Pa was just waiting for me to reach out to him. He bore no resentment, nor was he angry with me. If I was prepared to give the relationship a chance, he would easily be able to forget the pain I had caused him. Today I know that's how a father feels about his children. Always. But for a (very new) seventeen-year-old it was a big step closer to under-standing and wisdom.

The second was that my father was a brave man. Gentle but brave.

I knew that when I looked at Amanzi from the dam. There were the walls – already at window level – of the first eight houses on the southern bank on the eastern side of the town. Built with our bricks and our cement. The first of more than six hundred that were planned. The roads were made, the water, sewerage and electricity services were supplied. I thought of everything I saw and experienced this morning on the way to the Orphanage. My father had done this. Despite the dogs and the Jeep men, despite his inability to shoot people and snakes, or to stand up to the pastor or Domingo. Despite the winters and opposition and division. He had paid a price, you could see it in the lines on his face, the grey hair, his son who had so deeply insulted and hurt him. But it was his vision, he had accomplished this. In four years. He was a brave man, in his own way.

In that moment I felt an overwhelming compassion and love for my father. I decided I would do everything in my power to restore our relationship.

And I thought if I was in any way as brave as my father, I would push the letter under Sofia Bergman's door today.

We drifted closer and closer to the northern bank.

Suddenly Pa stopped talking. He had spotted something. I followed his gaze. Fifty metres away, against the opposite bank, was the mouth of a dry stream. It was densely overgrown, with branches overhanging the water and deep shadows underneath. A chance angle of sun, water and the position of our boat on the dam caused an unnatural reflection, a flash in the shadows. It came and went as the wind moved the dense foliage.

'What could that be?' Pa said.

'Let's go take a look,' I said and picked up the oars.

At first I thought we were mistaken, as it disappeared in the shadows between bushes and the water. I had to row right up to the overhanging branches, and Pa had to lift them up and push them away before we saw it.

'It's a little ship,' said Okkie.

It was a black rubber dinghy. The inflatable bow was punctured with holes, but only the boat's stern was underwater. The bow seemed to have snagged on a thick, dry branch.

'It doesn't look like one of ours,' said Pa.

Pa and I pushed and pulled the branches so we could go closer. The holes in the boat's bow were all of uniform size, it looked like it had been stabbed with the same knife. On the bottom of the boat lay a long, dark object. I leaned over to see. It was a metal pole – an iron standard like those used in wire fences. It was rusty, one end just in the water. The rest was dry. Near the other end it was darker, and the texture was different.

We knew dry blood when we saw it. Because we hunted and butchered animals, and I had shot people.

'Nico ...' said Pa, concerned. He was thinking what I was thinking.

I stretched as far as I could to see the pole closer up.

'Don't touch it,' said Pa.

I was certain it was blood.

'What is it, Nico?' asked Okkie, a bit scared, more curious.

I looked at Pa and nodded. 'I think we should go and tell Sarge.'

For a while that day I reverted to being the practically invisible shadow of my father, the chairman.

I rowed us back. We dodged Okkie's questions about why we couldn't fish any more and what was in the rubber dinghy and what it was we had to go and tell Sarge X.

Pa called Sarge on the radio. He came to fetch us in his pick-up and we dropped Okkie off at school, much to his disgust. Pa, Sarge and I drove around the dam, back to the dinghy. The three of us dragged the vessel out of the bushes. It was difficult, and took more than twenty minutes. Sarge said, 'Not one of our boats, I know all our boats.'

He carefully removed the bloodied standard using his handkerchief and carried it to the pick-up. It was blood, now black, that stuck to it. And hair, and bits of bone and brain. He said, 'I wish we had forensics.'

Pa said, 'This boat was left by someone who came from outside, Sarge.'

'Yes, I'm afraid it does seem that way.'

'I want us to keep this quiet.'

Sarge X nodded. He agreed.

'But we'll have to tell Domingo.'

We drove from there to the SpOT base. Alpha and Bravo were busy with lorry manoeuvres on the parade ground, jumping out of the Volvo and ERF's trailers. Domingo stood watching, hands on hips.

Sarge stopped beside Domingo, and we got out and walked to my commander. Pa told him about the metal standard and the boat.

Domingo listened carefully. Then he looked at me. 'Birthday party over, Storm?'

'Yes, Captain.' I badly wanted to hear the conversation between Pa, Sarge and Domingo, but I was not as much of a knucklehead as I had been. The path of least resistance was the only one that worked with Domingo.

He pointed at my comrades beside the Volvo. 'Off you go.'

'Yes, Captain,' I said and began jogging reluctantly back to Team Bravo.

All thought of the letter to Sofia was driven from my mind.

It was only two days later, on 24 August, that Domingo ordered us to fall in on the parade ground. We stood at attention as he said, 'What I am about to tell you is most confidential. If I ever hear that this information has reached a civilian, I will make it my sole mission in life to find out which one of you maggots snitched, and I will rip your tongue out with my bare hands, and I will consign you to shovelling horse shit for the rest of your days. Do you read me?'

'Sir, yes sir.'

He glared at us suspiciously, as if he didn't believe us.

'I kid thee not. If you breathe a word about this matter, then you are no longer a part of my Special Ops Team. That is a promise. Is that very, very clear?'

'Sir, yes sir.'

He stalked up and down, up and down, like a compressed spring. He said, 'Our enemy managed to launch a rigid inflatable craft into our dam. Our enemy managed to cross that dam, and they managed to murder a very good and gentle citizen of our beloved Amanzi. Why would our enemy do this? Why would they go to the considerable trouble of bringing a rigid inflatable craft all the way to our dam? Under cover of night. Why would they run the considerable risk of being confronted, and captured? Or killed? Why?'

We knew better than to try to answer.

'I'll tell you why. Because they are reconnoitring. Why are they reconnoitring? Because they are planning an attack. An invasion. Why do they want to invade us? Because they want to steal our women and our food and our way of life. Why am I telling you this? Because we will not let it happen. Are we clear?'

'Sir, yes sir.'

'I am also telling you this because you have the right to know why you will not sleep, you will not rest, you will not relax, you will not have a weekend off until we find and annihilate this enemy. Are we clear?'

'Sir, yes sir.'

'Stand easy.'

We followed the order.

Domingo lowered his voice: 'The Special Ops Teams are to be doubled. I am going to need leaders to help. Are you a leader? Show me. In the next eight weeks, show me.'

Sofia's SpOT test: I

Domingo wasn't exaggerating. We didn't sleep much, we didn't rest much, we didn't relax at all and weekends at home were history. All through September and the first half of October.

I didn't get the chance to deliver Sofia's letter.

The restoration of my relationship with my father was like a fruit, ripe and full of promise, that now remained just beyond my reach to pluck. There simply wasn't opportunity to see him.

Nero Dlamini

Those were troubled times.

Domingo came and convinced the Committee that the rubber duck ... You know, the inflatable boat, I think that's what they called it, the boat and the murder of Matthew Mbalo were connected to a pending invasion. He made the case that the absence of biker gangs on the roads was ominous. That the radio silence was an omen. You know, the fact that Number One and the Chair and the Sales Club were just gone. He said people like that, an organisation like that, did not just disappear. That they weren't stupid, they knew something had happened to the gangs we killed. And Amanzi must be the prime suspect, and now they were scheming, and planning their revenge. He said part of their tactics must be to get us to lower our guard, that's why they've crawled back into the woodwork. He really believed they were going to come for us big-time. Full force. That was the term he used.

And he was right, of course, he was absolutely right.

But when he started talking about spies ... I have to admit, I didn't share his sentiments. I ... Look, let me be honest; I wasn't one of Domingo's biggest fans. I respected him, make no mistake, but I didn't like him much.

Ideologically and philosophically, we were worlds apart. And he was aloof, he was antisocial, one of those people who just always believed they were right. He saw the world in terms of good and evil, black and white. I'm much more of a thousand shades of grey kind of guy. And he ... I think he actually liked violence. While I'm very much against it.

Anyway, troubled times ... So the Committee let him have his way. Again. Allowed him to double the size of the Special Ops Unit. To four teams.

And then he started with this espionage story. He approached it from a tangent, saying, we have to explain the military expansion, we can't let the people of Amanzi know we're expecting a big attack.

So we asked him, why?

He said, obviously because it would create fear and panic. But the real problem is, there may be a spy or spies in Amanzi.

So I said, come on, Domingo, get real, what are you now, a conspiracy theorist?

And he said, go and think about the time of the murder, and the place where it happened. And the circumstances. They knew when to cross the dam. They knew there would be nobody at the reserve entrance, that time of night. Matthew was there by accident. How, Nero? How did they know all those things?

Of course I had no answer.

And he said, because they have someone on the inside.

How do you approach that possibility? How do you manage it? How do you react to it? By mistrusting everybody? By changing your immigration policy of 'send these, the homeless, tempest-tost to me'? I mean, we had hundreds of new immigrants since the last battle, with the Marauders. If it were true, if we did have a mole in our midst, it could be anybody.

So we deliberated and argued for hours.

Eventually we put the matter to a vote. And it was decided: we would lie. We would tell the people of Amanzi we were doubling the Special Ops Teams because of the new trade routes we were developing. We needed more soldiers to safeguard these routes.

Of course, if you lie to people, you will be found out eventually. And there will be repercussions. And politicians like Pastor Nkosi Sebego will exploit that lie. And the repercussions. He was very clever, our dear pastor. He voted against the lie. And he made sure the record showed that he voted against it. And we suspected that he had a reason to do that. But what could we do?

Sofia Bergman

I was stubborn and pig-headed and later I regretted that bitterly. But I was so frustrated and unhappy. And I was a teenager, I know that's a poor excuse, but there you go . . .

I just wanted to get out of school and out of Groendakkies, and if I could have left town as well, I'm sure I would have chosen to do that too. With all the ordinary Amanzian, post-Fever and puberty reasons for my urge to flee. And one of those reasons was that, on top of everything else, I was bored. In the first six months I didn't do well at school. The work was easy, so I didn't go to any trouble and wasn't stimulated. Of course, my attitude was extremely negative. But in any case, they made me stay with children who were two years younger than me for the rest of the year. You know how it works at school, you normally socialise with the kids in your class. And usually they're your peers. But my age group were two years ahead of me academically, and they cut me out completely, because I was the dunce going to school with little kids. So I didn't fit in anywhere, and nobody wanted me . . . Frustrated, unhappy, angry and alone.

But then I heard they were going to expand Special Ops. I went to tell the headmaster I was going to do the test. He said no, and I said Amanzi's brand-new, just-approved constitution had moved the entry age for Special Ops up to seventeen. And the law said it was everyone's choice at that age whether they wished to join. And I was turning seventeen on 16 October. He tried to talk me out of it, saying, Sofia, please finish school first. But I was stubborn. And I was afraid there might not be any vacancies left in the Spotters, because there had been a lot of applications. So they sent Nero Dlamini to talk to me. He really did try . . .

Of course I was completely unaware that my path was so similar to Nico's. If I had known . . .

I don't know if it would have changed anything.

16 October

Domingo was a bastard. Domingo was as cunning as the devil.

He made us compete for leadership positions. He gave us each the opportunity to lead a team through intense training scenarios, but he never told us how we fared. He let each one believe they had a chance.

And then that morning Sofia arrived. She said she had heard there were still three places open, and she wanted to do the test.

Domingo called me. He knew how I felt about Sofia. The whole world knew how I felt about Sofia.

He sent the other troops on a run, so it was just the two of us left standing with him. He had a little smile on his face. I knew what that meant. Trouble. Domingo changed the selection test for a place in Special Ops whenever he liked. He liked to surprise, to invent new and inhuman challenges.

I looked at Sofia. She was indescribably beautiful. Her hair was in two long white-blond plaits. 'Good luck,' I told her. And I was relieved to see her nod her thanks.

Domingo said, 'Storm, take Bergman to the Q-store and give her kit.'

'Yes, Captain.'

'Give her a rifle, and give her a try-out rucksack.'

'Yes, Captain.'

'And then the pair of you run to Luckhoff, to the stone.'

'Yes, Captain.' What was he planning?

'And then run back.'

'Yes, Captain.' Where was the catch? In the time he would allow? In a new route? Would she have to carry me?

'You have eight hours.'

'Yes, Captain.' Eight hours? Why so long? Everyone knew Sofia Bergman could run. Like the wind, for kilometres on end.

'But she has to beat you, Storm. Do you both understand?'

I said, 'Yes, Captain.' She said nothing, only nodded in determination. It's too easy, I thought, where was the Domingo-catch?

'If she gets back to me before you, she's in.'

'Yes, Captain.' Maybe it would be a very enjoyable morning after all. Eight hours with Sofia, just me and her at a steady trot.

'The problem, Storm, is that you're one of my strongest leaders. You're on my shortlist. I want you as my sergeant of Team Bravo.'

'Yes, Captain. Thank you, Captain.'

'The sergeant job is yours. But you have to beat Bergman. You must be back before her.'

Cunning as the devil himself.

Sofia Bergman

Perhaps I should clarify one thing: Special Ops were the rock stars of that era, as far as the teenage girls were concerned. We knew the name of each member of the Spotters, we knew who was the strongest and the fastest and the toughest and the best-looking and the sexiest. So there I was, standing next to Nico Storm and looking at him, already a head taller than his father, taller than Domingo, he had these shoulders, and he was incredibly fit, just glowing with health. And I knew he was the second fastest over thirty kilometres and sixty kilometres; not even Domingo could shoot like Nico Storm now.

I had to beat him.

And he wasn't going to let me win because he liked me, because if he wanted to make sergeant, he could not let me win.

At that moment, nothing counted any more. It didn't count that I had seen him walking down the street with Okkie and his father, and that he had been kind to his kid brother. Now he was my opponent, my rival, he was the hurdle I had to leap over. And I thought, okay, then, I'll have to beat you.

Sofia's SpOT test: II

Sofia Bergman

It's one thing to run twenty or thirty kilometres every day with feather-light, comfortable running shoes. It's quite another thing to run in military boots and uniform with the helmet and the rifle and a rucksack stuffed with stones.

It was even weirder doing it with someone else.

Nico ran just behind me. And he would say, Sofia, no, stay in the foot-path. Look out for the sand. Careful of the thorn trees. Or he would say, run slower, don't burn up your energy too soon. I didn't say a word, I just ran. And I thought, why is he saying these things? He wasn't going to let me win. Did he really think I would like him more, or what?

And so we ran.

I ran a few steps behind her, because I loved watching her. She was beautiful and she was a beautiful runner as well. She had a rhythm and grace that I had never seen in anyone else. She ran with consummate ease, as if she were not exposed to the same gravity and drag as common mortals.

Initially she ran too fast. It was adrenalin. I told her to slow down. I knew the route like the palm of my hand, warned her about the holes, the difficult sections, the problem areas. Because I wanted her to stay in the race as long as possible. So that I had time to think, time to decide what to do. There was more than one thing at stake here.

There was the way I felt about Sofia.

There was Domingo, who always worked with a strategy. He was constantly testing us. I had to try to work out what he was testing this time: did he want to see how badly I wanted to be sergeant? The answer was: very badly. Surely he could have seen that in the past seven weeks I had worked like one possessed.

Perhaps he wanted to know if I would sacrifice myself for a fellow soldier, for someone else's desire. Or if I could suppress my own interests, if I could act unselfishly. Maybe that's what a leader ought to do?

Or he might want to know if I was ruthless, if I could put leadership and the interests of Special Ops above all else. Above the desires of my heart.

By the time we arrived in Luckhoff, I was certain it was the latter. Domingo was completely unsentimental. Domingo believed in animals. Domingo wanted to see if I could be an animal.

Of course I could.

It would be brilliant if Sofia Bergman could become a Spotter. It would be even more brilliant if I could be a SpOT sergeant and she was one of my troops. Then I would see her every day. Be near her, show her what a wise and balanced leader and brilliant soldier I was.

But if she didn't pass the selection test successfully, if she had to go home to Groendakkies, it meant that I could visit her there. I had to be clever. I had to let her believe that I gave her a fair chance to beat me.

So I kept on offering her advice.

Sofia Bergman

In Luckhoff Nico showed me where the stone was. He lifted it up for me. There was a letter that read: Shake a leg. Time's a-wasting. *There was a water bottle, which he passed to me. I drank some of it.*

He checked his watch and said, 'Wow, your time is very good. But you have to pace yourself. You can burn out. Rather come in a bit late. Domingo gave me seven hours, I didn't make it, but I was selected anyway. You can't always take him literally.'

Later he told me he really meant it well, but at that moment I didn't hear it like that. I thought, you arrogant little show-off. He thought I couldn't beat him. He was telling me he only got seven hours, and Domingo gave me eight. And what's more, he didn't think I could make it in eight?

I lost my temper. Totally. I said, 'Fuck you, Nico Storm. You can't beat me.'

And I turned round, and ran back.

You should have seen his face.

★   ★   ★

For nearly a year I had been fantasising over this beautiful girl, dreaming dreams of tender words about sweet things with her.

And there she stood at the stone and swore like a trooper and I could see she was livid and absolutely determined. I couldn't believe my ears. I couldn't believe that a word like that could come out of that mouth. And I couldn't believe that she really thought she could beat me.

I knew we had run an excellent time to Luckhoff – just as good as my very best time. But the return trip was another story. And she didn't know that.

I watched her run towards the mountain, and I laughed. To myself, of course. And I ran after her.

Sofia Bergman

It was only about seven or eight kilometres on the way back to Amanzi that my temper calmed and I found my rhythm. And something happened.

My elder brother Dawid won silver in the fifteen hundred metres at the Commonwealth Games. He was the first to tell me about endorphin euphoria. Only now and then, he told me, when he was training, while he was running, he would get the high, the euphoria. Then he felt as light as a feather, he felt he was running without effort, felt like he could keep going for ever. And he ran faster than he had ever run. I always wondered what it felt like; as a school kid I had never experienced it.

But 16 October in the Year of the Pig was my birthday. And nobody had given me a present.

Till I got one from my late brother Dawid.

On the way back from Luckhoff you have to run uphill first. It's a flat-topped mountain. You run for almost nine kilometres on the top before you have to go down a valley.

A kilometre before Sofia and I had to descend the mountain, she increased her pace.

'Slowly,' I said. 'It's more than twenty kilometres to go.'

She didn't listen to me. She just ran. Effortlessly.

I still believed I couldn't lose. I accelerated too.

Down the mountain. I remained five paces behind her, I felt a bit sorry for her. I would tell Domingo she had set one of the best times in the first thirty kilometres, she had a lot of potential.

We reached the bottom. The footpath that Special Ops had carved out here, over and over, ran all along the hills, to the Amanzi Dam. It ran in search of the easiest route between the inaccessible ruggedness of the dry gullies that drained away the water in the rainy season, and the energy-sapping, rocky hills themselves. It was never easy, it was never level, there was no chance of a breather, it just kept on testing you.

She kept up her pace.

Sixteen kilometres to go, and still she ran on with that light-footed grace.

Fifteen, fourteen to go. At thirteen her booted foot hooked on something and she stumbled and I thought she was going to fall. She regained her balance and kept on running.

At ten kilometres I was still in denial. I had never seen a civilian run like this. She couldn't keep it up.

At seven the possibility wormed its way into my mind: what if she did keep up this pace? Could I?

Of course I could.

At six kilometres I realised I would have to decide when I was going to speed up. I didn't want to leave it too late.

At five I knew the time had come. I waited for a stretch of terrain level enough for me to pass her, and I accelerated, caught up with her. She was in her own world, completely unaware of me. She was unbelievable.

I ran even faster, lengthening my strides. I had to build up a lead and then I had to increase it, step by step. I didn't want to be involved in a sprint finish over the last kilometre, in full view of my comrades. Break her spirit. Do it now.

Sofia Bergman

It was the stumble that broke my euphoria. All of a sudden.

I kept my pace, but I could feel my legs and my lungs, I could feel them. And I heard him running just behind me, and I thought he was going to win. I couldn't keep up this pace. It was the rucksack and the rifle, they were breaking my rhythm.

I didn't want to go back to school.

And I began to think of what Nico had said, how Domingo had accepted him anyway, how Domingo was a person you shouldn't always take literally.

Domingo had told him, 'If she's back before you, she's in.'

That's all. That was the only rule.

I had to be back before Nico Storm.

Then I had an idea. And I thought, it might not be fair, but it didn't matter, he was an arrogant, cheeky brat. All is fair in love and war. And this is war.

But then I thought, wait, it might not be necessary. Let me see if he can pass me. And then he passed me.

Four kilometres to go. Her footsteps behind me grew heavier. Slower.

My heart went out to her. Such terrible resolve, such delicate grace, such wonderful rhythm, but today she was not going to become a Spotter. Unless Domingo was in the mood for mercy.

I extended my lead, I wanted to deliver the *coup de grâce*, put the result beyond all doubt. I wanted to look back, but I had to think about our romantic future as well.

I heard her scream, a shrill scream of terror.

78

Sofia's SpOT test: III

I stopped, turned around.

Our first crossbow meeting still haunted me a year later. So many times I wished that moment could have been different. More romantic. More dignified. For me. Over and over in my bed at night in the SpOT barracks I had replayed that scene so that I could fulfil my leading role as hero and saviour.

And here it was now, dream turned real: Sofia Bergman was in distress, and I could save her.

I ran back, I couldn't see her. She must have fallen, over there at the big rocks and thorn trees.

'Sofia!' I shouted, really worried now, as I ran back on our tracks.

She didn't answer.

Perhaps she'd fainted. Exhaustion. It happened.

I was past the thorn tree, I reached the rocks. And then something hit me right between the eyes.

Sofia Bergman

I hit him with the butt of the rifle. All's fair in love and war.

He dropped like he'd been pole-axed and stayed there as I ran on. I didn't know if I'd hit him hard enough to be out for a minute or an hour. I would find out once I'd passed the test.

A bit further on I started to doubt: had I hit him too hard? Did he hit his head on a stone?

What if he's dead?

No, he's not dead. Just unconscious.

What if he's dead?

Three kilometres to go, I could see the dam, I could see the Special

Ops base there on the hill across the river, and I was worried I had killed him.

I would have to go and see. I ran slower and slower. I stopped and turned around.

Then I saw him coming. Fast. Five hundred metres away. Or four hundred. I spun around and bolted as fast as I could. Pumped full of adrenalin, because now I was scared of what he would do to me. You can't hit someone over the head with a rifle butt and think there'll be no consequences. He was going to be cross. Very cross. And the anger was going to make him run like he had never run before.

And if he caught up with me, ten to one he would hit me too.

Fear gives you wings.

I can't describe all the things that I thought in those moments, because my children are going to read these memoirs.

I was angry with Sofia Bergman. Angry at the poor sportsmanship, angry at the abuse of my goodwill, angry at my own naivety, but above all because I knew: that was exactly the sort of thing that Domingo would love. His lips would curl into a thin, mean, half-smile and he'd tell her, 'Welcome to the Spotters.' And he would smirk at me and say, 'Sorry, Storm. You are not my sarge. Better luck next time.'

That wasn't going to happen.

Rage is a powerful engine. But the knockout blow and the blood in my eyes and the concussion took their toll. I was closing the gap, but I didn't know if I was doing it fast enough.

And what was she going to do when I reached her? Hit me again?

We had to pass through the gate at the Havenga Bridge. She was still nearly three hundred metres ahead. I heard her shout to the guards, 'Open up, open up!'

I saw the guards run out to see what was happening, how they laughed and hurried to push the gates open so that she could run through.

'It's Nico, it's Nico. He's bleeding!' I ran past. My dignity in shreds, once again.

Across the bridge. She still had a lead of over two hundred metres, but I heard her boots on the tarmac, and I knew she could hear my footsteps too. She was going to look back. Looking back is bad. It robs you of your rhythm and speed. Then I would catch up some more.

We reached the south bank, on the other side of the bridge. Just over a kilometre back to base.

The bridge guards would have radioed ahead. The entire Special Ops would know we were coming. And that I was losing. And I was bleeding and tired, the pace relentless. But fury fuelled me.

A kilometre to go. She was a hundred and fifty metres ahead.

She looked back.

Sofia Bergman

I heard him coming, I heard how quick his stride was. I knew I didn't have any gas left in the tank, I was dead tired, my entire body burned like fire. He was right behind me, I wanted to surrender, I was afraid he would hit me or knock me down or something.

I looked back.

He was still more than a hundred metres behind. I was mistaken. I had a chance. I ran, I gave everything I had, up the slope, that dreadful steep slope to Special Ops.

I looked back again.

He had halved the distance, he was closing in.

Through the gate now. I was still ahead, his boots hammering behind me. Domingo was standing there, I had to reach him before Nico. The soldiers stood watching, cheering and yelling. I was going to win.

And then Nico tackled me. We crashed to the ground. He was on top of me; I was winded. He swung his leg across my belly and pinned me down with his weight, his hands on my forearms. I couldn't move, I couldn't breathe, I gasped, I made strange croaking and hiccupping noises, just like when I shot him with the crossbow, only our roles were reversed. I saw his forehead. The massive purple mark, the broken skin, the cut, long and ugly, blood all over his face, in his eyes, it had run right down to his neck.

Hit me again, you disgusting swine, hit me again, he said. He echoed what I had once said to him – it must have made a lasting impression on him.

I said to her, 'Hit me again, you disgusting swine, hit me again.'

And in that moment it felt as if my universe was back in balance.

79

Sofia's SpOT test: IV

Sofia Bergman

There is a part of this story that nobody knows. Nobody except Nico, and I only told him a long time afterwards.

At the moment it happened, it made no sense at all.

As I lay on my back on the parade ground, winded, heaving and gasping, I was afraid of Nico, he was furious with me. He was sitting on me, holding my arms. I looked up, saw his broken face, and I saw the aircraft.

It wasn't Hennie Fly's aeroplane. It was an airliner, a big airliner, though small now, little more than a speck, because it was flying so high. It winked brightly in the clear deep blue sky, a flash of light on metal, gone in the blink of an eye.

I couldn't say anything, I had no breath. I couldn't even point my finger, because my hands were pinned down.

The airliner flew north, towards Europe. And then it was gone, and Domingo's shadow fell across me.

Domingo said, 'Get off Bergman, Storm.'

I climbed off, stood up.

He looked at me. I didn't know how deep the gash on my head was, how terrible the blood looked, I just knew it was bad, and it was there, because I had to wipe the blood from my eyes with my hands.

Domingo looked at her. 'Bergman, you've passed the test. Fall in with Team Delta.'

He waited until she stood up and was out of earshot. He looked at me intently. I could see myself in the mirror lenses of his dark glasses. I looked pathetic.

Domingo sighed. 'Happy to see you have an anger management problem too. You're not yet ready for sergeant, Storm. I'm moving you to Team Charlie, until you learn to control that temper.'

I waited for him to dismiss me. I could see there were still words in his mouth. He held them back.

'Dismissed,' he said.

80

In the Year of the Pig I learned humility.

I was just another one of the troops in Special Ops Team Charlie, the weakest team of the Spotters. And the Sofia Bergman story oblit-erated my reputation. Overnight she became an Amanzi sensation, a legend, a heroine, thanks to her hit-him-with-the-rifle strategy to earn SpOT selection. When Domingo found out about her background, of the Bushman who had taught her to track, he let her share that knowl-edge with the Special Ops troops as a sort of informal instructor.

Overnight I became a figure of ridicule.

It was deeply painful for me, on more than one level. My prestige in the unit went out the window. I was still the top shot, the second fastest and a strong candidate for promotion. My own legendary tale – inter-woven with the diesel Cessna and Okkie and the twelve KTM men who I had shot – was eternally besmirched now. There is a special pleasure people take in cutting down tall poppies: the arrogant son of the chair-man, the founder, the author of the pamphlet. Everywhere I saw heads bowed together, the giggles and gossip hidden behind cupped hands, the way their eyes followed me with a mixture of fascination and pity.

But the greatest injury of all was the damage to my relationship with Sofia. Or rather, the damage to the potential of our relationship.

Just seeing her every day broke my heart all over again.

In the Year of the Pig I saw how my father's love worked.

A Tuesday late in October, a little more than a week after my fall. We worked hard at SpOT, from early in the morning. But nobody worked harder than I did. I was hell-bent on making Team Charlie the best team of all, even if I had to do it all myself. I may have been just another soldier, a humble private, but I gave it my all. I'd show them. It sapped my energy, because I tried to help everybody, I tried to push *and* pull. I was dog-tired every night.

I'd just come out of the shower next to Team Charlie's first-floor dormitory and was getting dressed before mess when through the uncurtained window something familiar caught my eye. Looking out, I saw Pa and Okkie walking away, past the edge of the parade ground towards the gate.

What were they doing here?

I hadn't seen them at all since the Sofia episode, as we didn't have weekends off any more.

My father and Okkie walking hand in hand, in the soft light of the setting sun. Pa gesturing with his free hand. He was explaining something to Okkie. The meaning of a word? The geomorphological history of the river down below? That the bats that swooped over them were mammals?

My heart melted, my body flooded with emotion. I jumped when someone shouted 'Storm!' in the corridor. I turned away from the window and nodded.

'Parcel for you at the front door,' I heard.

Pa had brought it.

I dressed quickly, and went to fetch it. A sturdy cardboard box. I carried it to the dormitory, put it down on my bed, and opened it.

The moka pot that Pa and I had used in the Volvo. And the little gas stove. And a mug. And four packs of ground coffee, vacuum sealed.

The universe was merciful to me, because thankfully I was alone in the dormitory – something that didn't happen often. I was intensely grateful, because I couldn't help but weep, silently, but irresistibly, the tears rolling down my cheeks. Because of the way my father reached out to me. He must have heard the gossip. He must have known how that made a young man of seventeen feel. And he couldn't make contact. He couldn't come in here and ask for Nico to come home on Sunday. That would have humiliated me more.

But he took his most precious possession and brought it to me. I didn't know he had hoarded coffee like this. It was a secret he had kept very well.

I wept over the love of my father, despite all that I had done to him. I wept over the memories of the moka pot, the months and months that Pa and I were on the road performing our little coffee ritual every morning.

I wept a little out of pity for myself too. Which wasn't necessarily a bad thing. It also heals.

And I put away the moka pot and coffee for another day.

In the Year of the Pig, summer was very hot and dry.

It didn't rain in October or November. In December it was so scorching hot that the grazing in the veld shrivelled and 30 per cent of our hens died. We hadn't planted pastures for the livestock, but there was enough straw and stubble to keep the herds and flocks alive.

In the Year of the Pig, Birdy finally agreed to go on a date with Domingo. Apparently she told Nero Dlamini that 'he just wore me down'.

On Christmas Eve he came to pick her up with the Jeep, and they drove across the Havenga Bridge and out of the gate in the late afternoon. They only returned the following morning. Nobody knew where they went, but Sarge's patrols reported seeing Jeep tracks on the road to the old Otterskloof Private Game Reserve, on the northern bank on the other side of the dam. The veranda of the old guest house had recently been swept, and it looked like the biggest and best guest room had been thoroughly cleaned.

I didn't want to hear about it. I begrudged Domingo his luck in love. Especially because it was Domingo, of all people.

The Year of the Pig was the last that my father was chairman of the Committee. Because Amanzi adopted a constitution, and in January of the Year of the Lion we would vote, and my father would become the first President of Amanzi.

The constitution took months of work to edit and tweak until everyone was happy with it. It began with:

We, the people of Amanzi, through our freely elected representatives, adopt this constitution as the supreme law of our community, so as to create and establish a democratic and open society in which government is based on the will of the people and every citizen is equally protected by law. Our constitution will strive to improve the quality of life of all citizens, free the potential of each person, and build a united and democratic society able to take its rightful place as a sovereign entity in the post-Fever world.

May God protect our people.

Along with the new constitution came new titles. Pa was the

President. The Committee became the Cabinet. It was bigger, every member was a minister with a portfolio. Sarge was elected as Minister of Safety and Security, which meant he was head of defence and police, but everyone still referred to him as Sarge X. He didn't mind. Domingo refused point-blank to accept a more notable rank or title. He said captain was sufficient, he wasn't a Cabinet member, he didn't take part in the elections and he remained head of Special Ops. He was still the person with the most power in Amanzi, despite his humble title.

In the Year of the Pig we produced enough diesel for all our agricultural and military requirements.

In the Year of the Pig people started paying tax for the first time.

We completed construction work on the mill in Gansie Street, opposite the Forum and started operating it. We used electricity to mill grain – our own wheat, for our own bread.

The old OK store was far too small to store all our surplus food. They redesigned and converted all the buildings in Disa Street into one big solid food warehouse.

Birdy Canary ensured electricity supply to Petrusville. Seventy houses in that town were repaired and equipped, and people moved in. Birdy said we would have to increase our electricity supply in fourteen months, because the two-hundred-and-twenty-megawatt hydro-electric generators would not be enough for the industrial and agricultural expansion that we planned.

There was much debate over the possibility of repairing the hydro-electric power plant at the Gariep Dam and diverting it here. But Domingo said we would have to protect and defend the power stations and that required too much manpower.

Pastor Nkosi Sebego supported Domingo. It caused quite a stir; people wondered what his agenda could be.

The result was that the Committee decided to start moving the wind turbines at Noblesfontein near Victoria West as soon as possible and erect them in the mountains of Amanzi's reserve.

In the Year of the Pig more than five thousand souls formed part of the Amanzi community. They lived in the town, in the SpOT barracks, in Petrusville and on farms along the river, as far as Hopetown. It seemed that Hopetown would be the next settlement to be revived.

People began to speak of the Republic of Amanzi.

The Year of the Lion

81

Annus horribilis

That was the final year of my father's life.

I so wish I had known it then. As I reminisce about those last months before his death, I think January, January especially was a good month for him.

Despite the heroic name, the Year of the Lion was an *annus horribilis*. It was the one that confirmed the rule: everything always happens at once, just when you least expect it. Betrayal and war, destruction and murder, and the excruciating pain that comes with knowledge. About everything.

January was hot and dry, just like the December and November preceding it. Crops were shrivelling, we needed rain badly. The election was on 5 January. There were three thousand four hundred and nine people over the age of seventeen who were eligible to vote, according to the new constitution. Altogether three thousand four hundred and eight turned up to vote. Everyone knew the single voter who abstained was Domingo. He didn't believe in democracy.

Free Amanzi, my father's party, gained 58 per cent of the votes, the Mighty Warrior Party won the rest. I was there, that night in the Forum when the pastor made his speech. He was a dignified loser. But he closed his speech by assuring his supporters, 'Don't worry. The night is darkest before the dawn.'

None of us realised he meant it as a promise.

Then, my father.

He spoke from the heart. He began by thanking Pastor Nkosi and his party for the manner in which they had taken part in the election. He quoted from Plato's *Republic*: 'Democracy is a charming form of government, full of variety and disorder, and dispensing a sort of equality to equals and unequals alike.' He said equality had been one of the cornerstones of democracy for hundreds of years; in 1790 Maximilian Robespierre made it part of his motto of Freedom, Equality and Fraternity. The problem was that true equality, in the fullest sense of the word, was a rare and evasive phenomenon. Everywhere in the world, but especially in South Africa, the Fever had wreaked terrible devastation, but it had at least one positive outcome – it made us all truly equal. In Amanzi there were no rich and poor, there were just people. And it was an honour and a privilege to serve them as the democratically elected leader.

Pa said he would like in all humility to add a short piece to Plato's view on democracy. He would like to say that democracy not only afforded a kind of equality to the equal as well as the unequal, but also a freedom to the believers and the unbelievers, to the Christians and the Muslims, Hindus and Buddhists, ancestor worshippers and agnostics.

Everyone knew he was talking to the pastor.

'I want to invite every member of our community tonight: embrace this freedom. Enjoy this freedom. Use this freedom. And come, work together to make it bigger and stronger.'

For the past four months Hennie Fly had been flying with his first trainee pilot, twenty-year-old Peace Pedi. Peace's first name was a misnomer, because he was anything but peaceful. He was skinny and slightly stooped, leaning forward so far when he walked that it seemed that at any minute he would tumble forwards into perpetual motion. Peace had a full, wide mouth curved in a permanent smile, and he was practically never silent. He talked, to everybody, about everything, he was a social dynamo.

He and Hennie were unlikely bosom buddies, united in their great passion and unquenchable love of talking. There was much specula-tion over how and when each got a chance to talk as they flew about in the small Cessna.

They flew patrols every morning, when the weather allowed. For four months they saw nothing, except livestock and game and our people, and migrants on their way to Amanzi.

Until 27 January. January was supposed to be the rainy season and the time for thunderstorms, so they took off in the early morning, just after dawn. But the clouds stayed away. Hennie chose a different route each day, so there was no predictable routine to his flights. Just in case Domingo's spy theory was true. They flew at varying altitudes.

On 27 January they flew above the R717 east of Amanzi before 07.00. About sixty kilometres from Amanzi, just outside the completely lifeless and deserted town of Philippolis, Peace spotted the motorcycles: four of them, at a distance just far enough away to allow for some doubt. He pointed them out to Hennie Fly and they both stared hard at the specks riding into Philippolis. They saw the motorcycles for about twenty or thirty seconds, until they disappeared under the big trees along the main road.

Hennie kept his head. He didn't deviate from his route, he didn't change altitude, fly slower or faster. He didn't want the bikers to realise they had been seen, but he reported it to Minister Xaba's radio operators in Amanzi. Sarge X let Domingo know, and eleven minutes after Peace's sharp eyes had seen them, the SpOT commander left for Philippolis with Team Alpha in the Volvo.

Fourteen minutes later Alpha found the imprint of a dual-purpose motorcycle's front and rear tyre in a strip of sand that had washed across the tarmac of the town's main road.

It was the first sign of gang activity we'd seen in nearly a year.

The next day the Volvo and the ERF, with Team Alpha and Bravo, drove to Philippolis and Jagersfontein, Bethulie and Springfontein, Trompsburg and Reddersburg.

They found nothing.

On 30 January Domingo asked Hennie and Peace to fly patrols at night too. Because he had his suspicions.

82

February: I

During the night of 2 February at 00.23 Hennie and Peace spotted lights between Koffiefontein and Fauresmith. Strange lights, single lights, it looked like six or seven motorcycles racing at high speed, but according to the pilots' calculations that was just veld, there was no road there.

They flew towards the lights, which were suddenly extinguished.

Very early on 3 February Team Alpha drove out in the Volvo to investigate. No road, but an old railway line, near Bellum Station. With clear motorcycle tracks running alongside. Perhaps up to ten bikes.

They followed the tracks until they disappeared on the tarmac road near Koffiefontein. Domingo summoned Team Bravo, and Hennie and Peace in the Cessna too, and sent them out to fine-comb the entire area all day and all night, all the way from Ritchie to Jagersfontein.

They found nothing.

But it was clear now: there was definitely something brewing in this scorching hot summer.

The four Special Ops Teams consisted of fourteen people each – two sergeant-instructors and twelve troops. Aram and Taljaard were the sergeants who trained Team Charlie. They had been ordinary soldiers with me in Bravo before their promotion. I was the only regular soldier in Charlie with previous experience. The rest were all new recruits.

When we heard the news of the motorcycle tracks and watched Alpha and Bravo drive out of base, Aram and Taljaard looked at each other, and then at me. All three of us longed to be with our old comrades, but we were busy with manoeuvres, preparing Team Charlie for operations. And I was enduring my punishment, though the nature of my offence was still not entirely clear to me.

*　　*　　*

On 3 February, precisely one year and two days after our last skirmish – with the Marauders – Sarge X's radio eavesdroppers heard voices for the first time on the forty-metre band of the ham radio.

'Clan Victor, Clan Victor, this is Number One, come in.' Our radio room had no idea how long Number One had been calling on this frequency. They heard the voice at 10.03 and immediately sent for Sarge X, Pa, Birdy and Domingo. The chorus continued for another fourteen minutes: 'Clan Victor, Clan Victor, this is Number One, come in.'

'It's him,' said Domingo. I knew he would never forget that voice. 'It's Trunkenpolz.'

At last the reply came: 'Number One, this is Clan Victor, repeat, this is Clan Victor. QRI.'

'Tone is good, Clan Victor. QRM?'

'Negative, Number One, negative. QRU?'

'Roger, Clan Victor, roger. I have an invitation for you. Sierra Charlie at Maseru on 6 February, Clan Victor, repeat, Sierra Charlie at Maseru on 6 February. QRV.'

'Roger, Number One, copy that, Sierra Charlie at Maseru on 6 February.'

'Number One, over and out.'

It took a whole hour to reach consensus on the meaning of the conversation. Domingo, Birdy, the engineer and Minister Xaba worked on the translation, which ran:

Vikings gang, this is Number One, come in.

Number One this is the Vikings gang, how is the tone of my signal?

Your tone is good, Vikings. Are you experiencing any interference? Which Domingo interpreted as: are you experiencing any enemy actions, or eavesdropping?

No, Number One. Do you have anything for me?

Yes, I have an invitation. There is a Sales Club meeting on 6 February at Maseru. Are you ready for it?

Yes, we are.

Then they confirmed the date and place, and signed off.

Much later Nero Dlamini told us of the big debate that followed this radio message at a special meeting of the new, expanded Cabinet, which, according to the constitution, replaced the old Committee.

They called Domingo in to hear his opinion too. Pa, as President of Amanzi, was the chairman of the meeting.

The big question they argued over was: should Amanzi send Special Ops to Maseru for the meeting, to try to capture or kill Clarkson and Meyiwa/Number One and the Chair?

Surprisingly, Pastor Nkosi Sebego was the aggressive one: 'It's been a year. They feel safe. We can't afford to let them slip through our fingers. Let's send in the soldiers. Let us take the war to them.'

Ravi Pillay gave his cautious support: 'I have to agree. There is no evidence to the contrary. I say we send SpOT.'

Beryl and Birdy found the coincidence troubling: within the space of one week there had been signs of gang activities within a hundred kilometres of us, followed by the conversation over the radio. All of a sudden, out of the blue, after a year of silence. And not just a how-are-you radio chat, but one that, in between all the Q-codes, made the date and place of a trade meeting crystal-clear. 'It's just too easy,' said Birdy. 'Too much of a coincidence.'

'Please,' said the pastor. 'Not everything is a conspiracy. I just don't think these terrorists, these devil's spawn, are that smart.' And so they argued back and forth, until eventually Pa called the Cabinet to order, and asked Domingo – who till now had sat listening poker-faced – what he thought.

'I think they got a big fright when they killed Mbalo in August. They must have thought then, let's wait six months, let the dust settle, let's not make these idiots suspicious. The dust has settled now. I think they're coming for us. 'Cause our harvests are coming in, and lots of canning and preserving is being done, and it's a very dry season, there will be hunger out there. I think the radio broadcast is a trap. They want us to send soldiers to Maseru. They want our Ops Teams away from here, so they can attack Amanzi.'

'Oh, please,' said Pastor Nkosi. 'It seems I'm the only one who isn't a coward. Give me a SpOT team. I will lead them.'

Domingo stood up before Pa could respond. Nero Dlamini suspected he was going to give the pastor a cuff on the ear. Instead he said, 'Mr President, I have said my piece. It's for this Cabinet to decide.' And he walked out.

They voted on the matter and decided the Special Ops Teams should stay home for now. If it wasn't an ambush set by Number One, there would be more radio calls and Sales Club meetings.

The next four days were ominously quiet. There were no further radio chats on the forty-metre bandwidth, nor any suspicious activity seen by scouts.

On 8 February all hell broke loose.

At 04.41 Domingo woke the entire Special Ops unit. It was still pitch-dark. He ordered us to fall in on the parade ground, said there had been an attack on our settlement at Hopetown just after midnight. Of the sixty-six people who lived and worked there, sixty-three were killed. Three girls of twelve and younger survived. When the first shots were fired, an adult told them to go and hide in the old graveyard across the main road. They listened in fear and trembling to the shots, explosions, the screams, the roar of engines, and the crackling of fires raging through their houses. They saw the flames, thought it was all over, and crept nearer. And they saw the attackers leave. On motorcycles, led by one pick-up, with a large machine gun mounted on the back.

The oldest of the children knew how to work the radio, and she had let Amanzi know when they were sure the attackers had all gone.

'The girls say the attackers came from the north, and left in that direction. Hennie Fly is in the air, combing the area. Alpha and Bravo, we are moving out immediately. Charlie and Delta, you are operational as of this morning. In my absence, your team leaders will be taking orders from Sarge X. He will be following our emergency defence plan, and I expect you to perform to the very best of your abilities.'

The big attack on Amanzi came in the darkest hours of 9 February.

Our best units, Alpha and Bravo, were near Kimberley, along with our best military brain: Domingo. They were hunting gangs that had disappeared like smoke into the wide, wild veld. Hennie Fly and Peace Pedi were providing air support.

Amanzi's big emergency defence plan was set in motion. It meant that Sarge X's entire defence force – the so-called Dad's Army – was deployed. Supported by reservists, about a hundred residents who were not officially part of Dad's Army, but at least had a bit of training in guard duty and firearms. They happily and in self-mockery called themselves Mom's Army. They had never been called up, as we had never had a true emergency. Until now.

On that night of 9 February there were more than two hundred people in and around Amanzi who stood ready to defend the town and community.

There were twenty heavily armed guards posted at each of the Petrusville and Havenga gates. Thirty were on duty at the heavily fortified main gate. Ten mounted sentries patrolled on horseback on the other side of the dam, the north bank.

And the rest, a force of fifty of Sarge X's best (middle-aged) soldiers, plus another fifty reservists, were in trenches and barricades back in the reserve, in Sector 3, the 'soft underbelly' of our natural mountain fortifications – the little valley that stretched from the dam up to the mountain.

The plan was one day to secure Sector 3 with a wall and a gate. It would have to be a long wall and gate. The scope of such a project required a great deal more resources than Amanzi had access to now, because the terrain was extensive and rough. Consequently, the defence force of one hundred people sheltered in a network of trenches and stone barricades. Sector 3's 'lines'.

Both the sergeants from Team Charlie and I had more than a year of intensive military training behind us. We had survived a KTM battle, we had gone to capture the Marauders' radio base. My fellow troops, the newer members of Team Charlie, could boast of four months of Domingo's relentless instruction. Despite our advanced skills, Charlie had the singular honour and privilege of standing guard with the weak reservists, the rest of Mom's Army, in Disa Street. We were the last line of defence around Amanzi's food warehouse, bottling factory, mill, bakery and police station – the heart of our community. We were deployed in pairs in strategic positions between the buildings, alternating with the reservists.

It was hard not to see this deployment as a slap in Charlie's face. But we knew it wasn't meant that way. The emergency defence plan's original blueprint placed Team Alpha at the main gate and Team

Bravo in Sector 3. But they were with Domingo, somewhere near Kimberley now.

Sofia Bergman was with Team Delta.

I thought of her where I lay waiting. I thought of her and wondered whether she ever spared a thought for me.

Team Delta's orders were only fractionally more exciting. They were up there, in the heart of the reserve. They served as support for the hundred brave defenders of our soft underbelly. They waited at the old game ranger's storage shed and offices, halfway between Sector 3 and the gate that separated our town and the reserve.

The attack on Amanzi came precisely as Domingo had predicted. They struck back in the valley.

The assault force was large. Larger than we had made preparation for. More than two hundred vehicles. About three hundred bloodthirsty fighting men. They fell on us two hours before dawn.

83

February: II

The Enemy. I remember: that's how we referred to them at the time, with a measure of frustration. An enemy without a name is a less hated and less feared enemy. Where were the days of the KTM?

The amorphous, amalgamated terrorists, the evil slave-trading partnership, the alphabet soup of motorcycle and pick-up gangs and the unfathomable Sales Club and other criminal, warmongering splinter groups metamorphosed in the Amanzi parlance to an unimaginative 'Enemy'. They had hidden from our Cessna and our patrols in the folds of the mountains and ravines of the valleys near the furthest upstream point of the dam, fifty kilometres from our town. It must have cost them many nights of slowly creeping closer to get them all there unseen.

They had evaded our best scouting attempts due to the amateur status of our defence force and the wide expanse of the Karoo. Last night after sundown they must have mobilised the massed vehicles and fighters to drive silently, slowly and carefully to their nearest gathering point, the place where they were still invisible and inaudible to us. It was about four kilometres from Sector 3, down the soft underbelly valley.

From there, at 03.25, just over two hours before dawn, they set off, in a mad rush, a race against time to confront the smallest possible defence force and utilise their strategic advantage best: the element of surprise, their superior numbers, their armour-plated pick-ups – four with the relatively heavy ordnance of twenty-millimetre cannon – and the cover of darkness.

They also had four problems. The first was what we now called Sector 3: the valley itself. The road from the plains below up to the reserve was a Jeep track up the steep slope – mountain on one side, valley on the other, along a treacherous canyon. There was no space for more than two motorbikes side by side. Four-wheeled vehicles had to drive in single file. Their assault convoy was thus a very long, winding worm.

The second was that the length of the Jeep track from bottom to top was two kilometres where they were completely exposed. There was no shelter for the long procession of vehicles.

The third: if they made it past the lines and trenches of Dad's Army in Sector 3, they had to pass through the rock fields. The mountaintop was strewn with extremely inconvenient, round rocks. Not small rocks. On average the size of a melon, the largest like soccer balls. Hundreds of thousands of them. It was hard to walk there on foot; horses hated the terrain. You could race over it with a four-by-four vehicle, but it would shake and rattle and break both man and machine. In the dark the damage would be severe, as they could not dare turn on their headlights. With a motorbike you could only ride at speeds of less than twenty kilometres per hour, picking your way very carefully over the stones. The only solution was to stay in formation on the sole vehicle track. Which made it much easier for your opponent to hit you. Team Delta, Sofia Bergman's team, lay beyond the rock field waiting.

The fourth: the old main gate of the reserve. It was the only place where any vehicle coming through the reserve could enter Amanzi. It was a strong steel gate. A motorcycle could not crash through it. A pick-up perhaps. But thanks to the rough terrain and the gate buildings, only one vehicle could pass through there at a time.

If they ever did get through, Amanzi was in great peril.

Sofia Bergman

It's just about impossible to describe what it's like to be in a battle. I think that's why most people can't talk about it. It feels as though everything were distorted. Time – what feels like hours, is only minutes. What feels like minutes, could be hours. Space is distorted, your sense of near and far and up and down and left and right, everything blurs into one and everything feels like a thousand broken pieces. And your senses, your decision-making, memory, the snatches you can remember, everything topsy-turvy. It's the

*most awful of all terrors that does that, the fear that you might die. And the
adrenalin and the survival urge and a kind of rage inside you, a rage at the
Enemy – how* dare *they try to kill you? It's what they call the 'red mist of
battle', that rage.*

*Nobody can be truly objective when they describe a battle. It's a patchy
memory. A partially imagined memory.*

I was fast asleep at 03.30. It was the urgency of the voices on the two-
way radios that woke me. Anxious voices calling, there's activity in
Sector 3, there's engine noise, lots of engines, vehicles racing, it sounds
like they are coming across the plains beside the dam. Dad's Army in
the trenches of the ravine wanted to know if the guards at the main
gate and Petrusville could also hear it.

No, no one else could hear it.

Minister Xaba's voice crackled over the radio, evident that he had
just been woken, but he took charge immediately. He asked each of the
four lookout posts in Sector 3 to confirm the noise independently.

They did that one after the other.

'We see sparks or something,' said one of them. 'Like a glow. It
might be from exhausts.'

'It's a loud noise,' another added. 'Lots of engines.' Voices freighted
with tension and fear.

Sarge X asked the other posts again, 'Is there any activity?' Again
Petrusville, the main gate and the gate at the Havenga Bridge
confirmed: no, the night was dead quiet.

'They're coming through Sector 3,' said Sarge X. 'Stand by for
action. If you have a target, fire.'

We waited.

Over the radio: 'Coming closer. Noise now louder. We think . . .
There are hundreds . . .'

A voice, shrill with fear: 'Send more people. Send more . . .' Shots
ringing out.

Sarge X remained calm, to his eternal credit. He gave orders to the
radio room to let Domingo know: the big assault is here. Bring Alpha
and Bravo, hurry back to Amanzi.

Domingo and company were more than two hours away. It was too
far to make a difference. This was going to be over soon.

Minister Xaba took his radio, climbed into his police vehicle and drove to the gate of the reserve, and then to the front.

The Enemy were cunning. They sent four armour-plated pick-ups up the valley first. Each of the four had a twenty-millimetre cannon bolted to the load bed, with two men loading and firing. Behind the pick-ups raced the first of scores of motorcycles.

Dad's Army was not equipped to stop these armoured vehicles. They had only R4 rifles.

The pick-ups raced through. Sparks showered where the bullets hit them. Our defence force personnel screamed over the radios to warn Team Delta and Amanzi. I listened and I jumped up, I wanted to do something, wanted to help Team Delta, as we were useless here, we would not be able to withstand a superior force here, we had to stop them before the gate.

Sarge X's voice stayed calm. 'Keep firing. Hold your positions.'

Our defenders told us through the chaos that they had hit some of the bikers. I remember one's jubilant yells, over and over: 'I got him, I got him!'

But most of the first fifty vehicles got through. They didn't want to attack our line in Sector 3. They wanted to breach it, right through to the town. They just raced, shooting wildly, past our lines, over the plateau on top of the mountain, on the way to where Delta lay in wait, now wide awake and ready behind their stone barriers.

And then, the first setback for the Enemy. Dad's Army got lucky. They shot two bikers almost simultaneously – just a hundred metres from the crest of the valley. Both fell in the Jeep track. The next two motorcycles were following too closely. They crashed into the two on the ground and tumbled down as well. The next two just managed to stop in time, but our defenders shot them. A pick-up came next. The driver ploughed over a fallen motorcycle, swerved to avoid the next wreck and his bumper slammed into the rocks beside the track. A plug in the bottleneck ravine. The Enemy's motorcycles and pick-ups dammed up behind them. They couldn't go forward, and they couldn't go back. They were exposed, with no shelter.

Our defence forces yelled and cheered and fired, ensuring no one could clear the pile-up.

But they shot too eagerly, because they were Dad's Army. Their ammunition would not last.

The Enemy's first fifty came across the flats towards Team Delta. Through the rock field.

We heard the voices of Team Delta's two sergeants over the radio. They were former members of Alpha, good leaders, experienced and cool-headed. 'We see them. Five hundred metres. Four hundred. Three hundred . . .'

Team Delta's sergeants gave the order to shoot.

And then, the Enemy's moment of madness. Perhaps due to the unexpected and accurate fire from Delta. Perhaps from bravado, or just sheer adrenalin. The rock field was generally flat; in the dark it seemed easily negotiable, seemed possible to run off the Jeep track and race beside your comrades. They raced at frightening speed, trying to reach the town before we could respond in an organised fashion. A pick-up with a mounted cannon on the back, and an over-enthusiastic driver, swerved off the road to drive beside the one in front of him, or trying to overtake him. Due to a combination of speed, rocks, darkness and poor skills, the driver lost control, just two hundred metres from Delta. The pick-up rolled and then somersaulted, sparks showering the night as it crashed down across the track. A following pick-up smashed into it with a resounding crash. The leading vehicle burst into flames, lighting up the veld and the Enemy. And blocking the track. The racing convoy came to a complete standstill.

Some of the motorcycles bypassed the fire through the veld, struggling, bumping, slow. Team Delta picked them off one by one.

The rest sought shelter behind the pick-ups. Some of the vehicles swerved out of the road and tried to drive through the rock field. At snail's pace, brightly lit by the fire. Team Delta focused their blanket fire on the cabs. They hit the drivers, the passengers, the gun operators. The pick-ups halted. Further back the remainder of the fifty vehicles jammed. The Enemy's soldiers jumped down and out, running for shelter behind rocks and bushes. And began to return fire.

Delta shot as freely as they wanted, because just behind them was one of Domingo's weapons caches. There was plenty of ammunition.

Suddenly it was trench warfare.

Suddenly it was a game of chess.

84

February: III

We hunkered down in Disa Street listening to the radios. Impotent. We could hear Sector 3 and Minister Xaba and Team Delta's sergeants. We formed a mental picture of what was happening up there, and eventually also the impasse on each front: in the valley our defenders were holding the majority of the Enemy's force back at the bottleneck, but their ammunition was depleted. At the rock field Delta had an enormous reserve of ammunition, but they were pinned down.

We had halted the invasion temporarily. As long as the plug in the ravine held. As long as Dad's Army and their reservist brothers had bullets to shoot and pin down the Enemy.

The minutes ticked by to the scattered voices on the radio, distant shots; it was like something happening in another world. On the other side of the mountain, very far from the quiet, calm town where we lay. It was almost impossible to sit still, to accept that this waiting was the best use of our experience and talents.

Bad news came from Sector 3: 'We're running out of ammo.'

If only we could help them. If we . . .

I thought back to my days as a shepherd. I thought about the alternative route that Jacob Mahlangu and I once discovered, when it had snowed so heavily that the road into the reserve was an impassable mud bath. We rode it a few times with that forgotten quadbike, an ancient sheep and game path that the animals had tramped out to and from the watering points.

Maybe I could . . . There was a way to get ammunition to Sector 3. I stood up. Sat down again. I dared not disobey orders.

But I couldn't stand it any more. I jumped to my feet. Ran to where Aram, my closest Charlie sergeant, was lying.

'What are you doing, Storm?' Angry, because I was abandoning my post in stressful circumstances.

'I know a way to get ammunition to Sector 3.'

'How?'

'I used to be a shepherd up there. For over two years. There's a footpath leading from the old township here. It might be overgrown, it's difficult, steep, but it's a shortcut. If we take horses . . .'

He looked at me, thinking. 'In the dark?'

I nodded. 'I often rode that route.'

He hesitated a moment. He jumped up. 'Come on,' he said. We ran to Taljaard, the other sergeant.

Taljaard called the minister on the radio and requested permission to supplement ammunition to Sector 3. Just that, as we suspected the Enemy were listening to our radios. Taljaard didn't say who was going to do it or how. Sarge X was quiet for more than a minute. 'Can you do it?'

Taljaard looked at me. I nodded, more certainly than I felt.

'Roger. We can.'

'Do it,' came the reply, and I took half of Team Charlie to the stables while the other half began carrying ammunition out of the police station and stacking it on the pavement.

We saddled thirty horses – fourteen for the riders and sixteen for ammunition – and we raced to the police station while listening to the radio. The battle continued. Sector 3 were only shooting single shots, their ammunition almost exhausted.

We loaded the boxes on to the horses. I led the group, we rode as fast as we could. It was nearly five kilometres, first to the old township, now fully occupied by Amanzi people, then along the winding path that had been trampled out by animals over many years. It was difficult terrain, the gradient very steep. The horses were heavily laden and we progressed slowly in the dark. Over the radio we heard the anxious voices of our defence force: 'They're coming, they're coming, help us!' The Enemy had launched an attack on foot when they realised return fire was diminishing. We heard the shots. We heard the cries of fear from our men in their last moments before death.

We came around the last bend of the mountain. Into the smell of cordite and burning rubber and petrol, the clatter of shots, at full gallop. Aram called them on the radio: Team Charlie on horseback from the west, don't shoot. But there were none of our men left to shoot, only the Enemy.

We jumped off the horses, sought shelter against the ridge. I had my R4 DM, scanned the scene through my scope – to the right, the Jeep track coming up the canyon. Another four motorcycles blocking the track and ten or twelve men working hard to clear the road, now that no one was shooting at them. Behind them, as far as I could make out in the dark, to the bottom, the long line of the Enemy's vehicles, and people who wanted to kill us.

I swung the scope to the left. I saw the lines and the trenches of our Sector 3. The Enemy's soldiers running up and down with torches, pistols and rifles, shooting the good people of Dad's Army who lay on the ground, making sure they were dead.

The Jeep track was our first priority. We had to keep the road blocked. I started there. I breathed in, aimed, fired. One shot after the other. This caught them by surprise, they thought our forces were wiped out. I was calm, controlled. I didn't waste a single shot. Seven of them down. The rest bolted behind the nearest pick-up and hid there.

They shot back, tentatively at first, then with more focus, from the left and the right. Wildly, all together, a curtain of lead, whining over us, smacking between us. Aram, Taljaard and I had experience. We had been trained by Domingo. We kept Team Charlie calm. Aram deployed us, directing half of our firepower to the left, the others to the right. 'Choose your own targets,' he said to me.

I shot at their front line, then again into the canyon. Until their lines were clear and silent. And the Enemy fire from the valley track also died down.

We didn't celebrate when we won the mini-battle. Because just beyond us, barely two hundred metres away, a hundred of our people were shot dead. People we knew well, likeable, good people, our amateur soldiers, who had given their lives tonight for Amanzi.

Aram let Sarge X know we had halted them for now. It was however just a question of time before they abandoned the trucks-in-the-kloof-plug completely and came for us on foot. There must still be a hundred and fifty of them left.

Sarge X was quiet again for a long time. Then: 'You'll have to hold your position, Charlie. Delta is pinned down for now. But the cavalry is coming.'

That meant Domingo. And Alpha and Bravo. Still at least an hour away, according to my calculations. What difference would they make, twenty-nine people, against this overwhelming force?

Sofia Bergman

One of the things I discovered on that night of 9 February is that I made a huge mistake becoming a Spotter. Becoming a soldier. It was when Killian . . .

I don't really want to talk about it, I don't want to remember it. The simple fact that you were lying there with your people, people with whom you had a strong bond, a Special Ops bond of mutual hardship and so many other things, you love these people, and there on the other side are people who want to kill you and your friends. Who were shooting at you. Who wanted to come and take everything you and your people worked so hard for. I . . .

Killian, he . . . He was hit by a twenty-millimetre shell.

Right beside me.

But I already knew by then that I wasn't cut out to be a soldier. Not because I was scared – we were all terrified – but because I knew the things that I saw and experienced that night were going to . . . They were going to change me. For ever. In a way that I didn't want to be changed.

By then of course it was too late.

Half an hour before sunrise the first wave of the Enemy came. They came on foot, they came from the east, from our eastern flank. We had expected them there, because on our right flank we had the advantage of height. And they couldn't come up the Jeep track; I took out every one of them who poked his head out from behind the vehicles.

In the dark we saw the attack very late. But Aram and Taljaard had made us dig in, as well as we could. And they kept us disciplined; we shot single shots, controlled shots. Despite their numbers – that first infantry assault was nearly sixty men – they didn't get closer than seventy metres. Then they fell back.

We only lost one member of Charlie.

And then it was quiet again.

We knew Domingo was coming. We knew daybreak was coming.

We just didn't know if they would come in time.

85

February: IV

It wasn't Alpha and Bravo led by Domingo, or daylight, that determined the outcome of the battle. It was the air force of Amanzi.

The second wave of infantry that attacked us on the crest beside Sector 3 was larger and more disciplined. They used the cover and charge tactic, which suppressed our return fire so they could advance faster. And come ever increasingly closer.

We suffered more losses. In the first ten minutes of the skirmish they shot dead three members of Charlie. One of them was our Sergeant Aram, as he ran fearlessly between us encouraging us and keeping us calm. Aram, the legendary Namibian, whose records for the Special Ops marathons of thirty and sixty kilometres have never been broken.

But the eastern horizon lightened and we could see them better, and we inflicted losses on them too. Still they approached, each wave of fire closer than the last.

I realised I was going to die here, on this very morning. Along with Sergeant Aram. I would fight to the last bullet, but unless a miracle happened, I would die here.

And then the Cessna came. Out of the north, behind us, from Amanzi's side. Just before the sun rose over the horizon.

Later I would try counting the number of times in my life that I have been surprised and happy to see the belly of a Hennie Fly aeroplane. But that morning must have surely been the best. Hennie Fly and Peace Pedi flew so low and fast over us that I ducked. It was, they later explained, so that the Enemy's reaction time would not be fast enough to shoot the plane.

They roared over us, and then came the explosions down the valley, one after the other. Our Cessna had become a bomber; the bombs were hand grenades that Domingo had found in the Defence Force arsenal at De Aar. He and Hennie had never mentioned this strategy. Hennie and Peace practised in secret. Not even the Cabinet knew about it, because Domingo firmly believed there was a spy in our midst.

The accuracy of this bombing run left much to be desired, but the Enemy were stunned for the moment, and that gave us a chance to lift our heads again, to drive the foot soldiers back with concentrated fire.

The Cessna banked sharply to the right and disappeared again behind Amanzi's mountains towards town.

And then it came again. Just as low. The grenades fell more accurately, Hennie and Peace had now spotted where the fighters were holed up. The Enemy shot wildly at the aeroplane. We fired at them, with deadly accuracy. The foot soldiers began to fall back.

The Cessna turned.

They came again, a third time. Hand grenades exploded, stones and shrapnel and the screams of the dying.

And then the cavalry arrived. Literally.

Apart from the Jeep track the Enemy had used, there was no other vehicle access route to the back of the reserve. Domingo and Teams Alpha and Bravo had to leave the Volvo and the ERF in the town and fetch the remaining horses. They didn't know my shortcut, and had to gallop up the longer way, from beyond the main gate, behind most of the mountains, on to the western hill beside the canyon where the Enemy were launching their incursion. And from there, from the heights, Domingo and company began to shoot. They were right behind the wave of infantry that were attacking us, so that together with Alpha and Bravo we formed a pincer movement.

The Enemy's foot soldiers and their big flanking manoeuvre were in full retreat. They retired to the shelter of the vehicles.

The Cessna made another bombing run. This time a few of the grenades fell on the vehicles, the long worm that was trapped on the Jeep track.

From there came their last, massive barrage.

For twenty minutes the battle was intense, they were shooting with everything they had – one remaining cannon, assault rifles, hunting rifles, handguns. They shot wildly, continuously, furiously, as though they meant to defeat us by sheer volume. The air was thick with noise and odours and smoke and lead. We lay low, only lifting our heads when the Cessna flew over, but we suffered losses. Of the forty-two members of Alpha, Bravo and Charlie we lost nineteen comrades, including three of our sergeants. They shot Domingo, first high up in the ribcage, just under his left arm. Then in his left hip, so that the bullet jerked and spun him around, brought him crashing to the ground. Alpha team members wanted to jump up and run to his aid, but the hail of bullets was too thick and deadly. Then, without warning, the Enemy's ammunition ran out. Within six or seven minutes from when their fire began to decrease, it suddenly ceased. A deathly hush.

Until engines began growling down below, and the great retreat began. At first it was reasonably orderly, the furthest vehicles turning around and racing away over the plains, while the others had to wait patiently. But as we picked off more and more targets, they left more hastily and recklessly.

The sun broke free from the eastern horizon. It lit a scene that is burned in my memory for ever. The towering plumes of smoke from the burning vehicles, dust trails from fleeing pick-ups and motorbikes, cordite clouds hanging down the canyon, before a morning breeze gently nudged them away.

And in the north, clouds in the sky. The first rain clouds of that unbearably hot, dry summer.

Only in late afternoon did the last of the Enemy surrender on the reserve plateau, where the first fifty vehicles were stopped by the rock field and Delta. We took the twenty-one survivors captive. Drove them like cattle to Amanzi. Team Delta and us. I saw Sofia Bergman. She looked like the rest of us. Dog-tired. The exhaustion was paralysing, greater than anything I had ever experienced before. In my mind I knew it was the after-effect of adrenalin, but my body said, no more. We were filthy, our eyes dead; we had won but it didn't feel like victory, so many people had perished. Too many of them, and too many of us.

And Domingo. We had no idea how Domingo was, he'd been taken away on a horse, and we didn't think he was going to make it.

Without Domingo we were lost.

We walked back to the town. Sofia looked at me just once. I didn't know what to read into that look. And then thunder rumbled over the mountain, and fat raindrops speckled the veld.

Sofia Bergman

I was so incredibly glad that Nico Storm was alive. Remember, it was my fault that he wasn't with Alpha or Bravo any more. It would have been my fault if he had died. I know, I know, it's not a logical argument, but that afternoon I don't think any of us was capable of logic. In any case, when I saw him, I felt like going to him and throwing my arms around him and saying I'm so incredibly glad you're alive.

If I hadn't been so dead tired, I would have. I swear.

86

March: I

Nero Dlamini

So, during the third Cabinet meeting in March, Nkosi drops the bombshell. Absolute bombshell.

   Usually he spoke without notes. That day he read from a written speech ...

Cabinet meeting, 24 March

Transcript by Willem Storm. The Amanzi History Project.
   Pastor Nkosi Sebego, Minister of Internal Affairs: *Mr President, thank you for this opportunity to make a special announcement.*

   Mr President, colleagues, friends, I must admit that I stand before you today with both great joy and great sadness in my heart.

   Great joy, because the Good Lord spared me to take part in and to witness the great victory over our enemy, the devil's spawn. Joy, because this was God's will, this was his answer to our prayers, this was his sign, to show me and my fellow believers that we should take the road he had opened for us. Great joy, because now our world is safe enough to follow that road.

   Great joy, my friends, because today, we faithful, we members of the Mighty Warrior Party, take the first step in the realisation of our future, our vision, our dream of a city and a community exclusively ruled by God. Joy, because I was chosen to lead my people to this Promised Land, to make this vision, this calling come true.

   But let us not forget the great sadness. First of all, sadness for the brave men and women who gave their lives for our victory. Sadness for the loved ones left behind. Sadness for those who were wounded and whose lives will never be the same again.

Sadness for those who passed without knowing the love and the grace of God.

And lastly, sadness for the big goodbye. For today, Mr President, colleagues, friends, I have to announce that we will be leaving you, we will be leaving Amanzi. As from tomorrow we will start our migration to the place you know as Gariep, the great dam just one hundred kilometres east of here. But we will not call it Gariep. As from tomorrow, that place will be known as New Jerusalem.

Of course, our migration to New Jerusalem will not be complete in a day or a week or even a month, but our journey starts in earnest tomorrow.

Yes, we are leaving, but we will remain connected, my friends. We will be physically connected by the same great river. We will be connected, I hope, through our mutual travails and suffering, through our mutual history, our mutual desire for peace and goodwill, and our mutual hope to make this world a better place, each in our own way.

Now, as you may know, my followers and I have fought beside you against a common enemy. We have toiled beside you these past years, to build this community. Our blood and our sweat and our tears have run together, we have lived and died together. Despite our differences, despite our disputes. We are part-owners, we are partners, I would like to believe, in everything we have achieved here. In that spirit of cooperation and co-ownership, I am calling on you today to grant us our due. Nothing more than our due. We only ask for our share. Our share in the food stores, the seed banks, the herds, the weapons and ammunition, the fuel, the agricultural equipment and the know-how. We ask your support in the months and years ahead, as you have received our support in the years past.

In exchange, of course, you will always be able to count on our loyalty, our friendship and our support, whatever the future holds.

In conclusion, I want to extend my most heartfelt gratitude to you, Mr President, for your wise leadership and counsel. Thank you for dreaming of a better world, and a fine community. Thank you for starting it, and leading it. Thank you, too, to our friends and colleagues in the Cabinet, and to every person who will remain in Amanzi. Thank you for sharing our journey so far. Thank you for your love and generosity. And most of all, thank you for understanding that we now seek the right to govern ourselves with God as our President.

Nero Dlamini

And there we sat, absolutely stunned. I mean, looking back, you could see all the little clues and signs, we ought to have seen it coming, I suppose. But I always sort of thought his references to a new dawn and the night being darkest before this new dawn were, you know, religious.

So, astonished silence. Which was awkward, because he delivered his speech like a fire-and-brimstone sermon, all dramatic and magnanimous, ending on this high note, so you instinctively felt there should be applause or an amen, brother, or a hallelujah, praise Jesus, or something, but we just sat there. And he waited expectantly . . .

So finally, dear old Sarge X, our Minister of Safety and Security, he says, 'But Pastor, Gariep, how are you going to defend Gariep?'

And Nkosi says, 'Please, Sizwe, it is now called New Jerusalem.' Like, he is totally into this whole new name thing, as if that is going to protect the place by itself. But I think it was an effort to deflect the question.

But then everybody piped up at once. Birdy says but that's a fair question, and I say but surely, if you're going to lead your people to this place, you must have given thought to how you are going to defend it. It's your responsibility. And Ravi, and Beryl, and Nandi Mahlangu's daughter, Qedani, and Frostie, that's Abraham Frost, our engineer and Minister of Public Works, they all chip in, and take him on.

Nkosi gets really flippant, he says, 'Defend it against what? We've won the war haven't we?'

Then President Willem Storm stands up.

Cabinet meeting, 24 March

President Willem Storm: *Mr Minister of Internal Affairs Pastor Sebego, thank you for your kind comments about me. And thank you for your candour.*

As I'm sure you could deduce from the stunned silence, your announcement took us all by surprise. I knew we had our differences, but I never thought you viewed them as so insurmountable that you would choose to leave Amanzi.

I'm not sure that it will make any difference, but it is my desire and my duty to at least try to persuade you not to go ahead with this. I can list all the obvious benefits of our strength in unity, and of a single republic; from economic and military, to technological and social. But I'm sure you are aware of it all, and have considered every implication of secession. So allow me to plead with you, not from the head, but from the heart.

This country, before the Fever, was one of perpetual separation. We have always been divided, and in our separation we were always at odds with one another. Among so many things, we were separated by tribe and clan, by colour and race, by legislation and religion, by language and culture, by our divergent economic realities and by our ideologies. And the more we argued and fought about the differences, the more we focused on them, the more they divided us.

Today, I want to ask you to help this community, this Republic of Amanzi, to change all that. Of course, we are not all the same. Of course, there are so many things that could divide us, if we allow them to. If we focus on them alone. But, please, take a look at all the things that unite us. We all passionately believe in freedom and democracy. We all believe in human dignity, in basic human rights. We all want to live in peace and prosperity. And our children . . .

That man sitting over there, our honourable Minister of Health Nero Dlamini, came here four years ago, on a bicycle. He tells the story of his journey, and his reasons for coming, with so much self-deprecation, wit and charm. But I always believed there was more to it. Therefore, a few months after his arrival, we sat in the Orphanage lounge and I asked him, 'Nero, what was the real reason for coming?'

And then he told me about John Bowlby, the British psychologist. Such a fascinating man, who did incredible research. But the bottom line was, Bowlby worked with war orphans after the Second World War. And he soon realised that the absence of good fathers, the absence of the fabric of caring families, had a huge and negative impact on people. And eventually on societies, I think. Nero told me that he thought that was the biggest problem in South Africa before the Fever. The damage done to the fabric of family in the disadvantaged communities was so great that society just wasn't able to recover. And that's why Nero took his bicycle, and rode it from Johannesburg to Amanzi. Because he wanted to make sure the children of this community, the children after the Fever, did not suffer the same fate.

Pastor, Mr Minister, surely this is something that unites us. This wish, this passion to create a singular, loving family for all our children?

Please, sir, reconsider. Please, I beg of you today. Don't go.

Nero Dlamini

And you know what Nkosi's reaction was?

He sat there, and he just shook his head, and said, 'No.'

87

March: II

Nero Dlamini

So Willem Storm called an emergency meeting of the Cabinet, the very next day. We took our seats, and the door opened, Domingo shuffled in. He was limping, that hip was pretty badly shot up, though we tried our best to fix it, but our knowledge and our resources were limited. Anyway, everybody was just so happy and relieved that he survived, he was our saviour, really. Everybody except the pastor, of course. So Domingo walked in without a cane, without anybody helping him, and we all stood up, we gave him a big round of applause. And he went and sat right across the table from Nkosi.

Our President said, very formal and dignified, ladies and gentlemen, I would like to welcome our military leader Captain Domingo to this meeting. We have called on him many times before, for his help, expert opinion, for his support. Today, he has risen from his hospital bed against medical advice, and has asked to be a part of this special Cabinet meeting. May I assume that this is in order with everybody?

Of course we all said yes. Even Nkosi. After that applause, he really had no choice. And then Domingo turned those eyes of his on the pastor. You know, that Domingo look that scares the living daylights out of you.

Cabinet meeting, 25 March

Captain Domingo: *Nkosi, on 5 January, when you conceded election defeat in the Forum, you told your people: 'Don't worry. The night is darkest before the dawn.' Can you remember that?*

Pastor Nkosi Sebego, Minister of Internal Affairs: *A little respect for this Cabinet and what I represent might be in order, Captain. Please address me as Mr Minister.*

Domingo: *Can you remember what you said on 5 January?*

Nkosi: *I certainly can.*

Domingo: *Can you remember the emergency meeting on 3 February, after we intercepted the ham radio conversation?*

Nkosi: *I . . . What is this about, Mr President?*

President Storm: *May I ask you to indulge us, Mr Minister, and answer Domingo's questions?*

Nkosi: *I will not be part of an inquisition. I will especially not be the victim of such a process.*

President Storm: *Mr Minister, we have tasked Captain Domingo with the responsibility of keeping this community safe. Part of that process, part of his job, is to ask strategic and sometimes difficult questions. This is not only about the security of Amanzi, it is also about the future of New Jerusalem. It would be wonderful if we could start out as neighbours who trust each other . . .*

Nkosi: *Mr President, you are manipulating me . . .*

President Storm: *No, please. We are asking for your cooperation. That is all.*

Nkosi: *Go ahead, Captain. Do your damnedest.*

Domingo: *Can you remember the 3 February meeting about the radio conversation?*

Nkosi: *Yes.*

Domingo: *Do you remember that you were very much in favour of Special Ops going to Maseru?*

Nkosi: *I thought we should go, yes. So did Ravi . . .*

Domingo: *And would you agree that the radio message was a trap? A diversion? A way to get our soldiers out of Amanzi?*

Nkosi: *Are you saying that I . . . This is an insult!*

Domingo: *Sit down, Pastor, I'm not saying anything. Yet.*

Nkosi: *I am done here.*

Domingo: *You want me to give you rifles and ammo, don't you? For your new city.*

Nkosi: *We demand what is ours. Our share. And this Cabinet will not deny us.*

Domingo: *If you want your share, you have to answer my questions.*

Nkosi: *You don't have the authority to withhold what is rightfully ours.*

Domingo: *You're right. I don't have the authority. But I have something that is much better. I have some exclusive knowledge. You see, two years ago, the old Committee withheld permission to move a large part of our arsenal to a secret location. Problem is, I don't trust anybody. So, let me make a confession, Pastor: I was a naughty boy. I was very disobedient. I went and moved 80 per cent of that arsenal anyway. Nobody in this Cabinet today knows where it's stashed. If you want weapons, you'll have to get my cooperation first. And if you want my cooperation, you have to answer my questions. Or do you have something to hide, Pastor?*

President Storm: *Domingo, this was never part of our ... This is blackmail.*

Domingo: *Only if he has something to hide.*

Nkosi: *I have absolutely nothing to hide.*

Domingo: *Then answer the questions.*

Nkosi: *Do you think I'm stupid? I can see where you are going with this.*

Domingo: *Where am I going?*

Nkosi: *I know you suspect that there were spies in Amanzi ...*

Domingo: *Suspect? No, Pastor. After Matthew Mbalo's murder, I was suspicious. After we found that rubber duck on the opposite shore, I was suspicious. But now, I'm absolutely sure there were spies in Amanzi. Let me tell you why. One: because they attacked just when most of our people were harvesting all along the river, in the irrigation fields, and sleeping outside our walls. Two: because they attacked through the canyon, specifically. Three: because of the way they attacked through the canyon; with overwhelming numbers and force, all of it aimed at only that soft underbelly. Because our main gate is almost impenetrable. Four: they attacked only once I took my teams away to chase the Hopetown attackers. There's absolutely no way an outsider, with no knowledge of our defences, can get that lucky. Five: what finally convinced me, was when we started interrogating our prisoners of war. They told me the attack was not about our food reserves, or our women. Although they did say they would have kidnapped them if they had the chance. The attack was about guns and ammo. They say Number One was aware of the fact that the De Aar weapons depot was stripped, and that we did the stripping. They say Number One knew we had all the weapons and ammo, and that we kept the bulk of them in the old nature reserve store. They did not want to get into Amanzi, Pastor, they only wanted to get as* *far as the warehouse. Because those are the most precious commodities out there at the moment: guns and ammo. The question remains, how did they know about the nature reserve warehouse? Only a few of my security team people knew, and the members of the old Committee knew. That's why I am so sure we have spies in our midst.*

Nkosi: *And you're saying I'm the spy? That is ridiculous.*

Domingo: *Is it?*

Nkosi: *Yes!*

Domingo: *And yet, you have the most to gain from providing our enemy with that information ...*

Nkosi: *You are a heathen and a liar. I have nothing to gain.*

Domingo: *If we lost the battle, and they stole the arsenal, you would have had immense leverage to force a new election. And a really good chance to win it. And if we won, you knew it would be safe to take your people to Gariep, because the threat of an enemy attack would diminish for long enough to build up that community. You were the only person on the planet in a win–win situation ...*

Nkosi: *Mr President, I will not sit here and listen to one more word from ... this Philistine. I am leading my people to New Jerusalem. With or without our share, with or without our weapons ...*

Domingo: *Why are you not denying my allegations, Pastor?*

President Storm: *Please, Nkosi, Mr Minister, please ...*

Domingo: *Why did you tell your people, 'Don't worry. The night is darkest before the dawn.' Why?*

Nkosi: *I am done here.*

Domingo: *I'm going to find proof, Nkosi. And then I'm coming for you ...*

Nero Dlamini

You have to hand it to Nkosi, he was nobody's fool. The next day, he came to see me and President Storm. Actually, he came to see Willem, and Willem asked me to sit in, because he needed a witness, he ... Well, he just wanted someone to confirm the record, for what it was worth.

So, the pastor says, 'You're blackmailing me, Willem.'

And Willem says, 'I do not condone what Domingo did.'

'But you didn't stop him,' says the pastor.

And Willem says, 'He had legitimate questions.'

And then the pastor says, 'Does Domingo control you, Willem? Does he run Amanzi?'

Which was a sore point, because there was some truth in that. So Willem does not answer. And the pastor says, 'You remember when we found the murder weapon that killed Matthew Mbalo? And that little rubber boat. You remember you lied to the people of Amanzi about why we wanted to enlarge Domingo's forces?'

So Willem says, 'We all lied, Pastor.'

And Nkosi says, 'No, Willem, you lied. You, personally. You told the people. And if you don't give me your word right now that I will get half of all the guns and ammunition, I will tell the people how you deceived them. How you knew there was a big attack coming. And still we lost so many people. Then we will see how many are willing to stay behind.'

We just sat there.

And Nkosi said, 'You have until 3 April to make your decision.'

88

February: V

We had been fifty-six members of Special Ops. Plus Domingo.

After the invasion we were thirty-four. And Domingo was injured.

For three long weeks we didn't see him, we just heard how he was doing when Sergeant Taljaard returned from the hospital and told us Domingo was in a critical condition. They didn't know if he was going to make it. Birdy Canary sat with him for hours through the night. Taljaard told us one night how he came quietly into the hospital room and Birdy was sitting holding Domingo's hand, and what a peculiar scene it was for him. You never imagine Domingo, the obstinate, incorruptible, indestructible Domingo, having his hand held. Later, Taljaard told us Domingo would live. And Domingo recovered. Though he would probably always walk with a slight limp.

But Domingo didn't need to walk normally, he would still always be Domingo. He would continue to be our commander; it was his mind, his character, his personality that led us, trained us and inspired us.

But we were good for nothing in those weeks. Even though Domingo gave us orders to reorganise into two teams of seventeen each. Even though we obeyed, though we put ourselves through our paces, our exercises, we were useless. We were sheep without a shepherd, drained, sore and sick. We were bruised by the loss of so many comrades, but above all, the loss of the reservists, the ordinary, good people who went to man Sector 3 with such innocent courage, such cheerful pluck. For me that scene was the one I found hardest to banish from my mind, the Enemy walking among them and executing the last survivors with pistol shots to the head. Another confirmation of Domingo's philosophy that we were animals, cruel animals, heartless and soulless.

It all blunted me, so though I saw Sofia Bergman at Special Ops – she was in the new Team Alpha, I was in my old unit, Bravo – it was as if she wasn't real, a ghost in a dream, a fantasy I once had that was slowly fading.

I knew thanks to my therapeutic talks with Nero Dlamini previously that I was suffering once more from post-traumatic stress. But I couldn't escape it, and Nero was too busy helping other people – civilians – to process their loss.

It was Pa who tried to make me whole in those first four weeks.

It began on 9 February, the day of the battle and the slaughter. We walked out of the reserve dog-tired, our rifles trained on the prisoners of war. I saw Pa on the other side of the big gate, where we entered town. He was waiting for me, he came up to me, put his arm around me, and said, 'I am immensely proud of you.' His voice was thick with emotion, his arm squeezed me tight. And then he let go of me, not wanting to embarrass me.

On 10 February we rested in the base.

On 11 February they came to collect us with a tractor and a long trailer, all thirty-four of us, and Hennie Fly and Peace Pedi. They paraded us through town. People lined the roads, more than three thousand, they shouted, sang, applauded us, they rained flowers and petals on us. I saw Pa with Okkie on his shoulders. I beckoned to them. Pa came up to the trailer. 'Can I come too, Nico, can I?' begged Okkie.

'You can.' I took him from Pa.

Pa wept when he passed Okkie to me.

This one time I wasn't ashamed of Pa's tears, it made me happy and sad. I wanted to cry too, but the tears got stuck somewhere.

Okkie rode with me on the trailer. He waved at the people, as if he had personally, single-handedly annihilated the Enemy.

That night Pa and I ate together, just the two of us. He made small talk about this and that, knowing I didn't want to talk about the battle. His voice and eyes were gentle. Just before I went to bed, he said, 'I would never be able to do what you did, I am too much of a coward. But I know where you got your courage . . .'

After that I saw Pa and Okkie every weekend, Saturday and Sunday, until March, until Domingo came out of hospital, until Pastor Nkosi announced what we later referred to as his Moses plans.

Every Saturday and Sunday I walked and drove with Pa on his

rounds, I didn't speak much, mostly just listened to him. And it was good to listen to Pa, he was so interesting to talk to.

I remember one conversation particularly well. We were outside the town, in the vineyards beside the river. The grapes were being harvested. And the three of us, Pa and Okkie and I, helped where we could. Pa talked to everyone. At four in the afternoon most of the people took a breather, in the cool underneath the willow trees beside the river. Pa looked at them and I could see he was enjoying this moment, this peaceful gathering, so shortly after the destruction of the battle. As if he knew this scene was what we had fought for, this was what had been preserved.

He turned to me and said, 'You know my project to make some kind of record of our history?'

I nodded. I knew about it, and to my shame for months I had thought it silly, a waste of time.

'Well, in January, I asked quite a few people what they didn't miss of the old world, and I got some interesting answers. It got me wondering, what didn't *I* miss? Was there anything? Because I . . . You know how I loved the world before the Fever. And you and I lost so much . . . The world lost so much, could there be anything that I wasn't sorry to see the end of? Something that's better, here, after the Fever? Then I remembered the longest research project in history, one that stretched over seventy-five years. It began at Harvard in America; they followed the lives of many men, from the time they were eighteen or nineteen years old, into their nineties. One of the big findings that came out of this study was that your happiness in life is primarily determined by good, strong, healthy human relationships. And they not only determined your happiness, but also had an effect on how long you lived. I remember this huge sense of irony when I read about the research back then. Because there we were, in a world where we couldn't have been more isolated from each other. Where it was increasingly difficult to have those healthy relationships, in marriages, in friendships . . . Even our friendships were more synthetic and digital . . . What I want to say is: that's the one thing I don't miss. Because look here. Look at the relationships here . . .'

'It's true, Pa,' I said. Because I could see it, just as he did.

Later we wandered down to the people and he talked with them. During my absence in the months of military duty I had forgotten how good Pa was with people. I sat watching him, and I saw again how he went everywhere, how he talked with everybody. He consoled and encouraged and led, but was purely and absolutely genuine, there was not a trace of the politician's agenda about him.

In that moment I realised that my father was someone I liked. He was someone I admired and respected all over again. I could see he had forgiven me for my stupid moment of teenage weakness eighteen months ago.

I realised our relationship was whole again.

Until 29 March. Until Domingo came out of hospital.

89

March: III

On 29 March Taljaard brought Domingo back from the hospital.

We lined up on the parade ground in front of Special Ops head-quarters. The black Jeep drew up and Domingo got out. It was the first time we had seen him after the Battle of Sector 3. We knew he was limping, but we didn't know how badly.

He handled it in the usual Domingo way. With controlled fury. It looked as if he hated his damaged hip, as if by sheer willpower he would deny any discomfort.

He walked without a cane, with sway-and-halt, sway-and-halt, the dark glasses on, right up to us.

His voice was the same, the tone, the volume, the suppressed menace. He said, 'You did well. I'm proud of you.'

Taljaard said, 'We are proud of you, Captain.'

We cheered Domingo. He raised his hand, sternly, his mouth turned down in distaste. We stopped.

'Enough,' he said. And he walked into the building, to his office.

Taljaard came to fetch me. 'Captain wants to see you.'

I jogged to his office and knocked.

'Come in.'

I went in, closed the door behind me. He was sitting behind his desk. I stood at attention.

'No. Sit.' The dark glasses lay on the desktop in front of him; his eyes were the colour of gunmetal.

I didn't show my surprise. Captain Domingo never invited you to sit down. But I did.

'I was hard on you,' he said.

If I said 'Yes, Captain', it might create the wrong impression.

With Domingo I had learned the best policy was, when in doubt, shut up.

'Do you know why I was hard on you?'

'No, Captain.'

'Because you were an arrogant little arsehole.'

'Yes, Captain.'

'You're "yes-captaining" me just out of habit now. You were an arrogant little arsehole, Storm. Because you can shoot straight and run fast, and you got lucky with the diesel aeroplane thing, and your pappa is the President. You were insufferable. The good news is, all those things would have turned just about everybody into arrogant little arseholes.'

'Yes, Captain.'

'You weren't ready for promotion.'

'Yes, Captain.'

'Why weren't you ready for promotion?'

'Because I was an arrogant little arsehole, Captain.'

He nodded in satisfaction. 'Quite right.'

And he grinned faintly, and shifted a little on the chair, perhaps to make his hip more comfortable.

'In the Battle of Sector 3, you made me proud.'

I said nothing, just enjoyed the rare moment.

'You showed a keen strategic mind, you showed respect for the chain of command, you showed bravery and discipline.'

Still I kept silent.

'You're not going to let the praise go to your head.'

'No, Captain.'

'You will for ever refrain from being an arrogant little arsehole.'

'Yes, Captain.'

'You are now ready for promotion.'

He opened a drawer. He took out a pair of insignia, three sergeant's stripes for each shoulder. 'Sergeant Storm. It has a ring to it.' And he put the insignia on the middle of the desk.

'I want to say something to you, Nico. Man to man.'

It was years since he last called me by my first name.

Domingo looked out of the window, down to the parade ground. 'There's nothing like bleeding like a stuck pig from a good hip wound to remind a man of his mortality,' he said. 'When I was lying there that day, I thought, damn it all, I won't have time to train my successor. And I thought of who that successor should be, and lo and behold, I could think of only one little man. Arrogant little arsehole that he might be.'

He looked at me. 'If you repeat this conversation, I will kill you, understand?'

'Yes, Captain.'

'From tomorrow we work hard. 'Cause I'm not going to live for ever.'

'Yes, Captain.'

'From tomorrow we work hard, because you are going to be the best sergeant, and you are going to stay very humble.'

'Yes, Captain.'

'From tomorrow we work hard, because you are my designated successor.'

'Yes, Captain.'

'Anything you want to say?'

'Just thank you, Captain.' But I lied, I wanted to tell him he was Domingo, of course he would live for ever.

'From tomorrow we work hard. So take the rest of your day off. Go and celebrate your promotion with your family.'

In March in the Year of the Lion there were three different modes of transport for Amanzi citizens. If you needed to travel a few kilometres, your first option was a vehicle, provided it ran on diesel. That was the only fuel we had for our trucks, pick-ups, tractors, a few cars, the single Jeep and, of course, the aeroplane. Because we produced the diesel ourselves, and the supply was still relatively limited, most of it was reserved for agriculture and military purposes.

Should your transport requirement fall into a more personal category, your best bet would be to travel on horseback. We had a growing number of good horses, but there was still a shortage of saddles, and most people had to learn to ride bareback. If, for example, you wanted to visit someone in Petrusville on the spur of the moment, you could probably get a horse at the stables across the Madeliefie Street crossing.

But not if you were a member of Amanzi's Special Ops Teams. We were required to walk, jog or run, according to the prescription of our commander. Unless he stipulated otherwise in person.

Therefore, on the morning of 29 March, between ten and eleven, I jogged from our base to the Amanzi town centre, so that I could tell Pa about my promotion. And we could celebrate together. I ran to the main gate first, then through the wide U, up the last slope, past the stable, through the town, into Disa Street.

Pa's work space was in the old post office, when he sometimes did his administration in an open door office.

He wasn't there. I asked if anybody had seen him.

No, not yet this morning.

Was there a Cabinet meeting?

No, not today. Perhaps the President was at the school, someone said. Or he might be helping at the Orphanage.

I thanked them all, and trotted off to the Orphanage.

It was quiet in the building, the children were outside somewhere. I walked through, and out the other side, towards the vegetable garden.

I heard something, a trace of a voice, a suppressed sound, half a word, or a cry. Behind me, inside somewhere. I turned round.

Maybe Pa was ill, in his room still perhaps. I went there, I didn't knock, because it was my father and barely yesterday I was still sharing a room with him – that's how it felt. I opened the door and saw him, with Beryl in his bed.

And they saw me.

90

The lions

Sometimes it feels like everything happens at once, just when you least expect it.

On 29 March I was promoted. And I opened the Orphanage door and saw a man I didn't know. But I recognised the scars of dog's teeth on his back: it was my father.

I walked back to base. I was bewildered. Dumbstruck. Angry. My father had betrayed me; Pa had hidden this thing from me, for how long? I suddenly thought of nights long ago when Pa would come back to our room late, I thought of moments when I came upon him and Beryl deep in conversation together somewhere. I always imagined the intensity of their conversation was over life-and-death Committee business.

It had been going on for years.

Why did he never tell me? Why didn't he trust me? What else was he hiding from me?

What about my mother, what about the memory of my mother that he was dishonouring?

It was as if I didn't know him, my brain couldn't process or categorise or understand this.

I was angry, and ashamed, mortification seared right through me, because it was Beryl. Jacob once said Beryl liked women. It was the conventional wisdom of the entire community; after all she was an ex-golfer with a muscular physique. There was always whispering behind hands about her and Nero Dlamini's sexuality. And that was the woman my father chose to have sex with. A lesbian.

So about eleven that morning I dragged my feet back to base, kicking stones along the way.

*　　*　　*

At more or less the same time, twenty of our people were at the wind farm on Noblesfontein near Victoria West, led by the engineer and now Minister of Public Works Abraham Frost. By road it was over three hundred kilometres from Amanzi, and just a fraction over two hundred for Hennie Fly and Peace Pedi's Cessna, who were supplying air cover and intelligence for the wind turbine expedition.

They had travelled in a truck and four pick-ups, on a mission to dismantle the first of the turbine towers, and at the same time try to work out how to transport the giant structures. The goal was to erect two or three in the mountains across the river at Amanzi, for a start.

All twenty men were gathered around the tower nearest to the substation of the wind farm, hard at work, arguing about the best methods and tools for the task. Each of them had brought an R4 along: no expedition left Amanzi without them. Some had radios on their belts. But their firearms were in the pick-ups and the truck, or leaning against them, as Hennie and Peace had assured them there was no human threat in the vicinity.

They were totally at ease. Until one of the men noticed movement on the ridge, two hundred metres from the tower. Later he would describe how he did a double-take, because the first impression was too bizarre to believe: two lionesses casually strolling towards them, neatly cutting them off from their vehicles. His second look confirmed his fears and he shouted out a warning to the rest.

There wasn't much they could do. All twenty jammed through the steel door on the other side of the wind tower and sought refuge up the ladder leading to the top of the turbine.

The lionesses nonchalantly walked up to the door and peered inside. They sniffed the air. One lion sneezed, the sound echoing loudly in the hollow tower. She shook her head as though to rid her nostrils of a stench. Then the lionesses turned away and went to lie down a few metres away in the long shadow of the tower.

For years afterwards the men would still rib each other over who got the biggest fright, and whose was the fart that made the lion sneeze. But at the time, none of them were laughing. The Minister of Public Works Abraham Frost radioed Hennie Fly to inform him of their problem.

Peace Pedi joked over the radio: 'Would you like us to make a bombing run, Mr Minister?'

And then, in the honoured tradition of everything happening at once, when you least expect it, Hennie Fly pointed at the horizon in the west. Thin lines of smoke drifted up into the blue sky, on the far side of Victoria West. Human activity where there should be none.

I stalked angrily back into base. My mates came rushing out in full battle dress on the way to the Volvo and ERF lorries.

'Come on, Sergeant Storm,' Taljaard yelled at me. 'Enemy activity other side of Vic-West.'

I ran to get my gear. Other members of Alpha and Bravo came rushing past. They called out congratulations with a 'hey, Sarge!'.

The news had spread.

On the day of my promotion I led my team to battle. It made me feel a little bit better.

Domingo sat up front beside the Volvo driver. He told us over the radio that Hennie and company had spotted a large group of people – it looked like more than three or four hundred – on the other side of Victoria West, barely sixty kilometres from the Noblesfontein wind farm. They were certain those people had not been there two days before when they scouted the area.

Hennie and Peace reported that they were wary of flying too low, in case they were shot at. From a safe altitude it was hard to see how heavily armed the group were.

We had to go and investigate.

It took us almost four hours to get there, because the roads were deteriorating fast. The summer rain had held back for most of the year, and came eventually in February in the form of three gigantic thunder- and hailstorms, cloud breaks and floods, which considerably worsened the condition of the crumbling roads. Domingo said we would stop in the tarmac road, the R63, and approach the suspect group from there on foot. According to Peace they were two kilometres into the veld, on a farm.

We stopped. I led my team out of the truck. There was a signboard reading *Melton Wold*. It looked like it had once been a holiday farm. We and Team Alpha jogged through the gate. There was a multitude of footprints on the overgrown farm ground track, here and there a hoof print. No vehicles. We spread out, through the veld, covering each other. We could hear the Cessna somewhere up above us, at high altitude.

It was strange to be back in action. The memories of the Battle of Sector 3 were fresh in my mind. The positions of fallen comrades in our formations were empty, other people ran in their places. I wondered how many would be dead by tonight, how many of these people – now under my command – would we bury tomorrow or the next day. Perhaps I would be one of them.

And yet, there was nowhere else I'd rather be.

Domingo's radio voice in our ears; he was waiting in the truck, suppressing the frustration he must be feeling. He relayed Peace Pedi's messages, telling us the enemy force was not showing any activity.

The dry bed of a stream ran beside the farm road, here and there pools of water remaining from the recent rain. We ran on the banks of the overgrown stream bed, the road to our right. We smelled the smoke of their fires, we smelled meat barbecuing on coals. We didn't see any guards or lookout posts. It was strange. Was this an ambush? Over the radio I warned my team to stay alert, there was an avenue of big trees ahead. Taljaard called Alpha to a halt, I did the same with Bravo. He was the senior sergeant, he sent two scouts ahead. They crept between the green thorn bushes, then along the avenue of trees. They let us know we could follow. We jogged through the undergrowth and suddenly we were among them, men, women and children, gathered around the old farmyard. We startled them, children began wailing, women screamed. I halted my team, and made them kneel with rifles at the ready. The men put their hands in the air, mothers grabbed children and held them tight, shielding the little ones with their bodies.

The folk were dirty, thin and starved, their clothes in tatters. Their eyes were full of fear and their body language said they knew this was the end.

They were the West Coasters.

Sofia Bergman

Something changed inside me, that day among the West Coasters.

Just as I had come to the realisation on the night of 9 February in the Year of the Lion that I would never be a true soldier, that I had made a mistake becoming a Spotter, so I did with the West Coasters. It wasn't quite a realisation, but it was a seed. A seed was planted, as I listened to them.

I'll tell you what's so interesting about life: we can make all the plans we want, but life does its own thing. Life with all its coincidences opens doors for you, and closes them. I mean, look at me. I was so absolutely sure I was a soldier. Because my father and brothers taught me to shoot, Meklein taught me to track, I could run like a gazelle, and I was angry at the world. Perfect recipe for a soldier, right?

Then came the Battle of Sector 3, and then the West Coasters.

There at Melton Wold we walked among those poor people, the West Coasters, and I helped, gave them water, encouraged them, and listened to their stories.

And it was the stories that moved me. That's what happened to me. I was touched by their stories and I was captivated by fate. Life. The things that happen to us. Destiny, I suppose.

I must say that was before I knew about Willem Storm's history project.

But today I believe he and I have this invisible bond. And you know what my greatest wish is? That he was alive still. Just for one day. And I want to spend that whole day just talking to him about why he recorded all the history. Was it for the same reasons?

I recently read this quotation from Cicero, the Roman statesman: 'To be ignorant of what occurred before you were born is to remain for ever a child. For what is the value of a human life, unless it is woven into the life of our ancestors by the records of history?'

I so badly want to ask Willem Storm if he also agreed wholeheartedly with Cicero.

My continuation of Willem's work began that day, there among the West Coasters. But on that day itself I didn't know that.

The Minister of Public Works and his nineteen helpers were trapped on the ladder inside the wind tower for six hours while the lionesses rested outside. They grew hungry and thirsty, they sweated in the hot confinement of the tower, fingers aching from holding on, their bodies cramped and sore. But they had to wait, because Special Ops had gone to Melton Wold first, and the lionesses stayed.

By five in the afternoon, when we had established that the more than six hundred West Coasters – as they would for ever be known

– were unarmed and harmless, and we could finally go and help the lion's captives, the two lionesses got up lazily and wandered off in a southerly direction.

Later Pa would speculate they must have come from the old Karoo National Park. But not in any conversation with me. I would still be too angry to talk to him.

That's why that year will be remembered as the Year of the Lion.

91

The West Coasters: I

Joe Drake

As recorded by Willem Storm. The Amanzi History Project.
    My name is Joseph Drake, I arrived here with the West Coast refu-gees. After the meltdown, I spent close to four years in Lamberts Bay. I was the first one who became suspicious about the origin of some of the groceries we were being offered for trade. You see, I used to be an assis-tant manager at the Spar in Table View, before the meltdown. And last year in January in Lamberts Bay, we had these travelling traders offer-ing us fruit juice . . . Spar had its own label of fruit juices, the 'nectars' . . . Now keep in mind, those cartons of juice came to us more than three years after the meltdown, every supermarket, cafe, spaza shop and farm stall this side of the Cederberg had been ransacked over and over again, but we are offered Spar nectar fruit juice, with expiration dates roughly corresponding to the last goods distributed to supermarkets before the meltdown . . . Sorry, you guys refer to it as the Fever. I'm so used to talk-ing about the meltdown, the nuclear meltdown; that was the thing that stuck in my mind.
    The fact is, if you looked at all the evidence, there was only one place the juice could have come from.
    And when I asked the traders, they said, 'Oh, so you want to steal my contacts, my sources . . .' They were very evasive.

Sewes Snijders

Yes, I'm one of the West Coasters. I actually come from Atlantis. My uncle got me a job on the boats and I've worked on the sea since I was sixteen, in Lamberts Bay. When the Fever came to town, I was twenty, and we were at sea on the boat, a trawler, that's what we call it, anyway, and just heard on the radio about everyone who was so sick and all the people dying.

You must know, we were at sea, and we were all healthy, we weren't on land when the virus came round; the skipper and two others of the crew, they heard over the radio that their wives and children had the Fever, and we knew that the virus was highly contagious. You could see the skipper was broken, 'cause he wanted to go to his family, but he had a responsibility to protect his crew as well. We told him, come, let's go home, go be with your family, say goodbye, but he said, no, he's the skipper, he had his responsibility, and it was to his crew. Until the night they told him over the radio, the skipper's wife was on her last; we said now it's mutiny, now we're really going back.

So we did. And I did see the last of the Fever. The very worst part. And the whole crew caught the virus, and the skipper died, and all the crew died, except me, and in the whole town there were four people left. Then I wanted to go to Atlantis to my mom and dad. I was pretty certain they were dead, and we didn't exactly have a good relationship, but in those times you want to be with your people. So I took a car and drove, and I hadn't even reached Clanwilliam, when we found the refugees, the people running away from Cape Town, and they said it's Koeberg, it's the nuclear reactors. There weren't any people to run it, it was in meltdown and everything burning, they said you could see the smoke, such a black smoke that never stopped. That smoke blew out over the sea one day, the next day over the Cape, just as the wind blew, and the people were getting nuclear disease or something, their skin peeling off their bodies, and the authorities said everyone who survives the Fever must get out, the radioactivity was going to fry the whole Cape.

Then I knew if the Fever didn't get my family, the nuclear disease would, 'cause Atlantis is just a stone's throw from Koeberg. So I turned back, and the refugees asked me, where are you going? And I said back to Lamberts Bay. And they asked what is there? And I said only the sea, but a person can survive. So they came along. And then more people came in the next two, three weeks. And the last ones said the Cape is a death zone now, and all the passes over the mountains are blocked, and the bridges over the Berg River as well, and there were big signs saying: Danger: Radioactivity. Do Not Enter.

So we made a life at Lamberts Bay. There were about three hundred of us to begin with.

It was a hard life, that first year. There were people who brought their old attitudes with them. I don't want to be funny, but white people who thought we brown and black people should work for them, look after them, 'cause they used to be rich people in the Cape. There was this brother and sister, twins, can you believe it, from Constantia, they moved into the grandest house in Lamberts Bay, and they gave us orders, do this, do that, be quick. Most of us ignored them, but some people got angry, and they cornered those rich whiteys in their grand house and just wanted to kill them. But Missus Irene Papers stood up. She used to be a school principal in Morreesburg, one of the refugees, she got up, went in the front door of the house, and said, there's been enough death. It's going to stop now. The rich whites must go, they weren't welcome in our community, they must pack their stuff and be gone before the next morning, but there will be no murder.

The next morning they were gone. I don't know where, I don't know happened to them.

But that's how Missus Papers became the leader of the community, and we made a life in Lamberts Bay. Really we just lived off the sea, every year the fish and the crayfish numbers grew, you could watch the sea coming alive again, slowly, and the birds; that's where you could see the Fever was actually good for the world. There are these blue gannets and cormorants on Bird Island at Lamberts Bay. And every year you could see there were more of them and their condition was better 'cause there was more fish for them to eat, 'cause there were fewer people to catch the fish.

Anyway, our numbers grew too, there in Lamberts Bay; people came from the north, and from Clanwilliam's side, they came looking for seafood 'cause there was nothing else really, and they found us, and they stayed. We filled up that town, and there were people at Graafwater who had sheep and cattle, and we bartered, and there were other people who siphoned out diesel everywhere, then they came to barter for fish and crayfish. We needed the diesel for the trawlers, of course.

And then, then the funny stuff began.

First there was the ghost ship.

Last July, we went out with a trawler. There weren't any weather reports any more of course, you had to go on your gut feeling, and what you remembered about the weather. And I remembered, after a cold front, there were often a few days of good weather. So there was this heavy cold front, and afterwards, looking out across the Atlantic the weather looked good, and we took a trawler out. I was the skipper now. Perfect sunshine, and we got snoek. I never in my life saw the snoek run like that, the water came alive in front of us. But I was the only fisherman now, the others were novices, and a snoek can hurt you badly, so I had my hands full catching them and teaching the others. I didn't see the mist; when I looked up, the bank was close. West coast fog. It makes you blind. We had seen that the GPS didn't work so well any more, it was giving funny readings in those days, so we couldn't depend on it. And I was the skipper, and a skipper takes responsibility for his crew, and I said, come on, let's go home, 'cause you get mixed up with direction very fast on the open seas when that mist comes in.

We had hardly got going when one of the crew says, skipper, look there. And we saw the ghost ship. I'm not an expert in ships, but if you've lived on the sea, then you hear, and you know some stuff. And that was a frigate. A naval frigate, military ship, not the big guns, little ones, and there were missile tubes on deck. It was light grey, but we just saw it there coming out of the mist, into sunshine, and then back in the mist. I wonder if it was forty seconds. But I swear it was a naval frigate. We all saw it, and it sailed towards the Cape.

Then, in early August, there were two children who were sneakily collecting gannet eggs on the island. Missus Irene Papers had told us to leave the birds alone, but the kids, they like treats ... And they came running to the grown-ups saying, come and see, come and see, there's a whale in the water, and the people who got there first saw a submarine diving, just the last glimpse of the conning tower and the aerial or periscope or whatever. They were trustworthy people who saw the submarine, they had no reason to lie. Then you think, well, somewhere there must still be military people. Maybe in America, or Russia, maybe the virus didn't kill so many in that Russian cold, you believe it must be people from another world.

Yvonne Pekeur

Near Graafwater the hills are like this, where the road goes through to Clanwilliam. There are two rows of hills. We lived between the two rows, in the farmhouse, six women and the three children who farmed with cattle, and we had a good herd; last November we had more than a hundred and twenty cattle. We just farmed for meat, some people in town were milking, but we just farmed beef. Now you see, we were just outside town, outside Graafwater, it was half an hour's walk, ten minutes on horseback.

In summer we moved around for grazing, to the Olifants River, but in winter the grazing was good in and around the hills, so we trekked with the cattle; we weren't more than, say, an hour or two from the house. And that was last July, it wasn't a very wet year, but the grazing was good, and I ... It was just a few weeks after the Lamberts Bay people told us about the submarine. We were just this side of the old gravel road that goes to Skurfkop, we had made camp for the night, and two of the children and I were with the cattle, we took turns. Everything was peaceful, man and beast, we had gone to bed long before, but I was the light sleeper. Must have been one in the morning. I woke up, and I heard the helicopters. No, not one. Two, or more. Who doesn't know the sound of helicopters? I heard them, but they flew over by the tarmac road. That's the main road, the one that runs from Lamberts Bay to Clanwilliam.

I'm not good with estimating distance and direction and such, but I think the tarmac road was about five kilometres from us. So the noise wasn't overpowering, it was sort of half in the distance. But it was clear enough.

Now you know, you don't want to wake the children, just now they get scared, but you also don't want to be the only one hearing the noise, you hope it comes nearer ... long story short, I listened to those helicopters for a good fifteen minutes. It's not like I was dreaming or anything. Precisely because it was so strange, I got up, and I walked into the darkness, a bit away from the children and cattle, to listen carefully. And I heard, yes, those were helicopters. For about fifteen minutes, and then the sound faded, as if they flew away. And the next day, I took a horse and went to look. And I found it there beside the tarmac road, more or less where I thought I heard the helicopters: I found the trader's wagon.

Let me say something about the traders, the pedlars and the wagons. There were seven pedlars. Three of them travelled alone with donkeys or horses and a cart, and there were the other four, who were a few people working together. Old Jan Swartz and company were five people who travelled together, they had a sheep lorry that they stripped, and they had eight pretty horses that pulled the truck. He was the big rooibos tea pedlar, and they also sold furniture, but pretty stuff, you could see they were antiques. And old Jan Swartz and his team would come and trade those for a few blocks of butter in town. The world was turned upside down, hey? Now, the pedlars that I found that morning beside the road, after the helicopters, it was Lionel Phillips's wagon. He had the dwarf who travelled with him, who was his helper, funny little man. And Lionel was a big strong man,

handsome, with a thick black moustache; he came from Vredendal origi-
nally, and the dwarf from the Cape, when everyone ran away from the
nuclear. Lionel and the dwarf went everywhere together trading with their
wagon. They had stripped a Ford Ranger to make it light and they harnessed
six horses in front; every now and then the horses would be bigger and more
flashy and then they would be towing a little Venter trailer as well.

So I knew Lionel's wagon.

I found the wagon there, and the horses were unharnessed, they were
grazing in the veld. Peacefully, nothing wrong with the animals. But Lionel
and the dwarf – I can't remember his name – Lionel and co were just miss-
ing. No sign of them. And the wagon was empty, completely empty. And
blood, on the wagon door, there where the driver would sit, behind the steer-
ing wheel. And the little hat the dwarf always wore, with a long peacock
feather, the hat was lying in the dust.

Those helicopters must have stolen all their goods, and taken Lionel and
him away.

I wouldn't have said anything about the helicopters if the Lamberts Bay
people hadn't told us about the submarine.

I mean, that's funny, isn't it?

And I still wonder: what happened to Lionel Phillips? And the dwarf. It
was like they had been snatched away.

Joe Drake

So, that was the funny thing, for me: this Lionel Phillips, the travelling
trader, he was the one who started bringing in the suspicious ... I suppose
suspicious isn't the right word, but I was pretty sure the stuff was coming
from the contaminated zone. I mean, why else would it still be available
four years after the Fever, with every town and village pillaged?

And fruit juice. That was the kind of stuff that went first. Or went bad.

Beginning of last year, this Lionel Phillips started coming round with
this merchandise, out of the blue. Reluctant to tell us where he got it.

And then he's the one that disappears after that cattle woman hears
helicopters.

My concern was that the produce might be radioactive. I tried to warn
people, but the novelty of fruit juice and peaches in syrup and even bags of
sugar ... Nobody would listen.

92

The West Coasters: II

I watched Sofia Bergman mingling with the West Coast refugees. I watched her pause with children and women, and the way she sat on her haunches beside two frail old grey-beards, how she touched them, gently, respectfully, and how they responded.

It was like the sun coming out in their faces when they saw this pretty young woman under the military helmet. The dawning of hope. And relief, as if they knew they were safe now.

I didn't watch her for long. I didn't want to get my own hopes up, I didn't want anyone to see my heart was still lost. Besides, I was a sergeant now. I had more serious matters to attend to: I made sure these refugees were who they said they were. I looked for any concealed weapons, or hidden enemy soldiers. I collected information, interrogated some of the refugees about their origins and history. I was a little impatient, a bit stern and self-important, so I only heard brief snippets about the attacks at sea, of privations during their journey this far, and of their hunger and thirst.

But even if I had taken more time and they had been more talkative, even if I had known their whole story, it would have made no difference. It wouldn't have saved any lives.

That was my consolation when I later gained access to my father's historical recordings for the first time. They were some of the last he made, with his usual keen interest, altruism and thirst for knowledge.

And by then it was too late.

Sewes Snijders

I had known Yvonne Pekeur for about three years by then, and I knew she wasn't one to tell tall stories. If she said she heard helicopters, then she heard helicopters. Certainly in her head, anyway. But deep down you wonder if they were genuine helicopters. But you think, okay, it's probably what people think about you when you talk about the ghost ship.

Anyway, it wasn't long after she heard the helicopters that the Bushmans Kloofers came. Bushmans Kloof is deep in the Cederberg, it must be about a hundred kilometres from Lamberts Bay. You drive through Clanwilliam, then you drive up the Pakhuis Pass, and down the other side, and that part is called Bushmans Kloof. There was this grand hotel, in the old days, in a very remote spot, and that's where these people lived. The Bushmans Kloofers. Hippies. No, wait, let me rather say they were different . . .

Andrew Nell

In the beginning there were only three of us in Bushmans Kloof, but at the end we were between twenty and thirty people living there, at the old retreat. It was a luxurious hotel and spa, deep in the valley, extremely remote. I personally was there for over three years. It was very safe place, with only one road in and we took down the road signs. If you pass it on the main road, you wouldn't even know it was there.

The crucial element was the good, clean water from the spring. And in time we had a nice flock of sheep, plus there was game, and the fish in the dam. We tried to grow vegetables, but the baboons robbed us blind, so we just tried to harvest some of the citrus fruit from the orchards over the mountain. And firewood from the hills. It wasn't an easy life. But because we felt safe, we stayed. People passing through talked about the dogs, dogs that ran in packs and attacked people, and of robbers and crazy men. So you stay, because you're reasonably safe where you are, and you're surviving.

We knew about the people in Lamberts Bay, because there was this one pedlar who came up the valley once, and he found us there. And he told us there were a bunch of people at Lamberts Bay and Graafwater, why didn't we go there?

We said no thank you. We had our own ways, you know. We knew other people might not like our ways. But we didn't tell the pedlar that, we just said no thank you.

Then the pedlar said, but those people had a better life than we did. And again we said, no thank you, we are safe here.

Then he said, are we working with the Wupperthalers?

And we said, we don't know about any Wupperthalers.

That wasn't actually the truth.

So he left, and we asked him, please don't tell anyone we're here. And he looked at us, and said, but there's nothing here, why would anyone care?

We didn't keep a calendar, so we didn't know the date precisely. The Lamberts Bay people said it was early September last year. That sounds about right. One night in September, they came for us. Without warning, they broke down our doors in the middle of the night and began hitting us with whips and cudgels, and they said, 'Go, go, take your stuff and go. We told you, stay away from Wupperthal. We told you.' And they said, 'Don't come back,' and there was one who said we were thieves, 'You damn thieving bastards' or something like that. It was horrible, to be attacked in the night suddenly, and we could only grab a few things, and they were hitting us, we had to run down the road. They said, 'Don't ever come back, if we catch you within a hundred kilometres, we'll kill you.'

Some of our people said the whippers all had the same boots on. They weren't dressed the same, but they had the same boots.

I don't know who they were. I think I know why they chased us away from there. I think it was about Wupperthal.

So we walked through the night and through the next day, over the pass, to Lamberts Bay.

Sewes Snijders

The Bushmans Kloofers ... Really different people ... they were polygamists; that Andrew Nell who turned up there, he had five wives. The oldest in her fifties, the youngest one eighteen or so, and three of them were pregnant at once. And all five of those women swore they were legitimate, Andrew Nell had married them and they loved him and he was good to them. That skinny man, with grey in his beard. Five wives ... that takes some doing – I don't have the strength for even one wife. And there were the other men too, from Bushmans Kloof, some of them had two or three wives. So they were a bit strange to us, we didn't know what to believe. About the people who came to chase them away with whips and sticks. But then we saw how those Bushmans Kloof people could work, they would be good for our town. So we decided, if they wanted their polygamy, then can have their polygamy. I mean, the world is a different place now.

And then, in November, the boat came into our harbour. In broad daylight.

Last year in November, we rowed out with the bakkies *for crayfish and fishing. That's a little boat, a rowing boat, we call it a* bakkie. *We rowed out in the* bakkies, *because it was months since the pedlars had come, and we had finished all the diesel they had sold us.*

Yvonne Pekeur

Yes, I meant to say that: once there were seven pedlars. But when Lionel Phillips and the dwarf disappeared when I heard the helicopters, it was the last we saw of any of them.

I don't know what happened to them all. No idea. But I'm just saying: when Lionel Phillips and the dwarf were snatched away by the helicopters, it was the last time we ever saw a pedlar. It must have something to do with it. I believe it.

Sewes Snijders

Anyway, the boat came and anchored in the bay, just outside the harbour, and the people came to call me and Missus Irene Papers, 'cause I was the seaman, and she was the … You could say she was the mayoress. They pointed out the boat out there.

It was big boat, a seventy-five-foot tuna pole boat; her name was the Atlantic Hunter *I noticed later when we rowed out with the* bakkie, *myself and two crew. Missus Irene Papers sent us out to see what this strange boat was.*

As we rowed towards it, people came on deck and said, 'Don't come any closer, don't come any closer, we are sick.' Just like that, in English. Not like South African English, but British. By then we must have been, I don't know, eight or ten metres from them, so I couldn't see too well, myself and the oarsmen. We could see the people were covered in boils, all over their faces and necks and arms, everywhere that wasn't covered by clothing. Ugly boils, they looked like bee stings that were rotting, if you know what I mean. And we just stopped there, 'cause you don't want to get those sores, and I asked, 'What do you want?'

And they said, 'We want water, please, we need fresh water.'

So we rowed back to fetch water for them. We filled bottles, and we tied the bottles in a net, and I tied a rope to the net and a buoy to the rope. We rowed out again, and threw the rope and the buoy in the water. We rowed a distance away, and they came closer and took the buoy and pulled in the net with the bottles. You should have seen how those people drank water, you could see they were extremely thirsty. They said, 'Thank you very much. We have to warn you, there's a new fever. Blister fever. We all have the blister fever. It kills you much more slowly. We were living in Saldanha and people came from Cape Town, they came with this fever and they infected us all. They are coming here, they are coming north. You have to flee before they get here. You have to go north. Go very far. Go to Luderitz, or Angola.'

And they had two corpses wrapped in cloth, and they said, 'Sorry, we have to give two of our people a sea burial, they died of the blister fever, it is a terrible death,' and they all stood on the deck when they threw those two corpses into the sea, and watched them sink.

I shouted at them, 'Why did you come bury those people here?'

And they said, 'We were too thirsty; we didn't have the energy, you'll understand, when you get the fever.'

They said thank you again for the water, you have to run away, the blister fever is coming, and they sailed away in the tuna boat, the Atlantic Hunter, *out to sea.*

Now what seemed very strange to me was that engine, that diesel engine ran like clockwork. As if their diesel were fresh from the oven.

And another thing that was strange to me: that overseas English. Not too strong, but to my ears it sounded foreign.

I didn't think to ask them where they got the diesel. Maybe they were like you guys. Maybe they planted canola or sunflowers at Saldanha and made their own diesel, who knows?

Anyway, we rowed back to tell Missus Irene Papers and our people that the blister fever was coming. And the whole town, we talked all day and late into the night, and we decided we weren't going to flee to Angola. We'd watch the roads for blister fever people from the Cape, and we'd tell them to turn back. Go back. And if they wouldn't go back, we'd have to shoot. But Angola? We were not going to Angola.

93

The West Coasters: III

Joe Drake

This might be a good time to mention that we had heard of you. Not the name of your republic, we didn't know it was called Amanzi. But we had heard there was a settlement on the Orange River, on a dam. I thought it was just a legend, you know, one of those stories that people make up. But then, when we heard it from another travelling trader, I thought it was perhaps at Gariep Dam, that's the idea I had in my mind.

I can't remember which trader first told us about you. It happened more than two years ago, he was telling us there's this community on the river, and they've got electricity, and irrigation, and they have a bakery and everything. And I thought it was nonsense. And then, early last year, another trader said he'd heard it was all true, that you made your own diesel, you had tractors and trucks and stuff, and you were even building houses. But it was very dangerous to get to you, because you had these motorcycle patrols to stop people from getting to you.

I think that's why nobody thought of coming, before the big attack.

Sewes Snijders

December and January we saw nothing. We had sentries out on both the roads, and on the railway, north and south, and there were no blister fever people anywhere.

Then we started wondering, maybe it was a bunch of loonies on that boat with the fresh diesel.

And then, 16 February, all hell broke loose.

Yvonne Pekeur

We heard the explosion as far as Graafwater. That's thirty kilometres away. After midnight, I'm the light sleeper, we were on top of the mountain with the cattle, and I heard that boom and got up and looked towards the sea. And I saw the glow.

Sewes Snijders

We were five hundred and forty-six souls in Lamberts Bay the night the missile hit the fish factory. Some people saw the missile coming in, from the sea. Like an arrow. And it hit the fish factory bull's eye. There must have been seventy people living in that factory, they slept there, we never used it as a factory any more, since the Fever it was for housing. Living space. They were all killed.

And then the helicopters came. We heard them coming, not over the sea, they came from the direction of Muisbosskerm, flying low over us, turning over the caravan park, and coming back. I would guess there were twenty helicopters.

They landed on the old school sports fields, and soldiers jumped out, hordes of them, and began hitting us with whips and batons, and firing their rifles in the air, shouting, 'This area is contaminated, this area is contaminated, in two days we will bomb this place, there is blister fever contamination, get out, get out, you have two days.'

It was terrifying; behind us the fish factory was burning after that helluvan explosion, and now we had soldiers jumping out of helicopters and the women screaming and children crying.

Missus Irene Papers was one of those who lived in the fish factory.

So we lost our mayor. And we left. That was six weeks ago.

Yvonne Pekeur

Yes, that following morning they came walking, streams of them, and they told us what had happened. So we Graafwater people also packed our things.

We trekked, looking for you. But what with the drought this past year . . . Lots of children and old people died on the road. And one of Andrew Nell's pregnant wives. You know, the polygamist.

Andrew Nell

Yes, some of us were polygamists. Not all. I was one. I am one. Amanzi's constitution says I may be one. Do you have a problem with it?

It just happened that way. There were more women than men, and it just happened like that. I don't think we have to say anything more about it.

You should rather ask me about Wupperthal. I believe Wupperthal is crucial. I believe Wupperthal could be the reason why so many things happened to us.

Yes. Things. Let me tell you about Wupperthal. I think the people who drove us out of Bushmans Kloof with whips and cudgels thought we had something to do with Wupperthal.

We didn't. I give you my word on that. We had nothing to do with those people. But we knew about them.

In the old days Wupperthal was a little place, a very pretty town and old mission station. If you drove up from Clanwilliam the road ended there, deep in the Cederberg. For most cars the road ended there.

But in truth it didn't really end there. There is a rough Jeep track that runs over the Eselsbank, and over the mountain. Down the other side and eventually to Ceres, and on to Cape Town. It's a kind of secret route, that Jeep track. There were so many other roads to Cape Town, main roads, tarmac roads, gravel roads. So very few people knew about the road behind Wupperthal, over the Eselsbank.

In Bushmans Kloof there were times of starvation, we had no choice, we were forced to make a plan. About two years ago I thought there might be something in Wupperthal, it was such a tiny place, maybe it was overlooked, maybe there'd still be some canned food or something. Three of us made the trek to Wupperthal with the donkeys. It was about twenty kilometres.

The main road to Wupperthal runs over a pass, or at least, a winding mountain road, until you see the place down below you in the valley. We walked all the way, and it was late afternoon, and we smelled the fires first, so we stopped, and hid away. When darkness fell, we saw the fires.

I left the other two with the donkeys, and crawled through the riverbed, to where the little hall was, and I saw a group of pedlars. One pedlar I had seen before, but the others, there must have been five others, I didn't know. But they all had old trucks or pick-ups and they had taken out the engines and stuff, and they pulled them with horses or donkeys. And all those trucks were parked there.

I heard the pedlars call someone. Then I saw there were four men walking away to the other side, with a string of pack donkeys, eight or ten, I suppose, and they were walking in the direction of Eselsbank. They were taking the secret path over the mountain, towards Cape Town.

We went back to Bushmans Kloof, because those people, those pedlars . . . I think they were smuggling. They were going into the radioactive places and bringing goods out, things that could make you sick.

People like that were dangerous people. That's why I just walked away and went home.

The people with the boots who came and whipped us and drove us away, the whip men, they thought we were some of the Wupperthal smugglers.

Think about what they said to us: 'We told you, stay away from Wupperthal.' And: 'You damn thieving bastards.'

We never stole a thing, why would they say that to us? It was because of the Wupperthal smugglers.

94

Pa

I want to slow down a bit at this point in my story. I want to waste some time; my courage fails me for the final part of this journey.

I also want to pause so that I can delve into my memory one last time, use that to draw the most accurate sketch of my father as he was in life. I want to describe his character in full, make him live again for the reader, so they can experience the same unbearable pain when I describe my father's death.

Shared pain is lessened pain, I think.

Perhaps I want the reader to understand me and have more empathy for my reaction to the death of my father, and my behaviour afterwards. I have never been able to rise above the sinful weakness of searching for sympathy.

The trouble is that I don't have the means to reveal my father's character fully. When I knew him, I was just a child.

I know that sounds like a poor excuse, an evasion of my duty as memoirist. But there's truth in it. I don't believe children want to analyse their parents' characters. I don't think they're interested in that. As a child I was much too self-absorbed, and now looking at my own children, I see it with them too. A child's obsession with self leaves little room for the study of others.

When I look back as a middle-aged man, it is still through the eyes of a child, so it's really hard for me to remember my father objectively. Take the moment I caught him in the act with Beryl. Even here, now, I have to force myself to get my head around their relationship. It was absolutely not about the fact that he was white and she was coloured, or that they hid their affair and everyone strongly suspected that she was a lesbian. It was simply that he was my father, and I didn't think of my father in that way.

There is the dilemma of perspective too. Daily I realise – more and more – that we are eternal prisoners of our own unique view. We try to see others equally and fairly, we truly believe we're objective enough to do that, but in the end it's largely an illusion. We can only see through our own eyes. Even as adults, objectivity remains elusive.

The final factor that made it impossible for me, was that all my life I wanted to be like my father. Even now.

And I will never achieve that.

On the one hand because in my mind my father is just as much an idea, a concept, an icon, as he is human being. The dead have that advantage, a life, terminated and summed up. And I am an incomplete, ongoing project, I am a personality and character still in search of himself, as yet undefined, still in development, still striving to be just a fraction of what Willem Storm was.

Even now, in my forties.

Then the insight: Pa must have felt this way too. Perhaps he lived in the shadow of his father. Or in the memories of his wife and their relationship, and all the pain that went with it. Inside he was unquestionably much more complex than I knew or understood. Pa must have had moments of self-doubt too, he must have been ever-changing, growing and seeking too. Pa was both more, and less, than the man I got to know with a child's and teenager's understanding, but how much more or less I will never know.

My attempt at a complete, balanced and insightful character sketch would be at best disrespectful, at worst a crime against his legacy.

And yet in moments of weakness I wonder: did he have an affair with Beryl because he loved her? Or was she a substitute because he had a weakness for muscular women, as my hockey-playing mother was – athletic, fit and supple? Or were he and Beryl consoling each other, making physical connections in the sense of Nero Dlamini's explanation of what we as social animals needed?

I want to believe it was love. And I believe it happened by chance. I think in those first Amanzi years they worked so incredibly hard for the children and the community, despite the threats and the setbacks, and I think one night, exhausted, they sought physical comfort from each other, and it became a matter of convenience and habit that eventually grew into love.

If I remember the way they were together – the genuine friendship, the kind that accepts and forgives everything, the respect and admiring mutual recognition – then it all made sense. Then they have my blessing, I am glad it happened. Now, as I'm writing this.

But when I was seventeen, when I was Sergeant Nico Storm of Team Bravo of the Spotters, the knowledge of my father and Beryl's liaison was like a big awkward reptile wriggling and writhing in my guts, and so I lost out on the last months of his life.

The Sunday after the West Coasters came, I was called to the front door of the barracks. 'Your father is here.'

I went down. He was standing there, with Okkie. It was the first time I had seen him since the day I had burst through the door at the Orphanage.

I was angry with him for bringing Okkie. I saw it as cowardice, as his way of avoiding an explanation or any discussion of his indiscretion.

He stood there with an air of embarrassment about him, like a child who has broken a minor household rule, his face full of unspoken apology, ready to break into a smile of relief if I gave the lead in amused forgiveness, to show it wasn't so bad, that my anger was just for show, tempered with compassion, understanding and love.

I can recall that scene with intense clarity, because we remember the moments of fear, loss and humiliation the best. And in this case it is humiliation. My humiliation, because I wasn't big enough to show him that compassion, understanding and love.

And so I can see them before me now: Pa and Okkie, hand in hand, silhouetted against the light outside. Pa looked smaller, each time I saw him he seemed smaller, as Okkie and I grew and his responsibilities and the political and social questions grew bigger and more burdensome. Pa searched my face for understanding and empathy. And I looked away, with disdain. I looked at Okkie, I said hello to Okkie, picked him up and held him and ignored my father.

'Do you want to walk down to the river with us?' Pa asked. His tone was a peace offering.

I lied and said, 'I can't.' I didn't look at him. I abused my power to the maximum.

Okkie begged too: 'Come on, Nico. We can shoot catties.'
'Another time,' I said. 'I have to work.'
Pa knew that was a lie.
'All right,' he said in resignation. 'Another time.'

95

April: I

Domingo sent for me. He said, 'Shut the door,' and then: 'Sit.'

I wondered if it was about my father, had he seen me turn my father away at the door yesterday?

'How much have you heard of the West Coasters' stories?' he asked.

'I know they've had a hard time. On the road—'

'Did they tell you about the helicopters?'

'No.'

'Okay. Short version: they said they lived at Lamberts Bay. They say first there was this boat with people with festering boils all over them, who came to tell them they must leave, because there was another fever spreading. And when they didn't leave, helicopters full of troops arrived to tell them to leave. A whole fish factory was blown up.'

'I didn't know.'

'Remember the Marauders?'

'Yes, Captain.'

'Remember Leon Calitz and the sparky, there where they kept the women locked up?'

'Yes, Captain.'

'Remember how the sparky went on about the "chopper"?'

'Yes, Captain.'

'We have to revisit that. For obvious reasons. And my problem is, I can't remember so well, I was pissed off that day. As you well know. I didn't pay attention. And you and I are the only survivors of the Special Ops there that day. So I want to know, what can you remember?'

I nodded, trying to recall. It was more than a year ago, but they were events that had made a big impression on me.

'Take your time,' said Domingo.

'He talked about the chopper. One chopper. That's how I recall it.'

'Check,' said Domingo.

'He said guys with rifles jumped out, and the rifles had lasers.'

'Check,' said Domingo. 'Laser sights. I remember that too. But how many men jumped out?'

I did my best, but I couldn't remember. 'I don't know.'

'Not important. Okay, what else?'

'He pointed at the bullet holes above the door, then said the guys shot at him while he was standing in the doorway.'

'Check,' said Domingo. 'They shot at him with laser sights, and they all missed him. That's why I schemed he was high. I mean, arriving in a chopper, the assumption is you know what you're doing. Arriving in a chopper with laser sights, and the assumption is you're really hot shit. And then you miss the target? But now these West Coast people say they were attacked with whips and sticks. Guys who blew up a fish factory with a missile and then jumped out of helicopters and hit them with sticks . . . It also sounds to me like a pothead dream, only problem is, all four hundred West Coast people couldn't have been high at once. So maybe those laser-sighted chopper troops missed on purpose. But why?'

We pondered that in silence together. We couldn't find an answer.

'Okay,' said Domingo. 'What else can you remember? About that sparky?'

'He said they asked him stuff about people he didn't know.'

'They asked about people he didn't know?'

'That's what I remember.'

'But he didn't say what people?'

'No.'

'Check,' said Domingo. 'What else?'

'He said they went to look for the radio. The chopper guys looked for the Marauders' radio.'

'I remember that. But then they just left the radio there?'

'Yes.'

'It's all a bit strange. Come on, we have to talk to those women too.'

Her name was Anna van der Walt. She was the oldest of the Seven Women we rescued from the storeroom where the Marauders had

kept them prisoner. She was forty-something; a year after her rescue
she was a cook in the community kitchens, but the experience still
seemed to be in her bones – she was still so thin and emotionally fragile. She briskly dried her hands on a cloth, told her colleagues she was
just going to talk to me and Domingo, and then she led us out to the
garden. We sat down under a pepper tree, on mesh metal chairs with
their paint completely worn off.

Domingo said I should do the talking. I think he was afraid he
wouldn't have the necessary sensitivity and diplomacy.

'Ma'am, we want to talk about the night before we found you, out
there on the mountain. We wouldn't bother you if it wasn't important.
Please, if it's okay, ma'am?'

Her eyes betrayed her, revealing how this thought scared her. But
she said, 'All right, Nico. Let's talk.'

'We just want to know about the helicopter that came that night.
That's all.'

'Good.'

'Ma'am, would you tell us what you can remember.'

Her skinny body tensed slowly, as if she needed to brace herself to
revisit that time and night.

'There were no lights in that storeroom,' she said.

She thought while the minutes ticked by. We waited, barely
breathing.

'And there was no window. In the day the light, the sunlight, shone
through the holes in the roof. And under the door. We . . . We were
inside so long, they never let us out. I never really knew when I was
sleeping and when I was awake. I heard the helicopter, and I thought
it must be a dream. But then I looked up at the roof and saw the light
shining through the holes, the long thin beams of light, and they were
moving, like tiny searchlights, moving over us. It wasn't the sun, it was
something else. They were pretty . . . And the loud noise of the helicopter . . . And people shouting, and shooting . . . Have you ever been
locked up?'

And Domingo said, 'Yes,' so quietly that I wasn't sure he'd actually
said it, and I didn't dare look at him, but Anna van der Walt did, very
intently and directly, and she said, 'You dream of being freed. You
dream of someone coming to fetch you. The whole time, you dream

you are going to escape that hell. I . . . the little lights in the roof, and the racket and voices and shots, and someone opened the door, the door of our prison, the storeroom door, and I saw the people standing there, they were soldiers, I saw them against the bright light of the helicopter, and I thought I was dreaming that these people had come to rescue us, maybe they were from heaven. I put out my hands to them. And they shouted. Then I thought they were just like the other men. And they closed the door again. And I thought, then, yes, definitely a dream.'

She looked away from Domingo, she looked up, to the blue sky, and slowly the tension drained from her body.

We drove back with Domingo's Jeep.

'What sort of people fly in a chopper, look like soldiers and close a door on seven women prisoners? What sort of people?'

I had no answer to that.

'What sort of people shoot a missile at a fish factory, and then assault the people with whips?'

He made a gesture that said it was a mysterious world.

'We'll have to get defences against helicopters,' he said.

'How?'

'I'll have to think. There were sixteen Starstreak missiles at De Aar, but I've never worked with them, and sixteen are not enough for experimenting. The upside is, these chopper guys don't actually want to kill. If you take the fish factory casualties as collateral damage. So, the question remains: what is their agenda?'

We drove pensively back to base. He parked. Before I could get out he said, 'You know, all the people who helped me move the lion's share of our arsenal to Sicily died in the Battle of Sector 3.'

'No . . .' I had never realised that.

'It's true. All four of those guys were reservists. Which means you and I are the only ones who now know where those guns and ammo are.'

'Okay.'

'You're going . . . There'll be an announcement on 3 April. That announcement might give you divided loyalties. And you are going to wonder if you shouldn't tell someone where the arsenal is.'

'I won't tell anyone.'

He gave me a long look as though weighing me up. Then he nodded. 'Okay, Sergeant. Dismissed.'

I climbed out and began jogging back to my team who were practising drill. Domingo called me back. 'Sergeant!'

I looked back. He beckoned to me. I went back and stood beside the Jeep.

'I asked Birdy to marry me. And she said "yes".'

He could see I was going to congratulate him, but he said sternly, 'No, you're not going to say anything. You will just listen. The wedding is in three weeks. And you can't attend. 'Cause why, if I invite you, I'll have to invite the whole of Special Ops, and that's going to get a little crowded. The bride is a bit of a pacifist.' And he grinned his Domingo grin.

I just stood there, as I wasn't allowed to speak.

'Just so you know. Information not to be shared. Dismissed.'

That night the message came: there would be a big announcement the next morning in the Forum at nine o'clock. The whole of Amanzi was to attend.

96

April: II

Déjà vu is that strong feeling that we have seen or experienced something before. We get the word directly from the French. In that language it literally means 'seen already'.

Pa gave me that language lesson when I was thirteen, but I remembered it on 3 April in the Year of the Lion, in the Amanzi Forum. Because the feeling of déjà vu was overwhelming.

Pastor Nkosi Sebego stood on the back of the old Tata truck, with a microphone in his big fist. Pa stood beside him, dwarfed as always. The pastor looked presidential and powerful, he exuded authority and self-assurance; my father looked beaten and defeated. I felt the angry shame that Pa could do this to himself and me.

Just about the entire population of Amanzi was crowded into the Forum. The old parking lot was almost full. People stood shoulder to shoulder in Gansie Street, and on the pavements and in the front gardens of the houses across the street. They stood dammed up east and west; not everyone could see, but thanks to the public address system everyone would be able to hear. There were nearly six thousand people, as the West Coasters were there, and our whole community – the river farmers, the Petrusvillers, the people who were re-establishing Hopetown, and the Spotters and most of Sarge X's guards.

Pastor Nkosi made the announcement. It was a repetition of the speech he had given to the Cabinet, I would later find out. He said he was going to lead his people to the Promised Land in New Jerusalem. He was a natural and brilliant orator who was at his best when the crowd and the business and the stakes were high. Now he didn't read the speech, he performed it, his voice was a drama that ebbed and flowed over the houses and buildings, resounding off the hills, and eventually echoing away over the waters of the dam.

After the main part of the speech everyone cheered him, even those who weren't following him, because it was that kind of speech, impassioned and inflammatory.

Then the pastor said the exodus would begin the following week.

'And' – his body talked with him, arms and hands that gestured and directed – 'I want to tell those who won't join us, that you must think very carefully. Do you want to be part of a community of truth and justice and fairness, or do you want to remain with liars and cheats? Oh, I hear you gasp, but how can Nkosi say that? How dare he? I wonder, would you still gasp if you knew the truth? Do you want to hear the truth?'

A few hundred voices shouted, 'Yes!'

'Do you want to hear the truth?'

'Yes!' More and louder.

Nkosi's voice thundered over the crowd: 'Do you want to hear the truth?'

Thousands answered with 'yes'.

'Then I shall reveal the truth, and the truth shall set you free. So, let me ask you, did my Mighty Warrior Party people and I work side by side with everyone in Amanzi to build this place?'

'Yes!'

'Did our blood and our sweat and our tears stain the soil of Amanzi, just like everybody else's?'

'Yes!'

'Is it fair that we ask for our share of what we have built? Just our share, nothing more, nothing less, just our share. Is that fair?'

'Yes!'

'Our proportional share. If 10 per cent of the people follow me to New Jerusalem, we only want 10 per cent. Is that fair?'

'Yes!'

'Of course it is fair. But this man,' and he pointed at my father, 'this man and his cronies are denying us that. They are hiding guns and ammunition. They are hiding our own weapons from us, weapons they know we will need to defend our land, our beliefs, our way of life. Our liberty! Why, my brothers and sisters? Why are they hiding them? Why are they denying us our liberty? Why are they refusing what is rightfully ours? What is their agenda? Do they want to throw us to the wolves? Do they want to see us suffer? Or do they want to attack us? Dominate us? Rule us?'

Deathly, shocked silence.

'I have asked them to give us our share, and do you know what they say? They say I am a spy!'

Cries of disbelief. My feeling of déjà vu continued, my respect for the political savvy of the pastor grew as well. And my disappointment in my father, who was snookered, left holding the short straw yet again.

'Can you believe that? Me? A spy? But there's more. This man and his cronies have lied to you. Last August, this man and his cronies knew that we would be attacked. They knew of the death and devastation that was to come. They knew! And they chose to hide that from you. They chose to lie to you about the reasons for enlarging our defence force. If you don't believe me, ask them for the record of that meeting. And if they don't want to give it to you, come and ask me, because I have kept a copy in a safe place. The truth, my brothers and sisters, is that they knew the attack was coming. And still they allowed hundreds of us to die. They knew, and they did not protect us. They knew, and they sent half of our Special Ops Teams on a wild-goose chase, while the Enemy was at our door. And they knew! Ask yourself, do you want to stay with people like this? Do you want to stay in a republic built on lies and deceit? Or do you want to be part of the truth?'

Pastor Nkosi Sebego spread his arms wide, as a question, as a man waiting to be crucified for his honesty, for his struggle against the forces of evil. The crowd cheered him, they screamed their encouragement and frustration and indignation.

The pastor stepped back. He indicated, flamboyantly and theatrically, that he was passing the microphone to my father. Pa took a step forward. The crowd jeered him. Pa waited, head bowed, for minutes, until Nkosi lifted his hands to show the crowd to be quiet.

Pa took a step forward, up to the microphone, and he looked me in the eyes and said, 'Yes, I have lied to you.'

There was a chorus of blame, but not as vociferous or extensive as Nkosi would have liked.

'I lied to you in the interest of good order and military security.' Pa's voice was calm and reasoned. 'At the time, I thought it was the right

thing to do. And today I still believe that. Yes, we suspected an attack
was coming. We did not know when, or where, or how. That is the
truth. We did everything in our power to protect you. We made
mistakes, and we lost too many people. All that is true. But we did our
best, and we did it in your interest. Those of you who choose to stay in
Amanzi will have the opportunity to elect a new President, because I
am resigning as from today. Our honourable Minister of Technology
Cairistine Canary will be Caretaker President until then. But before I
go, I want to make it very clear: as your democratically elected leaders,
we did not hide or refuse any weapons to Pastor Nkosi and his people.
We never did, and we never will. Thank you.'

The crowd was a restless beast, conversations and lamentation and
arguments flurried through it like gusts of wind, the people sensing
they were pawns in a larger chess game, and no one really knew if
there was going to be a winner.

I felt pride well up in me. Pa had used the pastor's own strategy
against him: nearly three years ago Nkosi had used the resignation-
move to improve his position on the board of power. Now Pa had
done the same.

While I stood there in the crowd, I suspected that my father was
politically much more astute than I had given him credit for. That he
thought in the long term, not for minor, immediate victory. He had his
own talent for theatre. Had he deliberately shrunk in on himself as he
stood beside the pastor? Did he want Nkosi to physically – and with
that preacher voice – overshadow him, so that Pa would look like the
victim, and Nkosi the bully?

Was Pa talking to me, in those moments, when he looked straight at
me? Was he saying, yes, I lied to you about Beryl, but it was in your
best interests?

I felt someone's gaze on me. When I looked around, it was Domingo.
The unspoken meaning was: do you understand now about the
weapons?

I nodded.

Birdy had climbed up on to the Tata. Pa adjusted the microphone
so that it was in front of her mouth. Birdy said, 'My fellow Amanzians,
it is with great reluctance that I take over the presidency, and I will

ensure a speedy election for those who choose to stay. That is a promise. But first, to ensure the fairest possible division of resources
between us and New Jerusalem, we need to know who will be leaving
us. Those of you who plan to join Pastor Nkosi must please sign the
list at the old post office. You can do so right now.'

Domingo drove his Jeep and we ran behind in two separate teams,
Team Alpha and Team Bravo, back to base. Past the old post office
where a long line of people was queuing up to sign the Leavers list. I
wondered how that made Pa feel? After all that he had done for these
people.

We are like the dogs, Domingo said back then. And I believe he was
right. Look at how the dogs turned on each other after the Fever,
when the food ran out, when they just had to survive. No loyalty to the
broader species.

We are animals, Nico. Social animals. Domesticated, social animals.

I was running behind the Jeep of the man whose philosophy that
was, and I wondered what he was thinking about behind that steering
wheel, behind those dark glasses. Because I had drawn my own conclusions. If Pa said that none of the democratically elected leaders had
refused weapons to Nkosi and his Mighty Warrior Party, then it meant
that Domingo had.

For the very first time I wondered whether my father and Domingo
were conspiring. I thought back to each time that Domingo had
manipulated or forced a standpoint or decision. Was it possible that he
and Pa had planned and managed it that way? Since I had walked in
on my father and Beryl, I realised how little I actually knew about him.

All those thoughts ran through my mind on the way back to base.

Domingo ordered us to fall in on the parade ground. He got out of
the Jeep. His hip had not fully recovered, he still walked with a slight
limp. He faced us, legs planted wide, and said, 'I'm going over to
Luckhoff. I will only be back tomorrow morning. 'Cause why, it gives
you time to pack your stuff, if you feel moved to join the good pastor.
He's going to need good men in his army, and you are the best of the
best. I'm leaving for the night so you don't feel any pressure from me.
If you join him, I say, no hard feelings. You believe what you believe,
and I respect that. If you do that, then I say thank you for your service,

thanks for your loyalty, thanks for your bravery, so long and good luck.'

He looked at us intently, turned and walked back to the Jeep.

He halted.

'Those of you who stay: the Cabinet has asked us to ride shotgun for the Great Trek to Gariep. And that's what we will do. To the very best of our ability.'

97

April: III

Cairistine 'Birdy' Canary

As recorded by Sofia Bergman. The Amanzi History Project, continued – in memory of Willem Storm.

   No, I didn't want to be President. I never aspired to that, I never dreamed. I mean, I will always serve. But President? It's just not for me. But when Willem came to me and said, Birdy, some are born great, some achieve greatness, and some have greatness thrust upon them. And I said, But Willem, how will it look, in those history books you write: President Canary. I ask you. Our descendants will just laugh.

It was a hundred and fifty-six kilometres from Amanzi's main gate to New Jerusalem.

   We drove it back and forth, up to eight times a day. The route ran via Colesberg; times without number we saw the spot where we had our first skirmish with the KTM, and by the fortieth or fiftieth time it was just a flyover in the dry, hot summer and you were bored and no longer alert to possible attacks, because there was nothing and nobody on the road – except of course the 2,300 people following Pastor Nkosi to the old Gariep Dam. Forty-six per cent of Amanzi's people. They walked, rode horses and donkeys and travelled on wagons and in trucks, pick-ups and cars. Along with 46 per cent of our tractors and collection of agricultural implements, 46 per cent of our irrigation equipment, vehicles, radios, 46 per cent of our diesel, our seed, our processed, tinned, milled and bottled food supply.

   Forty-six per cent of everything. Except the weapons.

   They received 80 per cent of the weapons and ammunition that were stored in the shed in the reserve. But Domingo said that was less than 20 per cent of our total supply. The remainder were still secure, only he and I knew they were on Sicily.

New Jerusalem got 0 per cent of the Special Ops people. The Spotters didn't lose a single member. This irritated Nkosi beyond measure, and sent him back to the negotiating table to ask Birdy and the Cabinet for 'instructors' to train his own army. 'But not Domingo. I don't want that heathen near New Jerusalem.'

Before long the pastor was the only one referring to the new settlement as 'New Jerusalem'. In the local lingo everyone spoke of 'NJ' – or En-Jay.

Domingo seconded Sergeants Taljaard and Masinga for three months to train NJ's soldiers.

Birdy Canary spent three weeks in NJ to help with the renovation, diversion and adaptation of the hydro-electric power station.

I found it interesting in that first week to spot the geographic and strategic differences between the two dams and towns. Gariep/New Jerusalem was larger. The dam was larger, and there were more houses and infrastructure in the town. There was a feeling of space, of a community with room to breathe. But at Gariep/New Jerusalem only about a third of the town was situated on a hill and defensible. The rest of the houses and an old holiday resort (more luxurious than Amanzi's) were exposed to attacks.

And oddly enough, there was less arable irrigation land in the immediate NJ area.

I noted all that and gained new respect for my father's early choices. And I felt an increasing pressure to forgive him for his sin with Beryl, and make peace with him. Later I would wonder if I had some sort of premonition, if the universe was hinting to me that our time together was running out.

98

The last day with my father

The first Sunday in May was the first weekend that we weren't on escort duty to NJ.

At eleven in the morning I went up to the Orphanage. I stopped in the sitting room, I never wanted to go to my father's room again. Beryl was the one who came in at that moment, as chance would have it, sent by fate. I saw her stiffen, a shadow cross her face, one of guilt, or discomfort and shame.

'Beryl, it's okay,' I said.

'Really?'

'Yes.'

'Oh, thank God,' she said. 'I'll call your father.' And she hurried down the passage, and I thought I saw her hand brush her cheek.

Okkie came running in. Okkie had an early warning radar that told him Nico had arrived before anyone else. He squealed with delight and threw himself into my arms, saying my name. I picked him up and he began babbling about horses, how he was going to learn to ride, Pappa said this afternoon he could learn to ride, because now all the En-Jayers were gone and there was enough time and horses, that's what Pappa said, are you going to ride with me, Nico? You can ride, we can ride together, but bring your gun, Nico, where is your gun today? Can I touch your gun today, please, Nico, just one time?

A stream of happiness and words, his arm around my neck in total love and trust.

Pa appeared in the passage. Again, he was smaller than I remembered.

'You've grown some more,' he said to fill the silence. 'Are you ever going to stop?' But he halted a few steps away, hesitant body language, uncertainty reflected in his eyes.

'It's okay, Pa,' I said.

Pa came to me and hugged me, with Okkie between us. I was more than a head taller than Pa. I was broader and stronger, and I suddenly recalled that night in front of the House of Light, when I was a kid, after shooting the two Jeep men, when I discovered that I would have to protect my father for the rest of his life. And that feeling, that desire to protect him, overwhelmed me as I held my father tight.

It was the last time in my life that I embraced my father.

It was the moment I return to when regret threatens to consume me because I didn't give him more time and love, more attention and respect. I want to crucify myself because I didn't tell him that day 'I love you, Pa'.

At least I did hold him for a while. I experienced a *lucidum intervallum*, after my stubbornness, my lunacy, my anger because he had an affair with Beryl.

Lucidum intervallum. It's Latin. A legal term. It means – according to Willem Storm, my father the jurist and lover of words – 'a moment of psychological normality', a brief moment when a mentally disturbed person regains his sanity, so that he can engage in a contract and speak for himself. And be responsible for his actions.

For the rest of my life I will be grateful for my *lucidum intervallum*.

We walked back to the stables, Okkie pulling us both by the hands; we were hopelessly too slow for him.

I asked how things were.

Pa was going to say it was fine now that I was here, now that he and Beryl were forgiven. I could read it in his expression. But he didn't say that in front of Okkie. He said he was enjoying not having an official position for a change. He was considering not standing in the next election on 1 June. 'To just farm for a term. I want to see if I can get potatoes going. There's new farm land we're going to develop, irrigation, beside the canal on the other side of Luckhoff. And now that our population has halved . . . There's less pressure on everything. And everyone.'

'Maybe you should just take a holiday, Pa,' I said.

He laughed. He said that might be a very good idea.

We had reached the stables. Okkie demanded Pa's complete attention. I stood watching them saddle the horse, Pa explaining the basic principles of riding to Okkie. I wondered where Pa had acquired that knowledge. And I knew: he had asked someone, he wouldn't have been able to suppress his curiosity. I saw how good Pa was with Okkie, I recognised him in that. He had been the same when I was small. Endlessly patient. And never condescending.

The saddle was on. Pa lifted Okkie onto it and adjusted the stirrups. Suddenly Beryl was beside me.

'I'm sorry, Nico,' she said. 'That you had to find out that way.'

'I was just shocked,' I said.

'I understand that. We would have told you, but every time when we wanted to, something happened. A crisis. A war. A pastor . . .' She smiled.

Pa looked our way. He saw Beryl's smile, and mine. His body relaxed a little more.

'How long have you . . .'

'Remember Thabo and Magriet? The first traders?'

'*Medicine. For trade. We come in Peace.*'

'Exactly. It . . . We liked each other a lot from the beginning. But in that time it became serious.'

'All right.'

'And now you're okay with it?'

'Almost completely,' I said.

'Almost is good,' she said. 'Almost is good.'

All four of us went riding, slowly, for Okkie's sake. We went down the gravel quarry road to the dam, and along the bank, Okkie and I in front, Pa and Beryl behind us.

We all ate lunch together and it was good.

Okkie and I dozed off on the biggest couch in the Orphanage sitting room, and at four we drank coffee and ate *koeksisters* and talked.

At five I went back to base.

At half past six Pa called Number One/Trunkenpolz/Clarkson over the radio. But I didn't know that. I would only find that out after Pa was already dead.

But that was more or less the way we spent the last day that we were together.

I've played it over and over in my mind, for nearly thirty years.

Over and over.

99

Send my regards to Cincinnatus: I

Commissioner Sizwe Xaba

That Sunday morning at around 11.30 the radio room picked up the broadcast on the forty-metre band. 'This is Number One, calling on Willem Storm, this is Trunkenpolz, calling on Willem Storm.'

Every fifteen minutes, the same call.

My radio room called me immediately. Of course my responsibility is to report such an incident directly to the President. The problem was, our Caretaker President Cairistine Canary was in New Jerusalem at the time, advising on their hydro-electric power station, and I was unable to report to her. My second thought was to report this to the former President, as it was him who this Trunkenpolz was calling for. I proceeded to look for Willem. I saw him and his two sons and our Minister of Social Development Beryl Fortuin riding horses along the shore of the dam, in the direction of the boat landing. I knew that Willem had been through a lot, and he hadn't seen his son the soldier for some time, so I made the decision not to disturb him yet. I proceeded to the Amanzi Special Operations Headquarters, where I informed the commanding officer of the unit, Captain Domingo, about the radio call. I did this because in my opinion Number One/Trunkenpolz was predominantly a military threat.

Cairistine 'Birdy' Canary

No, I knew nothing about it, I was in New Jerusalem, and that was the day of the voltage regulator fiasco, so I had my hands full, I couldn't go home. And they, Willem and Domingo and Sarge X, couldn't say anything to me on the radio because we didn't trust the pastor, and the pastor's people were listening in on our general comms frequencies, that much we knew. We'll probably never know if they were eavesdropping on the ham radio frequencies as well.

Commissioner Sizwe Xaba

Captain Domingo insisted on going to the radio room immediately after I informed him of the Trunkenpolz call. This was at about 12.20, so we had to wait until 12.30 before Trunkenpolz called again, on the same wavelength. This was, as Captain Domingo pointed out at the time, the same wavelength on which we picked up the conversation about the Maseru sales meeting a few months ago, which we believed at the time to be a trap.

Captain Domingo decided that, in the absence of President Canary, he and I should decide on the appropriate military response. His argument was that the calls might cease before the President returned, or before we could get the Cabinet convened. He argued also that the Cabinet would have asked for and followed our advice in the matter anyway. He was persuasive. Captain Domingo was a very persuasive man.

He then proceeded to respond to Trunkenpolz. On the ham radio, on the forty-metre band he said, 'Trunkenpolz, this is Domingo of Amanzi. I am authorised to respond. State the nature of your business with Willem Storm.'

And Trunkenpolz laughed, and he said, 'I don't speak to servants, I speak to masters. Tell Storm I have a proposition. I will be listening on this wavelength.'

Captain Domingo did not respond to this. He simply left the radio room. I followed him outside, and I asked him what he proposed we do.

He said we should get the message to Willem Storm. We proceeded to the Orphanage, where we saw Willem Storm and his sons having lunch with our Minister of Social Development Beryl Fortuin. Captain Domingo and I decided to postpone informing Willem about the radio call. We went and had lunch together. We did not discuss the matter with anybody. I am absolutely certain that my staff members on duty in the radio room that day did not discuss the radio conversations with anybody. I am absolutely certain. I asked them, and I believe them. They are good people.

Captain Domingo and I returned to the Orphanage at about 14.30. Willem Storm's sons were asleep in the lounge. Willem Storm was sitting with our Minister of Social Development Beryl Fortuin under the trees on the east side of the building. We informed them both about the radio conversation.

Willem Storm asked for our advice. Captain Domingo said he thought we should make Trunkenpolz wait.

Willem Storm asked, how long?

Domingo said a day or two.

Willem Storm said that he would think about it.

I then issued orders in the radio room to be notified of any further activity, and went home.

At 18.15, Captain Domingo and Willem Storm arrived. They informed me that Storm had come to a decision. He would call Trunkenpolz at 18.30. It was also decided by the three of us that Storm would not misrepresent his status, but he would also not offer information pertaining to the fact that he was no longer the President of Amanzi. We agreed that this would give us a fair indication of how informed Trunkenpolz was on matters in our community. We then proceeded to the radio room, and at the designated time Willem Storm called Trunkenpolz on the forty-metre band.

The conversation was brief. Trunkenpolz answered within a few minutes, and said he had a proposition for Storm. One that would be to everybody's benefit.

Storm asked about the nature of the proposition. Trunkenpolz said he would discuss this when they met in person. And would Willem Storm be willing to attend such a meeting?

Willem Storm said he needed time to decide.

Trunkenpolz said, ah, the vagaries of democracy, QRM all the time. He was using the Q codes that ham radio people used. QRM means 'are you being interfered with', so what he was saying was that in a democracy, you are being interfered with all the time. Which I believe was an attempt at humour.

We did not laugh.

Cairistine 'Birdy' Canary

I couldn't go back to Amanzi that Sunday night; when the mess with the voltage regulators was sorted it was already dark.

My escort said we would leave just before sunrise.

So I arrived home at half past six on Monday morning, and Sarge X and Willem and Domingo were waiting for me in front of the Orphanage. That's when I knew our troubles were not limited to electrical supply.

Send my regards to Cincinnatus: II

Domingo didn't wake us.

On that Monday morning, the first Monday in May in the Year of
the Lion, Domingo didn't wake us up. Every weekday morning it
was his habit to wake us, it was a rule, a ritual. He would come walking down the passage, opening every dormitory door, the first one
at precisely six o'clock. He would say: 'Rise and shine, ladies.' He
said that to the women's dormitory, and the men's. His words were
measured, his voice never raised, he had never needed to scream at
us.

On that Monday morning, the first Monday in May in the Year of
the Lion, I woke just before six, as always, and waited for the sound of
his boots on the cheap tiles, the halting step of the past months, but I
didn't hear it.

I checked my watch, saw that it was five to, then four and three and
two and one, it was six o'clock and Domingo wasn't here.

I jumped out of bed. Sergeants Taljaard and Masinga were still in
New Jerusalem, I was the senior officer present. I must wake the
troops.

I did so. I used Domingo's words and tone of voice. It felt false and
strange and just plain wrong.

Sofia Bergman

*That Monday morning I wanted to go and tell Domingo that I thought I
should go back to school.*

*I don't want it to sound like a big coincidence. The truth is, I had wanted
to do it the previous Monday and the one before, and the one before that too,
I had wanted to resign right after the Battle of Sector 3, but then something*

happened, and I thought, wait, I would stay a bit longer, it wasn't a good time to resign. Because I had gone against the advice of everyone in leaving school and joining Special Ops, I felt I had an obligation to at least leave at the right time.

But that Monday morning I was resolute, as we had spent almost a month driving patrols non-stop with the people of the Great Trek, to NJ and back, and all of a sudden it was done, and I thought, before the next thing comes up, I'd better tell Domingo. If he thinks I should stay another week or two or longer, then I will, but at least he would know I intended to leave.

And then Nico opened the door and said, 'Rise and shine, ladies,' and it was just so unexpected and so ... wrong, I knew something wasn't right. I had a very strong feeling of ... It was a sort of evil that I felt. Of course that's nonsense, it's just because you know what happened afterwards, and we were so accustomed to hearing Domingo's voice, and suddenly it was Nico's. But later I did feel that I had a premonition.

Domingo arrived at half past nine.

We were checking equipment after the weeks on the road. I heard Domingo's voice in the passage: 'Storm!'

'Captain!' I answered, and ran down the stairs to his office.

Birdy was sitting behind Domingo's desk. He stood beside her. Leaning against the wall was one of the West Coasters, a bespectacled man that I had seen before, but didn't know his name.

'Close the door,' Domingo said.

I closed it.

He didn't invite me to sit. He said, 'Is Bravo good to go?'

'Yes, Captain.'

'It's a hush-hush job. Strictly confidential. Are we clear?'

'Yes, Captain.'

'Birdy.'

She nodded and said, 'Nico, do you know John?'

'I know he's one of the West Coasters,' I said to the man.

He came closer and put out his hand. 'John Hahn,' he said.

'Okay,' said Birdy. 'I'm not going to get very technical. Let's just say for a hydro-electric system to work, you need voltage regulators. It's vital, critical. That's why there are always two voltage regulators on the control panel. One does the work, the other is the back-up, the redundancy. As in, the spare regulator. Understand?'

'I understand.'

'As you know, I helped the pastor and company to get NJ's hydro-power going. They basically have the same system as we do, it's just been five years since it was last used or serviced. We connected and diverted everything, got it all going. I was very careful, but when I threw the final switch, the voltage regulator blew. Completely fried, irreparable. So I knew I had made a mistake somewhere . . .'

'Maybe it wasn't you, Birdy. Maybe it was—'

'Shush, Domingo.'

Only Birdy Canary could tell Domingo to 'shush'. The dynamics of their relationship remained surprising and mysterious. And unthinkable. You expected him to pull out a knife or a pistol and say, 'Nobody tells me to shush.' But not when Birdy was involved.

'I made a mistake,' said Birdy. 'That's the long and short of it. I tried to track down the fault, and I was absolutely certain I had found it. So I switched everything on again, and I blew the redundancy regulator as well. So the Promised Land doesn't have the promised electricity. And there's no way to fix it. I had to tell the pastor and the pastor was not happy, to put it mildly. And then he asked me, what about our regulators at Amanzi. Would they work? And I said those are our regulators. And he asked again, will they work? And I had to say, yes, they would work. So, since it was me who fried the thing, it was my fault. And there is a strict share agreement, 46 per cent. So now Amanzi's voltage regulators are part of the share. We have two regulators and they are claiming one. It's our spare, Nico. Our one and only back-up. These things break eventually. If our one fries too . . . Anyway, it doesn't help to cry. When I told the pastor sorry, it's tough luck for NJ, he said I better go and tell the people. I must tell the people they have to sit in the dark and the cold, they must cook over fires while we in Amanzi live in the lap of luxury, 'cause why, we won't share an extra, unused voltage regulator. Nkosi said let's see how my people take that. Let's see if we can stop a civil war.'

Domingo grunted.

Birdy said, 'No, Domingo, it doesn't matter that we will win a civil war. Those were our people. Those people helped to build what we have . . .' She looked back at me. 'It's a tough choice, Nico. But I want to do the right thing. And to do that, I need more information. Fast. I told Nkosi to give me two days. Today is day one. Maybe there's hope, because John . . .' And she pointed at the West Coaster against the wall, '. . . worked at Eskom. John has been assisting me, these last two weeks at NJ. And John has strategic information. Tell him, John.'

Hahn stepped forward. He said, 'Yes, I was with Eskom. That was ten years back. I was Works Coordinator: Maintenance and Operations for Eskom in the Eastern Cape, I worked in Queenstown. I had to send the teams out to build the substations and maintain them. And one of the substations was at Teebus.'

'Do you know where that is?' Domingo asked.

'No,' I said.

'Between Middelburg and Steynsburg,' said Domingo. 'But John will show you. He's going with you.'

'You see, there are voltage regulators there,' said Birdy.

'There's a hydro-electric generator that actually no one knows about,' said Hahn. 'Underground. In the middle of nowhere.'

'Weird,' said Domingo.

'But true,' said Birdy.

'The Orange–Fish tunnel,' said Hahn. 'In 1975 they built a tunnel from the Gariep Dam, to bring water to the Fish River, for irrigation, and so that Grahamstown and Port Elizabeth would have enough drinking water. That tunnel runs underground, from the dam, for about ninety kilometres. As far as two pointed hills, Teebus and Koffiebus, named after a tea tin and coffee tin, because of their matching shape. Just past Teebus the tunnel emerges and the water runs down a canal for a few kilometres, and into the Teebus River, which is one of the tributaries of the Fish River. Now, just before the tunnel emerges, they built a hydro-electric power station. Underground. Under a hill just the other side of Koffiebus. You drive into a tunnel, slanting downhill, to a bigger tunnel. They call it the turbine hall, where the turbines and everything are.'

'And that's where I want you to go,' said Birdy. 'To see if the voltage regulators are still there.'

'They should be,' said Hahn. 'The funny thing is, the power station was never used, because it was damaged before it could be switched on. Some idiot forgot to pull the handbrake of his vehicle, and the thing ran down the slope in the tunnel and crashed into one control panel. At the time there was more than enough electricity, and the Teebus station could only generate point-six megawatt, so they didn't even bother to fix it. It's from the same era and the same technology as our power station and Gariep . . . I mean, NJ's. There should be two voltage regulators there. And they should work.'

'As a matter of fact, we want you to take out the whole control panel for us,' said Birdy.

'I'll help you,' said Hahn.

'If it's still there,' said Domingo.

'My little ray of sunshine,' said Birdy.

'I'm a realist,' said Domingo.

'He's right,' said Hahn. 'Those tunnels used to be closed for five weeks every year for maintenance. It's been more than five years since there was any maintenance. The tunnels might have caved in.'

'I have to give the pastor an answer the evening of the day after tomorrow,' said Birdy. 'You must let me know at the latest by lunch-time day after tomorrow if the regulators are there. And serviceable.'

'Take the Volvo,' said Domingo. 'You can't use the N1 or the N10, and I can't give you air cover. 'Cause why, I don't want a Nkosi spy seeing you travelling in that direction. Those voltage regulators are a very strategic asset now. You'll have to take back roads, and they are in a bad state. So drive carefully, but don't waste time. And we'll use Romeo as radio code. R, as in Romeo, for regulator.'

'Yes, Captain.'

'If you see the regulators are okay, tell me over the radio, Romeo is affirmative.'

'Romeo is affirmative.'

'Check. And if it isn't okay, for whatever reason, then you tell me, Romeo is a negative.'

IOI

Send my regards to Cincinnatus: III

Sofia Bergman

We watched Team Bravo climb into the Volvo, along with one of the West Coasters, and drive out of the gate. It was the first time since I'd become a Spotter that one team didn't know what the other team was doing. It heightened the feeling we all had that something wasn't right. And Domingo stayed behind. Domingo not going along? And then Birdy came walking out of our building, and she looked really worried.

It was strange.

Plus, both our sergeants were still busy with training in NJ, so we talked a lot among ourselves about what was going on.

Cairistine 'Birdy' Canary

It was a weird morning. We had to get the Special Ops Team on the road, because we didn't have much time. And then we had to sit down with Willem Storm and Sarge X over the Trunkenpolz message. I know his name is really Clarkson, and there are people who talk of Number One, but to us, I think, he will always be Trunkenpolz.

Anyway, Willem said he thought it was strategically a good thing to keep talking to Trunkenpolz. We didn't trust him, he knew we didn't trust him, let's see where it goes.

And Domingo said, yes, sooner or later he's going to make a mistake. So let's talk. Sarge X and I said okay, let's do it.

Domingo said it must be only him and Willem in the radio room. Sarge X said his people were trustworthy, but Domingo said, be that as it may, let's not take chances.

So it was only Domingo and Willem who talked to Trunkenpolz. And they came out of there, and said, okay, they agreed to a meeting, date and place to be determined.

Only the two of them would know what was said over the radio that day.

We drove from De Aar to Richmond, taking a lousy gravel road to Middelburg, and there was one spot where the road was completely washed away. We wasted three hours moving enough earth and stones with the spades that we carried in the back of the truck so we could get through.

In Middelburg we saw people. Not many, maybe eleven or twelve who came running out when they heard the Volvo's engine. I ordered the driver to keep on going. I saw the people waving, they were starved, neglected and wild. There had been no sign of life when we last passed through here, thirteen, fourteen months ago. It was different now without the KTM killer gangs racing around.

The old R56 was tarred, but it must have been a bad road even before the Fever. Where we had to cross the Rooispruit between two hills, a low-water bridge had entirely washed away. We wasted another two hours making our way across.

And then we saw Koffiebus and Teebus, the two distinctive hills, Koffiebus like a fat man on our left, Teebus slender and feminine on the right.

John Hahn, the former Eskom employee and West Coast man, sat up front. He told me over the radio: 'It's past Koffiebus, you can't really see anything from the road.' And at last: 'Slow down, slow down, there, turn left there.'

Through the peephole where Domingo usually stood, I saw the faded road sign that said Hopewell, Teebus Station, Bulhoek. We turned left, and scarcely two kilometres further was the old village: a few houses, a big swimming pool, now empty and dirty. I stared at it and wondered why a swimming pool, of all man-made structures, evoked the most melancholy when it fell into disuse and neglect. Maybe because we usually associated them with sparkling, blue water and the excited shrieks of children at play?

The entrance to the tunnel was just a few hundred metres further on, behind a high wire fence. The white signboard beside the road said nothing about a hydro-electric power station, only ORANGE–FISH TUNNEL: *Administration and Plant.*

We drove through the first big gate which was standing wide open. Not a good sign.

The second gate, in front of the few structures, was also open. To the right was a red brick building, on the left a shed where eight vehicles could park. It was overgrown, bleached and crumbling. Right in front of us, the tunnel. But it was walled up with poles, stones, bricks, planks, panels and roofing sheets.

I ordered my team to get out, take up their positions to cover the mouth of the tunnel. I had the Volvo back up, outside the gate and park at a safe distance. Cautiously I walked towards the entrance to the tunnel. It seemed as if someone had blocked it so they could shelter in the tunnel. Were they still inside it now?

I saw no recent signs of life.

And then there was a whirlwind of motion from behind the shelter, and shots boomed out.

Nero Dlamini

'Send my regards to Cincinnatus.' That was Willem Storm's distress call.

It went way back, to that very first winter in Amanzi, that terrible winter. When we had our first democratic election. Everybody wanted Domingo to stand, to make himself available as a candidate, because we were all a little scared of him – especially the pastor – and we all wanted him inside the tent pissing out, rather than outside pissing in.

Of course Domingo refused. And the pastor cornered him about it, and Domingo said he didn't believe in democracy in this crazy post-Fever world, he believed in a benevolent dictator. The pastor wanted to make a big song and dance about it, and that damn polymath Willem Storm said, hold your horses, Domingo has the ancient Romans on his side, they were democrats, but they knew the value of a dictatorship when they were in deep trouble.

And some time later, I think it was when Domingo saved the election for us, the second election. I think it was the second election, he saved it for us by telling the people he would leave Amanzi if Nkosi won . . . Anyway, that night, Willem Storm told Domingo that basically he was our dictator.

And Domingo said, well, you don't sound very upset about it, andWillem told us the story of Cincinnatus. He's the guy the American city of Cincinnati was named after, by the way. Cincinnatus was this ancient Roman guy, just another aristocrat that they elected dictator after Rome was attacked, and they were in real trouble. But when they defeated the enemy, Cincinnatus said, okay cool, guys, I'm all done here, he relinquished power and he went back to being just a regular aristocrat citizen, and he became a big democratic hero for letting go of power.

So Willem was saying, Domingo can be our Cincinnatus. One day he must just let the power go. And that's how it started.

When Willem was President, he insisted on going everywhere on his bicycle. No escort, no guards, no fancy presidential car, he said oh please, that's just nonsense.Which was all fine, most of the time. But then we were at war too, off and on. And Sarge X and Domingo were not happy, they called him our greatest asset, but Willem absolutely insisted. They demanded that he carry a radio with him at all times, and they gave him a special distress signal.It wasWillem's idea:'Send my regards to Cincinnatus.' He came up with that. It was a sort of reminder to Domingo, to let go of power one day.And Domingo just smiled, and said okay.

So if Willem was ever in real danger, life-threatening stuff, he had to say that on the radio: 'Send my regards to Cincinnatus.'

They leapt out right there in front of me, out of the chaos of rocks and bricks and metal sheets, with strange, unearthly cries. Panicked, I raised my rifle and fired. Behind me, my troops were shooting too, the bullets smacking left and right and over my head.

Two massive males raced out faster than I ever thought a baboon could run, dirty grey streaks of naked fear, one left, one right, up the hill behind the entrance.

Not one of the Spotters hit them. Despite all the hundreds of hours of training.

And then it was quiet, the baboons vanished.

And we laughed. My troops had the decency to wait until I began to laugh. But they carried on laughing much longer than I did.

102

Send my regards to Cincinnatus: IV

The people who had blocked up the tunnel had been gone for years.

When we began removing the barricades, the only signs of life were baboon shit, dassie droppings, and the shed skin of a very large puff adder.

The tunnel was in a terrible state – part of the roof had fallen in. It was going to take half a day or more to tunnel a path through it.

We started at once, while we still had a few hours of daylight left. We had brought candles and bundles of twigs to use as torches, but we had to save them for the delicate task of removing the control panels in the turbine hall – when and if we got that far. We were going to work deep under the earth in the pitch-dark and we would need all the light we could get.

Cairistine 'Birdy' Canary

At four o'clock they called me to the radio room; the pastor wanted to talk to me, all the way from New Jerusalem.

I wasn't in the mood, I knew he wanted to harass me about the voltage regulators, and I had nothing to tell him. But what can you do? I went to the radio room. He said, Madam President, I cannot wait. I have spoken to my people, and I have prayed over the matter, and I cannot wait. Tomorrow, I am coming to fetch that voltage regulator. We want what is rightfully ours.

I'm no shrink, but I always thought the pastor was a bit of an anal retentive, or obsessive compulsive, or whatever you call them.

And I said, Mr President ... Maybe I should just mention here, since they were in NJ, the good pastor insisted we call him Mr President too. So I said to him, Mr President, I will have to consult with my Cabinet.

And he said no, there's nothing to consult about. They want their share ...

Wait, it's important that I remember correctly what I said. Let no one ever doubt exactly what he said. On my word of honour, he said, 'There is nothing to consult about. We will no longer be denied. I want to make this very clear. We demand what is rightfully ours, and we will take what is rightfully ours. Our voltage regulators and our weapons.'

That's what he said.

Sofia Bergman

Domingo came at about six o'clock in the afternoon, and said we were to sleep on the dam wall until further notice, we were guarding the hydro-electric power station, and our voltage regulators. All of us, the entire Team Alpha. And if anyone came near the entrance to the power station, we had his permission to shoot.

Cairistine 'Birdy' Canary

We had the Special Ops Team stand guard on the dam wall, and we tried to reach Nico Storm on the radio at Teebus, but we couldn't make contact.

I have to add, Willem Storm was no longer in the Cabinet, so he wasn't at the meeting where we decided to give the pastor nothing before Nico had sent us word.

And finally, probably only half past seven that night, Nico called us on the radio, and the signal was poor, and the news was bad, we thought they weren't even in the tunnel, because Nico said, 'No news on Romeo yet.'

From just outside the tunnel entrance we couldn't pick up Amanzi on the radio at all. We had to drive back in the Volvo on the R56 to the other side of Teebus and try again. I stayed within protocol by saying: 'No news on Romeo.'

Domingo said, 'Really bad news. When can news be expected?'

'Perhaps tomorrow around twelve,' I said.

'That is really bad news,' he said.

From that I knew they wanted us to hurry.

We drove back. I divided my people into three teams – one to dig with minimum light, one to stand guard, and one to sleep. I rotated them. And I barely slept at all.

Beryl Fortuin

Willem went to Witput in the afternoon. Witput was the irrigation area west of Luckhoff, the farm alongside the canal where he wanted to plant potatoes in the spring. He was planning the layout of the fields, and he had gone to look for the right spot to install the old diesel water pump, as of course there was no electricity there.

He went alone. I think he enjoyed the solitude. Remember, for many years he could never be alone, he had always been surrounded by people, solving their problems, pleasing them, all the time. So I think he enjoyed being alone very much.

In that time ... I don't believe he considered it dangerous to go alone. Witput is ... There's nothing and nobody, not even a decent road. And it was after the Battle of Sector 3, there was no reason to be afraid ...

He came back at sunset and we ate together in the Orphanage, and Birdy and Nero came in and told him the news of the pastor's new deadline, and that Special Ops were guarding the dam wall now. And Willem said he thought the pastor was trying to intimidate Birdy, Nkosi had always been a bit of a bully. Then Willem said, 'Birdy, tell Nkosi you are prepared to share the regulators, but Willem Storm has the keys to the power station, and he won't give them up. If you have to, you can say that. Put the blame on me.'

And Birdy said thanks very much. And they left again.

That was the last night we were together.

We worked through the night, and through the morning. By Tuesday afternoon just after twelve the tunnel was open and safe, and we could go down to the turbine room. There were signs that people had lived here, perhaps two or three years ago. Empty cans, empty bottles, bedding, jewellery in a box.

The control boards with the voltage regulators were untouched. Covered in dust, damp in the humidity, but John Hahn said they would definitely work when they were dried out.

I drove back in the Volvo to where the radio reception was good and called the radio room. They sent for Domingo.

'Romeo is affirmative,' I said.

The signal was weak. 'Repeat,' he said. I repeated it.

'He's in good health?' Domingo asked.

'Romeo seems to be in good health,' I said. And I wondered who might be listening in on our general communications wavelength. If Pastor Nkosi's people heard this they would know we were doing something secretive, but they would have no idea what it was about.

'Excellent news,' said Domingo. 'When will you be joining Juliet?'

John Hahn said we should be finished about three o'clock.

'Some time tonight.'

'Safe travels,' said Domingo.

Cairistine 'Birdy' Canary

At lunchtime on Tuesday Domingo came to tell me the Teebus voltage regulators were good, they ought to arrive tonight. I got the Cabinet together and we decided we could take the risk, I had to let the pastor know we would be bringing him his regulator the next day.

So I went to the radio room and we called New Jerusalem, and they answered, but said the pastor was not available.

And when I asked them when he would be available, they said they didn't know, maybe only tomorrow.

And when I asked them where the pastor was, they said none of your business.

Sofia Bergman

Domingo was with us, at three that Tuesday afternoon. He brought us food and water for the night, he had his pistol and his radio on his hip and his R4 in the Jeep; the rifle was upright where he always kept it in a holder.

He shared out the provisions, chatted to us and then he drove off. He didn't say where he was going.

And then, at half past three, we heard Willem Storm on the radio, crystal-clear. On our wavelength, the military channel. There was great urgency in his voice. And I grabbed the radio and turned the volume up louder and I heard Domingo's voice saying, 'Repeat, Willem, repeat.'

And Willem said, 'Regards to Cincinnatus from Witput, regards to Cincinnatus, I am at Witput.' But you could tell he didn't really mean to send regards to anyone, you could hear he was ... excited. To be honest, if I allow my imagination to ... Let's just say his voice was very excitable.

And then it went quiet on the channel and Domingo said, 'Affirmative, Willem, I will send regards to Cincinnatus.'

That's all.

103

Send my regards to Cincinnatus: V

We arrived back at Amanzi at eight that night. The sun had already set.

The guards at the Petrusville gate seemed subdued. I didn't make anything of it.

The guards at the main gate were silent and stiff. They usually welcomed us with genuine friendliness, but not tonight. I suspected it might be because they were tired from the longer shifts now that there were fewer people left. More than 40 per cent of Sarge X's defence force and reservists had gone to New Jerusalem in the Great Trek.

We stopped in front of the base, I let my team get out; we were weary, hungry and thirsty. We knew the Special Ops kitchen would have something special for us, as they always did when we came home from a mission.

We offloaded the electrical control boards, and my team carried them into headquarters.

The others walked to barracks, while I stood waiting for the Volvo driver to come too. I wanted to do as Domingo would – I wanted to be the last to go in.

I wondered where Domingo was.

Birdy and Sarge X, Nero Dlamini and Beryl Fortuin came walking out of our headquarters. Right past the control board with the volt regulators, they didn't even look at them. I could see from all four of them that something was terribly wrong.

Birdy, little Birdy, President Cairistine Canary broke into sobs before she could reach me. She said, 'Nico, oh, Nico,' her voice completely broken.

'What's wrong?' My heart went ice cold.

'Your father,' she said.

I knew. I didn't have to ask because I could see it in her and Beryl, in Nero and Sarge X, she didn't have to say another word.

I felt the blood and life flow out of me, so fast, empty. I felt my legs wobble, my knees give.

Birdy grabbed me, embraced me. I felt Birdy's body flutter and shake. Beside us Beryl began to weep inconsolably, and she put her arm around us as though she wanted to be part of this grief.

Birdy's face on my chest. She said, 'Domingo too, Nico. Domingo is also dead.'

I don't remember much about those first few hours.

I remember that Birdy and I tried to comfort each other. We sat like that for a long time, holding each other tight.

I didn't cry, everything seemed surreal. I couldn't. I wanted to, I knew the tears were inside me somewhere, but I didn't really believe it: Pa *and* Domingo? Impossible.

We sat in Domingo's office. Somebody brought us sweet tea and fresh baked bread. I couldn't stomach it, asked for water.

Everyone spoke quietly. The whole barracks was silent, the news spread and left everyone dumbstruck.

Nero talked. He was the strongest of us all, I thought. He spoke so beautifully and calmly to us. He reassured us.

Eventually I couldn't stand it any more. I asked them what had happened.

Nero said, yes, he understood. He understood I needed to know.

Yes, I said, tell me, please.

He said my father had been at Witput.

Between one and three o'clock this afternoon Pa had spoken to the irrigation farmers over the agriculture-reserved frequency many times, asking for advice about the diesel pump and the system he was busy installing. Pa had been making little jokes about his lack of technical know-how, but he never gave any indication that anyone was around or that he saw anything threatening.

Until half past three.

Pa used his emergency code phrase over the radio. Just that. Nothing else. Domingo had raced to him in his Jeep. The radio room also alerted Sarge X. Sarge wanted to send his Luckhoff patrol, the one that covered the north shore of the dam as far as Philippolis. But they didn't answer. Sarge had a shortage of people and vehicles after the Great Trek; he immediately ordered the only other available team to drive to Witput, but they were in Hopetown, and it took them twenty-five more minutes to get there.

At Witput Sarge X's two defence force men found Pa and Domingo. They were lying close together, on the edge of the salt pan, the snow-white, dry salt pan beside the old irrigation circles of Witput.

They had been shot. The defence force members loaded up the two bodies and raced back to Amanzi, to our hospital. A hopeless mission, because they were pretty certain that Pa and Domingo were already dead, but what else could they do?

Sarge X said, 'By the time I got out there, to the crime scene, it was almost dark. There wasn't much we could learn . . .'

And he hesitated, and I saw Sarge X and Nero and Birdy look at each other, and I said, 'What is it?'

'I want you to know, I had Hennie Fly in the sky. I had every available patrol out and searching, but there is just so much territory to cover . . .'

Nero Dlamini said, 'We have no evidence, Nico. We don't know for certain who did it. We really don't.'

I realised what was going on. 'But you suspect someone.'

'Nico, we have to be very careful . . .'

'Who, Birdy?'

'Sit down first, Nico,' and I realised I was on my feet.

'We need cool heads,' said Nero Dlamini. 'Perhaps you should get some sleep first.'

'Very cool heads,' said Sarge X.

'No,' I said.

'Sit, Nico.'

I couldn't.

'Please, Nico, we need you to be strong. We need you to be very strong tonight,' said Nero.

Nero always had the ability to calm me down, ever since he had treated me for the PTSD after they stabbed Okkie. And now it made me suddenly tired. I sat. My body shuddered. I gripped my knees

because I knew they would start shaking. I felt emotion for the first
time. I kept it at bay, I wasn't ready to believe it was all true.

They didn't say a word. I regained control. After a while I looked
up, at Birdy.

'Please. Tell me now.'

It was too much for Birdy. She looked at Nero. He nodded. 'I'll tell
him.'

It took him a quarter of an hour. He told me the whole story. He began
with the radio contact from Trunkenpolz. He said two days ago, out of
the blue, our arch-enemy wanted to arrange a meeting. Pa and
Domingo eventually responded to Trunkenpolz alone, nobody knew
what had been said there.

'It's him,' I said. Rage and hatred ignited suddenly and I leapt up
again.

Nero gently touched my shoulder. 'Sit down, Nico. We don't know
that it was him. We really don't. There's other stuff. You need to hear
everything.'

'But he's the one who—'

'Please sit down first.'

'Please, Nico,' said Birdy. There was something in her voice that got
through to me, a tone and an emphasis that said she couldn't hold out
much longer. And then from the depths of my own loss I saw her, I
realised she had lost Domingo. She had lost her fiancé. Her heart was
just as broken as mine.

I sat down.

Nero took a while before he got going again. He told me about all
the events involving Pastor Sebego: from the moment when he
announced the Great Trek during the Cabinet meeting, until yesterday, when he said he was coming to fetch the voltage regulator and the
weapons. He talked of Domingo's spy allegations and his confrontation with the pastor, and my father's conclusion that it was possible,
though highly unlikely.

'You're not making sense, Nero,' I said. I was bewildered, the shock
and emotion and fatigue and adrenalin and pain were all coursing
through me, and I knew I wasn't processing the information as I
should.

'Your dad wasn't happy to confront Nkosi like that. But he had little . . . You know how it was, how tough it was for anybody to refuse Domingo. We owe our lives to him. So your dad didn't have a choice, really. And afterwards, he said we should let it go. There just wasn't any real evidence, other than circumstantial.'

'Wait,' I said. 'I don't understand why you're telling me all this.'

'Patience, Nico,' said Sarge X. 'That was just to give you the background. Because something else happened this afternoon.'

'What?'

Nero said, 'First I need you to promise me something.'

'What?'

'We're going to tell you, and then you're going to take a sleeping pill, and I'm going to put you to bed,' said Nero.

'What?' I said again, and looked at Sarge.

'Will you do what we ask, Nico? Will you take the pill and go to sleep?' said Birdy, pleading, as if she just wanted this day to end.

'I will.'

Sarge X looked at Nero. Nero looked very intently for a long time before he nodded to Sarge.

'As you know, I have a Luckhoff to Philippolis patrol during the day,' said Sarge. 'Two men in a Nissan truck. They do the farm roads, all along the northern shore. It's a slow trip. They leave in the morning, they have lunch in Philippolis, then they take the Jeep track for a quick look at Luckhoff, just before they return here, at about five. They were the team I called when I received your father's distress call. But they did not answer. Turns out their radio wasn't working. And they never checked. Just one of those things, because the radio is quiet, they just assumed. Today, of all days . . . They got back about an hour after dark. They came straight to me, to report an incident. They didn't know about your father and Domingo at that time.'

'What incident?'

'They saw three vehicles, speeding off . . .'

'Motorbikes?' I asked, with the first spark of rage.

'Nico, please, just listen,' said Nero.

'My patrol came via the little Jeep track into Luckhoff from the east, and they saw the three vehicles speeding off on the tarmac road towards Koffiefontein. The timing, that was the significant thing. It was just after four. About ten past.'

Why didn't he tell me who it was? 'Did they see who it was?'

He made a gesture with his hands. There was despair in it, but I didn't understand it. 'What did they see, Sarge?'

'They think it was our vehicles. Our pick-ups.'

'Ours?'

'Yes. Until three weeks ago, when we gave them to New Jerusalem.'

104

The investigation of my father's murder: I

Birdy broke the silence of Domingo's office. 'Nico, they think they were ours. They aren't sure.'

'They gave chase, but they couldn't catch up,' said Sarge.

'What made them think they were NJ's pick-ups?'

'There were three Toyotas. All three.'

'Of course, that doesn't constitute proof,' said Nero Dlamini. 'And they weren't absolutely sure.'

I shook my head. I didn't agree with Nero. If there were three Toyotas, the odds were good that they belonged to New Jerusalem. We gave them all the Toyota pick-ups in Amanzi, to simplify the situation with spares and maintenance. It was part of the final agreement. We kept the Fords and the Nissans. And who else in this region had diesel to keep three pick-ups – of any make – running so far from a town? Only Amanzi and New Jerusalem.

'I have to know, Nico,' said Birdy. 'I have to know who did this thing. I won't rest until we find out. I promise you that. But we must have proof. Not just allegations. That's what your father would have wanted. And Domingo. We mustn't let this destroy what they built here.'

'We need cool heads,' said Sarge X.

Nero Dlamini poured more water into my glass. He took a plastic pill holder out of his shirt pocket. 'I want you to take two of these,' he said.

'We'll start again tomorrow,' said Birdy. It sounded as if she were talking to herself.

I held out my hand. Nero shook the pills into my palm. I took the glass. I pretended to toss the pills into my mouth. I swallowed only the water, while my right hand slipped the pills into my trouser pocket.

Sofia Bergman

I don't think anyone could sleep that night.

Domingo was dead. It was unthinkable. Domingo was invincible. Immortal. Like a superhero, you never thought anything could happen to him. And if they could kill him, what chance did we have? And Willem Storm. He and Domingo were . . . They were Amanzi. They were everything about Amanzi. The members of the Cabinet, the rest of us were just bit players.

We were distraught, but we were also afraid. Who would be our leader now? What would happen to us?

That was the dominant emotion that night, I think, a sort of . . . suffocating anxiety. And incredulity. It couldn't be true. Willem Storm and Domingo? Impossible.

The heartbreak of loss would come later. Remember, we were children of the Fever. We had all known death and loss. So we had ways of dealing with it. To a degree. But so many of us in Special Ops were children. Seventeen, eighteen, nineteen. Willem Storm and Domingo were like fathers to us. Or at least surrogate parents to us. Authority figures . . . No, that sounds so . . . When I was little, lying on my bed on the farm, hearing my father's voice, or smelling the pipe tobacco he used to smoke, I would feel safe. I would know the world was okay.

That's what Willem and Domingo had given us. That feeling that we were safe and the world was okay.

But that night we couldn't articulate it. We just sat on the dam wall, in dazed silence. Team Alpha was still on guard duty, as Domingo had instructed as. Our sergeants, Taljaard and Masinga, were still in NJ, so we were completely leaderless. Entirely.

Since Domingo died . . . no one had thought to bring us food and water; just past twelve that night our food and water had run out, and I volunteered to fetch more. I walked back to base; via the shortcut it was just over one and a half kilometres.

Dead quiet, everything was silent. Just past midnight.

I passed the front door of HQ, and Nico Storm came out. He startled me, and I almost burst into tears, for him, for his loss, for everything. I expected that he couldn't sleep, that he just wanted some air, somewhere to grieve. But he held a finger to his lips, and I could read the 'please' in his eyes and

*it made me wonder, why? It wasn't what I was expecting, it wasn't the way
I imagined someone would behave if their father had just died.*

*I stood there, not saying a word, watched him walk past me, and go to
Domingo's Jeep, which was parked where Sarge X's people had left it. Nico
got into the Jeep and drove out the gate.*

*He doesn't look heartbroken, I thought, he looks . . . determined. And I
realised his rifle was slung over his shoulder.*

*I had no idea he was going to New Jerusalem. We knew nothing of all
that.*

I should have protected my father.

It was my job, my vocation, my responsibility. And I didn't. I wasn't
here, but that didn't matter, I should have protected my father.

I lay sleepless on my bed, I felt empty and rage began to fill the void
inside me. It was rage that was a long time coming, a rage at myself
that morphed into a rage at this world, this broken, unjust, wicked
world, that morphed into a hatred for Nkosi Sebego, because I saw
that he was responsible for all of it. At least, at the very least: if he
hadn't gone to New Jerusalem, Pa would still have been President, Pa
wouldn't have wanted to go farming at Witput. At the very least. But
there was more. Much more. The more I thought of it, the more I
knew it, I *knew* and I got up from my bed, dressed and picked up my
pistol and rifle and I left the room, went down the stairs, out of the
door.

I saw Sofia Bergman coming in. The sight of her brought me into
some sort of clarity, so that I realised that for what I was about to do
there must be no witnesses. I gestured to her she must keep quiet. She
mustn't tell a soul. Her eyes widened. She nodded.

I went to Domingo's Jeep. Switched it on. The tank was nearly full.
Enough fuel. I drove away.

At the main gate the guards were respectful and subdued, they
expressed their sympathies. I said thank you, I was just going for a
drive to clear my head.

They said they understood.

At the Petrusville gate it was the same.

And then it was just me, the darkness and the lights of the Jeep on
the road. The road to Colesberg, and then Gariep. New Jerusalem.

It was a hundred and fifty kilometres. I knew this stretch of road, we had driven it over and over these past weeks of the Great Trek. With the Jeep it would take me just over ninety minutes.

My rage at the pastor grew to a light-headedness. I had listened to Nero describing Domingo's allegations of espionage against him. I put all the clues together, and realised that Domingo was right. Nkosi was a traitor and a spy. I remember what he had said in the Committee back then. And I remember how he had humiliated my father time and time again. He was obsessed with power, had been from the beginning. I remember that very first day when he arrived, how he had looked at Domingo, as if he wanted to say: one day you're going to stand in my way, and I'm going to kill you.

Domingo was dead.

Nkosi had murdered my father, and he had destroyed Domingo's immortality.

By the time I turned off the N1 my fury was a white-hot flame. I knew where Nkosi lived. He had chosen a modest house in Hamerkop Street in the lower part of town. That had surprised most of the Spotters who escorted the Great Trek. I think it was a lesson he learned from my father.

NJ was pitch-dark. So different from Amanzi.

They had a temporary barricade at the town entrance, where the column with the words *Gariep Dam* still stood beside the little building with the pitched roof. NJ's guards huddled round a fire; they looked scared and inexperienced as they walked in front of the Jeep with their rifles. They recognised me and wondered what was going on.

I was cold and calm. I said I had an urgent message for the pastor.

They said they must first let him know I was here.

I realised then that I hadn't thought this through.

I said go ahead.

If he had guards who tried to stop me, I'd shoot them first.

Sofia Bergman

I packed my rucksack full of food and water and walked back to the dam wall. All the way I was thinking of Nico. Thinking of his expression, what had I read in it? There was something . . . familiar. In the finger on his lips, in his eyes, something I had seen before.

And where was he going in Domingo's Jeep? In the middle of the night?

Should I tell anyone?

It took an eternity to wake the pastor. I couldn't hear what he said, only the deep rumble of his voice over the guard's radio. The guard walked up to me and said, 'The pastor wants to know what this is about.'

'I have a message from my father.' Let me see what his response to that might be. Let me see if he betrayed himself.

They relayed this to him over the radio. No response. His silence gave him away. His silence gave me the assurance that I was looking for.

He stayed silent for so long that even the gate guards became uneasy.

'Send him in,' said Nkosi.

Sofia Bergman

At three in the morning I remembered where I had seen that look in Nico's eyes before. It was the day that I shot him with the crossbow. The day he tackled me, in front of HQ, after I had hit him with the rifle.

The eyes of someone beyond fury.

But where had he gone?

105

The investigation of my father's murder: II

I stopped in front of the house, holding the R4. I switched off the Jeep, climbed out, and walked up to the front door.

He must have heard my boots on the gravel; he opened the door. He was wearing a dressing gown, somewhere behind him a lamp was burning, and I saw him in silhouette. I shifted the R4 to my left hand, and I hit him in the face with my fist. I hit him with all the rage and pain and hate in me.

I hit him on the mouth. 'I'm going to kill you,' I said as he staggered backwards into the house. But he didn't fall.

He swung at me. He was a big man, taller than me, his shoulders wide and powerful. And he was much faster than I had expected. He caught me on my right cheekbone, lifting me off my feet. I crashed down, half-deafened in my right ear, black specks floating before my eyes. I tried to stand up, but I staggered, off-balance. He aimed another blow; I could see the whites of his eyes, his mouth bleeding. I could see he was capable of murder, he was wild, dangerous. I rolled to the left, up against the wall. He missed me, then he hit me, somewhere on my ribs. I pushed against the wall to roll away, suddenly realising this wasn't going as I had planned; tonight I was going to be beaten to death.

Adrenalin.

I stood up fast, he was waiting for me. I moved quickly, hit out at him with everything I had, on the bridge of his nose.

He gave a deep roar and came at me, a bloodied bull. I knew how fast he was now, and as he swung I jerked my head away, just in time. The blow connected my left shoulder, the violence of it throwing me against the wall. My left arm felt dead. I hit out again, my only hope was that I was faster than him. I punched with my right fist, every ounce of strength. He bent his head down. My knuckles connected with the top of his shaven skull. I could hear my knuckle break, a sick, loud noise, and pain shot up my arm. He fell to his knee, grabbed something on a table. I had to hit him again, swung my left hand, but he hit me first, with something in his hand, against my hip and my pistol. The sound rang like a metal bell, because he had hit me with a pan, a big cast-iron pan. I stumbled and fell and he was on me. He lifted the pan, ready to hit me again, and I jammed my right elbow into his eye as hard as I could. I knew my knuckle was broken, the pain sharp, I would not be able to use my fist again.

He bellowed again, shook his big head, dropped the pan, gripped his massive hands around my throat. I hit him on the forehead with my left fist; in his eyes I could see the blow had shaken him, but still he strangled me. I hit my right elbow against his mouth. He spat out a tooth, choked me harder.

I couldn't breathe.

I hit him again with my elbow, on the mouth again, desperate, I couldn't breathe. He spat blood and spittle over me, throttling me harder still.

I grabbed his hands, I had to loosen them.

I had to get air.

I couldn't.

Only then did I realise: it was too late, his hands were too big and strong, his grip too tight; the world spun around me. I jerked and dragged on his hands, and kicked and twisted and wriggled and strained, my mouth gaping in search of air, but I couldn't get any in my lungs. I couldn't see, I was dying, I was – like my father – going to be murdered by this man.

Sofia Bergman

Remember, no one had told us about Pastor Nkosi and spies and hidden weapons and the three Toyotas that raced away from Luckhoff. That would only come out later. Much later. So that night I sat with my Alpha team-mates, and never said a word about Nico. To anyone.

*　　*　　*

I regained consciousness when Pastor Nkosi threw a bucket of ice-cold water over me. I coughed and spluttered, groaned and choked and snorted, I dragged the air, the heavenly oxygen, deep into my lungs, and he said, 'What the devil is the matter with you?' The words slurred through his broken mouth.

I tried to get up. 'I'm going to kill you.' My voice was hoarse, my body weighed a ton.

He tramped a big foot on my chest. He pushed me flat on the floor. My right hand hurt. My ribs too.

'But why, Nico?'

'You know,' and I tried to sit up, I grabbed his foot, but my arms weren't working well.

He pulled the pan on the table nearer. 'I will hit you again.'

'Kill me. You had better kill me.'

'I am not going to kill you, but I will hit you again if you don't tell me what the hell is going on.' He raised the heavy pan, threatening.

'You killed my father, you bastard.'

'I did what?'

'You killed my father.'

The pan dropped to the floor with a hollow clang. I saw Nkosi's whole body react, saw his shock. 'Your father? Your father is dead?'

He was a swindler, a liar. 'We saw your pick-ups, yesterday.'

'Pick-ups?' He looked completely dismayed, defeated.

'Three Toyota pick-ups in Luckhoff.'

'Yes,' he said. 'That was me.'

Rage blinded me, I grabbed his foot which was pressed on to my chest. He jerked it out of my grasp, stepping away from me. He said, 'Nico, please! I had nothing to do . . . Tell me, when . . . how did your father die?'

I stood up. I walked towards him lifting my left fist. 'You shot him yesterday at four o'clock.'

'Oh, God,' he said. 'Oh, dear God.' And he staggered backwards as if I had hit him, and sat down on a kitchen chair.

My father told me an asteroid ten kilometres wide struck the earth two hundred million years ago.

It formed a three-hundred-kilometre-wide crater, the largest on Planet Earth that we know of. The crater has long since disappeared completely due to erosion, but in the middle is a geological structure, a half-moon of hilly terrain that we call the Vredefort Dome, near Parys in the Free State.

Only months before the Fever scientists discovered an extensive series of caves in the hills of the dome. It was in those caves that my father and I lived when the Fever destroyed the world.

It was in those caves that I fell ill with the Fever.

What I relived in that night in Pastor Nkosi Sebego's kitchen were the dreams of delirium. While he sat with his head in his hands at his kitchen table and prayed to the Most High, I remembered that my father was also sick in those caves, but less so than me. Pa nursed me while the delirium dreams ran through me like heatwaves, they came and went, I didn't know if I was awake or sleeping. With every feverish dream the sensation was the same: it seemed to me like looking at the world through a very narrow, misty window. My limbs, my hands especially, felt fat and swollen, heavy, strange, but they weren't. From head to toe I felt slow, as though swimming through thick, bitter syrup. It was strange and frightening and completely surreal.

In Nkosi's kitchen I felt that way again.

I towered over him, filled with hate and physical and emotional agony, but I felt slow, I felt trapped, my head, hands and fingers thick and useless, and I wanted to give my pain to someone else. Nero says that's what you do when you experience unbearable pain.

'I loved your father,' said Nkosi. The words were like lead, heavy, sluggish. I absorbed them slowly, took an eternity to process their meaning. I said he was lying, lying, he hated Pa and Domingo.

And he said, 'No, I'm just scared of Domingo,' and I screamed at him, 'You killed him because you're scared of him?' He stared at me as if I'd gone mad and then asked in confusion, 'Domingo?' and I could now see he was in the same delirious dream, we were both lost.

'You killed Domingo.'

'Domingo is dead?'

'You killed him, and you killed my father.'

'Heaven help us.'

I took the pistol out of the holster on my hip. I looked at Nkosi through the narrow, steamy window of my fever, and I pressed the pistol against his temple. He just sat there, blood dripping from his split lips on to the table, slowly shaking his head as he said, 'I didn't kill anybody, Nico.'

I pressed the safety catch to off.

'You let your people do the killing?'

He didn't say a word. Just shook his head to say no.

He closed his eyes.

106

The investigation of my father's murder: III

I couldn't pull the trigger, because beyond the fever and hatred, the rage and overwhelming emotion, I knew he was telling the truth. I could see it in the way his head drooped, with his eyes shut, I could hear it in his voice, I could feel it in the way he resigned himself to the executioner's bullet. In the way he stopped fighting, in the way he had let me be free. In his pyjamas and bloodied dressing gown he was a broken, innocent man. And he was grieving. For my father.

I stood there with my pistol to his head, waiting for the fever to abate, to flow out of me. It took the pressure and the intensity with it.

I clicked the pistol's safety up again and I sagged, gripping the table for support. I went and sat down opposite him.

He slowly opened his eyes. 'How did they die?'

'They were shot.'

'I am so sorry, Nico.'

'But you were there.'

'I was in Luckhoff.'

'They were in Witput.'

'Dear Lord . . .'

'Why were you there?'

'I went to fetch my rifles. And ammunition. Our share.'

'In Luckhoff?'

'I was sure they were there. I was so absolutely sure. You used Luckhoff for military purposes. That whole town. It was Domingo's playground. Exclusively. In the Cabinet we often talked about settling people there, it was closer than Hopetown, it had lots of canal water. And Domingo just refused, he said it was Special Ops' training facility, you needed it. So I thought that's where he hid the arms. We went there yesterday. We searched the town. We looked in every house. We even had a metal detector, we thought they might be buried somewhere . . .'

His voice trailed away.

We sat there in the deep twilight, the paraffin lamp burning low, taking deep breaths.

I didn't want to believe him. He was such a sly man.

'You spied for Number One,' I said.

A sound popped over his lips, blood sprayed over the table.

He shook his head.

'I saw you, that first day,' I said to him. 'I saw you.'

'What first day?'

'When you came to Amanzi.'

'You saw me?'

'Yes. I saw how you looked at Domingo. You hated him.'

He looked at me. I couldn't really see his expression. It sounded like a brief and bitter laugh. Then he got slowly to his feet. 'Would you like some brandy?'

I had never drunk brandy.

'Yes.'

It tasted like horrible cough mixture. It burned my mouth, throat, made me choke.

Pastor Nkosi Sebego would probably have smiled if his mouth had been whole and circumstances different.

He sat down again opposite me. He said, 'Do you know what that tattoo on Domingo's hand stands for?'

'No.' I had long forgotten about the tattoo on the back of Domingo's hand, two curved swords and a rising sun. It was so much a part of him, I was so used to it, it had no meaning.

'It means he was a member of the Twenty-Sevens.'

'The who?'

'The Twenty-Sevens. The Numbers gangs? You've never heard . . .? Never mind. They were prison gangs, the Numbers, in the old days. Before the Fever. You had three divisions. There were Twenty-Sixes, who were the least violent, they were the thieves and the con men and the burglars and the fraudsters. Then you had the Twenty-Eights, they—'

'How do you know this?' I asked him because I didn't want to believe anything bad about Domingo.

'As a pastor it was my duty to visit those parishioners who were in prison, Nico.'

'Domingo wasn't a criminal.'

'Then why did he have that tattoo? The sign of the Twenty-Sevens? The most violent of all the prison gangs, the killers. The assassins.'

'It was just a tattoo.'

'I've seen many of them, Nico. He was a Twenty-Seven.'

'That's not true.'

'Go ask Sarge X.'

'Why?'

'He was a policeman. And . . . Do you remember when Matthew Mbalo was killed? Our first murder.'

'Yes.'

'Can you remember who the only person was that Sarge X interrogated, right after the body was found?'

I could remember. We had watched, there at Luckhoff, how Sarge and Domingo stood and talked beside his pick-up. How angry Domingo was. But I said nothing.

'Sarge X didn't tell us about it,' said Nkosi. 'Until I confronted him, about a week after the murder. I called him lazy and inefficient, because there was absolutely no progress in the investigation. Then he told me, he said he had interrogated the only real suspect. The only Amanzian with a known criminal record who had been up and about that night, moving freely according to his responsibilities. Domingo. So I asked Sarge, how do you know Domingo has a criminal record? And Sarge says, that tattoo, Pastor. And he told me what I already knew. Domingo had been in prison, and he was a member of the most violent Numbers gang.'

I still didn't want to believe it.

The pastor saw that. 'I know you were very fond of Domingo.'

'Yes. He was my hero.'

'I know.'

'He was a very brave man, and he was a good man.'

'Yes, he was brave. And we can be good and bad, Nico. We can do good and bad things. That's the way God made us.'

He stood up, went to the cupboard where the brandy bottle was and poured another for himself. I never knew he drank alcohol. He held up the bottle, asking if I wanted more. I shook my head. The stuff was horrible; I still had some in my glass.

'You have my deepest sympathy for the loss of your father,' he said, sipped and came back to the table. 'I had the utmost respect for him. He was an exceptional man. I did not leave Amanzi because of him.' He sat down. 'I left because of Domingo. Because there was no real democracy. No real liberty. No real freedom of religion. Because there was one state religion in Amanzi. Domingo's. He ruled that place. With an iron fist.'

I shook my head. 'That's not true.'

'Just think about it, will you? Just look at the facts. Ask yourself: why did he hide the arsenal?'

'Because you're a spy.'

Again he made that snorting sound. He touched his mouth, it must have hurt.

'Really, Nico? Really? A spy? Okay, so I might be a spy. But answer these questions: do you know who else is called "Number One"? Go ask Sarge X. In the Numbers gangs, the top structure are called Number Ones. If you're a leader of the Twenty-Sixes, you are a Number One. And do you know what the speciality of the Twenty-Sixes was in prison? Smuggling. Smuggling and selling. Remember when Trunkenpolz came to Amanzi the first time, do you remember how Domingo didn't like it at all? How uncomfortable he was that night? Why? Because maybe he saw a tattoo on Trunkenpolz. And Trunkenpolz saw Domingo's? Go ask yourself, when Trunkenpolz could have killed Domingo, when he was standing there with a pistol to Domingo's head, why didn't he just pull the trigger? Because, perhaps, he saw somebody he could blackmail? Ask yourself: who arrived at Amanzi on a motorcycle, Nico? A motorcycle. Think about it. Ask yourself: who killed that Marauders man, the one you took prisoner, what was his name . . .?'

'Leon Calitz.'

'Yes, that one. Who killed him, who shot him and their radio man before you could bring them back for questioning about human trafficking?'

'That was because of the . . . Domingo saw the women, the Seven . . .'

'Okay. Do you remember when the KTM attacked us, that day when you shot ten or eleven of them?'

'Twelve.'

'Yes. Twelve. Do you remember, there were two of the attackers trapped in the truck? And they were shouting, "We give up, we give up!" and Domingo walked up to them and he executed them. Shot them right between the eyes. Do you remember?'

'Yes.'

'Why would he do that?'

'Because they were animals.'

'I wonder who the real animal was, that day. Why did he have to kill them? Why were there never any people to interrogate? Just ask yourself why, that's all I'm saying.'

I shoved the glass away and stood up.

'I don't believe you.'

His gesture said he didn't really care.

'I'll find out if you're lying.'

'I took my people away from Amanzi, because they deserved better than Domingo's tyranny.'

'Domingo's tyranny was good enough for my dad.'

'Are you sure, Nico?'

When you are seventeen, and you're tired and confused, and everything you know and believe is threatened, the easiest solution is to flee.

I didn't answer him. I just walked out, so that the darkness of New Jerusalem could swallow me and the Jeep.

107

The investigation of my father's murder: IV

To this day I don't know how I reached the bridge over the Seekoei River.

It is forty kilometres north of Colesberg, just before the old R369 becomes a gravel road.

That was where I regained my senses at about four in the morning, when the Jeep's headlights lit up the silver of the steel railing and the grey concrete, and I suddenly hit the brakes, for no good reason except that I was suddenly awake, back in the real world.

I stopped, because I had to, because I didn't know where to go.

I switched off the Jeep and its lights and got out and walked to the front of the vehicle. I looked out at the incredible firmament, billions of stars twinkling. Pa said the night sky was a time machine, each star in its own era, so many light years away. I need a time machine, Pa, to turn the clock back.

I didn't see the breathtaking beauty. I just felt small, immeasurably small, insignificant and lost, but above all to this day I recall the over-whelming unbearable weight of loneliness that pressed down on me. My mother was dead, and my father was dead, and Domingo too. I was a real orphan now, fit for the Orphanage.

Part of the weight I felt had to do with loss of confidence, loss of certainty. Who did I believe? What did I believe? Where was truth? Another addition to this mass was the loss of an ideal, of an idea, as Amanzi had been my father's idea. His vision, his dream. Suddenly there was nothing. No future, just the pitch darkness.

I didn't feel self-pity. I was just aware of the absolute loneliness. I don't know how long I stood there staring at the heavens. It could have been ten or twenty minutes.

And then I heard the crackling of the radio in Domingo's Jeep, and

I heard the voice of one of Sarge X's guards: 'Base, this is Sector Three. Four o'clock, and all's well.'

I was close enough to pick up the radio signal.

I lowered my eyes to the horizon. I could see the faint glow of Amanzi. Our place of light.

Sofia Bergman

I was lying asleep on the rock-hard tarmac of the road across the dam wall when I felt someone pressing my shoulder very gently, and I woke with a start. It was Sarge X. He said, 'Sofia, I need you to track for me.'

I felt embarrassed that he had caught me sleeping, I wanted to explain. I said, 'I wasn't on duty,' and he said, 'I know, my dear, I know. But the sun will be up in half an hour, and I want to start searching the crime scene for tracks as soon as there's enough light.'

'Yes, Sarge,' I said and got up and I wanted to ask if I had time to wash and brush my hair and teeth, but he was already walking to the three parked APS vehicles, the pick-ups of the Amanzi Police Service, each with hand-painted stars on the doors.

I stopped in front of the Orphanage, when the eastern horizon was fiery red over the dam, and got out. The pain in my broken knuckle throbbed non-stop, and I wondered, had they told Okkie? Did Okkie know our father was dead?

I went inside where I could hear people already moving around in the kitchen. I didn't want to face them, I just wanted to sit and wait for Birdy. I had to talk to Birdy. I walked into the sitting room and saw her standing at the window, she couldn't sleep either.

She heard me enter and turned. She seemed old and tired. She looked at me with compassion, and then with concern. 'What happened?' she asked, seeing the blood on my cheek.

'Was Domingo in prison before, Birdy?' I asked, because the question weighed so heavily on me, and when it was out, when it was so irretrievably out, I realised how mean and selfish the question was.

Birdy stumbled. I reached her, held her up, she pushed towards a chair, sat down. Looked up at me.

She said, 'Yes, Nico. He was.'

Sofia Bergman

Sarge X showed me where the bodies had been lying. I remember the softness of the light of the rising sun, the purple of the dried blood in the bone-white dust.

'Domingo was here, Sofia,' he said, 'and Willem was right there.' Old Sarge X was a small man, he must have been in his fifties by now, and when he stood pointing out to me, I wanted to hug him, because he looked so dazed, like he didn't want to be there. As if he didn't want to investigate this scene, would so much rather have them back. I was too young then and too upset and tired myself to realise how heavily the responsibility rested on him. He was the only one of the senior military men left.

He showed me that Domingo and Willem Storm had been lying only three metres apart.

He showed me the spatters of blood beside the tracks, and the two places they had been lying, and how there was surprisingly little blood.

I never liked that area. It was . . . I don't know . . . Spooky. There were the pans, the dry, flat pans, as white as skeletons, and no good for planting, their soil sick and brackish, and then there was the canal flowing nearby, and the old centre-pivot irrigation circles; you could still make out the outlines. I . . . I always got goose bumps there. In any case, Willem Storm and Domingo had been lying in the pan, just a few steps from the edge, the edge of natural veld. And Domingo's Jeep had been parked in the road, near the old farmhouse, probably three hundred metres away.

And then I asked Sarge who else had been here yesterday. He said just his patrol from Hopetown, and himself. And he called the two men from the patrol to come over. I checked their boots, and I looked at Sarge's boots, and I asked if any of them knew what shoes Willem had been wearing. One of the patrol men fetched them and brought them to me: Domingo's shoes, and Willem's. They put them down in front of me. The empty shoes.

It was a very bad moment for me. I can't explain it.

Cairistine 'Birdy' Canary

Yes, you see, that Christmas Eve, the last one before he died, Domingo took me to Otters Kloof. It was once a grand guest house and game farm across the river, and he'd cleaned the place on the quiet and made it beautiful, and when we arrived there was a little table set with a tablecloth, can you believe it, and wildflowers, and I laughed and said, who did that, it can't be you. It's so romantic. And he didn't smile, he was terribly serious, and he said, Birdy, I want you, but first you must know who I am.

And he told me everything.

I think it was a release for Birdy to tell me the truth about Domingo that morning. I think carrying that knowledge alone had been a burden to her.

We sat side by side on the couch. She held both my hands. She was so focused that she didn't register how swollen they were, the grazes and blood on my knuckles.

She told me about Domingo. His name was Ryan John Domingo. He grew up in Riverview in Worcester, where in summer the south-easter blew the stench of the sewerage works into their little house. His mother was a cleaner at the De la Bat School for the Deaf, his father was scum, a man who didn't work, only stole, lied, cheated and boozed. A man who never held down any job longer than three months. A weak man, but outwardly strong, a big man, a man who had been physically abused as a child and who continued the tradition by beating his wife and six children with fists and belts, ropes and anything he could lay his hands on, whether he was sober or drunk. A man with a terrible temper.

His father's names were also Ryan John.

Domingo was the oldest. He was always the first to feel the force of his father's fury. Later he would stand up for his brothers and sisters, and for his mother. When he saw they were about to bear the brunt of his father's rage, he intervened and took the thrashing in their place.

At high school he tried to fight back for the first time, and his father beat him so severely that he spent a week in hospital recovering. Nursing staff and a social worker asked him who had beaten him like that. He said he had fallen.

The social worker said he should know that he could put an end to the abuse. He just had to talk.

He thought about it, and he decided, yes, he could put an end to it. And so he planned the murder of his father.

He was in grade eleven. Sixteen years old. Some of his school friends' fathers worked at the Brandvlei Prison. He had heard stories of how the prisoners killed each other there. One method involved a bicycle spoke.

Cairistine 'Birdy' Canary

Domingo may have been at the table talking to me, but really I could tell he was back in Worcester. You didn't often see Domingo's eyes, I think because he knew his eyes were windows to his soul. I saw his eyes were distant, and hurting. He said, Birdy, for weeks I sharpened that bicycle spoke, its tip was sharp. I wanted to kill him, but didn't have the courage. I wanted to kill him, I pictured it in my mind, as he lay dead drunk, how I'd slip the spoke between his ribs, just like they did in Brandvlei Prison, but I didn't have the courage. It's a big step, to kill another human being. Even when you have the heart and the motivation. Even when it's in self-defence. A very big step. For weeks I sat and listened to his drunkard's tales, you know those stories, Birdy? They're all the same, every time, over and over, long and rambling and all the same, until you want to throw up. Drunkard's tales about what a hero my father was, all the things he had done, the guys he had beaten up, the bosses he had told just keep your stupid job, over and over, over and over. And then one night he hit my ma, and I tried to stop him and he hit me, he beat me black and blue, Birdy, and my little brother tried to stop him, and he hit my little brother, he was just eleven, he beat him to a pulp too. That night, Birdy, I shoved that bicycle spoke between my father's ribs, and I killed him, in his bed.

Sofia Bergman

I told Sarge and his people to wait there and I began studying the tracks as Meklein had taught me. Remember, I had been training the Spotters to track for over a year, so it was all fresh in my mind. And I wanted to know what happened there, who had killed them. So I was focused.

The first thing I noticed was that there were four people whose tracks came from the north, from the canal. And not one of those four was Willem Storm or Domingo.

It seemed that later they had carried Willem and Domingo to that spot in the pan.

It made no sense.

108

The investigation of my father's murder: V

Birdy said Domingo had gone to school in mortal fear. And when the headmaster sent for him, and he saw the policemen waiting at the office door, he knew they had come to get him for the murder of his father.

But they just told him his father was dead. Died in bed. Heart attack. They were so sorry. The deepest sympathies. He could go home now.

He did go home, to console his mother and brothers and sisters.

He didn't know why they hadn't noticed the tiny wound. Maybe because they knew that Ryan John Domingo was drinking himself to death anyway? Maybe because the mark was so small? Maybe because they didn't bother to do autopsies on coloureds from Riverview?

So they buried his father. And he was left wondering: how long before the body decomposed, and the evidence along with it?

Sofia Bergman

The tracks showed that they put Willem and Domingo down in the pan, and they joined up with the other one, and headed north. The third one was carrying something heavy. For over five hundred metres I tracked them — that was where the old irrigation circles were, in patches you could see the tracks clearly — and then there was a big bloodstain in the sand, and you could see that one guy had fallen.

Tracking is actually just very careful observation, and logic.

You check how close a man's steps are to each other, then you know how fast he is walking or running. You check how deep his tracks are compared to the others, then you know if he's carrying something. And drops of blood ... Meklein taught me, when we tracked wounded buck, that each droplet tells its own story.

So I followed them, closer and closer to the canal. I saw how they ran, but not very fast. I saw one was bleeding, and the bleeding was getting worse.

There was no wind, just a light breeze, a morning breeze, and out of the corner of my eye I saw something that ... It was out of place there, unnatural. I looked, almost reluctantly, because I only wanted to focus on the spoor, and the thing must have been five paces ... No, ten paces away from the tracks, something fluttered, something white. I looked and I walked over to it, and it was a photo, of Willem and Nico, and a pretty woman, but Nico was still small. Father, mother and son. And I knew it must have been in Willem's pocket. I picked it up and went back to tracking.

A ditch ran between the irrigation circles. I don't know if they had pipes in the gully or what, but it was a deep one. And I saw there was somebody there. The ditch ... Remember, it must have been six, seven years since people last ... There were bushes in the ditch, weeds and thorn bushes, and the man lay half hidden under the bushes; it seemed as though he were hiding, and it gave me a fright, because I had nothing with me, my rifle was still in Sarge's pick-up. Then I realised that the man was dead.

On the couch in the Orphanage Birdy held my hands tight and she told me that Domingo's father stayed buried, nobody asked questions, nobody looked at Domingo suspiciously, and slowly he began to realise he had got away with murder. Weeks and months went by, and he was even more convinced it had been the right thing to do. He watched his mother heal. How his brothers and sisters recovered and blossomed. How they lifted their heads again.

He heard of young Correctional Services men who went to Britain to join the British Army. The Brits were at war in Afghanistan, and they were encouraging people in the Commonwealth to join their army. He heard they were making good money, sending large sums back home, to their mothers and fathers and grannies and grandpas and little brothers and sisters. He talked to his ma. At first she wouldn't hear of it. She said finish school first. He said of course he would, but then he wanted to go. She said no. But he worked on her, over months, more than a year. Until she agreed.

In January after he had passed matric, he got his passport.

He saved and borrowed money for the plane ticket. Twelve months later, in the following January, he was in Afghanistan as a member of the Third Battalion of the British Parachute Regiment.

Sofia Bergman

The tracks showed that the other three had dragged the man into the ditch, and then they ran.

He was as dead as a doornail, shot between the eyes. And he was wearing a drab grey uniform, which looked like some sort of military uniform, and his boots were black.

I went to call Sarge X, and fetch my rifle, and I told Sarge I was going to run on the tracks of those three men, and if I saw anything I would shoot in the air. But he said, no, rather use the radio.

So I forgot about the photograph in my pocket. I followed the spoor at a trot, through the second irrigation circle, to the canal. There I saw the men had turned left, to the little bridge.

And I saw more blood spatter, more and more.

Every two hundred metres or so there was a footbridge over the canal, but some of the bridges were broken or washed away, and every kilometre or so there was a bridge for vehicles. I saw the men had crossed one of the footbridges over the canal and run across the next old ghost irrigation circle. The one who was bleeding was dragging his feet more, and the tracks came together as the other two helped him. I ran and ran, and suddenly their tracks disappeared.

I stopped and retraced my steps. I saw they had been running, and just before the tracks disappeared, they weren't. They were walking.

And then their tracks disappeared entirely.

Ryan John Domingo of 3 Para was promoted to lance corporal and later corporal and after five years of service to sergeant. Every month he sent money to his mother, and came home once a year for two weeks – with gifts for his brothers and sisters – and then he flew back to Britain and Afghanistan.

He was a good soldier. He was awarded medals. He took care of his family. He neither drank nor smoked. In Riverview, Worcester, he was a legend, and when he came home, the girls would saunter slowly past the Domingo family home. Not surprisingly, as he had become a handsome, strong young man, a steady man and a good breadwinner.

On leave in his fifth year of service he went to a high school athletics event, where his sister was competing. He met a young teacher, Yolande Goedeman. She was a sensuous young woman, with voluptuous lips and body, her lively nature shining with the same light as her flawless complexion.

It was love at first sight; he phoned back to base to request an extra week's leave, so he could strike while the iron was still hot with the fire of passion. They spent every possible moment together, they were the couple that everyone talked about, people said they were so lucky to have found each other.

He didn't want to go back, he was afraid of losing her. She didn't want him to go, because Afghanistan was the land of death. He promised her he would apply for a position with Correctional Services, they should give him credit for his military experience, and he ought to get a good rank.

He went back, first to Britain, and then to Helmand Province in southern Afghanistan for Operation Herrick, as part of 16 Air Assault Brigade. Fourteen of his comrades were killed, forty-five were wounded.

Domingo survived. He sent his letters to Correctional Services in South Africa to apply for work. Only to receive a letter from his oldest sister. 'You must come home, Yolande Goedeman is mixed up with the wrong people.'

Sofia Bergman

Tracking is acute observation and logic, and if something doesn't look right, if you can't explain it, then you approach it from another angle.

I had tracked the spoor of the three guys as they ran away, but now I traced them as they arrived. I confirmed that there had first been four. And I saw more or less what had happened. Willem Storm was in the old farmhouse. I don't mean that the farmhouse was actually old, it was just ... It had been standing empty for a long time, and was neglected like all the farmyards of that time, but you could see that Willem had started to clean up. In the house we found papers on a table, and pencils, evidence that he was making a map of the area, and planning his irrigation system.

I believe he was occupied with that in the house when the four men arrived. And Domingo. There were lines and marks in the dust, windows and doors broken, there had been a struggle.

The four men . . . Their tracks were very strange, because they began in the middle of one of the centre pivot irrigation circles on the other side of the canal, probably three kilometres from Willem's farmhouse. I couldn't understand it, the tracks just started there.

While I was wondering how on earth that made any sense, the pick-up arrived, people from Ou Brug, looking for Sarge. Ou Brug is on the far side of Hopetown, where a quaint old bridge was built across the Orange River. Some of our people had planted sunflowers there, our furthest western outpost. And Sarge called me over the radio, and said, 'You had better come and hear this, Sofia.'

Domingo requested special leave from his unit. He said he had a family crisis at home. They were grateful for his bravery and service in the terrible months of Operation Herrick. They said take as much time as you need.

He flew from Kabul to Frankfurt, and from there to Cape Town. He travelled for twenty-one hours, arrived at night, rented a car and drove through to Worcester, dog-tired and jet-lagged and still full of the bitter battles and violent tension, the great loss of his comrades in Afghanistan. His sister told him Yolande Goedeman was involved with Martin Apollis. Big drug boss of the Breede River Valley, the one who drove around in a Mustang.

Domingo knew where Martin Apollis lived. He walked out of his mother's house in the middle of the night. His sister tried to stop him, but he was unstoppable. He drove his hired car to Martin Apollis's house, and he saw Yolande Goedeman's little Toyota Tazz parked in front. He didn't knock, he kicked open the front door and walked down the passage. Calling her name.

Apollis came down the passage, naked, pistol in his hand, furious. Who dared come into his house? He was Martin Apollis, you took your life in your hands barging in here.

Ryan John Domingo took the pistol from Apollis and shot him. Between the eyes. And he walked to the bedroom, and there Yolande Goedeman, with her ripe, full body, was lying naked in bed. And he shot her too.

Cairistine 'Birdy' Canary

He told me, 'Birdy, I want you to know I have my father's temper. I didn't know that, Birdy, but that night, I discovered it.'

They sent Domingo to jail.

When the Fever came he was still in there, at Buffeljagsrivier. Then everyone got sick, the prisoners, the guards, everyone. But not Domingo.

Sofia Bergman

The people of Ou Brug told us they'd seen a helicopter the previous afternoon.

They heard it first, around three o'clock, further west. They tried to spot it, but it was too far away. And then, some time after four, it might have been half past four already, they heard it again, and when they looked up they saw it flying. High, and far to the west, but they saw it. Three of our people, all three reliable and honest, they were absolutely certain they had seen the helicopter.

109

The investigation of my father's murder: VI

Sofia Bergman

Boy, there's so much I have to say about that morning, not just about what happened, but how I felt as well.

But the biggest thing that happened that morning was that I fell in love with Nico Storm.

Just like that.

One moment there was nothing, and the next moment I was in love.

It was a very strange morning. Nico always says, nothing happens and then everything happens at once, just when you least expect it.

That's the way things were that morning.

We were sitting in the Orphanage sitting room, side by side on the couch. The morning was cool, the autumn sun shining through the window. I was so dreadfully tired, my hand hurt, my thoughts were consumed by the story of Domingo and the murders he had committed. The murders that I understood, the murders I wanted to forgive him for, if that was the whole story. I wanted to ask Birdy if Domingo had been a member of a prison gang. I wanted to ask her if he and Number One had been involved. I had a thousand questions.

Then Beryl came in and holding her hand was Okkie, and they both looked scared. He saw me and said, 'Where is Pappa, Nico?'

Beryl said, 'I don't know what to do. I'm sorry, Nico, he keeps asking me where his father is.'

'Where is Pappa?'

I stood up, and held out my arms to him. He approached me warily. He knew something was wrong. He could see it in my and Birdy and Beryl's faces, and because Pa was not there. Pa was always there.

I picked him up and squeezed him tight and said, 'Pappa isn't here any more, Okkie.'

Then he cried for the first time.

Sofia Bergman

Nero Dlamini still teases me about it, how I fell in love with Nico in that instant. He said he would love to know what Freud would have had to say.

Sarge X and I walked into the Orphanage, and there was Nico on the couch, and he was holding Okkie, and he and Okkie were weeping, they cried like little children, that sort of crying you can't find consolation for, there is nothing you can do, you have to wait until it's finished.

That is when I fell in love with Nico.

Weird, hey?

I cried, and in a way I knew it was a good thing.

I cried for everything that I hadn't cried for before. And there was so much.

I saw Sofia come in with Sarge X, I saw they had something important to say. I knew I should listen, but I had to finish crying first.

It took so long. So long that Sicelo Kula came in. Along with Nero Dlamini.

Sicelo Kula. They called him Thula Kula. The Quiet One. I barely knew him.

Everything happens at once, just when you least expect it.

Sicelo Kula was one of the West Coasters.

He was sixteen. He was in school. He lived in the Groendakkies, where Sofia used to. He worked at the stables, because he had a feel for horses. He was very quiet and shy. Introverted, said some people. A bit strange. They speculated that he was like that because he was one of the polygamists, the Bushmans Kloofers, the hippies, the gypsies. He was one of them.

Nero Dlamini had been treating Sicelo over the past months because he exhibited the symptoms of post-traumatic stress. Sicelo trusted Nero.

That morning Sicelo walked down from Groendakkies to the stables. He saw Sarge X's pick-up and, lying on the back, the man in a uniform that looked familiar. He went closer to have a look.

Sicelo recognised the dead man in the grey uniform. He didn't know what to do. He wavered, and then went to find Nero Dlamini. When he had told Nero, they came to the sitting room of the Orphanage.

By that time I had done my crying.

Okkie clung to me. His sobs were quiet, his head pressed to my chest.

Sarge X cleared his throat politely. 'There have been some very strange events,' he said. 'We believe a helicopter brought the men who killed Willem and Domingo.'

Sicelo Kula couldn't contain the information any longer: 'I know that man,' he said

'What man?' asked Sarge X.

'The dead man on your pick-up.'

Nero Dlamini made him sit down, and helped him to tell the whole story, because Sicelo wasn't fluent in English.

Sicelo Kula's parents were working on a farm near Citrusdal when the Fever came. He attended the little farm school.

He was the only one who didn't fall ill. He was twelve years old. He survived for eighteen months on food from the town and farmhouses and the orchards. When he saw people he hid.

Then it grew quiet, the stream of refugees from the Cape suddenly stopped.

He thought he might never see other people again. But one day he saw Jan Swartz's sheep truck. Jan Swartz, of whom the West Coaster Yvonne Pekeur had said: *Old Jan Swartz and company were five people who travelled together, they had a sheep lorry that they stripped, and they had eight pretty horses that pulled the truck. He was the big rooibos tea pedlar, and they also sold furniture, but pretty stuff, you could see they were antiques.*

For two weeks Jan Swartz searched for trade goods in Citrusdal. Sicelo Kula hid, but watched Jan Swartz and his four assistants closely. He realised they were harmless, looking for food and goods to trade.

On the eighth day he found the courage to show himself, he was tired of being so alone. It wasn't easy: Jan and his helpers were Afrikaans, Sicelo was Xhosa, and nobody's English was that good. But by the eleventh day Jan recognised how well Sicelo worked with the horses, he indicated he was now one of the team. The care of the horses quickly became his responsibility.

They drifted on, and Sicelo enjoyed that life. From January to March they cut rooibos tea around Citrusdal and Clanwilliam, over the mountain and through the Botterkloof, to beyond Nieuwoudtville. They sweated and fermented the tea and trampled it underfoot until it was ready. Through the winter months they peddled it to the communities at Lamberts Bay and Sutherland, and once to Bushmans Kloof.

Jan Swartz was strict, but he was fair. He liked to tell stories and sing around the campfire. Sicelo didn't always understand the stories, but he enjoyed the songs. He sang along and taught the rest of them his Xhosa songs.

Every August they went to Wupperthal. Because that was the month of poverty and hunger, the whole tea supply had long been bartered for food, the West Coast was battered by wind and rain, the veld food would only be edible by September.

Wupperthal was a secret place.

They trekked with the horse lorry, a difficult journey to Wupperthal. There were other pedlars there too, with their own transport. In the first two years Jan Swartz told Sicelo: 'You stay here. Look after our stuff. I don't trust these other rascals.' Then Jan and the others would go with the other traders, and they would follow the track. Then they came back, two days, sometimes three days later, with the donkeys, now laden with boxes of stuff to barter. Food, mostly food. Rice and pasta, tins with the sweetest fruit. Boxes of long-life custard. Good stuff. They would divide it among each other.

Then, three years ago, the pedlars stopped going over the mountain. They waited there, and other people came with the donkeys and the goods. Strange people, but it looked like Jan Swartz knew some of them.

And then, the last year, they waited there, the pedlars, at Wupperthal for the donkeys and the smugglers to come. But this man, this dead man on the back of Sarge's pick-up, he was the boss of the grey uniforms, a whole bunch of them, all in the same uniforms and black boots. They came suddenly at night, in the dark, over the mountain and they shot the pedlars with automatic rifles, they shot Jan Swartz and his people, and all the other traders, they shot them all dead.

Sicelo was with the horses. At Wupperthal there was always booze, some of the pedlars distilled their own *witblits* brandy from citrus fruit, and there was a lot of drunkenness around the fire. Sicelo never liked that, so he would go and sleep with the horses. It saved his life, that night.

The grey men shot everyone, and they burned all the lorry wagons. Some of the buildings too, where the pedlars would sleep. Everything burned, the fire lit everything up. That's why Sicelo thought the man would see him.

The horses were in the building to one side that they used as stables.

Sicelo was terrified, and hid among the animals; they were wild and restless, pushing against the poles across the door. Four grey men approached. They held up their rifles, Sicelo was sure they were going to shoot him and the horses. But this one who was now lying dead on the back of Sarge's pick-up was in charge of the four, because he said, 'Wait.'

Then the boss of the grey men came closer and closer, with his rifle ready to shoot, so that he could see into the darkness of the stables. And Sicelo saw him in the light of the big fires burning around them. He saw the man had leaves on his neck.

'Tattoos,' Nero Dlamini interpreted. 'The dead guy outside, he has these Maori tattoos on his neck.'

Sicelo nodded. He said that's right, they looked like leaves. He looked at the grey boss man for a long time, he was sure it was the same man. And then the grey boss man said, 'Let the horses out.' And Sicelo clung to the side of a horse as they ran out.

And when they were at a safe distance, he sat up properly on the horse's back and rode away.

That was how he ended up with the Bushman Kloofers. He was never really one of them.

When he had finished, Beryl said, 'Wupperthal . . .'

'Yes,' said Nero Dlamini. 'I know what you're thinking.'

'What?' I asked.

'The recordings . . . Your father talked to the West Coasters, they also mentioned Wupperthal, more than one of them.'

'Where are the recordings?' I asked.

'Nico,' said Sarge X, 'I think you need to listen to Sofia first.'

110

The investigation of my father's murder: VII

I listened to Sofia Bergman. Her voice was soft, full of compassion and loss and exhaustion, yet still musical. Her skin glowed in the morning light of the sitting room, her pretty, delicate hands talked along, and the gestures that she used were just as beautiful as the sound of her voice. With the help of Sarge X she reconstructed the murder scene. She said she had interpreted the spoor to the best of her ability. Here is what she thought; this was what possibly might have happened.

Pa was in the farmhouse busy drawing up his irrigation plan. Then he heard the helicopter. He must have run outside, the first helicopter in more than five years, so soon after the West Coasters' stories of choppers, he had to see it. Maybe he did, the area was very flat around there. But we'll never know. The helicopter landed nearly three kilometres away.

Four people jumped out of the helicopter. All four rows of tracks showed the same kind of boots, so one could guess that all four were in the same grey uniforms.

Pa's single set of prints showed that he had walked quickly in the direction where the helicopter had landed. Perhaps it was then that he gave his emergency call over the radio? He must have been worried, said Beryl, because the West Coasters' chopper stories were full of violence and destruction.

Sofia thought Pa must have seen the four grey men coming. His tracks showed that he suddenly stopped and turned back. He ran back to the farmhouse. She said the tracks could only tell a part of what happened next; she thought Pa must have locked himself in the house. The four grey men reached the yard and hid behind the trees around the house. It looked like they spent some time waiting behind the trees.

Then they broke open a window and a door, and there were signs that there was a struggle with Pa in the house.

There was no blood spilled there.

They hauled Pa outside, and dragged him along with them in the direction from which they'd come.

Then Domingo arrived.

She thought they must have held a gun to Pa's head. On the edge of the nearest irrigation land Domingo stopped, and so did the four with Pa. For quite some time. A hostage drama?

And then someone fired.

We knew that right there Domingo shot one of them between the eyes.

Pa fought back against them. The footprints sketched the lines of struggle.

Pa was shot there.

Domingo as well.

That is what the blood and bullet casings showed.

Two of the grey men carried Pa and Domingo to the salt pan. The other one waited with their own dead man. Then all three ran north. The deeper prints of one of the men showed he was carrying their fallen comrade.

She deduced that Domingo hadn't died immediately. She believed Domingo took his R4 and aimed, and he shot another one of them. Five hundred metres away. An astonishing shot, because Domingo himself was very seriously wounded. But he got one last shot in.

Then the grey men had a problem. They were burdened by their dead, and they had another wounded man as well. So they pushed the dead man's body under the bushes in the ditch.

She wondered why the helicopter didn't come closer?

Why were they in such a hurry?

The three, one of them wounded and bleeding, went to the helicopter. And the helicopter flew away first west, and then south-west.

In the direction of Wupperthal, I thought.

'That's all we know, Nico,' said Sarge X.

I showered in the Orphanage. They gave me food. They said I should get some sleep.

I declined. I wanted to listen to Pa's history recordings first. I wanted to know about Wupperthal.

Birdy, Beryl and Nero spoke to me. They said sleep was the best medicine now. I said I wouldn't be able to sleep until I knew.

Beryl went to fetch my father's laptop, showed me how to locate the files with the sound recordings of the West Coast interviews.

I lay on the couch with earphones on and listened. My hand throbbed, my face and ribs as well. But I lost myself in the stories. I heard Pa's questions and the people's answers, as if they were sitting with me talking.

The longing for him returned, acutely painful. I stopped the audio.

I pictured Pa in the farmhouse drawing up his plans. I saw him at a table with a pencil in his hand.

I believe he was tired of being in charge, tired of leading, tired of responsibility. I think he just wanted to bury himself in the simplicity of potato farming. Potatoes don't betray you. I think he wanted to be alone. He had fitted out that farmhouse so he wouldn't have to share an entire orphanage with other people, so that for the first time in so many years he could spend a bit of time on his own.

And even that was denied him.

I was going to get the people who took that from him. I would find them and kill them.

I switched the recording on again.

Somewhere along the line I fell asleep. Beryl came to wake me in the evening and led me to a bedroom, where I slept some more, through the night, deeply and soundly.

I woke the next morning at five knowing instantly that I must go to Wupperthal.

They said no.

They said 'no, you can't', and 'no, not now', and 'no, not on your own'.

I told them they couldn't stop me. I was going as the son of my deceased father, not as a member of the Spotters.

Ravi Pillay, the oldest member of the Cabinet, came to have a good long chat with me. He said, rest, recover, get over it first. Think it through.

I said it would make no difference.

'It will, Nico,' he said. 'You're emotional now. That's not good for making decisions.'

I told him the decision to go and find answers would never change. He asked then why not wait for a week or two?

I stammered, searching my mind for reasons, I wanted to try to explain that they deserved it, these good people, my father's supporters and friends. Eventually I simply told him what I felt, because it was my only truth. I said, 'Ravi, there's nothing else I can do. If I don't go now, I'll explode. I'll burn up inside. I won't sleep, I won't breathe. I'll die slowly. I have to go. Now. So please, just let me go.'

It took them two days. Then Beryl, Birdy, Nero and Sarge X, my colleagues Sergeants Taljaard and Masinga, Sofia Bergman and Hennie Fly, they all came to see me. Birdy was the one doing the talking.

'Nico, here's the deal. Hennie Fly is going to take you as far as Calvinia in the Cessna. You and Sofia Bergman. No, shut up and listen. This is not negotiable. Taljaard and Masinga are here, 'cause why, if you don't agree to all our terms, they'll take you to the brig. And they'll lock you up until you grow ears to listen. Understand?'

'Yes.'

'Okay. Sofia's going with you, 'cause, we talked to Sicelo Kula again, and he said that Jan Swartz said loud and clear "at Wupperthal, you just follow the tracks". So she is going with you to follow the tracks, and to be your back-up. We would send more troops with you, but Hennie says it would be too much for the Cessna with the weight, he only has room for two. We're scared to fly you further than Calvinia, we know too little about those people with the helicopters. And Calvinia is the nearest decent airport to Wupperthal that should work. The West Coasters say from what they remember, everything looks okay there. So what do you say? Okay?'

'Okay.'

'It's about a hundred and fifty kilometers from Calvinia to Wupperthal. Taljaard said three days' slow march. Three days to there. Then we give you three days to search. And then three days back. Nine days, then Hennie will go back to Calvinia. Okay?'

'Okay.'

'If the weather's good, you fly tomorrow morning, just before dawn.'
I didn't get a chance to thank them.

Sofia came to me that evening. She had a first-aid kit with her, and said, 'We must bandage that hand of yours.'

'How did you know?' Because I thought I was hiding the swelling and pain of the broken knuckle very well.

'I saw it the other morning, when you and Birdy were sitting on the couch. Every time Birdy touched that hand . . .'

She must have seen my concern, I didn't want to give the Cabinet a reason to delay our expedition. She said, 'I won't tell anyone.'

'Thanks.'

'Will you be able to shoot?'

'Yes. I just can't fight.'

'I promise you I won't hit you first.'

I smiled for the first time in days.

She sat down, opened the first-aid bag, took out the hand splint and bandages.

'They'll see the bandage,' I said.

She shrugged. 'But nobody will know what's going on under it . . .'

'Thanks, Sofia.'

She blushed. And then she focused intently on applying the splint and bandage, and we didn't say any more. When she had finished she jumped up and walked swiftly out of the room.

I sat there thinking I would never understand women.

III

The investigation of my father's murder: VIII

The Cabinet and the Spotters came to see us off. They were the only ones who knew about our expedition. There was something subdued about our departure. When Hennie Fly took off and banked and flew back over them, I thought they looked lost down below – the Cabinet without Pa, Special Ops without Domingo. As if we were all waiting for them to come back and lead us again.

The weather was perfect, the morning was crisp, but the sky was clear. Hennie Fly talked up a storm, as usual. Sofia sat beside him. He asked if she'd flown before. She said she had. In the old days when she was in the Free State cross-country team, they would sometimes fly to Cape Town for competitions.

Had she ever flown in a small plane before?

No, never.

Did she like it?

No.

He laughed.

We flew over the wide expanse of the Karoo. Just before Carnarvon we saw springbok, a massive herd of thousands racing across the plains. We saw the dust from their hooves rising up like red-grey smoke in the morning air.

We flew with the R63 either just to the left or the right of us. There was no traffic. None. Not even a horse wagon or donkey cart. We flew over Williston, and the Karoo flattened out and we could see the Cederberg for the first time on the distant horizon.

Two and a half hours later we flew low over Calvinia's single tarred landing strip. It seemed to be in good shape still.

Seven minutes later we were on the ground and picked up our

rucksacks and weapons. Hennie Fly stood beside the aeroplane and he hugged us, first Sofia and then me.

'I'll come back in nine days, you hear. You better be standing here. I beg you. And if you're not here, I'll come back a week later. Okay?'

It was strange to see the little Cessna fly away, and leave us standing there, Sofia and me in the middle of this arid country, five hundred kilometres from home.

We stood gazing after it until we couldn't see or hear the plane any more.

'Come on,' I said. I hoped she wouldn't hear the uncertainty that I suddenly felt.

She just nodded, and then she swung the rucksack over her shoulders, picked up her rifle and began walking.

Our conversation began awkwardly, with vague, neutral subjects and pregnant silences, and then both of us would talk at once, and then fall silent again. We were both burdened by self-consciousness, and the trauma of the past week, and I was struggling to disguise my feelings for her. Despite everything I still knew she was my future wife, but I had given up hope of making it happen. And now, on the crumbling R27, all my desires surfaced again, and I was terrified she would notice.

But slowly things began to flow, as we found our walking rhythm, and as we moved, and felt, further from our Amanzi reality. Sofia deserves most of the credit for that. She had a way, I found, of asking questions as though she were truly curious, and as though my answers were interesting and worth listening to.

Just before we turned off onto the rutted, overgrown gravel road of the old R364, we looked for shelter from the sun in the old white shed beside the road. As we ate, she asked me how it was, before Amanzi? How was the coming of the Fever for me?

And I told her that in comparison to other stories mine was easy. Sometimes I felt ashamed when people began talking about it. But it was my father who made our experience much less traumatic.

'Why?'

'Because my father ... We were quite lucky too, we were in a secluded place, but I think what saved us was that my father remained calm and made the right decisions. And one of those decisions must have been very difficult for him.'

'Why?'

'You sound like Okkie . . .'

She smiled. 'You don't have to tell me.'

I said I didn't mind telling her. But so that it all made sense, I had to start at the beginning.

She said we had a hundred and twenty kilometres still to go.

Okay, then, I said. And I told her about my father who would read to me at night, ever since I was tiny. Not story books. Non-fiction books about this wonderful world we live in. Books about moon landings and voyages of discovery, books about animals and geographic regions, philosophers and history. Sometimes he just brought an atlas or a news magazine to my bedroom. He would read to me with all the passion and fascination he had for things that excited him, and that he wanted to share with me.

From my ninth year we had those conversations in the kitchen, every evening after supper. Books and maps, an iPad or a laptop on the table, and Pa showing, reading, explaining. Ma and I listened and learned, laughed and chatted.

I could choose any of these things I wanted to see.

NASA and Trafalgar Square, the Eiffel Tower and the Great Wall of China would have to wait until I was older, he said. But in southern Africa I could choose. Almost every holiday.

So we went to the Tsitsikamma Forest. Kosi Bay. The Johannesburg Stock Exchange. Parliament. Kruger National Park. The Apartheid Museum. Aughrabies Falls. The Women's Memorial. Table Mountain. The Namib Desert. Khatse Dam . . .

Sometimes my mother came too whenever her job allowed. Otherwise it was just me and Pa.

In those months before the Fever, Pa told me they had discovered caves in the mountains of the Vredefort Dome. He showed me the dome on Google Earth, how you could see it from space, it was so big—

I interrupted myself at this point, because we had finished eating and there was a long road ahead. 'Come,' I said, 'we have to go.'

We packed up and walked out of the shed. 'Were you an only child?' Sofia asked.

'Yes,' I said. For the first time in years I wondered what the real reason for this was. My parents often used to say that when I was born, they knew they didn't want any more, and I loved hearing them say it. But that was then, when I was still a child.

'I don't think my mother wanted another child.'

'Why?'

'I remember how busy she was.'

I had nothing more to add. She filled the silence by saying, 'You were going to tell me about the Vredefort Dome.'

I resumed my story. One of Pa's many contacts in the geography world whispered in his ear about the discovery of the caves in the Vredefort Dome. And how the discovery was being scientifically investigated first, before the crowds could pollute it. They would have announced the news later that year, but we had the opportunity to go and explore and experience it before the public had access. But we had to go soon.

So I said to him, yes, please, let's do it.

That was the time when the Fever was in the news every day. But governments kept announcing that they could control it.

Pa woke me up one night and said, come on, we're leaving now, because with the Fever he didn't know how soon we would have the opportunity again. And in any case it was nearly school holidays, it wouldn't affect my school work.

Pa and I drove up with the car – the old Subaru Forester that Pa swore by – from Stellenbosch. Over the radio we heard that Europe had closed its harbours and airports. Experts said the American government was lying about the death toll. Medical people said they were working hard on a vaccine.

I asked Pa, did he think we were going to get sick? Then he said the people would make a plan, the doctors and governments and institutes, I needn't worry. Humanity always made a plan.

We slept in Bloemfontein. The next morning we bought provisions there. On a local radio station they asked people not to go to the city's hospitals any more as they were full.

We drove to the campsite beside the Vaal River, just a few kilometres from the caves. We were the only ones there, except for the owners. They didn't want to come close, asked us were we sick? We said no. We pitched our tent and drove to the caves.

The caves were incredible. We went every day, for over a week.

We tried to phone my mother, every night, but she didn't answer. Pa said she must be helping out at the hospital in Stellenbosch.

Every night Pa watched the news on his phone. Then he said it looked like the Fever was getting worse.

By the end of the week the campsite owners didn't come out of their house any more. We went to look for them. They were lying there, dead. I think that must have been when Pa got sick, when we caught the virus.

Pa said he didn't think it was safe to go home now.

Pa said it might be safer to hide away in the caves, because there was unrest and violence and chaos.

Pa and I fell ill and we lived in the caves. We got the Fever. But we didn't die. We only came out three weeks later, and Pa tried to call Ma. And then he said, 'Nico, I think Ma is dead.'

We cried that morning, me and my father, beside the Vaal River.

112

The investigation of my father's murder: IX

When the afternoon cooled down, I suggested we run and see how far we could get tonight. She said that was fine.

We found a pace that suited us both. I thought about the day she ran for selection in Special Ops, when she hit me with the rifle. I laughed out loud. She asked why I was laughing.

I told her.

'Will you ever be able to forgive me?'

'I'm working on it,' I said. And then: 'It was probably a good thing. I was very full of myself.'

'Sofia Bergman, therapeutic rifle-clubber,' she said. 'Let me know if you need more treatment.'

I smiled and looked at her as I ran. And she looked at me. It felt as though I could see her a bit more deeply and in sharper focus.

The sun just touched the horizon when we reached the top of the Botterkloof Pass. The road zigzagged down ahead of us.

'Are you still okay?' I asked.

'Yes, I'm still okay.'

We jogged down the pass as the sun set. She asked me questions about those months before Amanzi, and I told her about the trips Pa and I made up north, always giving the cities a wide berth, always avoiding other people, to the north of the Kruger Park. And then slowly south again, to Amanzi.

And when she had heard everything she wanted to know, I said, 'Now it's your turn.'

And so we ran into the darkness and we ran in the moonlight.

★   ★   ★

Just before the bridge across the Doring River there was an abandoned farmhouse, where we called a halt for the day, and made a fire in the hearth, and ate and drank.

It will remain with me till the day I die, that scene of Sofia Bergman sitting there. Looking so beautiful in the glow of the firelight. Her voice made music as she spoke, and the motion of her hands and arms so feminine. I felt an overwhelming urge to get up, go over to her and kiss her.

But I didn't stir.

At first light we were over the Doring River, and Sofia pointed out the tracks on the other side in the dust of the road. 'I think it's a leopard. He must have passed here last night.'

Behind us the sun rose, ahead of us lay the mountains.

We had had a very long day yesterday, we had travelled far and fast, but this morning we were paying the price. We were slower, our adrenalin less too. But our conversation was relaxed. We had become friends.

We walked along the winding road together.

By nine o'clock we heard the bark of a sentinel baboon, then another one, and another. The mountainside to the left of us came alive, and hundreds of them scurried higher up, little ones peering inquisitively from where they clung under their mothers' backs.

By ten we were back on tarmac road, and at the turn-off to Wupperthal. We had studied the maps carefully in Amanzi. We knew from here it was another thirty kilometres plus to the old mission station.

We stood a moment, as if to take a breather. Then we began to walk, and Sofia said, 'I heard a helicopter once. After the Fever, I mean.'

'Where?'

She told me of the night she slept on the veranda of a farmhouse, with the corpse of a woman in the bed inside, of the droning noise she heard, and the fiery stripe in the night sky, and the helicopter later, nothing seen, only heard.

I pondered over this, and she told me that it was that morning that she decided she wanted to live, and it was a decision with a lot of implications, because she wanted to live, but she didn't know what she wanted to do with her life; she had thought she wanted to be a Spotter, but after all maybe not. And I was walking with her in the Cederberg, on the way to Wupperthal, grateful that she was sharing that with me. I felt somehow privileged that she trusted me with it.

And she asked, 'What do you want to do with your life, Nico?'

'I knew that last week,' I answered. 'But now I don't know any more,'

She asked me what I thought the helicopters signified.

I told her about the one that landed at the Seven Women in the night.

And I said I had no idea what they signified. Hennie Fly said there aren't any helicopters that fly on diesel. Just before the Fever they were doing diesel tests on helicopters in Europe, but if there were helicopters still flying today, they must have access to aviation fuel. And that was the big worry.

'Do you think we will find something at Wupperthal?' she asked.

'Maybe not. Then I'll have to do more searching later. But that will be okay. I just had to get away from Amanzi now. I can't explain it. I just had to get away.'

'So you can see clearly?'

I realised then that she understood me.

'Yes, Sofia, so I can see clearly.' A look passed between us, something small yet meaningful.

After three in the afternoon we came in sight of Wupperthal. We saw the blackened burned-out skeletons of buildings in the narrow, green valley between the mountains. We saw wild horses grazing near the stream. These were the only signs of life.

We left the road, and climbed up the mountain. Domingo had taught us the advantages of height.

Wupperthal was situated in a ravine in the Cederberg, where three tributaries of the Doring River flowed together. We sat on the side of the eastern mountain, looking down on the centre of the abandoned village, the ruins of the old church and hall. We could see the roofs of the houses on the southern slope of the mountain.

We hid behind rocks and studied the terrain, then moved on, checked things out again.

By half past four we were certain the place was totally deserted. We studied the other side, where the path zigzagged southwards up the mountain. That was where Sicelo Kula said the 'tracks' ran. That was where we had to go.

'Do you want to wait till tomorrow morning?' Sofia asked.

'No,' I said.

'Nor do I.'

The old bridge had been washed away, we had to cross the shallow stream to get to the other side. We were moving slower now; Sofia's eyes were searching for tracks, my eyes were watchful, alert to threats.

We walked with our rifles at the ready.

Up the mountain, a kilometre or more, a steep climb, something glittered higher up, at the first hairpin bend.

We were almost upon it before I realised what it was: razor wire, thick rolls cutting off the road. The hand-painted signs attached to it were faded and weathered. All of them were a variation on one theme: *Danger. Gevaar. Ingozi. Radiation. Don't pass this point. You will die. Nuclear Disease!!!!*

Sofia studied the area. 'It's a few years old,' she said.

'No tracks?'

'Nothing.'

'You know you can wait here if you want.'

'I know, thank you. We can go that way to get round the razor wire.'

Nero Dlamini told us the symptoms of radiation sickness showed within two hours after exposure to severe radiation. With moderate exposure it could take up to six hours. We should be on the alert for fever, nausea and vomiting.

We clambered down the cliff, and then up again, so that we could get around the wire. And then we were back on the Jeep track, up and up the twisting hairpin bends. It was ages since the route had been used. It was in a poor state and overgrown.

Every now and then we would ask each other: 'How do you feel?'

'Hungry,' was my last answer, before we reached the top of the mountain, and the track suddenly turned very sandy, and on either side the rocks loomed huge and high. Sofia stopped and called my attention in an urgent whisper: 'Nico!'

She cocked her rifle and dropped to one knee.

I raised my rifle, looked around, I couldn't see anything.

'Tracks,' she said. 'Very fresh.'

I saw what she was pointing out. In the path's white sand, just beyond the big rocks on either side of us, were footprints leading out of the veld on the left. They led into the mountain on the right.

We looked, listened.

Nothing.

She straightened up slowly, moved forward, closer to the tracks.

She knelt down beside them.

I crept up beside her, my eyes still scanning the rough mountain veld around us.

'Boots,' she said. 'The same boots as the men who shot . . . The grey men.'

113

The investigation of my father's murder: X

Sofia studied the tracks carefully. 'They passed here about two hours ago. Three at the most,' Sofia whispered.

'How do you know?'

She pointed out the tiny animal tracks that ran over the boot prints. 'Birds and a lizard. But the outlines of the tracks are still sharp. Remember the wind that was blowing this morning?'

I couldn't remember, I hadn't noticed. But I nodded.

'The wind softens the sharp edges,' she said, and stood up. 'Should we follow the path or the tracks?'

'What do you think?'

'Nothing has used this path in weeks. But those tracks are fresh.'

I pointed in the direction that the boot tracks had taken. 'Then we must go and find them.'

Within a hundred metres the boots began following an ancient foot-path that first turned east, then south.

Sofia walked with her eyes on the ground, and I tried to see as far ahead as possible. But it was difficult. Around here the Cederberg consisted of layer upon layer of dragon's-teeth rocks, sometimes you could see for a kilometre, sometimes only thirty metres.

I spotted something to the left of us, something out of place in this landscape. 'Look,' I said. It was a pole. On top of it was a solar panel. With a small battery, and a lot of loose wires.

'The tracks suggest that . . . I think they tried to climb the pole.'

'How many are there?'

'Eight.' No doubt.

'Still two hours ago?'

She looked again carefully. 'Yes, about that.'

We followed the path again until it went down beside a cliff, and sixty metres below we could see a valley. The sun was in our eyes, it was dropping lower, but the little valley seemed deserted. Behind it the Cederberg made one rough fold after the next, up to the impassable peaks further on.

There was only one way out – follow the footpath to the bottom, and then down the little valley.

We began to walk again.

Sofia and I smelled it almost simultaneously, a rare scent: coffee. Percolated or filter coffee, but coffee.

We immediately squatted down on our haunches.

'Coffee,' I whispered.

'Yes.' And then: 'The wind is from that side.' She pointed south. 'And I don't see anything.'

'Maybe they're on the other side of that fold.'

'Coffee,' she said. 'Where do they get coffee?'

The wind turned, or died down, I'm not sure. The aroma disappeared.

We walked slowly and carefully down into the valley, then along it, south. The sun set behind the mountain peak in the west, even though it wasn't yet six o'clock. Suddenly the breeze chilled.

Her eyes were still on the footpath.

'Are those tracks still two hours old?' I wanted to know.

'Yes,' she answered, but I could see she felt as uneasy as I did. The coffee aroma had spooked us. It wasn't strong, but it was unmistakable. It meant they couldn't be far away.

A klipspringer leapt away from behind a rock. I jerked my rifle up, had the safety off, ready to shoot. I only just stopped myself in time. The buck ran light-footed down the cliff, stones rattling down the mountainside.

We dropped to one knee, watched and listened.

Nothing.

But it felt as though someone were watching us.

We moved again. More slowly. There were clouds blowing in from the west, so low we felt we could touch them.

The valley turned left, south-east. In the growing dusk it was increasingly difficult to see far ahead. The folds of the mountain were now both to the left and to the right of us, rugged, looming and ominous.

In a muted voice I said, 'I think we should find a place for the night.'

She didn't reply. She was staring intently at the cliff on the right of us. 'There's something . . .'

Movement drew my attention, in the middle of the narrow valley, about three hundred metres away. People running. In step, like soldiers. Six, maybe more. No, definitely more. And they were running straight towards us.

Sofia and I were both dressed in Defence Force combat fatigues, camouflage in shades of brown and green. I gripped her arm and directed her to the left, to the nearest mountainside. The rocks and clefts were big, light was fading enough for us to hide away here and it would be very hard to find us.

She followed me, immediately understanding what I wanted. We ran, searching and then I spotted the hollow between two massive rocks. I led her there and we crawled in as deep as we could; she was in the deepest part, and I was in front. I looked towards the entrance, my rifle ready, but unless they knew we were here, unless they could follow our tracks over the rocks, it was unlikely they would find us.

Just the sound of insects, birds and our breathing.

We waited. I tried to gauge how long it would take before they passed us.

The minutes dragged.

A big black bird flew low over the gap in front of us.

I heard boots, some crunching on the stones as they ran, but on the other side of the rocks and rises, maybe twelve metres away.

And then a voice.

'They're here.' The call was only just audible to us.

I shifted backwards, Sofia too, we wanted to be as far into the hole as possible.

Would they be able to see our tracks?

They had crossed rocks and stones. It was dusk.

I doubted it.

Voices. More than one. The words unclear. But they sounded nearer.

I heard the safety clip on Sofia's rifle click very quietly. I did the same with mine.

I realised we were trapped. It was too late to run now, they were nearby. There was only one entrance, right in front of me. And it was narrow, barely two metres high, not even a metre wide. They would have to stand right in front of the entrance and look carefully if they wanted to see us. And they couldn't know where we were. They were too far away. At the most they could have seen us disappear behind rocks.

'No, no. Go left,' I heard the voice of one. Still nearer.

'Nine metres north-east.'

What was he talking about?

'There, go around there. Halt.'

Silence.

Then, the voice calling: 'We know you're in there, and we know you're armed. Come out with your hands in the air and we won't harm you.'

Sofia and I pressed close, frozen.

'We know exactly where you are. I'm going to throw a rock . . .'

A stone, as large as a man's fist, hit the rock at the entrance to our cleft.

'You are there. We know you are. Now please come out.'

In that instant I recalled the history recording I had been listening to, the one of the West Coaster Sewes Snijders. He had said: *Just like that, in English. Not like South African English, but British.* This soldier's accent was British.

I didn't know what to do. I waited.

Silence.

'All right. I'm going to count to ten. If you don't come out before I'm done, I'll throw a grenade where I've just thrown that rock.'

There were at least eight of them.

'One.'

We didn't have a chance, if we rushed out shooting . . .

'Two.'

. . . we might get one or two.

'Three.'

Maybe three or four, if we were lucky. Even five, because I could shoot.

'Four.'

I turned my head as far back as I could.

'Five.'

I wasn't afraid as I stood there. My biggest emotion was one of shame and disappointment, that I had let them catch us so easily. What would Sofia think of me? That I was stupid?

Sofia Bergman

I remember clearly how I hunkered down behind Nico and thought we weren't going to get radiation sickness. Because these men lived here somewhere, it was their coffee we smelled. And they didn't sound sick to me. So we should be okay. If they really wanted us dead, the easiest would be to just toss the hand grenade between the rocks. And they hadn't done that yet.

I whispered to Sofia, 'I'm going to . . .'

'Six.'

'. . . tell them we're here.'

'Seven.'

'Okay,' I whispered.

'Eight!' he called out there.

'We're coming out!' I yelled.

114

The investigation of my father's murder: XI

They were professional. They stood either side of the opening. We walked out, rifles held high over our heads, I looked to the right, where the voice came from, and four of them came from the left and tackled me to the ground. Then Sofia fell on top of me, they pinned her down too. They grabbed our rifles. Jerked mine out of my hand so roughly that the jolt to the knuckle sent pain shooting up my arm.

The others pushed rifle barrels against us, boots on my back, and I lay pinned to the ground on my belly.

'Search them,' said the one had called out the countdown. It sounded as if he was the leader. Hands in my pockets, hands turning me over onto my back. Now I could see better. Two of them searched Sofia. There were eight of them, all dressed in the same grey uniforms as the corpse on Sarge X's pick-up. I didn't recognise the rifles they carried, they weren't R4s or R6s.

One of those who searched Sofia took something out of her shirt pocket. White and square, it looked like a slip of cardboard. He looked at it, frowned, looked at the leader, then back to the object in his hand. He took something off his belt. Clicked it on. A torch.

I realised they must have electricity, because the only batteries that would still work in a torch were rechargeable ones.

He shone the torch on the cardboard. Now I could see that it looked like a photograph. He examined it attentively. Then he shone the torch on me, then on the photo, then back on me.

'What are you doing?' asked the leader.

'You'd better have a look at this,' said the one with the torch, walking over to the leader and giving him the photo.

'I'm so sorry, Nico,' said Sofia.

'What for?'

'Shaddup,' said another grey man and prodded his rifle barrel roughly into my chest.

'It's your father's photo,' she said.

The grey man pushed the rifle barrel against her chest. 'I said, shaddup.'

'If you hurt her, I will kill you,' I said.

He laughed.

The leader came closer to me; he had his own torch now that he shone in my face, then at the photo.

He bent and gestured at the photo, shining the torch on it. 'Is that you?'

It was the photograph of Pa and Ma and me. I was ten years old.

'I'll tell you if you let us go.' I saw he had a chin microphone extending from his helmet.

'It's him, sir,' said the first torch man.

'Is it?' the leader asked me. 'It really is better if you tell me.'

'Let her go, and I'll tell you.'

'I can't do that,' he said, more reasonably than I expected.

He straightened up, walked a short distance away. 'Tie them up. Blindfold them,' he told the others. Then he walked further away, and talked to someone else. I only heard the word 'chopper'.

We lay side by side on the cold, hard rocks, we were blindfolded and tied up. We heard them talking to each other in muted tones, a stone's throw away from us. They sounded excited. Probably because they'd captured us. Because I was such a fool.

But the photo in Sofia's pocket was inexplicable. 'Where did you get it?' I whispered to her, with more urgency than I intended.

'It was your father's.'

'I know, but where did you find it?'

'In the veld, at Witput.'

'At Witput?'

'Yes. I think it must have fallen out of your father's pocket when they . . . When they carried him.'

Fell out of his pocket? Pa kept that photo in his bedroom, in a tin. A tin of expensive chocolates that we found in a supermarket in

Nelspruit, only weeks after the chaos of the Fever. We ate the chocolate together, and then Pa put his most valuable possessions in the tin.
Three photos – this one, and two others of him and my mother, his ID
book and driving licence.

'Are you sure?'

'Of course I'm sure.'

'How much of my father's stuff was in that farmhouse?'

'At Witput?'

'Yes.'

'Nothing. Just the pencils, and a few big sheets of paper. And his
water bottle, and . . . His hat was also lying there.'

'Was there a silver tin?'

'No.'

I wondered, had Pa felt guilty because I had discovered him with
Beryl? And then started carrying Ma's photograph in his pocket?

And I felt remorse again for my poor handling of the situation, and
an intense desire to have him back again, to beg his forgiveness, to
make everything right again.

But why were the grey men interested in the photograph?

Did they know Pa?

And then I heard the helicopter.

The blindfold was effective, I couldn't see a thing. It completely
covered my eyes, but not my nostrils. In the helicopter I smelled sweat
and fuel and the sour tang of vomit. I heard the thunder of the engines
and the faint sound of voices on the radio. I felt Sofia's body against
mine; we were sitting on the floor of the helicopter, back to back. And
I felt her right hand in my left hand, and I gripped it tight.

Nothing about the helicopter and the grey men made any sense.

I tried to think of everything I knew. From the helicopter that Sofia
heard that night at the deserted farmhouse – just weeks before the
Seven Women encountered a helicopter at Tarkastad. And the helicopters of the people who had chased the West Coasters at Lamberts Bay,
and the helicopter that brought my father's killers.

And none of it made any sense at all.

★   ★   ★

Sofia Bergman

My mouth was very dry in the helicopter, and I was nauseous. Because they had blindfolded me, because of the movement of the helicopter, and we were tied up, we couldn't even have a drink of water.

It suddenly occurred to me that a couple of these eight grey men who had captured us might have been at Witput. That was why they were looking at the photo. Because they recognised Pa. The man they had killed, only days before.

Then they noticed that I was also in the photo, and put two and two together.

It might even be the same helicopter. The one that took them to Witput.

And I thought of the man who talked to Pa over the radio, just before his death. Trunkenpolz/Number One. Things were beginning to add up. In my mind I sifted through everything I knew, and I felt I was close to understanding.

Maybe Pa had told Trunkenpolz to come and meet him at Witput.

He knew what Pa looked like.

Trunkenpolz could have sent the helicopter to Tarkastad, to see what the Marauders were up to.

How had Trunkenpolz progressed from a guy who arrived in Amanzi in a minibus in order to steal a few guns, to a man who could send helicopters hundreds of kilometres away?

I was going to kill him.

The hatred, now that I suspected he was behind it all, was pure and strong, it rose in me, filling me, while the helicopter flew for what felt like for ever.

Then the pitch and volume of the engines changed, and I could feel us slowing, and then the helicopter began to descend, I felt it in my belly.

It landed, the engines were suddenly shut down and the door of the helicopter slid open.

I could smell the sea, that overwhelmingly powerful aroma. I heard noises. The diesel engine of a lorry. No, two or three of them. And then I could see the glow of sharp lights under the edge of the blindfold.

Hands helped us up and out. Not the rough handling of the soldiers in the mountain. Hands that were more careful. And voices. One of them was a man's voice, ordering quietly, 'No, keep the blindfolds on. But be careful. Bring them to the car.'

Sofia's hand slid out of mine, people pushed and steered me, and I let them. I smelled other scents that I couldn't place. Oil or grease. Fish? The salt of the sea.

A hand pushed my head down. 'You need to get in the car, sir. Please bend down. Careful now, lift your right foot, that's it, okay, now get in.'

Their hands guided me, I sat in the car, felt the soft leather of the seat, felt someone shift in beside me.

'Sofia?'

'Yes,' she said. 'I'm here.'

'I'm glad,' I said, like an idiot.

'Me too,' she said and leaned against me.

It was in that car, with Sofia pressed against me, that I wrestled with the choice before me for the first time. I was going to kill Trunkenpolz if I got the slightest chance. I didn't care if they killed me afterwards.

But what about Sofia?

I would have to free her first.

But how?

I would have to wait and see.

115

The investigation of my father's murder: XII

The smell of the sea was strong when we got out. There was the sound of engines, people calling, people talking, the clang-clang of a hammer on metal. A helicopter flew overhead.

Hands pulled and directed me, my feet – and those of at least three other people – rang on metal grids under our soles. We turned right, we turned left, right again.

I felt unsteady on my feet, light-headed.

Our footsteps sounded hollow. We were in a corridor, but it wasn't a normal one, something was different.

Hands pushed me to the left.

'Okay,' someone said. 'Take it off.'

A hand pulled off the blindfold. Three grey men with me, one with the blindfold in his hand. I was in a room. It looked like a flat. There was a table and four chairs, metal cupboards against the wall, a single bed, neatly made. The other three walls were also metal. The floor moved.

The other grey man said, 'We're going to untie your hands. Please sit at the table.'

'Where is Sofia?'

'She is safe.'

'Where is she?'

'Please, sir, I need your word that you will sit down, and be civil.'

'Civil?'

'Yes, sir.'

I realised something when the floor moved again. 'We're on a ship,' I said.

'Yes, sir. Do I have your word?'

'Yes.'

'Cut him loose.'

The other one used a pair of pliers to cut the cable ties from my wrists. Immediately I lashed out at him. I caught him on the back of the head, as he turned away. The pain in my broken knuckle was so intense that for a moment I felt I would pass out. I swung at the other one, the talker. He shouted something and dived into me. Another three came through the door, their boots loud on the metal floor. They swore in English, pinned me down on the floor.

'Where's Sofia?' I screamed in helpless rage.

The talker said, 'Tie him up again.'

The one I had hit smacked me behind the head.

'Don't hurt him, you idiot,' Talker said to him. 'Just tie him to the chair.'

They dragged me to my feet, wrestled me into a chair. I did my best to break free, but there were too many of them and they were too skilled.

They tied me to the chair.

'We tried,' said Talker. 'We really tried to be civil.'

'Where's Sofia?' I demanded.

'Sir, I said she is safe.'

Then they all walked out, and closed the heavy metal door behind them.

The sound of their boots disappeared down the passage and then it was quiet.

We could be in Saldanha. There was a harbour there. The only other harbour was in Cape Town, but that was very close to the nuclear reactor meltdown at the Koeberg. It would be impossible.

Saldanha. Trunkenpolz was in Saldanha. We hadn't guessed that.

A new sound in the corridor. The tick-tack of shoes on metal floor. The tick-tack of a woman's shoes.

Mecky, the Zulu princess?

The door opened. A grey man stood there. He poked his head inside. He nodded to someone outside my vision. He stood aside.

A woman came in.

She stood there for a moment.

We each made a sound, both of us. Her sound was high and emotional. Mine was different. I don't know how to describe my sound. I will never know.

Because the woman in the doorway was my mother.

*   *   *

She started to cry.

She came walking across the floor to me and she was weeping, and she embraced me and I remembered my mother's scent and her embrace, and I knew that none of this could be real.

'Please cut him loose,' she said and the grey man came and clipped the cable ties. I stood up and she hugged me and said, 'You're so big, you're so big,' and she wept.

She held me so tight. My hands hung by my side, because this was a dream, this wasn't reality. The floor moved and this hallucination, they must have injected or dosed me with something, it wasn't real. I wanted to get away from her, I had to recover consciousness, I had to get away, find Sofia. I pushed her away.

'Nico, please,' she said. 'I'm so terribly sorry. I did everything I could to find you. I'm so dreadfully sorry about Papa. It was an accident, it all went horribly wrong. They were supposed to fetch you both . . . then the other man came and he shot at my men.'

'Ma, your men?' I moved further away from her.

She seemed to shrink, I could see she was hurting when she heard the rage and rejection in my voice. She grabbed a chair, pulled it away from the table. She looked at the grey man at the door and said, 'Please leave us.'

He nodded and walked away. The door stood open. I stared at it.

'Nico, sit down, please.'

I don't know how long I stood like that.

Then I sat down.

Sofia Bergman

They kept me in a restaurant. It was completely empty, just a few people in the kitchen who brought me food. One even asked me, 'Would you like some wine?' I wasn't tied up, or blindfolded, but I could see two grey men outside, at the door. The restaurant had windows, but it was dark outside, I couldn't see where we were.

I thought I could hear the sea. Surf. But you must remember, it was years since I last heard the sea, and it was only at Hartenbos, where we went on holiday three times. So I wasn't sure.

And they brought me fish and chips. With tomato sauce for the chips.

And a Coke. Can you believe it? A Coke. When will I ever drink a Coke again?

I can't remember the exact sequence of that night's conversation. I can't put her in these pages in her own voice. It's all so mixed up in my mind, there was too much emotion when I needed to listen.

And I didn't just listen. Sometimes I jumped up and walked to the door, slammed my palm against it until the metallic sound echoed through the ship. I asked questions. I cried. I screamed at her, out of pain and rage and inability to understand.

And she kept talking, explaining. She said, yes, hate me, Nico, but first hear my story.

Later they brought us food and drink. Neither of us touched it.

Her story was not a linear, chronological narrative at all. It was mixed up, mainly due to my interruptions and outbursts and my flood of questions. Some things I knew, back then, as a smaller child, and she refreshed the facts for me. Some I could vaguely remember, but just from my childhood perspective. But the bulk of it was new to me.

She had a way of talking that I had forgotten. There was a sort of pained but deliberate and total honesty about it – like someone who absolutely could not tell a lie, no matter what – and a sort of lack of social skills and consciousness. It was as though she didn't really realise how her honesty made you feel, and that served as mitigation, as the reason why you could and wanted to forgive her for it. She told me, in the cabin of that ship, that she was going to tell me everything that was relevant. And actually everything is relevant, she said. Because we make our future with who we are and with what we do. 'I want you to understand, and I want you to still love me. That's all part of my agenda.'

And that was why, she said, she had to start at the beginning.

This is broadly what she said, in a way that will make sense, it's what I remember.

116

The investigation of my father's murder: XIII

My mother was a mathematician. Her name was Amelia, her maiden name was Foord.

She was one of those children who took eight subjects in matric and got distinctions in all of them. She played good hockey. Behind her back on the hockey field they called her the Terminator. And it wasn't a positive nickname.

She won a big bursary for university, where her favourite subject was applied mathematics; it was her sole academic passion. In her third year she met my father. He was everything that she was not. He wasn't sporty and he was funny, he had a wide-ranging intelligence, and interests – a lamp to her searchlight. His personality was warmer, he was the proficient extrovert compared to her awkward misanthropy.

She was given to extremism, he was politically and economically moderate.

And she loved him. So she told me, over and over. 'I loved you and Papa very much.'

In her second year at university she joined Greenpeace Africa and marched in protests against nuclear energy, fracking and global warming and for every possible ecological cause. In her studies, she shone – spectacularly. That was the main reason that the Centre for Complexity Studies at the University of Stellenbosch recruited her even before she graduated.

'Come and do your honours in Complexity Theory,' they invited her. It was a discipline wrestling with the great problems of Africa and the world, such as sustainability and combating pandemic poverty. There were biochemists, philosophers and economists and, if she joined, mathematicians. And that was just the beginning.

She thought it over, and then joined them. She also married Pa. And they had me. They were happy in their little house in Die Boord.

Within the first few years they realised she was the star, the genius with a growing international reputation, the one who was going to open doors for them for study and accommodation overseas, something they were very keen on doing. She was the academic racehorse compared to my father's carthorse.

So she concentrated on her career, and Pa on us. On me.

'Everything would have worked out, Nico.'

Her voice changed when she got to this. I don't think she realised it. It was very subtle, but I suspect the fact that I had last seen her years before, and that there was distance between us, allowed me to recognise the change more easily. It reminded me a little of Pastor Nkosi Sebego when he was on the defensive, though believed he was treading the moral high ground in the Divine Light.

Just after I started prep school, she was invited to deliver a paper at an international congress in New York. With the approval of the Centre for Complexity Studies she chose her favourite subject: 'Pandemic poverty and global warming: no future without a sustainable planet'. Her argument was that spending billions of dollars – mostly in vain – to lift Africa out of its cycle of poverty was merely rearranging the deckchairs on Planet Earth's *Titanic*. If global warming was not halted and reversed, it was all futile.

Four people who were in the audience that night invited her to dinner. Four scientists, world-renowned for speaking out on global warming, but who were dismissed in conservative circles as alarmist and extreme. The four – three men and a woman – took her measure: her green militancy, her religious convictions, life and world view. My mother had never been afraid to state her views bluntly, and that evening she didn't hold back. She believed she was among people who saw things her way, shared her viewpoint completely.

And yet the atmosphere was muted when she left, and they ignored her for the rest of the congress.

Up until a few hours before she was due to fly back to South Africa.

The female academic came to see her alone in her hotel room. And asked, 'Do you really believe we will stop global warming?'

'No,' said my mother. 'There are simply too many conflicting interests.'

'Can you think of any other way?'

'Oh, I can, but nothing that the world would find acceptable.'

'And what is acceptable to you?'

'Anything.'

'Truly? Anything?'

'Yes.'

'Do you know what David Attenborough said of the human species?' the woman asked her, with reference to the famous British presenter of nature television programmes.

'Yes. He said the human species is a plague on the earth. And I feel that way too.'

'Truly?'

'Absolutely.'

'And do you believe this plague should be controlled?'

That was when my mother realised there was something going on. This was another kind of test. An extension of the dinner, but more careful, more secretive, and with much more at stake.

'Look,' my mother replied to the woman, 'if I could develop a virus tomorrow that could contain ninety per cent of that plague, I would do it.'

Sometimes I think back to that night, and that specific moment in the conversation, I rethink and relive it, then I wonder if the universe didn't intend me to be seventeen when the tumblers of understanding dropped into place.

Seventeen is the perfect age for it, of course. Seventeen, with Domingo as mentor – Ryan John Domingo Junior, the man who hated his first names because they were his father's. Domingo who bequeathed me his belief in, and rejection of humankind as animals. Which was tangibly and undeniably proven by the men in an aircraft hangar near Klerksdorp who stabbed little Okkie for absolutely no reason, by the Marauders who kept women caged, and by the Enemy who executed the good souls of our reservist force with cold-blooded shots to the head.

Cairistine 'Birdy' Canary

Domingo told me that in Worcester he believed only his father was an animal. In Afghanistan he thought many people were animals. In court, when they prosecuted him for the double murder, he believed he, too, was an animal. In prison, he saw things, things that people did, prisoners and guards, and then he knew we are all animals.

At seventeen I had a vague sort of understanding of my mother's point of view.

Perhaps a younger me – or older, without the influence of Domingo – would have keened and mourned and torn my clothes when I had the first suspicion that the Fever was not an accident nor a chance natural phenomenon, that the story of the man under the mango tree might be partly or entirely a fabrication.

But that night I just sat there and felt the terrible weight of this knowledge pressing me down into the chair. In a way, I understood.

It made me think of my father's words: *You are your mother's child.* He had said that to me in the winter of the perfect storm when I gave my food to the little ones, and when I shot the KTM off their motorbikes in the Year of the Jackal.

You are your mother's child.

And I was Domingo's creation.

For a brief moment I evaded this revelation of the Fever, as one does when the knowing is too great a burden. I looked at my mother, and remembered her as she had been – the athletic, energetic, timelessly beautiful and intelligent woman of my childhood, my primary school years. The one just out of reach, the one whose embrace I longed for and occasionally found comfort in when it was available. The one for whom I called after the dog attack at Koffiefontein. And I realised she had aged. More rapidly than my late father. The lines on her face etched deeper, the grey in her hair more pronounced. The keeping of the Great Secret had taken its toll.

She was speaking rapidly now, as if to convince me quickly, before I rejected her and her choices. She told me of the state of the earth before the Fever. Of the pollution in the oceans, eight million tons of plastic that humanity dumped in the ocean every year, plastic in the sea that already weighed more than all the fish in it. Of deforestation, air pollution, carbon dioxide that was making our planet overheat. Of species that had already died out, large and small. And the hundreds of species on the brink of extinction – rhinos and elephants and vultures, orangutans and gorillas, wild dogs and whales, pandas, tortoises and tigers, not to mention the less photogenic species, the caterpillars and frogs and coral creatures and fish.

She asked me, with rousing passion, what right did we have, the plague species, the pestilence, to do this to all the others? What right did people have, as just another animal, to commit such mass murder? And with evangelical conviction she said, 'Mankind can't change, Nico, mankind can simply not change. Evolution programmed us to keep consuming, until everything is used up.'

Later on I realised it reminded me of Ravi Pillay's story and his restaurant, where people always dished up more than they could eat. But while Ma was talking I said nothing. I sat across from her and tried to remember the times, in a house in Die Boord in Stellenbosch, when we three laughed together. And I couldn't.

Less than a month later they came to talk to her. Three of them. One was a South African, a zoologist and owner of a rehabilitation centre for vultures in Limpopo. They told her about Gaia One, the organisation of people – scientists, business people, politicians, technologists, medics, even a few soldiers – who all shared her conservation sentiments. They invited her to join Gaia One, to work with them on what they called 'Project Balance'.

She agreed. She promised them her loyalty, confidentiality and silence. They didn't believe her, and they tested her, until they were certain. The closer she was allowed to the inner circle, the more she recognised that these people were serious and unrelenting. In the next few years two members of Gaia One got cold feet. They wanted to go to the press with their knowledge of Project Balance. Both died in unusual circumstances.

Yes, they were serious and unrelenting. But global warming was just as serious. And so was the threat to the planet, and the scale of the plague species' damage.

In the end she decided to support it. As long as she could take her husband and her son with her to the new world after the Fever.

117

The investigation of my father's murder: XIV

The virus was developed in a laboratory. It was a select blend of corona viruses, as the media described it. But man-made. The vaccine came from the same laboratory, meant only for the chosen ones, the members of Gaia One and their nearest and dearest.

Preparations were made: the vaccine was distributed, and the deadly virus was taken to every corner of the world, so that it could be released according to a specific plan, to mimic natural spread. The survival centres' preparations began. There were seven bases where Gaia One people would be protected and civilisation preserved. Places that were geographically isolated – like the Cape Peninsula with its encircling mountains – and with access to nuclear, sun or wind power to keep the lights, systems and technology going.

And the countdown began.

Ma injected us with the vaccine herself, three weeks before V-Day. She simply came home one evening and told Pa she had bought the flu vaccines at the chemist, because an academic colleague in Germany had warned her about the virulent flu spreading from Europe, a bad flu that was making people really sick. 'Let me inject you, and then it's done.' First me, then Pa, and then herself, chatting all the while. 'It might make you feel a bit off for a day or two, but nothing serious.'

That night, after I went to bed, she told Pa. She told him everything.

My father, my good, gentle, sensitive, people-loving father. He was angry that she'd kept the secret from him for so long. She had been expecting this and understood. He was angry because his entire philosophy was based on the idea that mankind had solved every problem time and again, and the dilemmas of infestation and species extinction and global warming would also be overcome, with intelligence and renewed thought and astounding technology. Ma had expected this and understood.

Pa didn't scream and shout that night. It wasn't in his nature. When she had told him everything, he calmly and reasonably told her what he thought of it. And then told her that his integrity demanded that he not remain silent. His conscience prescribed that the next day he go to the media with this information.

This too Ma expected and understood. She said nobody would believe him. And he would be killed. There were Gaia One people who were specially trained and stood ready for that possibility, who would kill him. And her. And me. She had had to agree to that before she could receive the antivirus.

Pa and Ma were watched. All three of us would die, before the war against the Plague even began.

Pa agreed to do nothing, because Ma and I were his first priority.

Ma had expected that and understood.

But he gave her a sleeping pill, and he took me and the Subaru Forester in the night, and we disappeared. Until after the virus was released. She phoned him, but Pa's phone was off.

She hadn't expected that, and she did not understand.

She asked me where we went.

To the caves in the Vredefort Dome, I replied. Pa tried to phone her during that time – why hadn't she answered?

She said she never heard from my father again. He must have been pretending to call. She said she thought she knew why he did it. It was his way of distancing himself from the annihilation, and from her deceit. It was his way of giving his theories a chance, and to be part of that himself, to demonstrate that mankind's ingenuity can overcome even the Fever.

That was when I thought back to my father's speech that night after Pastor Nkosi Sebego founded his Mighty Warrior Party and called an election.

Aren't you also amazed by what we're capable of? Look at our journey, Homo sapiens' journey, look at how incredibly far we've come, from savannah prey to a robot on Mars and the splitting of the atom and the decoding of DNA. And democracy, reason and rationalism. Science above superstition, facts above myth ...

The Fever, it's horrible, the billions who died in the Fever, I know, it's
terrible, but I wonder if the greater harm wasn't the interruption of what we
were on the road to accomplishing.

I realised he wasn't just talking to the remainder of the Committee
that night, but to my mother. It was his plea to her, his counter-
argument against the Gaia One solution.

Yearning for my father was like a fire in my chest. I understood it all.
I understood why he couldn't praise me when I shot the KTM from
their motorcycles. He was terrified that I was so much my mother's
child.

And I was, to a great degree.

My mother said she had no right to be angry with Pa because he
left that night. After all her secrets and plotting. But she was enraged
that he took her son away from her. He didn't have the right, just as
she surely didn't have the right to conspire to practically wipe out the
human race.

She never heard of my father again. Until Trunkenpolz told the
Marauders over the ham radio: 'Willem Storm of Amanzi. You kill that
guy, and I'll give you gas for ten years.'

Ma knew Pa and I wouldn't die from the virus. She knew we would get
very ill, like everyone who had the inoculation against the virus, but
we wouldn't die. However, she had no assurance that we would survive
the chaos of the epidemic. She kept hope alive. She was one of the
executive committee members of Gaia One's Cape Town Base. She
asked them to listen over the ether for the two names she yearned for:
Willem and Nico Storm.

She gave them a photo so they could put it in the database of their
military computers. They were employing the same systems once
used by the USA to hunt terrorists, with military MQ-9 Reaper drones
flying higher than the eye could see, but with such powerful cameras
that computers could scan the video stream and identify faces to
compare with what was in the database. And we were in the database,
thanks to the photograph.

She kept hoping the drone camera would spot us somewhere in the
vast expanse of the country, and that the program would set off the
alarm when the system identified us.

So we could come to her. So we could have a better life. In a better world.

Because she had done it all, she had become involved and worked and planned and kept the secrets so that there would be a better world for us, and more specifically for me. Because she loved us, intensely and overwhelmingly, and she would understand if I wouldn't accept that, but she begged me to think it over: a sustainable future for all species. For mankind too. And also for her son, Nico Storm, and his children and their children. Was that not what true love meant?

So she continued to hope that the radio operators would hear news of us, or the flying drones record us, even though the statistical chances of that were minimal.

There were only two drones at Cape Town Base. The Gaia One members who had been in the US military sent them by ship along with their operators, once the worst chaos was over. They were to keep an eye on threats, like the rise of communities on the edge of the mountain borders, the people of the West Coast, Lamberts Bay, the Bushmans Kloof and the much smaller one at Villiersdorp, where they had to send their troops and helicopters to frighten and drive them away.

Because the big lie about Koeberg's nuclear reactor – and the fictitious threat of radioactive contamination – worked for more than three years. The reactor never malfunctioned. It was maintained by Gaia One and managed as the primary source of electricity for Cape Town Base. Back then, during the chaos after the Fever, they transported load after load of used tyres to Melkbosstrand and burned them to create the clouds of thick, black, stinking smoke. People saw and smelled it. The natural survivors who weren't part of Gaia One's conspiracy sensibly fled from the danger. Nobody looked back to see who stayed behind.

And then they sealed the borders – every mountain pass and tunnel into the Cape. They took car wrecks and dead bodies to the important access routes – Du Toits Kloof, Sir Lowry's Pass, Piekeniers Kloof, Bains Kloof – so that it would seem as if the radiation and the virus had destroyed everything. And so, for three long years they had no invaders or curious people.

Until the pedlars and smugglers began coming in via Wupperthal, driven by hunger and curiosity. Some of Gaia One's own soldiers and workers began trading with them. The way people do, people who always want *more*.

She told me first about the radio message that mentioned Pa's name, and afterwards I asked her about Sofia spotting the helicopter. Later I had to work out the chronological order myself to make sense of it.

The droning that Sofia heard, the night on the strange farm's veranda, and the streak of fire like a meteorite that she saw in the night sky, was one of the two Cape drones. It had mechanical problems, caught fire in the air and had to make an emergency landing in the mountains outside Richmond.

The helicopter Sofia heard the next morning was the mission to recover the drone. It was successful.

And then, weeks later, the radio message. 'Willem Storm of Amanzi. You kill that guy, and I'll give you gas for ten years.' I knew it was Trunkenpolz, to the Marauders. But my mother and Cape Base didn't know what it meant, except that my father's name was mentioned.

They had the technology to determine the location of the two radio towers. One was in the mountains of Lesotho, the other was in a farmhouse on the mountain beyond Cradock. She had to beg the Cape Council to approve a mission, because there was great reluctance to move beyond the mountain borders with technology like a helicopter. At all costs they wanted to keep their presence and, naturally, the Great Conspiracy from the rest of the unenlightened world.

The breakthrough came when she said their radar showed that there was an aircraft used by someone beyond the mountains, a common survivor, not a member of Gaia One.

Then the Gaia One's Cape Council approved the mission. They sent a helicopter with soldiers to gather intelligence at the radio sources. The mission extended over a few days, because the distances were too great for a single helicopter flight. They had to establish refuelling points and supply them.

The radio in the Lesotho mountains wasn't there. There were tracks of vehicles and signs of life, but the people had already moved on.

At the other radio, near Tarkastad they found people. One man, wild and bearded and high on cannabis, and a room of dirty, unkempt women. The soldiers asked the wild man where Willem Storm was.

And where Amanzi was. But they could see he didn't know. They asked the women, but the women seemed drunk and just stared at them.

Then the helicopter returned and the Gaia One soldiers said there were obvious signs at the Tarkastad radio that the wild man was part of a larger team of people. The helicopter visit was perhaps just poorly timed.

So they had the drone survey the area a few days later, for weeks long. But the radio mast was gone and there were no signs of life. My mother lost hope of ever tracking us down.

Just over a week ago, the voice was heard on the radio again, the same voice that had been broadcasting from Lesotho, so many months ago. And this time the voice said: 'This is Number One, calling Willem Storm, this is Trunkenpolz, calling Willem Storm.' The radio operators of Gaia One's Cape Base sent for her, because the voice called over and over. She had sat down at the radio with earphones and heard the voice herself. Her heart wanted to burst with hope.

Then another voice: 'Trunkenpolz, this is Domingo of Amanzi. I am authorised to respond. State the nature of your business with Willem Storm.'

And the Trunkenpolz voice laughed and said: 'I don't speak to servants, I speak to masters. Tell Storm I have a proposition. I will be listening on this wavelength.'

My mother waited by the radio. The ether in the forty-metre band was silent for hours after, but the technicians later told her the Trunkenpolz-voice radio was in the mountains near Ficksburg, and the Domingo-voice was at the Vanderkloof Dam.

My mother made the connection between Vanderkloof and Amanzi almost instantly. And simply knew that was where my father was. And perhaps I was too.

She waited beside the radio. At half past six she heard her husband, Willem Storm, speak on the radio, and in their radio room of Gaia One Cape Town Base she burst into tears of relief and gratitude and an overwhelming feeling of guilt. She cried so much she didn't hear everything that was said over the radio. They had to replay the recording for her later.

The Trunkenpolz voice offered Pa fuel. Ethanol. And peace. No attacks for five years. In exchange for weapons. Pa said no, thank you.

There was no mention of Nico Storm.

Then my mother pleaded with the Cape Council for one last mission. A last chance, because time was running out. The Cape Base was to be evacuated in ten days' time.

118

The investigation of my father's murder: XIV

My mother said she was responsible for the mathematical models and algorithms that predicted how many people would naturally survive the Fever – in other words, people who were not recipients of the Gaia One vaccine. And how many would die in the ensuing chaos when civilisation collapsed. She also had to try to predict how long it would take the survivors to organise themselves into communities and begin to produce food and energy, and trade and explore.

She studied the statistics of world and civil wars, or uprisings and revolutions, she analysed the effect of the Ebola virus in Africa and the swine flu and bird flu viruses in Asia. Her computer models predicted that all of Gaia One's carefully selected bases would be secure and intruder-free for at least ten years, specifically also that after the Fever the Cape Base would be a safe harbour for Gaia One in Africa – also the only one they would maintain on this continent.

But mankind's ingenuity, the ability to achieve the impossible, to solve problems and overcome circumstances, proved her mathematics wrong. Everywhere, on all the continents, the Gaia One drones showed that groups of people recovered and organised and produced far faster than they had predicted. That vehicles like lorries and even small aircraft kept driving and flying much longer than they thought fuel would still be usable. Which meant that someone was producing petrol and diesel.

Daring explorers had crossed the Cape Mountains much sooner than expected in search of tradeable goods, despite the clear warnings of radioactivity.

The rapid recovery of communities, the growth of curiosity and the will to explore didn't only occur in Africa and the Cape. Gaia One's bases in North America, Europe and Asia all came under pressure.

And they were not nearly ready to tell the common survivors about their man-made pandemic to save the earth, nor to share their conserved technology and supplies with those people.

Initially they tried using non-violent strategies to scare those communities and drive them back, such as a boat full of people with artificial abscesses and simulated fever, because they were terrified that harsher measures would reveal them, and their terrible secret. Sometimes the strategy worked, but mostly – as with the 'blister fever' and the West Coasters – it had no effect.

Eventually they had to send in troops and helicopters, which led to unforeseen casualties on both sides.

Consequently the organisation collectively decided to take their people, technology and equipment to the safety and isolation of a few islands across the earth, to gain a few more years of secrecy: Mauritius, Sri Lanka, New Zealand, Hawaii, Cuba, Ireland and Sicily. The translocation process had been going on for months.

The last ship from the Cape Town Base would leave the next morning.

That was why there was such urgency to fetch Pa – and hopefully me.

Ma sent the MQ-9 Reaper drone and the helicopter with Gaia One soldiers, armed with a photo of the three of us.

Thanks to Pa's radio chats with other irrigation farmers from his location at Witput, the drone tracked Pa down and kept an eye on him.

Ma saw him, on the screen in the control centre at Cape Base. She sat watching her husband walk down the streets of Amanzi, get into a pick-up and drive. She said it was a highly emotional experience to see him, so near and yet so far. She wished he would walk or drive to his son while the high-resolution camera tracked him, so that she could see me. So that she could see that I was alive, so that she could see how I had grown.

But there was no sign of me, and in those few days she began to doubt that I had survived.

She sent the helicopter and soldiers in because the image showed that Witput was isolated. They would be able to reach Pa without anyone else witnessing it.

That afternoon the drone watched Pa disappear into the farmhouse at Witput. The helicopter with the soldiers completed the last leg of their journey and landed north of the farmhouse.

The drone recorded Pa as he ran, and it relayed his emergency call on the radio back to Cape Base: 'Regards to Cincinnatus from Witput, regards to Cincinnatus, I am at Witput.' My mother didn't know what it meant.

Ma was riveted to the video screen as the drone cameras showed Pa come out of the house and walk in the direction of the helicopter. Then he turned and ran back. It showed her four Gaia One soldiers carry out their orders to get Pa out of the farmhouse.

The plan was to take Pa to the helicopter, where he could talk to Ma over the radio. And she could plead with him to come to her. And bring her son, if he was still alive. This was the only chance before the last ship left for Mauritius.

But then the man in the black Jeep arrived.

From an altitude of fifteen thousand metres with the drone camera pointed at Pa and the soldiers, the Jeep was a surprise. And then my mother saw Domingo get out and run towards the soldiers, and the firefight broke out. And how my father was shot in the skirmish. How he fell.

My mother screamed, in front of the operators in the control room. She screamed like a wounded animal.

She heard the soldier relay the news: Willem Storm was dead.

By that time we had been in the ship's cabin for five hours. Right at the beginning, when she came in, she hugged me, but I pushed her away. After that there was a distance between us, for the duration of the conversation. Both she and I moved, paced up and down to control emotion or express it, but we didn't touch each other again.

She told me she had seen Pa, her husband, die. At last she crumbled, she broke down, physically and emotionally. Sobbing, she said, 'It was an accident, it was an accident, it was my fault, Nico,' totally crushed, and I got up and embraced my mother, held her tight, comforted her. And I shared in her – in our – loss, I grieved with her. For that moment. Until the rage and loss, the disbelief and inability of a seventeen-year-old to handle all these revelations at once, forced me to push her away again.

Later she would tell me the drone had seen three white Toyota pick-ups in Luckhoff. Because of them the helicopter couldn't take off for a while to pick up the grey men.

Later she told me the drones even had infra-red cameras able to isolate and identify the heat of a human body in the landscape. That was how they knew Sofia and I had bypassed the razor wire at Wupperthal earlier today, how they had guided the troops directly to our hiding place in the rock cleft.

I remember that was the last thing I registered before exhaustion overcame me.

I remember her leading me to the narrow bed and saying, 'My child, my child. I'm so glad I found you, my child. I'm so happy you're coming with me.'

119

In the Year of the Lion the Enemy attacked us. We defeated them.

In the Year of the Lion I lost my father, and found my mother.

And Domingo died, but his story lived.

And I became a sergeant in a unit without a commander.

In the Year of the Lion the West Coasters came, and Pastor Nkosi Sebego and his followers in the Mighty Warrior Party left.

In May in the Year of the Lion a vibration rippling through the steel hull woke me. I opened my eyes, and saw my mother sitting at the table. I smelled coffee, the divine aroma of coffee.

And I asked my mother what's doing *that*? And she said it's the ship's engines.

'Where's Sofia?' I asked.

'Come on.' She led me out of the cabin. I felt the ship moving under my feet.

We walked down the passage and out onto deck. The day was dawning over Table Mountain. We were in the Duncan Dock of Cape Town harbour.

My mother pointed at the concrete dock, beside the cranes. There was the helicopter, its propeller turning, engine whining. 'There she is. In the helicopter. They're taking her back to Wupperthal,' my mother said.

I stared at the helicopter. A thousand thoughts ran through my mind.

I hugged my mother. I held her very tight.

Sofia Bergman

They blindfolded me. They just led me to the helicopter, and told me to get in, and I asked them, 'But where's Nico?' And a guy said, 'He won't be joining you.' I dug in my heels and said they couldn't do that, and the guy, one of the grey men, said to me, 'But he wants to go, miss.'

And I said, 'I don't believe you,' and I started to feel afraid. What would they do to Nico? I got angry too, and I bumped into the grey man, on purpose, and I rubbed my head against his chest, hard, because I wanted to get the blindfold off, and I did. Suddenly I could see everything, and it took my breath away. We were in Cape Town, at the harbour, Table Mountain was here, right in front of me, so beautiful! And there was a ship, a big ship just leaving, and there were cranes and a few trucks and the helicopter, and six grey men. One of them grabbed me to put the blindfold back on, but the main guy said, 'Too late, just leave it.'

I said, 'I want to speak to Nico,' and he just shrugged and said, 'Please get in. I'll try to get him on the radio. He's on that ship.'

Now, understand I knew nothing. All I knew was that it was dawn, we were in Cape Town, and Nico was there on the ship and he wanted to leave. What could I do? So I climbed into the helicopter. And they started the helicopter, and one of the grey men nudged me, and pointed, and there on the ship I saw Nico standing with a woman. It must have been sixty metres, but I could see the woman was familiar, and the helicopter engines made a terrific racket and it began to move. I kept staring at the woman, why did she look so familiar, and then I knew: it was the woman in the photo. I couldn't believe it. I thought, okay, I understand, I understand, I don't know why she's there, I don't know why they're on a ship, but I understand. His father is dead, and he found his mother, I understand. I really badly want to be with him, I love him, my heart hurts so much. But I understand.

The ship was moving, I watched it edge away from the quay.

And I waved to him, I waved at Nico, and the man said, 'He can't see you, miss.' But I kept waving, and the helicopter rose up, beside the crane, and I looked at Nico and his mother, I saw Nico hug his mother and hold her tight. And then I started crying. And through my tears I saw the ship moving further and further from the quay, and we rose higher and higher, and then I saw Nico jump into the water, he just dived off the ship, and he swam to the quay. And I called to the grey men, I said, look there, look there!

The helicopter just flew on.

And then the helicopter turned. And went to fetch Nico.

120

The beginning

We remember the moments of fear, loss and humiliation best.

I remember what it felt like to hug my mother tight. I remember the cool of the morning, the sea breeze, the ship's deck vibrating, the dampness of my mother's tears.

I told her: 'Ma, you know where to find me. But I have to go back to my family. To my blood brother Okkie, and my stepmom Beryl, and my sister Birdy and my uncles Nero Dlamini and Sarge X, Ravi Pillay and Hennie Fly. And my comrades in the Spotters. And my future wife, Sofia.'

Ma sobbed on my chest, but she nodded. She said, 'I know where to find you.'

I held her tight, and the ship moved further from the quay, and she said, 'You better hurry.'

I still wanted to tell her there were secrets to unravel, about spies, and the Sales Club, and a pastor in New Jerusalem, but there wasn't time for that. I had to jump.

I also wanted to tell her I was my mother's child. But I was also my father's child. And that made me very proud.

I wanted to tell her Pa told me the origins of the word 'fever' go all the way back to the ancient Indian word *jvárati* which can also mean 'he glows'.

As I was, at that instant. I was glowing and burning with pain and loss, I was glowing with longing for my father, and for Domingo, and for a world without the Fever. But I was glowing with knowledge, and anticipation for what lay ahead, the adventures to come.

ACKNOWLEDGEMENTS

Fever took four years of research and writing, and from start to finish it was an enriching experience – especially thanks to the many people who generously and patiently shared their knowledge, insight, imagination and time. I am for ever indebted to them. Any errors and omissions in this book are mine alone. The rest is due to their unselfishness. Many, many thanks to:

My agent, Isobel Dixon, and publisher, Dr Etienne Bloemhof, who provided more support and advice than ever, especially because *Fever* ranges a bit beyond my usual subject area. Hester Carstens of NB Publishers had outstanding editorial advice. I am incredibly privileged to work with them.

Professor Wolfgang Preiser, head of the Division of Medical Virology, Department of Pathology at the University of Stellenbosch. I asked him to design a virus, and not only did he assist enthusiastically, he enrolled the help of Professor Richard Tedder of University College London. It was an honour!

Cliff Lotter, my good friend for forty-five years, the best pilot I know, and a researching writer's dream when it comes to anything to do with aeroplanes.

The formidable and brilliant Dave Pepler, formerly associated with the Department of Conservation Ecology, University of Stellenbosch. I will for ever remember our discussions about dogs, crows, sheep and the Cederberg in a post-apocalyptic world.

Anton-Louis Olivier, for the extremely valuable information about South Africa's well-known and lesser-known hydro-electric turbines and volt regulators. Cairistine 'Birdy' Canary and I and the community of Amanzi will always be grateful to you.

The real Cairistine Canary, for permission to use her wonderful name and surname.

Nathan Trantraal, for permission to quote from his work.

Laura Seegers and all my other translators, who each in their own way make a contribution to my books, as well as the proof readers, Liesl Roodt, Annie Klopper and Marette Vorster, for their eagle eyes.

Many thanks too for your endless patience and support, Marianne Vorster, Lida Meyer, Johan Meyer, Marette Vorster, Hannes Vorster and Bekker Vorster.

For the people whose names were lost between notes, digital notes and dropped phone calls: many thanks!

BIBLIOGRAPHY

Apps, Peter (ed.), *Smithers' Mammals of Southern Africa – A Field Guide*, Struik, Cape Town, 2000

Dartnell, Lewis, *The Knowledge: How to Rebuild Our World From Scratch*, Penguin Press, New York, 2014

Harari, Yuval Noah, *Sapiens – A Brief History of Humankind*, Vintage Books, London, 2014

Homer, Trevor, *The Book of Origins*, Plum, London, 2007

O'Leary, Joe, *The Wilderness Survival Guide*, Watkins Publishing, London, 2010

Sheridan, Sam, *The Disaster Diaries*, Penguin Books, New York, 2013

Sherwood, Ben, *The Survivors Club – The Secrets and Science that Could Save Your Life*, Penguin Books, London, 2010

Shorto, Russel, *Amsterdam – A History of the World's Most Liberal City*, Doubleday, New York, 2013

Vosloo, Hein, *African Survival*, Survival X-pert Events, Johannesburg, 2010

Weisman, Alan, *The World Without Us*, Virgin Books, London, 2007

http://www.flyingmag.com/pilot-reports/pistons/cessna-172td-skyhawk-bang

https://www.psychologytoday.com/blog/the-camouflage-couch/201008/criminal-behavior-is-not-symptom-ptsd

http://discovermagazine.com/2005/feb/earth-without-people

http://www.netwerk24.com/Nuus/Eerste-aanleg-vir-hidro-krag-byna-klaar-20141224

http://io9.com/everything-you-need-to-know-to-rebuild-civilization-fro-1566170266

http://www.qsl.net/w5www/qcode.html

http://www.news24.com/Columnists/AndreasSpath/how-global-warming-is-pummelling-the-oceans-20160208

http://www.survival-manual.com/gas-to-alcohol-conversion.php

http://www.popularmechanics.com/outdoors/survival/tips/how-to-survive-absolutely-anything-15341044

http://www.buzzfeed.com/tomchivers/how-come-no-one-mentioned-evolution-by-naturalselection

http://kitchenette.jezebel.com/if-we-dont-cut-back-on-eating-meat-were-screwed-1710769158

http://en.wikipediaorg/wiki/Immortality_Drive

http://www.theguardian.com/books/2015/sep/25/industrial-farming-one-worst-crimes-history-ethical-question

https://en.wikipedia.org/wiki/John_Bowlby

http://www.theguardian.com/commentisfree/2014/sep/02/limits-to-growth-was-right-new-research-shows-were-nearing-collapse

http://www.swaviator.com/html/issueAM00/basicsAM00.html

https://en.wikipedia.org/wiki/List_of_South_African_provinces_by_population_density

http://www.theguardian.com/environment/earth-insight/2014/mar/14/nasa-civilisation-irreversible-collapse-study-scientists

http://www.netwerk24.com/Stemme/Nathan-Trantaal/nathan-trant-raal-uber-atheist-is-soos-om-n-liverpool-fan-te-haat-20151119

http://www.netwerk24.com/nuus/2014-10-14-groeiende-bevolkings-beskadig-ons-planeet

http://www.gestampwind.com/en/business/innovating-projects/noblesfontein

http://www.osric.com/chris/phonetic.html

http://www.defenceweb.co.za/index.php?option=com_content&view=article&id=9747:denel-showcases-a-21st-century-r4-assault-rifle-at-aad&catid=50:Land&Itemid=105

http://www.theguardian.com/environment/2015/sep/15/tuna-and-mackerel-populations-suffer-catastrophic-74-decline-research-shows

GLOSSARY

Aerie – Slang for 'aeroplane'.

Bakkie – Afrikaans for 'pick-up truck'.

Blikslater – Softer version of the mild Afrikaans profanity 'bliksem', used as an adverb: 'You blikslater = 'you bastard'. Or an exclamation or adjective ('Damn!' or 'damned').

Dassie /Dassies – small, furry animal found in the western semi-desert region of South Africa called the 'Karoo'. English name: Cape hyrax.

Donga – South African English for a gully, or gulch.

Duiker/s – small African antelope.

Jakkalsdraffie – 'Jakkals' = 'jackal'. 'Draffie' = 'to jog'. It refers to the way the African jackal jogs through the veld, an effortless gait.

Jinne – Jeez (as in much softer version of the exclamation Jesus!) (Afrikaans.)

Jissie – Jeez (as in much softer version of the exclamation Jesus!) (Afrikaans.)

Kinta – Slang for 'child'.

Klipspringer – small African antelope. English name: African chamois.

Koeksisters – Traditional South African sweet treat – dough fried in oil, and dipped in syrup.

Koppie – Afrikkaans for a small hill.

Kudu – Magnificent African antelope.

Kwaai – Mostly used in slang form to indicate coolness, it is an Afrikaans word with a very wide application. Literally meaning someone who is hot-tempered, bad-tempered, ill-natured, harsh or severe, it is also often used as an exclamation: 'Kwaai!' = "Cool!' (or 'Heavy!').

Lapa – A popular South African structure, usually consisting of a thatched roof supported by wooden poles. Lapas are commonly used as semi-open entertainment areas, a variant of the widely known gazebo.

Lieplapper / maaifoedie / skarminkel – Cape Afrikaans slang for a never-do-well, a rascal, an unstrustowrthy or criminal person.

Rooijakkals – red jackal.

Roosterkoek – griddle bread. Bread baked on the griddle over coals, popular at barbecues.

Scheme (vb) – 'I scheme' = I think, I reckon' . . .

Sjoe – 'Wow'. (Afrikaans.) With wide, broad application.

Spaza shop – general dealer in an African township, a small supermarket.

Steenbuck – small African antelope.

Witblits – South African home-made vodka, or moonshine.